Praise for the Leo Stanhope series

'Highly original'
Guardian

'One of the most inventive series out there'
i

'Leo is a brilliant hero: clever and flawed, infuriating
and at the same time someone I root for at every turn'
Stephanie Butland

'Wonderfully atmospheric, each page carries the whiff of
sulphur and gaslight'
Red

'A deeply atmospheric thriller with more twists and turns than
the grubby streets of London, and a central character we really
care about'
Heat

'This tense, emotional journey through late-Victorian
London has an unusual and memorable young hero at its
heart, carrying the weight of the world on his shoulders'
Sunday Express

'A thoroughly enjoyable excursion into Victorian London's
underbelly with a unique investigator as our guide'
William Ryan

'The writing sings with gorgeous description but, more than
that, achieves poignancy through Leo's keen sense of how
it feels to be misunderstood ... Immaculately researched,
sensitively written and, as ever, highly exciting'
John McCullough

THE
BLOOD
FLOWER

ALEX REEVE

RAVEN BOOKS
LONDON • OXFORD • NEW YORK • NEW DELHI • SYDNEY

RAVEN BOOKS
Bloomsbury Publishing Plc
50 Bedford Square, London, WC1B 3DP, UK
29 Earlsfort Terrace, Dublin 2, Ireland

BLOOMSBURY, RAVEN BOOKS and the Raven Books logo are
trademarks of Bloomsbury Publishing Plc

First published in Great Britain 2022
This edition published 2022

A catalogue record for this book is available from the British Library

ISBN: HB: 978-1-5266-1279-3; PB: 978-1-5266-1275-5;
EBOOK: 978-1-5266-1276-2; EPDF: 978-1-5266-5039-9

2 4 6 8 10 9 7 5 3 1

Typeset by Integra Software Services Pvt. Ltd.
Printed and bound in Great Britain by CPI Group (UK) Ltd, Croydon CR0 4YY

To find out more about our authors and books visit www.bloomsbury.com
and sign up for our newsletters

For Chris, Andy, Josie, Brogan, Ellie and little Arwyn

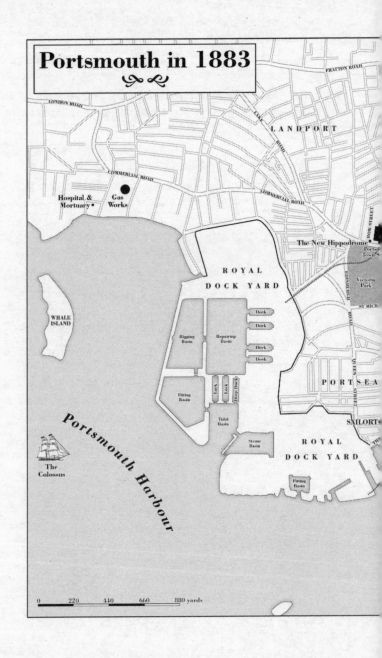

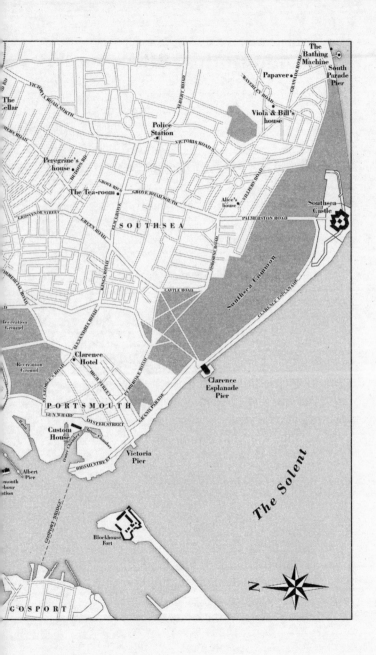

The Bathing Machine

South Parade Pier

Papaver

WATERLEY ROAD

Viola & Bill's house

Police Station

VICTORIA ROAD S.

ALBERT ROAD

VICTORIA ROAD SOUTH

Peregrine's house

HUDSON RD

GROVE RD

The Tea-room

GROVE ROAD SOUTH

Alice's house

Southsea Castle

PALMERSTON ROAD

GROSVENOR STREET

GREEN ROAD

ELM GROVE

KING ROAD

VILLIERS ROAD

OSBORNE ROAD

SOUTHSEA

The Cellar

VICTORIA ROAD NORTH

SOMERS ROAD

COMMERCIAL ROAD

CASTLE ROAD

Southsea Common

CLARENCE ESPLANADE

Recreation Ground

Recreation Ground

ST GEORGE'S ROAD

ALEXANDRA ROAD

Clarence Hotel

HIGH STREET

PEMBROKE ROAD

Clarence Esplanade Pier

PORTSMOUTH

GUN WHARF

OYSTER STREET

GRAND PARADE

Custom House

Outer Camber

Inner Camber

Basin

BROAD STREET

Victoria Pier

Albert Pier

mouth bour ation

GOSPORT BRIDGE

The Solent

Blockhouse Fort

GOSPORT

N

LITTLE SAM WAS THE first of us to see it, or perhaps Lillian saw it first and nudged him, but certainly Sam was the first to leap up and press both hands and his nose against the carriage window.

'Look! Is that the sea?'

I exchanged a glance with Rosie, who affected a nonchalant air, as though the sea was something she was perfectly familiar with, even though she'd seen it only once before, on a trip to Southend with her first husband, and was as eager to paddle in it as the children.

'I believe it is,' I said.

We crowded at the window with two of our fellow passengers, an elderly couple, and watched the mudflats glide past, glaze-cracked and barren under the blazing sun. The buildings became more numerous as our train arced inland, and we issued a collective sough as the view was obscured behind a row of houses.

The final person in the carriage was showing far less interest, and was instead reading a book, making rapid notes in the margin with a pencil. She was notable not only for her studiousness, but also for her skin. It was the brown of a kestrel's feather that had once floated down in front of me, fallen from such a height that when I looked up, the bird was just a dot in the sky. She could not be a servant. Her hat was belted in lace too fine to be a hand-me-down from a generous mistress and her dress fitted too well, made from fine taffeta the blue-green of a dunnock's egg. These clothes were her own.

If I found her presence noteworthy, the elderly couple seemed positively alarmed. Rather than share a bench with her, they had spent the journey crammed together next to Sam and Lillian.

'Portsmouth Town!' the conductor bellowed down the corridor. 'End of the line! Opposite platform if you want the harbour.'

As our train screeched and clattered into the station, a young fellow ran alongside and leapt on to the footplate of our carriage, pulling open the door and swinging inside. On his shoulders he was carrying a pole hung with the plucked carcases of birds, swaying together like a row of convicts at the gallows.

'Partridges,' he announced, not even out of breath. 'A treat for your table.' He leaned towards me, dangling the birds unpleasantly near my face. Their beaks had been removed, giving them a startled expression. 'Welcome, my friend. Would your lovely lady wife be wanting a partridge for your supper this evening?'

I'd never been to Portsmouth before and, if I was honest, hadn't wanted to come on this occasion, but a pretence of familiarity seemed to be part of his patter and he refused to let my glum expression dim his bonhomie.

'Only fourpence each, my friend,' he added. 'Or a shilling for four.'

'No, thank you,' said Rosie. She was already reaching up for our bags.

'They're the finest quality.' He held one of them to his nose and inhaled the scent. 'And fresh. Shot this very morning on my cousin's farm.'

Rosie cast a brief glance at the birds. 'They're crows,' she said. 'Not worth a halfpenny.'

The young fellow, who, I now noticed, had a thick neck and grazes on his knuckles, drew himself up. 'That's a slander, that is, madam. I'll thank you to withdraw it.'

The train was coming to a halt, wheezing and popping, sending gushes of steam and smoke over the people waiting on the platform. The door was still open, flapping against the side of the carriage, and I squinted through the miasma, hoping to catch a glimpse of Peregrine's giant frame.

The fellow took half a step towards Rosie. 'I told you they're partridges, and a man's word is all he has, my old dad used to say.' He turned towards me. 'Are you going to let your wife insult me this way? What kind of man are you?'

It was a complicated question, and not one I felt inclined to answer.

Rosie sighed and adjusted her spectacles. 'Well, *my* old dad was a butcher. Partridges have red eyes.' She poked one of the birds, setting it to swinging. 'Theirs are black. You've clipped their beaks, but they're clearly crows. Now please stand aside.'

She went to move past him, but he moved too, blocking her path. I started to rise – no one will stand in Rosie's way while I have breath in my body – but the studious young woman with skin the colour of a kestrel's feather clicked her tongue, folded her book and barged in front of me. She was short in stature, barely reaching the claws of the birds on their pole, but even so, she did not look the slightest bit scared. Indeed, the expression on her face was one of calm concentration, as if she was learning the steps of a dance. The fellow attempted to shove her aside, but as his weight went forward, she arched her back so swiftly and neatly that he grasped only thin air, and stumbled, emitting a low, porcine grunt. I thought he might fall on her, but she sidestepped him, ducking under his arm, and took two steps backwards out of the carriage, landing on the platform with the grace of a dancer. The fellow flopped against the seat vacated by Sam and Lillian, upending his pole and allowing the birds to slide down in the direction of the elderly couple, who bolted out of the carriage like gingered horses.

Rosie and I followed at a slower pace, stepping around the fallen crow salesman and collecting the children and our bags. Rosie scoured the platform for the young woman, but she had disappeared without a word. In fact, she hadn't spoken at all since she joined the train in London.

Rosie scratched her head. 'Well! I was going to give her my thanks, but apparently, she's not one for conversation.'

I glanced back at the fellow in the carriage, who was muttering to himself and rubbing the dust off his birds with his sleeve.

3

'We should go.'

I took Lillian's hand in mine, and we processed along the platform, resembling a normal family, though we were about as far from normal as it was possible to imagine.

'Where's Mr Black?' asked Rosie. 'I thought he was going to meet us.'

'He's always late. It's an affectation. Shall we go straight to Viola's house?'

'No.' She hoisted Sam higher on her hip, wincing with the effort. He was five years old now and plump on her pies. 'We should wait for Mr Black. He's most likely in the foyer.'

I felt an inner scratch of resentment. I was starting to suspect that Rosie wished to keep me apart from her sister. This was especially galling because I knew they weren't close, exchanging guarded, formal letters every month, Rosie explaining that the weather in London had been very fine and business brisk, and Viola replying that she was very well, thank you, and in Portsmouth the sun had shone for a few days until the easterly winds brought the rain. But Viola's recent announcement of a pregnancy – much wished-for but unexpected after eight years of marriage – had prompted Rosie to express a desire to spend time with her sister. And when my work as a journalist required me to visit the south coast, a family trip seemed fated.

I peered around the foyer, but there was no need. If Peregrine had been there, we would quickly have spotted him, and would have heard him before that. Like most actors, his voice carried a certain weight, and his personality was ... considerable.

Rosie tapped her foot, a sure sign of worriment. 'You don't suppose he's with the police again, do you?'

Lillian looked up at me. 'The police? Why, Mr Stanhope?'

She was an earnest girl who liked to join in with grown-up conversations. But still, I wasn't going to discuss a brutal murder with a seven-year-old.

I leaned down and looked into her eyes. 'Do you remember the story I told you about the boastful dog who liked to sing and dance?'

She nodded solemnly. 'His friends were cross with him, so he went to all the other dogs' houses and entertained them instead. And he was happy.'

Of course, she remembered. I'd told it to her a dozen times at least while she acted it out with her peg dolls.

'Exactly. Well, that's like Mr Black. Sometimes people get impatient with him. And sometimes he gets impatient with them too. And then, well ...' I cast around the room. 'Anyway, he'll be here soon, I'm sure.'

But he wasn't. We waited, pressed against a pillar to avoid the crush, the sunlight slanting down on us through the roof lights, making me feel oddly conspicuous even among a horde of strangers.

Little Sam's eyes strayed to the stall selling boxes of toffee. 'I'm hungry.'

He had a sweet tooth, doubly so because Robbie was not with us, having been left with my friends Jacob and Lilya so he could continue his schooling. Sam was looking forward to telling his older brother about all the treats he'd missed.

I pulled out my wallet for some change, but Rosie shook her head. 'We haven't the money, Leo. You bought them fudge when we left, and ...' She closed her eyes, and when she opened them, they contained a look of such gentle reproach I was hard-pressed not to take her hand. 'You've a kind heart, but truly, you mustn't spoil them.' We gazed at each other, and the distance between us, not five feet in reality, seemed a chasm.

It was another ten minutes before I became aware of a disturbance in front of us, like a quivering in the long grass before a dog bounds into view. It was quickly accompanied by a booming bark, though of the human variety.

'Let me through! I'm here to meet an important dignitary. Stand aside.'

The populace parted and Peregrine appeared – and what a sight he made. He was sporting chequered trousers, a green velvet jacket and a waistcoat that might have claimed to be tan, but was verging on yellow, matching his hat. Together with his doleful chestnut eyes, he resembled a mastiff that some unkind soul had dressed up for their amusement. He tipped his hat to Rosie and enveloped my hand in his, shaking it so vigorously I thought it would fall off.

'I've reserved a taxicab,' he announced. 'Hurry now. We don't have long.'

'Until what?' I asked.

He hadn't apologised for being late. He turned towards the entrance and began wading through the crowd. 'Come along, quickly. There's been another ...'

I couldn't hear end of his sentence as he was already lost in the throng. We trailed him outside to the forecourt, a feeble miniature of the one at Waterloo Station in London, as if that most exuberant of squares had accompanied us on our journey, eroding mile by mile until it was merely *this*, a dull place of function, where one could get off a train and, with any luck, get back on one again as soon as possible. I was missing home already.

Around the edges, pressed against a metal fence, tradesmen were holding up painted signs advertising fresh fish, trips on boats and the hiring of bathing machines for the ladies. Their shouts were quite deafening, and one couldn't hear individual words so much as a tumult, an assault of supplication on our ears. I felt Rosie's fingers on my forearm, the gentlest of touches.

'Keep going, Leo.' She pointed towards a line of broken-down hansom cabs, their horses stewing in the heat. 'We'll be out of this in no time.'

A young man, no more than sixteen, sidled up to us. 'Looking for somewhere to stay? I know all the right places. No fee neither.'

Peregrine batted him aside without a word and skittled three more – the first offering high-class accommodation, the second, seats at the world's finest circus and a third, occasional, yet well-paid employment for Rosie – in similar fashion before the rest of them realised we were well defended and went off in search of easier prey.

The cabbie looked up from his newspaper. 'You never said nothing about kids. I don't take kids. They vomit.'

Peregrine appeared nonplussed, turning to us and noticing, apparently for the first time, that Lillian and Sam were standing on the pavement next to us.

'You brought children?' he exclaimed, his voice rising even above the cacophony. 'To a murder scene?'

Lillian took a stronger grip.

'Mr Black,' said Rosie. 'Please be more careful with your language.' She covered little Sam's ears, although, in fairness to Peregrine, the boy was oblivious.

Peregrine gave her a contrite bow. 'Of course, my apologies, Mrs Flowers. I mean, Mrs *Stanhope*, of course. And congratulations, by the way, on your nuptials. Marriage is a marvellous institution.'

One which he had roundly abused, I thought, though perhaps a man can approve of a thing without being inclined to practise it himself. After all, I encouraged truthfulness in the children, yet I deceived them constantly.

Rosie offered him the kind of smile which really ought to come with a warning. 'We bring *our* kids with us when we travel, Mr Black.'

He failed to notice the emphasis, perhaps deliberately, and emitted a rumbling sigh, which made the horse widen its nostrils and take a half a step sideways. 'The thing is,' he explained, 'there's been another ...' He glanced at Sam and flapped a pudgy hand, trying to think of the right word. 'Another *event*. Similar to the first *event*, I gather. It happened this morning.' He leaned forward and whispered in a voice louder than I was able to shout: 'The, ah, the *remains*, as it were, are in the same place, near the Gosport bridge.'

The cabbie folded his newspaper and started gathering up his reins.

Peregrine pointed a finger at him. 'You stay where you are.'

I frowned. 'Another, in addition to the one you wrote to me about?'

'Yes, exactly. Weren't you listening? Now, Leo, we have to go. I told the police that a top newspaperman was coming down from London to report on the story. They're waiting for you, all agog, poor lambs. They think they're going to be famous.'

'Of course.' I was about to climb into the cab when Rosie stamped her foot.

'What about us?'

She was ever my partner in such endeavours. I could do my usual reporting on scientific discoveries – planetary movements, medicines and new strains of tea – on my own while she ran the pie shop. But, on those few occasions when the subject was murder, we came as a pair.

Peregrine shrugged. 'There's no time to lose and you can't bring children.'

The cabbie stuck out his chin. 'No, you can't. Them seats is newly cleaned.'

Rosie looked furious. 'Very well. We'll go to Viola's house and meet you later. I see no other choice.'

'Tomorrow, perhaps,' said Peregrine. 'Leo will stay with me tonight, of course. I've made arrangements.'

I hadn't expected this. My preference was to stay with Rosie at my sister-in-law's house. But before I could decline Peregrine's offer, Rosie nodded and accepted his card.

'Good, yes. We'll stay with Viola and Leo can stay with you. That's perfect.'

She picked up her neat little bag and handed me the drawstring hessian tater sack containing my essentials.

'Lillian, Sam,' she said. 'Come along. We're not needed here.'

I watched them head off to the back of the line for a cab, feeling more than a pinch of guilt. They were the most precious things I could imagine, along with Robbie, who by now would be beating Jacob at chess. My friend's faculties were not as they had once been.

'Stop daydreaming and hop in,' said Peregrine. 'The police are expecting us.'

The cab seemed crowded even with only the two of us. Peregrine took up a great deal of space, both physically and conversationally, prattling on about the play he was in and complaining that the local audiences weren't nearly as receptive as they'd been in Brighton and Margate where, he claimed, they'd begged for three encores. I was only half-listening, watching the narrow streets glide past, stunned by the smallness of everything. In central London, most buildings were six or seven storeys tall, but here they were two at most, and I felt as if I could step over them like dolls' houses and stride my way home across southern England.

Peregrine pulled down the window, allowing a light breeze into the cab.

'Wake up, laddie, for goodness' sake.'

The stink of fish and salt, which I had assumed was limited to the stalls at the station, grew stronger. The whole city must reek of it.

'I'm sorry. Tell me about this murder.'

His expression darkened. Beneath his bravado and, it must be said, occasional tendency to violence, he was a soft-hearted man. Indeed, his anger was only ever engaged in service to that soft heart. He couldn't bear injustice. He'd once remarked that we had that in common, though I wasn't so sure. If my experiences had taught me anything, it was that injustice was the natural way of the world and could come upon us any minute, any second, without warning or purpose. No resistance or readiness would help. If the cab were to throw a wheel, I could split my head on the doorframe or be pierced by a stray wheel-spoke in a second. My life would have no more meaning than that of the fly presently crawling across my knee, and could be swatted just as easily.

'I don't know much about this one,' Peregrine acknowledged, waving a fist at the fly, which had flown up towards his face. 'The body was left in the same place as the first. A girl this time, I believe.'

'How did you hear about her death?'

'My landlady, Mrs Mackay, told me just as I was coming to meet you. She said the police were swarming around the place, asking questions of everyone. Naturally, I went down there, but they wouldn't let me anywhere near. They're all in a tizz.

9

I mentioned you to the chap in charge, and he seemed rather impressed.'

I rolled my eyes. 'What on earth did you tell him?'

'Top man at the *Daily Chronicle*, knows all the best people, that sort of thing. I may have mentioned the Home Secretary.'

'You may have *what*?' I sat back, marvelling at his cheek. 'I'm a science writer. I don't know anyone important. I'm lucky if I get one article in the paper a *week*.'

He sniffed. 'Truly? Oh. Well, that is disappointing. I was under the impression … well, anyway, it doesn't matter, does it? This is the provinces, after all. He doesn't know you're a nobody.'

Our cab was delayed by a queue of traffic. Alongside the road, a great work was being carried out, men crawling over a pile of rubble the height of a horse and breaking it further with sledgehammers, passing lumps of rock – each the size of a loaf of bread – from hand to hand along the line. Around them, other men were standing in bowler hats, carrying what I thought, at first, were rolled-up umbrellas – hardly necessary in this weather – but then realised were rifles. The labourers were linked at the ankles with leg irons and chains, making their work precarious and slow.

Peregrine eyed them with pity. 'They're building yet another barracks, I'm told. The Navy owns this town.'

We rounded the junction, passing a formal garden, bountiful in the sunshine, and more military fortifications bearing masts and flags. From the saline smell and the weeping of the seagulls, I assumed the sea lay beyond, out of sight. As the street broadened out, the buildings became more colourful, and the people more numerous and better dressed.

Peregrine rapped on the ceiling to catch the cabbie's attention. 'On the left here.'

We threaded between warehouses to where the road ended at an open metal gate wide enough for three carriages to pass through side by side. Beyond it lay a stony beach and a grey expanse of sea.

'Can't go no further,' the cabbie called down. 'Sixpence half-penny, including the wait.'

We climbed out, but Peregrine made no move to produce his wallet. 'I'm merely your guide. I assumed the newspaper would be paying.'

My boss, J. T. Whitford, had been resistant even to covering my train fare, hinting that my reluctance to visit the seaside in the middle of a heatwave was an elaborate bluff. Only after I had come into the office as normal that morning did he relent, instructing Miss Chive, who looked after the cash box, to give me ten shillings, not a penny more, and to make darned sure I signed a chit.

I paid the cabbie, half-choking from the wretched stench of the shoreline. Above us, the sun, which had previously been clear and bright, had become a hazy disc, ringed with green. I put my sleeve across my mouth and followed Peregrine towards the gate.

'Christ,' he croaked, as I caught up to him. 'What a place to die.'

2

IN FRONT OF US, the sea was smothered in a sulphurating fog. Vast grey shapes hovered within it, some darker, some lighter, some with sails hanging like paupers' rags.

'Where's this bridge?' I asked, as we crunched across the pebbles.

Peregrine pointed towards a jetty to our right, oil-black and skeletal, mounted above the stones on wooden posts. 'Not a real bridge. Gosport's more than a mile away. There's a chain from one shore to the other and the ferry goes to and fro along it. Cargo mostly.'

'You seem to know a lot about this town for someone who's only been here a few weeks.'

His ample face twitched with irritation. 'I have curiosity, that's all. I like to know things.'

I too have curiosity, I thought. Peregrine had never told me where he came from or who his family were, nor anything about himself beyond the immediate and obvious. Even his name was surely a fabrication; *Peregrine Black* was like a character in a book by Mr Poe, sophisticated, idiosyncratic and dangerous. It was perfect for him as he was now, but what parent in their right mind would choose it for their newborn child?

Ahead of us, ghostly shadows formed into silhouettes of people, strutting about in a manner both authoritative and aimless, which could mean only one thing: policemen. Above them, seagulls were bickering and spiralling in the sky, dipping and veering away, greedy for whatever lay below.

'We're here!' Peregrine called, in a voice so booming I was surprised no answering foghorn came from out of the murk. 'I've brought the journalist!'

A figure came towards us, stooped and weary. He coalesced into a uniformed fellow, peering at us from under his helmet. I'd never seen a policeman so old. Despite the sagging of his skin, falling around his jowls like pastry dough, his moustache was coal-black, and his eyes were sharp.

He shook my hand. 'Sergeant Dorling. You're the important fellow down from London, are you?'

'Yes.' There seemed no other sensible answer. 'My name's Stanhope. I'm a journalist with the *Daily Chronicle*.'

He gave me a quick once-over, taking in my narrow-brimmed hat, my woollen jacket and my shiny Oxford shoes, size eight, and appeared satisfied. Apparently, I matched his idea of what a London journalist should look like. He couldn't know that my feet were size five and Rosie had constructed leather insoles to prevent my shoes from falling off.

We followed him across the stones towards the jetty, the reek of the sea getting stronger. Though the sun could scarcely penetrate the fog, the heat was unbearable, made worse by the damp air. I wiped my forehead on my sleeve, leaving a dark stain in the wool.

Dorling seemed determined to ingratiate himself.

'I met Sir Richard Mayne once, you know,' he said conversationally, unaware that I had no idea who he was talking about. 'He knew how to get things done. A great shame he's gone. He wouldn't have let the bloody Irish explode bombs in our capital. He'd string up every Paddy he could find first.'

Briefly, I was glad Rosie wasn't with me. 'I see.'

'I've no time for this new chap, Henderson.'

Light dawned upon my slow-moving brain. Peregrine had told him that I knew powerful people. Henderson was in charge of the police force in London, and I supposed Mayne must have been his predecessor.

'I haven't spoken to Henderson,' I replied, as if this omission was purely by chance and I was otherwise quite familiar with gentlemen of his rank.

He accepted this with a nod, his eyes resting briefly on my cheek. In certain lights, people noticed the sheen of it and probably wondered whether my malady was due to burning by fire or a defect of birth. The answer was fire. My defect of birth was otherwise.

On such a calm day, the waves were small, swishing and sighing against the stones, reminding me of little Sam's snoring at night, tucked into the bed he shared with Robbie. Those everyday noises: the rattle of carriages in the street, the hooting of distant trains and Rosie's singing in the kitchen; for a second, I wanted nothing more than to be back in our tiny home, where the smells were of ash in the grate and pies in the oven and ink in the books on the shelf.

A young constable stood aside as we approached, starting to doff his helmet before thinking better of the idea.

A curled figure was lying on the stones in the shade of the jetty, surrounded by policemen.

Peregrine stopped walking before I did. I heard him mutter, 'Dear God,' and the scrunch of his shoes on the shingle as he turned away.

The body was of a young woman. Her feet were bare, but she was otherwise fully clothed in a floral dress and light cotton jacket, one hand thrown above her head and the other tucked under her chin. She was resting on her hat as if someone had wanted her to be comfortable. Her eyes were closed, and her face was serene, pinkish-blue lips pushed out in a childish pout. In the curve where her jaw met her neck, a neat cut had been made, an inch wide. It was as efficient a killing as I had ever seen; no desperate slashing, no remorseful rending of her clothes, no fearful attempt to hide the body. She had been dispatched as neatly as a bobby calf.

One constable made a remark I couldn't hear, and the others sniggered. I had the urge to push them away from her. I knew their humour was motivated by fear, but still, it should be saved for the pub later, when they could clink their glasses and drain their ales and numb themselves to the certainty that their own bodies would one day be as still and cold as hers.

I crouched down beside her. 'What's her name?'

Dorling sniffed, wiggling his moustache. 'We don't know. She's not local.'

'What makes you say that?'

He pulled a pen from his pocket and twitched back her sleeve with it. He was too squeamish to touch the dead. 'See the tattoo?' he said. 'It's foreign.'

I took her forearm, having no similar compunctions. It was oddly heavy and dense, more like a man's. She had been remarkably muscular in life. I placed my own hand against hers, wondering, for a brief second, whether she might be like me, or my mirror image anyway, but her hand was small and her fingers slim. She wasn't wearing a ring and there was no sign – no indent or paleness – to indicate she ever had. I felt her palms, and they were as hard as boiled pigskin and marked with circles like ringworm, though no infestation could have penetrated so tough a leather. I ran my finger around the circles, determining that they were callouses, rubbed down and remade so often that they no longer left any ridges on her flesh.

'What are you doing?' asked Dorling.

I supposed my actions must have looked rather intimate, though they weren't intended that way. I felt an affinity for the dead. Had we been alone I would have spoken to her, helping her along her journey with gentler words than the last she'd probably heard.

'She was strong. And she worked hard.' I leaned down to sniff her hair and the collar of her dress. 'No smell of ammonia. I doubt she was a maid or a laundress.'

'A factory girl?'

'Perhaps.'

But I didn't think so. I'd visited factories that made pencils and lampshades and jute, and always it was the men who did the heavy labour, lifting, pulling and ratcheting. Women did the more dexterous tasks, no less difficult, their fingers darting into the machinery like sparrows' beaks. But this woman had power in her shoulders and neck. Remembering the events of the previous year, I checked her knuckles, but she was no fighter.

There were no healed cuts or bruises on her face. I examined her forearms, searching for other damage. Near her right shoulder, her skin was grazed, as if she'd fallen against a harsh surface. Her elbow joint felt strange too, bumpy and misaligned, as though it had mended badly after a break.

'She's led a hard life, but these aren't defensive wounds. She was surprised by the attack.'

'Makes sense,' said Dorling, though I could see he wasn't truly interested. He was looking out across the harbour at the ships.

'She may have been ill-treated.'

And yet ... was that right? Her hair was newly cut and styled. Her dress was pleasant and well sewn. She didn't seem like someone who'd been held against her will.

Dorling was becoming impatient. 'What of the writing?'

I straightened her arm. The tattoo was in dark blue ink and not recent; silky hairs had grown through it. I read the words out loud, slowly picking through the syllables, having no idea what language they were in. 'Urodzona by latać.'

'What does it mean?'

'I don't know. Any ideas, Peregrine?'

He shook his head, standing a few yards away, covering his mouth and avoiding looking directly at the girl.

'I'll find out,' I said.

Dorling clapped his hands together in a manner that might have appeared genial had his teeth not been clenched into a grimace.

'Of course,' he said. 'Your newspaper will have resources in London we don't have here. Translators and so forth.'

'Exactly.'

I ducked my face, unable to keep from smiling. I was picturing the resources available to me at the office: my colleague Harry, whose knowledge of languages was limited to the few words of French he'd learned in an attempt to seduce a young governess who turned out to be Portuguese, and a copy-boy whose father had taught him some Arabic swear words. No, my resources in this matter had nothing to do with the *Daily Chronicle*. They were an irascible old Jewish man with a failing memory and his blind wife; the wisest two people I knew.

'How does this compare with the last murder?' I asked Dorling. 'Tell me about the victim.'

He snorted. 'One of *those* lads, taking money from perverts, selling themselves like women. What can they expect?'

I gave him a thin smile. 'To live, I would have thought. Failing that, justice, at the least.'

He drew himself up. 'You may think us primitive, Mr Stanhope, and lacking in your London proprieties. But I assure you, we are as ready to defeat crime as any police force on the south coast. Don't confuse us with those buffoons in Bournemouth or Worthing. We're already on the track of the killer and, I have no doubt, will soon apprehend him.'

'Or her.'

He gave a knowing smirk. 'Oh no, ladies don't commit murders like this. They don't have the constitution for it.'

'I suppose their parasols get in the way.'

He narrowed his eyes, uncertain whether I was being sarcastic. 'You have an unpleasant mind, Mr Stanhope. Very unpleasant.'

'That's true enough. Who's your suspect?'

'I can't tell you that. Not yet. Don't want to spook the fellow. But we're on his trail, make no mistake about it.'

I wasn't sure whether to believe him. He was so keen to demonstrate the competence of the local police force that he may have been constructing a story for my benefit, and in fact be completely clueless.

'And the first victim's name?'

'Micky Long, though we don't know if that was real. Probably wasn't. They make up names. Aged nineteen, give or take. He was killed in this exact place, six days ago.'

'In the same way, I gather. Does he have any next of kin? A mother?'

'A younger brother, I believe, in the same game.' The sergeant folded his arms. 'You're asking a lot of questions, Mr Stanhope.'

I chose not to meet his eye. 'In the interests of our readers. I'm sure you'd rather I wrote about how the police were informative, rather than obstructive. Commissioner Henderson would be most concerned if—'

'All right, Mr Stanhope, all right.' He pursed his lips. 'We assumed it was one of his deviant customers until ...' He waved in the direction of the girl. 'Until this. They were killed in a similar fashion. There was more blood with him, though of course it rained this morning, and it was dry last week. When the holiday-makers came down to the beach, there was quite a to-do, seeing him posed that way.'

'Posed?'

He twitched again. 'Yes, *posed*, much like this girl. It's not a natural position for a murder victim, is it? Though I can't see why you'd need such details. I can't imagine the readership of the *Daily Chronicle* will be interested in the posthumous position-ing of the body. Surely, they're more interested in our hunt for the killer, knowing that the redoubtable boys of the Portsmouth police will be ...'

'Was he *exactly* the same?'

It was Peregrine who answered, his voice, normally so power-ful, quavering like a goat's. 'Yes, the same. His eyes had been pecked out by the gulls. It was awful.'

'Was Micky Long from around here?'

'Probably,' said Dorling. 'No one mentioned an accent or any tattoos. Born at the docks I should think, like most of 'em.'

He hadn't consulted his notebook. I wondered whether anyone had bothered to find out for sure.

'Did he have any other injuries? Grazes or broken bones?'

'Cuts and bruises, I think. Nothing unusual, given his choice of occupation.'

I sighed, wondering whether an examination of Micky Long's body at the mortuary might reveal something more useful than Dorling's vague pronouncements. But it was a fleeting thought. I was here to write my article and then go home, and there was no time for distractions.

I contemplated the young woman again. It seemed that these two killings had many features in common – the slit throats and bodies left in the same place and posture – but also some differences. What connected a lad who earned his living on the street to a well-dressed, foreign young woman? The thought occurred to me that, rather than being a second killing by the same person, this might be a response to the first killing by someone else. I might be looking at an act of revenge.

I wished Rosie was here. She could summon insights I could not and had a knack for understanding people. To me, they were a language I would never wholly understand, but Rosie was fluent. I pictured her now, settled with a pot of tea, nattering with her sister about pregnancy and parenthood and perhaps, if her patience was already running thin, her experiences of childbirth. I had never met Viola, but I gathered, as much from what Rosie didn't say as what she did, that the woman could be somewhat trying. But still, I wanted to meet my sister-in-law. Why was Rosie so keen to keep us apart? Our marriage was one of convenience, but I *was* her husband. Was I so ill-made that she was ashamed of me?

We were about to leave when a young constable arrived with a shirtless fellow in tow, his substantial belly barely hidden beneath a bib.

'This gentleman owns a shop on the Pembroke Road,' the officer said. 'He saw a girl who fits the description.' He indicated the victim. 'Is this her?'

The poor fellow seemed close to tears, pulling off his cap and running his fingers through his hair. 'Yes, I think so, sir. We're next to the gardens and we sell souvenirs and the like, for the ladies. She bought a brooch for sixpence. Pretty thing, made of pewter. My wife makes 'em.'

I gently rolled the girl so we could see her jacket lapel and, sure enough, a rough-made brooch of Celtic design was pinned to it.

'This one?'

'Yes, sir.' He turned away.

'Was she on her own?' I asked, and he nodded. 'Did she seem relaxed? Happy?'

'Certainly. Lovely smile, and not in a rush neither. I told her she should get a ring to match, but she wouldn't. She said a ring would hurt her fingers.'

'What did she mean by that?'

Dorling was listening to this exchange with growing irritation. 'Constable, take this man to the station. We can interview him properly there.' He turned and shook my hand, effectively dismissing me. 'I hope what you write reflects well on the Portsmouth police force,' he said. 'We do what we can with the thin resources we have.'

'I'm sure.'

'And should you require more information towards a *positive* article, I'm always available.'

'Thank you, but this is a brief trip and I'll be returning to London tomorrow. The day after at the latest.'

'Well, that's a shame.' He looked mightily relieved. 'It's not often we get gentlemen of the press down here from the capital.'

Peregrine and I crunched back to the road. He was unusually quiet, his hands thrust into his pockets and his face lowered. As we reached the giant metal gate, I stopped and faced him.

'Did you know the lad? The one who was killed here first.'

There was a minute's pause before he answered. It would hardly have been noticeable with anyone else, but Peregrine was rarely reticent. He loved to fill the air with words.

'Only vaguely.'

'How?'

He looked away and wiped his eyes. 'It's no matter. I have nothing of interest to offer, I assure you.'

'He worked as a … a molly-lad? Is that the right word?'

Peregrine pulled a face. 'It's one of them. There are many, none of them kind. He worked mostly on the ships, I believe. Like I said, I hardly knew him.'

And yet, I thought, he had taken the trouble to write to me requesting that I come all the way to this dismal town to investigate the lad's murder. I'd thought he simply missed my company, but now I wasn't sure.

'And did you know the girl?'

'No.'

21

This time, he was telling the truth.

We turned the corner on to a larger street, which was surprisingly industrious, crammed with people. They were ignorant of the tragedy that had occurred only a few dozen yards away. Many were what one would expect in such a spot: dockers hauling sacks on barrows, seamen smoking and chatting as they wandered home, their lean faces black with oil, and the occasional woman, heading to the market for provisions. But in amongst them, a few gentlemen could be spotted in top hats or bowlers, portfolios gripped in their hands.

Peregrine noticed my curiosity. 'They're here to argue down their excises,' he said, in a tone of disgust, as if describing maggots crawling on carrion. 'The Customs House is back there.'

'Does that mean there's a telegraph office nearby? I'd like to send a telegram.'

As we headed north along the shoreline, I felt strangely precarious. To our left, the mudflats stretched out, merging with the harbour, veiled in fog and smoke. To our right, warehouses were crushed together like teeming carcasses, interspersed with tiny shops as vivid as butterflies among the soot-stained walls and rotting wood paving. Most of them sold tobacco, but one was a barber with a queue of customers straggling along the pavement, another a tailor and yet another a dolly-shop, where a gambling man might leave his wife's jewellery and hope to reclaim it the next day. I closed my left eye and could believe I was in the heart of a city, but when I closed my right, I felt as if I was on the brink of the sea and might be washed away at any minute.

The telegram office was small but seemed efficient. The clock behind the desk told us it was six-fifteen. I hoped Jacob would have time to send me a reply that evening.

'What's your address, Peregrine?'

I wrote out my form and handed it to the clerk. He read it back to me letter by letter.

'Trnslt ths pls: Urodzona by latac. Rssn? Germn? Ydsh? Rply 19 Hudson Rd, Ptsmth.'

The clerk was about to send it when I stopped him. 'Please add the following. "P to K4".'

This last was a chess move: pawn to king four. Jacob had placed a set on his table at home, and I planned to do the same in Portsmouth, so we would be able to play a game remotely by telegram, keeping the two boards synchronised. However, my set was in the bag at Rosie's sister's house, along with my spare clothes; one more reason to curse our separation.

I paid the man and we left, Peregrine picking up the pace as we headed inland. We scurried like mice under the shade of another barracks, and onwards into a maze of streets, each lined with terraced houses as identical as the sausage rolls Rosie cut in her shop every morning.

'I told Mrs Mackay you'll be staying,' announced Peregrine. 'My landlady. Best you don't talk to her about … well, anything. Just stay away from her.'

'Why?'

He didn't reply, but bellowed: 'It's us!' as he pushed open the door, making me recoil briefly back on to the pavement.

Inside, the hallway had a faintly leathery smell and was decorated with wallpaper in bold black and gold stripes. A corridor led to a kitchen at the back, and I caught a glimpse of a dining table not unlike ours in London. I pinched the flesh at the crook of my elbow with my fingernails, almost breaking the skin. I was tiring of my own homesickness. I'd never been one to get attached to a *place* before and had lived in a dozen homes at least, some of them without the owner's permission.

A stairway led upstairs, and I followed Peregrine, his bulk blocking out the light. At the top, a landing led to two bedrooms.

'I'm paying for both,' he declared, as though he'd hired twin yachts for us, with gaggles of servants.

In one of the rooms, I heard a stirring and a yawn, followed by the sound of feet on creaking floorboards. Peregrine's face took on a stony look – not easy for one with such an abundance of flesh – and he attempted to usher me into the other. But he was too late. A young man emerged on to the landing, wearing only a pair of drawers. He was as skinny as a newborn eel, with a pale, hairless chest and a hungry face. His eyes were slow and full of sleep.

Peregrine glowered at him, though not without a degree of fondness. 'I thought you were going to leave before I got back.'

The lad yawned without covering his mouth. 'I fell asleep. It was comfy.' He glanced at the hessian sack I was still clutching and thumbed towards Peregrine. 'Watch out for this one. He has an actor's temperament.'

Peregrine ushered the lad back into the bedroom. 'Mr Stanhope is a friend visiting from London. Now get dressed and go.'

I confess, I was shocked. I thought of myself as a man of the world and was well aware of my friend's liberal approach to matters of the heart and flesh, but this was a level of blatancy surprising even to me.

Peregrine frowned, correctly interpreting my expression.

'We are who we are, Leo. You should know that better than anyone.'

'What of Miranda?'

His wife had been left behind in Holborn with their child, whose name and gender I couldn't recall, if indeed I had ever known. Peregrine rarely talked of them.

His mouth formed a hard line like the top bar of a closed gate. 'Miranda and I are honest with each other. And it's no business of yours.'

'You're right, of course. I apologise.'

He grinned and clapped me on the shoulder. One of his endearing qualities was how swiftly his tempers passed. They blew in and out like March winds.

'It's wonderful you're here, Leo. I've been bored without a true friend to argue with. Now, I have to get ready for the theatre, but we'll have a nightcap when I get back, yes?'

He closed his door, and I could hear low voices through the wall. The young man was teasing Peregrine.

I opted for discretion, ensconcing myself in my temporary bedroom. It was plain and unfurnished aside from a narrow bed, but was warm enough, and I was grateful to have it. The window looked out on to a pleasant garden and the houses behind, damp laundry hanging hopelessly from lines tied between the fences.

I pulled out my notebook and began writing my article. I was planning to send it to the newspaper office to be typed up by Miss Chive. As ever these days, I covered the simple facts in a sensible order, adding no colour or postulations of my own. I had no doubt the subeditors would enhance my bald text, perhaps creating a nickname for the killer such as the 'Seaside Stabber' or 'South Coast Sweeney Todd', but I would not. I'd made that mistake before.

The first paragraph was scarcely completed, detailing the exact dates and location of the murders, when I heard the visitor padding down the stairs and the front door opening and shutting. Not fifteen minutes later, Peregrine's heavy footsteps followed.

I was glad of the peace and quiet, which lasted until I heard a loud knock at the front door. There was no sign of the landlady, so I went to answer it, meeting a messenger boy, who handed me a telegram with my name at the top. I felt a brief rush of excitement. I still found receiving a telegram thrilling; much more urgent than a letter and you never knew what they might contain.

It was a reply from Jacob. I read it out loud as I climbed the stairs, translating the cryptic strings of consonants into words. He started with the chess: *Pawn to king's knight five.* I pictured the move in my head, our two pawns venturing forward, each unopposed, for now. Knights and bishops would soon emerge from the rear-guard to sweep them away.

The second part was more significant: *Not Russian or German but a Slavic dialect. It means Born to Fly.*

I took a moment to marvel at Jacob's command of languages, gained of necessity as he and Lilya had fled across Europe, escaping from … well, if I was honest, I wasn't certain what from. He never talked about it. He regularly harangued me about the failings of young people today, squinting pointedly through his overflowing eyebrows, or boasted about his long-ago exploits on the docks, or expounded endlessly, endlessly, endlessly about the intricacies of jewel settings, carat measurements and patination. But never about why they had left Nikolaev thirty or more years before. But he was Jewish, and I knew how Jews were treated in London, so I supposed I could imagine.

I pinched myself. I needed to concentrate.

What mattered was that I had gathered new information about the girl: she came from far away. I wondered whether she was newly arrived by boat in this city. If so, I might never discover who had killed her, or even what her name was.

And then, there was that tattoo. *Born to Fly*? What could it mean?

3

IN THE MORNING, I awoke with a sore neck and a throbbing head.

I had lain awake for an hour or more thinking about that poor girl, left in open sight on the beach. It wasn't up to me to uncover her killer, yet somehow I couldn't stop thinking about her. *Born to fly.* Fly where, and how? Fly as in 'flee', from wherever she came from to wherever she was going? Or was she a balloonist? She didn't seem like one, though I had no idea what one would seem like.

My attempts at sleep had been interrupted by Peregrine, who returned full of elation at the encore his play had received, including, he claimed, a particular blooming of the applause as he took his own bow. To celebrate, he produced a bottle of perhaps the nastiest liquid I had ever tasted, which he insisted was Danish schnapps. Unlike most drinks, it failed to improve after four or five glasses, retaining a sickly sweetness that made my tongue swell. Now, with the sun shining through the curtains and piercing the backs of my eyeballs, I dearly wished I'd been more temperate.

A rush from my stomach prompted an urgent grovelling under the bed for a chamber pot. I located it just in time for a thorough and purple evacuation. Thus relieved, I managed to stand, clutching the bedpost as the room tipped and slid around me. I reclothed myself, taking an age with each button and buckle, stuck my hat firmly on my head and stumbled down to the privy to empty my chamber pot and my bowels.

On my way back through the house, I passed the open door of the sitting room and caught sight of Peregrine's landlady, a woman in her forties. She was dressed in masculine riding attire and tending to what appeared to be a legless horse supported on a wooden frame. For a moment I wondered whether last night's excesses had permanently sundered my mind from reality. But no, it truly was half of a horse: a head, neck and back, complete with saddle, withers and tail, but no legs or, I now noticed, belly. Behind it, a bucolic scene had been painted on the wall showing trees, fields and a distant house, smoke rising from its chimney. As I watched, the woman climbed on to the abridged beast and sat in the saddle, bouncing up and down as if the thing were trotting, occasionally flicking its rump with her crop.

I climbed the stairs again.

Peregrine was in his room wearing a quite hideous shirt, with stripes that reminded me of the recent contents of my chamber pot.

'Dear God,' he said. 'Have you died? Are you a walking corpse?'

I ignored him. 'Your landlady …'

'Mrs Mackay. Don't talk to her.'

'Yes, but she has a …' My hands made the inadvertent motion of a rider holding reins, though the only horse I'd ever mastered was a rocking one in the vicarage as a child.

'I know. I did the backdrop for her. Do you like it?'

I was briefly dumbfounded. My brain seemed to be malfunctioning. In fact, it seemed to be trying to beat its way out of my skull.

'But why?'

He smiled patiently. 'It's for portraits. People like to be captured on horseback. Mrs Mackay does photographs, but it can't be with a real horse, obviously. Sometimes I paint them instead. Look, I'll show you.'

He pulled aside a sheet, revealing five small canvases leaning against the wall. Four of them portrayed men apparently cantering through the countryside. They were identical with respect to the background, the horse's flowing mane and their grip on the reins, each of their jackets billowing behind them. Even their delighted smiles were eerily similar. The last canvas was much like the others, except the rider was nothing more than an outline, a blank space, yet to be filled.

Peregrine bowed sarcastically low, showing considerable grace for so large a man. 'It's my talent.'

As he wrapped them up again, I noticed one further canvas, bigger than the others, that he hadn't shown me.

'What's that?' I asked, ever eager to tease my friend. I knew he didn't mind hackwork to augment his actor's salary, but he retained higher artistic ambitions as well. He'd once compared his work to that of George Frederick Watts.

'That's nothing. A portrait.'

My mind slipped unwillingly back to my childhood, sitting in our parlour with my hair tied fiercely back, trying to stay still while one of my father's parishioners, who fancied himself an artist, wielded a brush and snapped at me to *stop damn well fidgeting*. The resulting artwork resembled a monster of Mary Shelley's imagination and was banished to the maid's quarters. I still shuddered at the memory.

I snatched up the canvas before he could stop me. It was quite beautiful. Pastel swirls and touches of paint suggested a woodland setting, but it was indistinct, framing the subject and casting a halo of light about her face. Her hand was at her chest, caressing a red jewel hung on a chain around her neck. She was older than me, though not by much, with a blush in her cheeks and hair curling to her shoulders. Her stare was frank, and her expression relaxed, though also in the set of her mouth curious, as though she were trying to work out what to make of me.

Peregrine grabbed it out of my hands. 'It's not for ...' He paused and hugged the picture to his chest. 'It isn't finished. And you shouldn't look at people's private things.'

'But it's lovely.'

His face fought a brief battle with itself, indignation giving way to a kind of simpering assent. 'It was a commission. No one you know.' He rolled his eyes. 'Definitely not someone you *want* to know.'

'Why not? Who is she?'

'It doesn't matter.' He patted his stomach. 'All this talk is making me hungry.'

I couldn't say the same. I was feeling nauseous.

'We'll have to be quick. I want to know more about the girl who was killed. Where did she come from? And what does "Born to Fly" mean?'

'What?'

'It's the translation of her tattoo.'

He thought about it for about a second before returning to pulling on his trousers. 'Who knows? Probably nothing.'

'Then why did she choose it? Those exact words. It must mean *something*.'

'Must it?' He waved a dismissive hand. 'I knew a fellow once who wanted a tattoo of his wife's name on his back. The tattooist was drunk and put his own wife's name there instead, and the poor fellow had a terrible time explaining the mistake. His wife tried to burn it off with bleach and he ended up in the infirmary.'

I didn't have time for Peregrine's narrative perambulations. 'That cannot be true.'

'But it *should* be, don't you think? And my point stands. You can't assume much about the poor thing from a tattoo. She may have kept birds in her spare time or enjoyed looking at butterflies. Girls can be romantic like that.'

I supposed he had a point, at least about us not knowing the origins of the tattoo. But it was the only clue we had. Fortunately, I knew someone who might be able to discern its meaning. She was a genius when it came to understanding people, especially young women.

'Get dressed,' I instructed Peregrine. 'We're going out.'

'Excellent. I'm starved.'

'Breakfast can wait. First, we're going to fetch Rosie.'

Once Peregrine had prepared himself – including oiling his hair, polishing his shoes and twice trying on a different jacket, but not, despite my urgings, changing his shirt – we headed out of the front door.

I was feeling more perky. The air was pleasantly warm, though it wasn't yet nine in the morning, and the volcano in my stomach had become dormant.

We had barely gone twenty yards before a hansom cab pulled up and Rosie herself climbed out.

'I left the children with Viola,' she announced, though neither of us had asked. She looked me up and down, the beginnings of a frown forming on her forehead. 'What happened to you?'

'We celebrated.'

'Ah, I see.'

Peregrine cleared his throat. 'I know a wonderful place for breakfast.'

Over an insipid pot of tea, I described the murder scene to Rosie. As usual, she asked questions about things I simply hadn't noticed.

'That poor girl. Did she have a bag with her?'

I looked at Peregrine, who pulled a don't-know face while munching on his sausage. Having been bilious earlier, I was now starting to wish I'd ordered food. Rosie had almost finished her porridge.

'I didn't see one,' I replied.

'Did her jacket have pockets?'

'I don't know. Why didn't you have breakfast with Viola?'

'I left early. She wasn't up.'

'We were on our way to you.'

She finished her mouthful, swallowed and wiped her mouth before answering. 'Then I saved you a trip, didn't I?'

Peregrine glanced at each of us in turn. 'Are we discussing your morning's travel arrangement or a murder?'

I drained my tasteless tea. 'Very well. I don't know if she had a bag or pockets. She seemed as if she'd been ill-treated at some point in the past. A healed elbow and graze on her upper arm.'

Rosie pondered for a few seconds, staring at the walls. Peregrine had, typically, picked a theatrical tea-room, plastered with posters for plays, poetry readings and other highbrow entertainments. My embroidered place mat pictured a ballet dancer in épaulement, her hand reaching out towards Peregrine's fried bread.

'And if she'd been a man,' said Rosie, 'would you assume that he'd been ill-treated in the same way? You might have thought he'd been in bar fights or had a dangerous occupation.'

Rosie had, over the past year, become involved with the suffragist movement, and was prone to making such comparisons.

I shook my head. 'Men and women are not the same.'

She blinked four times quickly and sat back, speechless, while Peregrine choked on his sausage. Several of our fellow patrons looked round, and our waitress, who had hitherto spent most of her time preening herself in the mirror, came rushing over to check we had no complaints, a copy of *Robert the Devil* poking conspicuously out of her apron pocket.

I waited for my companions' hilarity to pass. 'What I mean is, people's *attitude* to men and women is different. Their position in society.'

Rosie raised her eyebrows, her eyes fixed somewhere over my left shoulder.

'So, your summary is that she was very strong, a bit bruised, or grazed, with formerly broken bones. Otherwise, she seemed well and had been chatting with a local shopkeeper. And she possessed enough money to buy a brooch she liked. Is that right?'

'I suppose so.'

I was aware that I was sounding peevish, but I was famished, and still feeling a pinch of resentment at her sudden arrival, once again keeping me from meeting her sister. Also, I had the remnants of a headache and my tea tasted as if the same leaves had been used two dozen times before. All things considered, I was out of sorts.

'Was there anything else of note? Any scars on her hands or feet?' Rosie's eyes were still focused on something behind me. I looked over my shoulder, but there was no one there.

'Yes. The skin on her palms was hard and blistered.'

Peregrine applauded Rosie, using just the ends of his fingers. 'Ah, yes, of course, Mrs Stanhope. I see what you're thinking. How clever of you. It's the only explanation.'

I stared from one to the other. 'What is?'

Rosie produced a self-satisfied smirk. 'It's often the way, Mr Black, between myself and Mr Stanhope, though my contributions usually go uncredited.'

I threw up my hands. 'What are the two of you talking about?'

She smiled and pointed her spoon, wafting the smell of porridge in my direction. 'See there, Leo? On the wall behind you.'

I looked back and there was a poster picturing two women. One was flying through the air, her flimsy skirt rising to reveal shapely calves, while the other was dangling upside down, her teeth gripping a rope from which was hanging, despite all the rules of common sense, a full-sized cannon.

'You think she was a circus performer?'

'It would explain her injuries, don't you think?'

I shrugged, unwilling to admit that she might be right. 'No one could hold on to something that heavy. She'd pull out all her teeth.'

Rosie rolled her eyes. 'Artistic licence, Leo. And it's worth investigating, isn't it?' She produced her spectacles from her bag and put them on, squinting at the poster. 'Quinton's New Hippodrome. We should go there later and make enquiries.'

Peregrine finished his last mouthful. 'Why not now?'

Rosie smiled. 'Because, Mr Black, my husband has a clear case of the collywobbles and he needs to get some food into his belly before he becomes even more unbearable.'

Peregrine declined to go with us, declaring, as if the matter were self-evident, that circuses were vulgar and lacked aesthetic merit. This, from a man who, when I first met him, sang in the music halls dressed as a shepherdess with a live lamb in his arms.

So, Rosie and I were alone, her arm looped in mine as we strolled along the pavement in the sunshine. For the first time since arriving in this place, I was feeling almost normal, having consumed a plateful of toast and jam, followed by two boiled eggs and another pot of awful tea. Rosie's reluctance to introduce me to her sister now seemed, to my eyes, less a product of embarrassment than an unfortunate, yet understandable reticence. After all, we were married only in name.

I hoped we might leave this very afternoon and be home by the evening. Tomorrow, I could file a story about an unsolved murder in Portsmouth that would appear on page 14 if I was lucky. My mind was already wandering to an announcement by a doctor in India, who had apparently discovered a cure for venomous snake bites.

One final stop and we would be on our way.

The circus was adjacent to the railway station, housed in what was clearly a former industrial building. Its modest brickwork and plain windows might have retained some pleasantness of form, or at least dignity, had it been left that way, but sadly some-one had attached to the front wall a gold awning and three flags, above which was written 'Quinton's New Hippodrome' in gold lettering. The whole ensemble gave the impression of a plain man in a prodigious blond wig. The doors were locked, and the blinds pulled down, so we couldn't see inside. Rosie knocked on the windows, but there was no reply.

'We'll have to wait till this evening,' she said.

'Or forget the whole thing.'

We were deafened as a train came in on the other side of the high wall, the roar and spit of its engine pierced by a shrill whis-tle. I wondered if the poor dead girl had screamed that way too, her voice lost in the wash of the waves.

Looking up, I was surprised to see a fellow staring at us from the other side of the road – not huddling in a porch or in the shadow of the railway bridge, but simply standing in the sunshine, his gaze locked on to us. I caught his eye, and he didn't look away.

'What is it?' asked Rosie.

'Nothing, I'm sure.'

The fellow was already striding away along the pavement, but he glanced back at me from under the brim of his hat. I didn't know him, but I recognised the style of that gait, regular as a clock. My impression was reinforced by his dark, well-pressed suit, which could only be described as *civilian*. My guess was that his more usual garb was a naval officer's uniform.

Rosie gave me a wifely look – a mix of disbelief, irritation and tolerance – and issued a sigh that seemed to come all the way from her feet. 'You've been grumpy since we got to this place. I would've thought a trip to the seaside would be fun, but you're drooping like a lost puppy.'

'I'm not.'

'You are.'

I was about to explain that I was still slightly hungover, that I had slept badly in a strange bed and that I disliked this place and everything about it, when a young lad appeared from our left, pelting headlong down the pavement, leaping out of the way of other pedestrians, his hand pressed on to his flat cap to stop it flying off.

We didn't have time to react. He arrived, breathless and red-faced, and started tugging furiously on the handle of the doors to the building, so hard I thought he might pull out the screws. We watched, mouths open, but he didn't take the slightest notice of us. He was my height or a fraction taller and his cheeks were red from his exertions. He glanced back the way he'd come and balled his fists, seeming to reach a decision, and then rushed around to the side of the building. My curiosity overcame my bad mood, and I followed him. He pulled on a side door, which was also locked, and on the window next to it, managing to prise his fingers under the frame and lever it open. In one movement he hoisted himself up and tipped inside, his feet being the last parts of him to disappear from view.

We had no time to make sense of the lad's sudden arrival and even more sudden exit. A man approached, and I recognised him immediately: the naval fellow who'd been watching us earlier. He, too, was panting, though he was making a strong effort not to appear to do so, tightening his shoulders and taking long, slow breaths through his nose. He tried the main doors, with equally little success, and then turned to face us. 'Did you see where he went?'

He seemed like a man who rarely had need of being polite.

Rosie looked him squarely in the eye. 'I didn't see anyone.'

Inwardly, I smiled. *Rosie, Rosie, Rosie.* Not for one second did I think she would give the lad away to a fellow such as this.

He clenched his teeth, glancing up at the garish frontage of the building as though his prey might be clinging to the awning like a monkey.

'I'll come back later,' he said, apparently of the view we would take a note of his movements and prepare accordingly.

We watched him march away, his boots pounding on the wooden paving: tock, tock, tock. Rosie raised her eyebrows at me. 'You know there's only one thing we can do now, don't you?'

I grinned, all thoughts of leaving this place melting away.

We headed around the side of the building to the window the boy had opened. My better mind was insisting that this was folly. We would certainly be caught and, even if we weren't, how would we question anyone, having broken in? They would assume we were thieves. But another part of me relished this adventure with Rosie, regardless of the consequences. We were at our best at such times.

We looked up at the windowsill together. She claimed to be five feet tall, but I had my doubts, and she always refused my offers to fetch a tape measure and prove the matter one way or another.

'You'll have to go first,' she declared.

4

IT WOULD BE AN exaggeration to suggest that I landed in the building with anything approaching elegance. At least I was saved the indignity of attempting, and no doubt failing, to haul myself up from the ground, as the lad had done. Instead, we had dragged a bin from the alley and positioned it underneath the window for me to stand on. Through the grubby glass, I could see a small room with cupboards, a vase of dead flowers and a Kitchener stove, covered in dust.

Rosie watched me with a smile growing on her face.

'This was a stupid idea.'

'Yours, as I recall.'

'No one's infallible.'

She was enjoying herself as much as I was, and for those few seconds we were exactly as we had once been: two friends on a quest, linked by a bond of trust that neither of us felt the need to verbalise.

The opening was too small to perform any kind of swivel, so I had no choice but to wriggle through head-first and land on the straw-strewn floor. There was a key in the lock of the side door, so I was able to facilitate a more gracious entrance for Rosie. A connoisseur of kitchens, she gave the room a single, dismissive glance.

'Come on,' she whispered, poking her head into the corridor. 'No harm in looking around.'

I hoped she was right.

I could see some light up ahead, where the entrance must be. Rosie led and I crept behind her, trying to keep the contents of my stomach in check despite the stink of lye in the back of my throat. I could hear sounds: a strange rustling, like autumn leaves blowing across a path, and a metallic squeaking, followed by a brief, truncated shout of encouragement and a woman's laughter. I shivered, but not from fear; in fact, I was feeling strangely elated. But I was also chilly, after the warmth of the sun outside. My fingers were going pink.

We reached the entrance, facing the locked street doors. If the blinds had been raised, I guessed we would have been looking at the spot where the naval fellow had spoken to us. Opposite, a pair of curtains obscured what I assumed from the scattered laughter coming from within was the main auditorium. I tweaked the curtain aside and, shoulder to shoulder, we peeked through.

We were looking at the backs of rows of seats facing a proscenium stage, which at first appeared splendidly framed by a pattern of gold relief, reflecting the light of four chandeliers, but I quickly realised was painted on. Indeed, the whole vista had a temporary air, aping the opulence of better theatres, as though the building might at any minute be turned back into a factory, brewery or produce market; whatever it had been before.

A group of eight or so people was on the stage, three of them stretching and the rest looking up and pointing at something above their heads. One of them, a burly fellow wearing black pyjamas, picked up a rope that was hung from a pulley, making me shudder with a dreadful memory: the flailing and kicking as they had hauled, higher and higher in the smoke and ash, until a ghastly silence came upon us all.

It was all I could do not to sink down to my knees and weep.

I felt a hand on my shoulder and met Rosie's green eyes. She gave me a brief nod of understanding and I felt steady again. This was simply a group of circus performers practising their act. No one was about to be hanged.

A young woman, wearing striped bloomers that finished above her knees, took the other end of the rope, looking up at the pulley to check it wasn't knotted. The burly chap took up the slack and wrapped it twice around his waist, setting his feet well apart.

Rosie elbowed me in my ribs and hissed: 'Look, that's her! That's the girl who was on the train. The one I wanted to thank.'

She was right. The young woman was unmistakeable. Her skin the colour of a kestrel's feather was amply exposed by her outfit, but it was more than that: just as in the carriage, she had an air of self-containment, even among the other performers.

She gave the rope a shake and, remarkably, put the end of it into her mouth. It terminated with a leather pad, which she bit on, nodding to her accomplice to pull. As the rope grew taut, she angled her head upwards and was lifted from the stage, all her weight hanging from the leather pad clutched between her teeth. Up and up, she went, spinning slowly, arms outstretched, knees lightly bent, with only the strength of her jaw saving her from a fall that would surely be injurious. What muscles she must possess! My teeth ached watching her.

With each draw on the rope, the squeak of the pulley grew louder and higher pitched. When she arrived at the very top, she reached up and I saw that she was holding something in her hand: a brass oil can. She squirted some oil into the pulley and switched hands, attending to the other side also. As she descended, the pulley gave out a last, feeble mew and thereafter worked in silence.

She alighted on the stage arms outstretched, like a butterfly on a lily.

No wonder she'd proven adept at eluding the crow salesman. She was an acrobat.

In the front row, a broad-shouldered gentleman started clapping, his bald pate bobbing up and down like an egg in boiling water. 'Bravo, Miss La La!' he shouted. 'They'll be queueing all the way to Fratton for tickets.'

The young woman performed a minimal curtsy and disappeared into the wings.

Rosie nudged me. 'I've heard of Miss La La,' she whispered. 'She's famous. On posters.'

'Truly?'

'For a journalist, you're not very observant.' She pointed to the edge of the auditorium. 'I bet you haven't noticed *him* either.'

Crouching by the wall, out of the view of the front-row applauder, was the lad who'd broken in. He wasn't exactly hiding, but he seemed keen not to be noticed, keeping his head down, his flat cap barely showing above the seat backs.

'I'm going to talk to him,' I said. 'I'm sure the girl had a connection to this place.' I gestured towards the stage. '"Born to fly" seems appropriate, wouldn't you say?'

A voice came from behind us. 'What do you know of "born to fly"?'

I was holding on to the curtain and was so surprised I almost pulled it out of its track. I turned, and Miss La La was standing there, now wrapped in a dressing gown, her head cocked to one side. Her approach had been utterly soundless; neither Rosie nor I had heard a footstep or a breath. And she didn't seem nervous to be confronting two strangers either, half-dressed though she was.

Rosie essayed a polite smile. 'We've met before. On the train from London. Do you remember?'

Miss La La shrugged. 'Yes, certainly. You didn't want to buy one of those birds.'

I detected an accent in her voice, reminding me of my friend Lilya's, except fainter, only present in her intonation and a slightly extended sibilance in the word 'yes'. I surmised she had left her home as a child.

'Exactly.' Rosie nodded enthusiastically to show she was friendly and therefore harmless. 'You saved us. I wanted to thank you, but you rushed away.'

Miss La La looked at each of us in turn, a frown forming on her face. 'Is that why you followed me here?' Her eyes strayed to the closed and bolted doors.

'Oh no,' Rosie's fanatical nodding turned quickly to shaking. 'No, we didn't know you were here. We're seeking information about ... about someone who might be from the circus. A young man broke in and we ... well, we wanted to ask some questions, not to follow you.'

'Or steal anything,' I added, earning an eye-roll from Rosie.

The other gave a deep sigh. 'Someone from here. Of course, I should have known straight away. "Born to fly". Where is she? What's she done?' She closed her eyes wearily. 'Do you want money? You can keep her. I have no more money and no more patience. None.'

I shook my head slowly. 'We didn't come for money.'

She shrugged. 'Well, what do you ...' She faltered as the awful possibility seeped into her irritation. 'Has something happened to Natalia? Is she all right?'

I swallowed hard. In a previous job as assistant to a surgeon of the dead, I had occasionally been required to impart bad news to relatives: the dead body, bloated beyond all recognition and gnawed at by fish, was indeed that of their beloved father, husband, brother, whose presence at the Surrey dock, barefoot and trouser-less, could not easily be explained. But at least those families had a degree of preparation, waiting in the hospital chapel, fearing the worst. Telling this young woman, who had no clue until this moment that her friend might be dead, felt altogether different.

I took a deep breath and spoke as gently as I could. 'Did Natalia have a tattoo?'

She pulled up her sleeve to reveal a tattoo in exactly the same spot on her forearm as the deceased: *Urodzona by latać*.

Born to fly.

———

We sat in the back row as the troupe of performers gathered round. They wanted to know every detail of the murder scene and asked, tears making tracks through their chalk face powder, why anyone would want to murder little Natalia La Blanche? Yes, she was a wild one, but also sweet and kind, and she could charm the stars down from the sky. Sometimes, they said, she would leave them for days at a time, fall in love and return heart-broken, only to do it all again a fortnight later. She loved to fall in love. And when she couldn't find someone for herself, she would matchmake for everyone else. Two of them, the burly fellow and an almost equally well-built woman, briefly touched hands and smiled, their eyes wet.

When they had asked all their questions and accepted that we had no more answers, they drifted away, sitting in twos and threes on the edge of the stage or in the front row, talking in whispers – all save Miss La La, whose real name turned out to be Olga Brown.

'I'm only Miss La La on the stage,' she explained, her voice halting and cracked. 'Or other names. Olga the Negress, Olga the Mulatto, the African Queen. I've never even been to Africa.' She shot a fierce look towards where the bald gentleman had been sitting, but he was no longer there. 'Whatever sells tickets.'

'Was Natalia an aerialist too?' asked Rosie.

Miss Brown smiled, though her face was still wet with tears. 'Oh yes, on the trapezes. There was no one to match us, not anywhere. Natalia was light and strong, and she had no fear. She would fly and spin and I would catch her. Sometimes she used to close her eyes, knowing I would be there. And I always was.'

She put out her arms and closed her own eyes to show us how it was, and I imagined being at the top of a perfect parabola, and that fraction of a second's panic until those hands took hold of mine. Miss Brown opened her eyes again.

'We were called The Flying Sisters. Foolish, I know, given …' She indicated her skin. 'But we were *like* sisters. We came over from Prussia together.' She gave a little shrug. 'Back when there *was* a Prussia.'

'To Portsmouth?'

She shrugged. 'To everywhere. Portsmouth, London, Amsterdam, Paris. We're here for the summer and after that … I don't know.' She wiped her eyes. 'When I said you could keep Natalia, I didn't mean it. I hope you understand. She frustrated me, that's all. I've got used to not knowing where she is. Sometimes I'd wish she'd go home and …' She ceased speaking and lowered her forehead into her palms, her shoulders shaking. Eventually, she lifted her face and glanced anxiously around the auditorium. 'Where's Honey? Does he know? Oh, God, what will he do when he finds out?'

'Honey?'

'The young man. The one you followed into here. They were friends.'

She stood up, spotting the young man still crouching by the wall. He lifted his eyes to meet hers, and I could tell he knew that Natalia was dead. I wondered whether he had known before he came in or had simply overheard us.

I exchanged a glance with Rosie. In truth, we'd gathered all the information I needed. My article might be promoted from page 14 to 12 on the basis of the dead girl's profession; the gentry of London did enjoy being shocked by the flutter of skimpy clothing and, by implication, skimpy moral virtue. But a provincial story would never make it to the front page, so there was little point in staying any longer. Uncovering the killer might take weeks or months or might never happen at all, especially with Sergeant Dorling on the case. If we were quick, we could catch a train and be back to our normal lives by that evening.

But something was still tugging at me. Not knowing the truth was like leaving a book half read. And here we were. What harm would it do to find out just a little more?

'Miss Brown, when we first saw Mr Honey outside, he seemed to be running from someone. A gentleman. Do you have any idea why that was?'

'Always, it's *men*.' She pulled a face. 'Always. He's probably the one who killed Natalia. You should write that in your article.'

'Do you know who he is or why he was chasing Mr Honey?'

She blinked quickly and dropped her eyes. 'I have no idea.'

I hoped for her sake that she was better at acrobatics than she was at lying.

I was about to suggest we leave when there was a sound behind us. Sergeant Dorling was striding into the auditorium accompanied by two constables in ill-fitting uniforms, each with a billy club in his fist. They were followed by the bald-headed fellow who'd been watching earlier, a look of grim satisfaction on his face.

'That's him!' he shouted, pointing at Honey, who was still crouching by the wall.

Olga Brown turned and gave the fellow a look that would have bored through rock. 'What are you doing?'

Dorling's mouth turned downwards in an ugly sneer. 'Arresting him for murder, not that it's any of your business.'

Olga Brown stood in the way. 'You'll do no such thing.'

Dorling sucked on his teeth. 'Jenks, move this ... obstacle aside. If it objects, stick it in the Black Maria.'

I felt a rising rage inside me. I might have been called 'it' as well, in other circumstances, but I was human and so was Olga Brown.

'Now, look here—' I began, but she shook her head.

'There's no need,' she said.

A youthful-looking constable stepped forward and attempted to shove her sideways but found himself grabbing air as she swivelled and ducked under his reach. He raised his billy club but was restrained by the bald gentleman.

'Oh no, matey,' he said. 'She's on stage tonight. Star of the show. You don't touch her.'

Dorling cleared his throat. 'Apologies, Mr Quinton. I'd forgotten she was here on your bidding. We'll arrest Honey and be off.'

Miss Brown glared at them both and raised her fists, and the confrontation seemed likely to take an unpleasant turn. I knew I shouldn't intervene, but I was irritated by the arrogance of these men.

'You should at least tell us what the evidence is against Mr Honey, before you remove him.'

Dorling turned and, from his expression, he was not one bit pleased to see me. His mouth hung open for ten seconds before any sound emerged.

'Ah, Mr ... Winthrop, was it?'

'Stanhope.'

The bald fellow, Quinton, vibrated like a simmering pot. 'Who the hell are you?'

Dorling forced a facial expression that might have been described as a smile, had the person doing the describing never seen a real one. 'Mr Stanhope is a journalist from London, Mr Quinton. He's taken an interest in recent events, for which we're all very grateful, I'm sure.' He pulled his face into a still greater deformation, adding a display of blackened teeth. 'As you can see, Mr Stanhope, we're apprehending our suspect and will be questioning him at the station. All very right and proper.'

'And I'm Mrs Stanhope,' announced Rosie, who hated to be left out.

Olga Brown shook her head. 'This is ridiculous. Timothy would never hurt Natalia.'

Quinton pointed a finger at the lad. 'Nonsense. He was always mooning around after her. And he knew the boy who was murdered too. He's the link between the killings.'

For the first time, Honey himself spoke. His voice was light and oddly detached, as though he was vocalising thoughts in his head rather than addressing anyone in the room. 'Everyone knew Micky.'

Dorling took him by the chin. 'You harboured lustful thoughts about Miss … about the victim. And you murdered her. She rejected you is my guess.'

Olga Brown snorted loudly. 'That's even more ridiculous. You know full well what he does for a living.'

Dorling shied away from Honey like a horse from a dead cat in the street. 'I was told—'

Honey interrupted him. 'I'm a picture-framer. And you don't really think I killed him.' He turned to me, his pale eyes looking right into mine. The skin was so taut on his face, you could see the architecture of his skull beneath. 'Are you truly a journalist? You should ask some questions of Mr Quinton. He knows what's true and what isn't.'

'What do you mean?' I asked, but before he could reply, Dorling interrupted.

'If nothing else, Master Honey is guilty of trespassing here. Take him away, lads.'

Olga Brown looked up despairingly at the corrugated ceiling above our heads. 'I won't let this stand. I won't.'

Quinton, seemingly a habitual finger-pointer, prodded her forehead. 'You'll stay out of it, Miss La La. You're due on stage tonight. It's in your contract.'

The constables dragged Honey away towards the entrance, squashing him tightly between them, deliberately impeding his feet so he was forced to hobble and trip.

'Wait!' I called after them. 'Mr Honey, what did you mean earlier? What *truth* were you referring to?'

I could see that he'd heard me. His head came up sharply and his flat cap fell on to the floor behind him. 'Ask Mr Quinton,' he said. 'Such a *fine* gentleman. Ask him how far he'll go to get his hands on the Blood Flower.'

5

AS THE DOORS CRASHED shut behind them, I turned to Quinton. 'What did he mean? What's the Blood Flower?'

I had sounded more brusque than I'd intended. Quinton scowled at me, his fingers interlocked in front of him as if resisting the urge to point. He was a stocky man, a couple of inches shorter than me, with wide, vaguely froggish features. Nevertheless, I had to admire his tweed suit, which was stylish and well tailored, fitting closely around his shoulders and chest – no easy feat on a man of his proportions. His boots were likewise shiny and fashionably pointed, and his shirt was the purest white. Taken as a whole, the man knew how to dress, and had the capital to match his taste.

'Mr ... what was it?'

'Stanhope. I'm with the *Daily Chronicle*.'

'Never heard of it.'

'And I'm Mrs Stanhope,' said Rosie, now with an unmistake-able edge of irritation. 'We're working together on this. Perhaps you can help us and our readers by explaining what Mr Honey meant. What is the Blood Flower?'

Quinton sniffed loudly. 'I have no idea.'

Sergeant Dorling put his hand on Rosie's shoulder, an act more courageous than he could know. 'Now, Mrs Stanhope, you can't take the slightest notice of what a person like Honey has to say. It's like the wind rustling through the trees. It doesn't mean anything.'

I admit I was surprised. I hadn't thought him capable of such fanciful imagery. A shame it was employed towards such an unpleasant sentiment.

Olga Brown folded her arms. 'What do you mean, "a person like him"?'

A look of pure distaste crossed Dorling's features. 'I'd keep quiet if I was you. Only Mr Quinton's good standing is preventing me from putting you on a boat back to Africa. And you said yourself what the lad does for a living.'

Miss Brown raised her shoulders as though she might be about to fly at him, and God help him if she had. But he gave her a little smirk, tempting her to do it, happy to have an excuse to throw her in the cells. She had no choice but to turn away, her jaw clenching and unclenching.

Rosie looked from one to the other with practised innocence. 'Mr Honey said he was a picture-framer, didn't he?'

Quinton released his fingers and pointed one at her. 'It doesn't matter what he is, does it? The fact is, he had no business mooning after one of my employees. He followed her around like a lapdog.'

Olga Brown glared at him. 'They were friends. That's all.'

'He was in love with her. We both know it. Crime of passion.' He straightened his jacket, proving how perfectly the lapels were aligned. 'Now, Miss La La, you should be rehearsing. All of you should.'

The burly fellow looked aghast. 'You can't expect us to perform tonight. Not after this. I can barely *think*, let alone entertain an audience.'

Quinton looked at him squarely. 'You'll perform as planned or you'll be reimbursing my profits from your pay.' He turned back to Rosie and me. 'And as for you two, I suggest you clear off before I instruct the sergeant to arrest you for trespassing.'

———

Outside, I sheltered under the shade of the awning. Rosie seemed altogether more comfortable, basking in the sun's full glare, turning her face to greet it like some old friend. Her green eyes were glinting.

'Miss Brown is an interesting person,' she said. 'Very talented.'

I sensed that Rosie had taken a liking to the young acrobat. She tended to form instantaneous opinions of people, for better or worse. Usually, she was proven right, but not always.

'She has the physical strength to commit a murder, certainly.'

Rosie narrowed her eyes at me. 'She said they were like sisters.'

'Yes, but people aren't always truthful, and jealousy could be a motive.'

She gave me a look, at once sceptical and indulgent. 'Not everyone in the theatrical world is like Mr Black, you know. And what about the boy? What do you make of him?'

I didn't answer immediately, still considering the talented Miss Brown. To challenge the police, as she had, a woman of her skin colour would either have to be very brave or very naïve. If they ever suspected her of murder, she could not expect a fair hearing. She would be hanged, no question.

For a moment I felt dizzy, and my nostrils were filled with the scent of hot ash.

I shook myself. 'Sorry. Do you mean Mr Honey? I don't know. What motivation could he have? He seemed more shocked than anything. Sergeant Dorling certainly seems to think he's guilty though.'

'That man couldn't find the shoes on his feet. And did you smell him? Like sour milk.' She scrunched up her face. 'We can't leave this matter to him.'

Part of me wanted to. I could hear a train pulling out of the station, its slow breaths becoming a pant and then a roar as it gathered speed. I longed to be on it. And yet, the deaths of two young people were preying on my mind.

Rosie interpreted my silence as indecision. 'And the Blood Flower? What do you suppose that means?'

I was having trouble concentrating. My brain was fogged. 'Could it be the name of a ship, something of that kind?'

She pondered, her lips pressed together. 'Strange name for a ship.' Her eyes flicked towards me and away again. 'I have to go.

I said I'd spend the afternoon with Viola at the pleasure beach. The kids are desperate to visit the pier.'

It seemed I would have to remain in this hellhole for one more day, whether I liked it or not. I told myself it was for the best. Not only would I have more time to investigate two murders, but Lillian and Sam would get the chance to play in the sea and I would finally meet my sister-in-law.

'All right, then. Lead the way.'

Still, she didn't meet my eye. 'Why don't you spend some more time with Peregrine? You know you've missed him these last weeks. It'll give me a chance to talk with Viola properly, while Bill's at work.'

Bill was Viola's husband. Aside from his role in her pregnancy, I knew nothing about him.

'All right. I'll meet you there later, shall I?'

'No need. You'll be bored by the two of us, I promise you. She does nothing but bring up ancient grudges. She still remembers the time I pushed her off a stool and she cracked her skull.'

I wasn't surprised that Rosie showed no sign of contrition at this act of violence. I knew first-hand how cruel an older sister could be.

'Very well.' I shoved my hands into my pockets, hoping she could detect the terseness in my manner. 'I'll see you tomorrow morning, I suppose.'

She gave me a stiff wave goodbye and set off on foot, as ever spurning the idea of a taxicab. I knew exactly what she would say if challenged on that: *On a beautiful day like this? What's wrong with your legs?* And she'd give me that smile that said she was very fond of me even if I was an idiot. But I was an idiot who would do anything for her. Anything at all. No hesitation, no equivocation.

I was still chewing on my resentment when I realised that I was being watched. On the other side of the road, in the dimness of the alleyway, that naval fellow was leaning against a wall taking a long draw on his cigar.

I considered going over to speak with him, but I was too angry, and I told myself it didn't matter anyway; I'd be gone from this place tomorrow. Let him watch, if he chose to. More than that: good luck to him!

I cared nothing for him or any of it.

———

As I plodded up the stairs, Peregrine was resurfacing from his regular afternoon nap – his *restoration*, he called it – with hair in disarray and a dressing gown scarcely covering his belly. He insisted on lunch together, and an hour later we found ourselves at a fish restaurant with metal tables and nets strung across the ceiling. I would have found it quite amusing had I been in a better mood, and had the place not been worryingly empty for a lunchtime in high summer.

'Do you know a man named Quinton? He owns the circus.'

Peregrine paused, his fork halfway to his mouth. He had ordered scallops, which I considered risky in the circumstances.

'He's a hoodlum, or near enough to one.' He inserted the scallop and started chewing, talking through the masticated mush. 'He owns a good many buildings in the city, though the Hippodrome is his favourite by all accounts. Aside from Papaver, of course.'

'What's Papaver?'

'A club. A bar, you know. Nothing you need concern yourself with.'

'You know him?'

'Only a little. Everyone knows *of* him though.' He peered over at my plate. 'Are you going to eat that?'

My food remained untouched and was getting cold. I'd only ordered it out of habit and wasn't really hungry. Still, I pronged a lump of hake and put it in my mouth, finding it to have roughly the taste and consistency of wet newspaper.

'Are you familiar with something called "the Blood Flower"? We think it might be a ship.'

'Doesn't mean anything to me.' He thought for a second. 'What's the context?'

'A lad was arrested by the police. He mentioned it.'

'What lad?'

'His name's Honey. Do you know him?'

Peregrine's eyes were fixed on his food, but his cheeks flushed red. 'I may have seen him somewhere.'

I sat back and contemplated my friend. Why exactly had Peregrine insisted I come to Portsmouth to write about the murder of Micky Long? He obviously knew more than he was telling me.

'At the club you mentioned, was it?'

He glanced at me from under his eyebrows. 'Don't try to be clever, laddie. Yes, I saw Long and Honey at Papaver, but I haven't *partaken* of either of them. I feel sorry for lads like them, that's all.'

I decided to believe him, at least for now.

'I'd like to visit that club.'

'You wouldn't enjoy it.'

'Why not?'

He gave a huff of amusement. 'It's a place of … freedom, I suppose. You're …' He spun his knife deftly between his fingers, trying to find the right words. 'You're a *reliable* fellow. You have *principles*. And I'm *very* fond of you. But your waistcoat is buttoned too tight for somewhere like that.'

'You think I'd be shocked?'

'Well, perhaps, but that wasn't what I meant.'

Everyone I knew seemed to want to keep me sequestered. Was I truly so unpalatable?

'Then what did you mean?'

'I don't wish to offend you.' He looked at me squarely. 'But you wouldn't fit in. You're too obviously law-abiding. The patrons would think you were there to collect their taxes or inspect the building.'

I folded my arms; not a position I usually favoured. 'I can relax, and I'll prove it to you. We'll go tonight.'

'Don't be prideful. We all have a natural place in the world. I myself would make a poor journalist, believing, as I do, that I'm far more interesting than anyone else.'

'Wearing a yellow waistcoat doesn't make you interesting. In fact—'

He held up his hand. 'Very well. Since you insist, I'll take you to Papaver. Come and see me in the play tonight and we'll go after that. I'll put two tickets on the door for you.'

'One will be enough.'

Neither of us spoke for a few seconds, until he pointed his fork at me.

'Where is Rosie, anyway?'

'Not here.'

'Obviously.' His expression changed from jovial to one of concern. 'Ah. I sense there might be a worm in the apple. Married life not all you'd hoped?'

'We're not really married. I mean we are, but ... not.'

'I see. "Things are seldom what they seem, skim milk masquerades as cream."'

'What are you talking about?'

He looked up in surprise. 'From *Pinafore*. Gilbert and Sullivan. Really, Leo, you should get a musical education.'

'I had one. It didn't work.'

He inserted another scallop into his mouth and ruminated on it. 'So, you never ...' He widened his eyes at me. 'I was going to say, you don't put your pie in her oven. But you're, you know, *pieless*, so to speak.'

I sat back, not trusting myself to answer. I didn't hate my physical self, but I hated any reference to it. For everyone else, their mind and their body were two parts of the same thing, as inseparable as the stars from the night sky. Not me. I was two things, the soul of a man and a body that simply didn't match. God had made me a thing of contradictions and I would never forgive Him for it.

But Peregrine was more concerned with mechanics than metaphysics, and he continued, oblivious. 'But there are still *ways* though, aren't there? All the delights don't have to be removed from you merely because there's no ... no actual *baking* possible.'

I clenched my jaw, feeling almost cross enough to punch him, though his arms were thicker than my legs. Quite apart from the views I held about myself, he was bordering on impertinence towards Rosie, and that I wouldn't tolerate.

'It's not how we are. We got married because she didn't want any more suitors eyeing up her business. Or anything else. She said one real husband was more than enough, and she'd settle for a fake one this time.'

Peregrine was thoughtful for a few seconds, scooping peas on to his fork and staring at them as if he'd never seen such things before.

'I suppose it's convenient for you as well. A bachelor above a certain age tends to get asked awkward questions, doesn't he? Questions of a *Hellenic* nature.'

'Like you.'

'I'm married.'

'After a fashion.'

I wouldn't normally have made such a jibe, but I was annoyed with him. And besides, he was a fine one to judge me. I hadn't forgotten encountering the young man outside his bedroom the previous evening.

'I fulfil my husbandly duty, laddie. Yearning for a steak doesn't mean you can't enjoy a dainty scallop too, once in a while.' He popped one into his mouth and chewed, making a play of its deliciousness.

'Good Lord, Peregrine, I heartily wish you'd stop talking in food metaphors. You're making me feel ill.'

He swallowed and smacked his lips. 'As I see it, you can either let this come between the two of you, or you can do something else. Home cooking can be charming, but if it's not available, there are always restaurants.'

'I don't want ... *restaurants.*'

Peregrine popped the last of his scallops into his mouth. The flesh looked worryingly pink and translucent, but it was his decision. 'You know what you have to do, don't you? Tell her about your frustration.'

'Maybe. She's gone to the pleasure beach with her sister, whom I have never met. Rosie's ashamed of me. Of my ... lack of pie, I suppose.'

Even I had to smirk. Truly, the whole conversation was so ludicrous and Peregrine so utterly lacking in normal propriety that there was no point in staying angry. I would be gone tomorrow, and he would be stuck in this town for another month and then be off to the next one as his touring company made their meandering progress along the south coast. He wouldn't be back in London until the autumn, and I hated to part on bad terms.

He picked up his plate and licked it thoroughly, making me glad we were alone.

'Do you need her permission?'

Deep down, I thought I probably did, but I didn't want to admit it.

'No. You're right.'

I stood up to leave, but Peregrine placed a restraining hand on my arm. 'Before you rush off, remember that you and Rosie have something I don't. Something I envy. The two of you belong together. Don't lose sight of that.' His doleful eyes looked almost tearful. 'And do pay the bill before you leave, won't you?'

'I'll see you at the theatre later, Peregrine.'

As I left, he was tucking into the remains of my hake and potatoes.

I made a single stop at the telegraph office to send two telegrams; one to J. T. Whitford explaining I would be travelling home tomorrow, and he could expect me in the office on Saturday; and the second to Jacob with my next chess move, which was pawn to queen's bishop four. A bold advance, but it was the mood I was in.

After that, I chose to walk the two miles to the beach, not, like Rosie, because I enjoyed toiling in the eighty-degree heat, but because, having paid for lunch, I was concerned about the cost of a taxicab. I had only about half remaining of the ten shillings I'd been given for expenses, and I dreaded to think what J. T. Whitford would say if I overspent and had to ask for more.

Unlike the parts of the city that I'd seen until now, the beach at Southsea was pleasant and the air clear. Even the sea was different: deep blue and stretching to the horizon, with only a few ships dotted decoratively along it.

I scanned the beach as I walked: families playing on the stones, an old man with a fishing rod and a net, a dog straining on its leash, two dippers smoking on a wooden barrel, their trousers rolled up to their knees. I knew Rosie wouldn't be pleased to see me, but I hoped I could make the argument that her renunciation was more of a suggestion. And she could hardly acknowledge the truth, could she?

Nearer to the pier, everything became more numerous: more tourists, sitting on the stones beneath windbreaks, and more seagulls, swooping hungrily among them; more bathing machines lined up like huts on wheels at the water's edge for modest ladies to swim from; more shops selling postcards, and more noise too, from the bandstand and from children whooping and throwing stones at the groynes. I looked closely to see if any of them were Sam and Lillian, but they weren't. Nevertheless, their gleeful expressions and the rush and hiss of the waves made me want to run into the sea and splash about. I was a decent swimmer, much practised in the ponds and rivers around Enfield when I was young. I missed the water, that enveloping cold and the vast nothingness beneath my feet. Who knew what was living down there. Sharp-toothed fish with human faces, blinking in the darkness and contemplating their existences. Did they have their own piscine god, I wondered, to hate for condemning them to such a place?

I had walked beyond the pier, almost as far as the pond where a few young couples were gliding about in rowing boats, when I heard a shrill voice behind me.

'Mr Stanhope!'

It was little Lillian, wrapped in an unfamiliar towel, a look of delight on her face.

She led me down the beach, to where Rosie was sitting under a parasol with her back to us, dressed exactly as when I'd last seen her. She waved in greeting, though not to me: a woman was coming up from the sea, her loose frock whipping around her legs, scattering droplets of seawater in all directions. She could only be

Viola. Her likeness to Rosie was uncanny; the same dark hair and round face, the same sharp eyes, though I could already see that Viola's were more forthcoming, less reserved. Her smile was broad and came easily to her mouth, as though it was her most common expression. Behind her, a rather portly fellow was huffing and puffing in a billowing bathing suit, his hair sticking to his scalp.

Sam leapt from Rosie's arms and ran to me. I picked him up, and Rosie turned, her motherly expression quickly curdling.

'Mr Stanhope is here,' announced Lillian unnecessarily. Always it was 'Mr Stanhope', not 'Father'. I supposed it was a compliment, as their actual father, dead these last three years, had been a brute. Robbie and Lillian still blanched whenever they caught sight of my belt hanging in my wardrobe.

'Leo,' said Rosie, without affect. 'I thought you were remaining with Mr Black this afternoon.'

'I came for a walk.'

Viola had made it to within hailing distance of us, her hands clutched to her rotund belly. 'Mr Stanhope, I assume! What a joy to meet you!'

'Of course, Mrs ...' I realised I didn't know her surname.

'Well, fancy not knowing!' she chuckled. 'Truly, Roisin, have you told your husband nothing of us? Well, it's Broadman, but you can call me Viola and I'll call you Leo.'

I was confused. 'Roisin?'

Rosie closed her eyes. 'In Ireland, yes. No one can pronounce it here.'

Viola threw her head back and laughed harder, sending a spray of water over Rosie and me. 'Not only do you not know *our* names, but you don't know your own wife's name either.'

She was right. It seemed that my Rosie had been born Roisin Dolan and had become Rosie Dolan, Rosie Flowers and then Rosie Stanhope. She'd had almost as many names as me.

The portly fellow thrust out a hand. 'Bill Broadman,' he said. 'Please forgive her, she's as giddy as a schoolgirl, being in the motherly way.' He had a strong Welsh accent and a pleasant face, with cheeks like apples and a drinker's red nose. 'You must come swimming, mate.'

'Thank you, but I'd prefer not.'

He clenched his fist and I thought he might punch me on the arm in a jovial, yet potentially painful, way, but instead he just motioned it towards me. 'Come on, man. Can't you swim? I do it most days, winter and summer.'

'I'd rather remain on the beach, thank you.'

Viola frowned. 'But why? Bill can go back to the house for some things, and you can change under a towel.' She nodded to her husband. 'Why don't you go anyway, in case Leo changes his mind. He can always just paddle.'

She had the kind of manner that liked to jolly people into things. I imagined in her youth she'd got a good many men into a good deal of trouble.

'Really, Mrs Broadman, it's not worth the trouble. I'm competent at swimming, but I have no wish to at present.'

Of course, this was a lie. I longed to swim, to feel the water around me, duck my head underneath and search for those wicked fish. But how could I? A soak in the sea and that other part of me, my female physique, would become all too apparent. I was only able to appear masculine through precise choices of clothes: tall hats, overlarge shoes, boxy jackets, loose-fitting trousers and, most of all, the binding of cotton I wore around my chest. My cilice. It was my saviour and my torturer, abrading my skin with every breath.

Viola pressed her lips together. 'Well, you are a pair, you and Roisin. You stay here then, and we'll take the kids. At least they know how to have fun.'

Lillian and Sam cheered and ran ahead of them, leaving Rosie and me alone.

'You may as well sit down,' she said.

'Why aren't you swimming?'

I knew she could if she chose. We shared an intimate knowledge of when the other's monthly blood arrived.

'I don't feel like it.'

We had little to say to one another, so we watched the children skipping and jumping in the surf, annoying the horses. Viola was sitting on the edge of the shore, legs stretched out in front of her, water lapping around her thighs. She truly was quite daringly modern, exposing the bare skin of her calves and arms.

When they returned, Viola clapped her hands. 'Of course, you'll come to dinner tonight, won't you, Leo? We need to know everything about you. Roisin has told us almost nothing.'

I detected a brief splutter from Rosie's direction.

'I would like that very much,' I said. 'But I have another appointment this evening.'

'Oh no.' Viola looked aghast, as though I'd declined an invitation to the Palace. 'Tomorrow then. Please say you'll come.'

Having expended so much goodwill with Rosie to meet my sister-in-law, it seemed perverse not to accept an invitation to spend more time with her, even at the cost of remaining another day in this godforsaken town.

When I acceded, I honestly thought Viola would rush up and kiss me. She seemed exactly the type. But I dare say something in my manner discouraged her, and she restricted herself to jumping up and down, her belly and breasts remaining curiously unmoving as if determined to counterbalance her enthusiasm.

Rosie folded up the blanket and thrust it at me. 'It's time to go.'

That decision made, we gathered their belongings and headed up the beach to the common. The children were barefoot, and they danced over the pebbles as though on hot coals. In the end, I picked up little Sam, wet to the skin though he was. He put his head on my shoulder.

As we walked, Rosie's expression shifted between impatience and irritation, a nuance with which I was familiar. The internal conflict was such that her face became quite purple, like Sam's when he needed the toilet. In the end, she tapped the end of her parasol on the stones and looked up at me.

'What appointment do you have tonight?'

'Two, actually. First, I'm going to watch Peregrine in his play. Shakespeare, I believe.'

Rosie shuddered. We had previously acknowledged that neither of us believed Peregrine would be any good. The music hall was one thing, but a proper play with a director who would prefer his actors not to attack members of the audience or invent their own additions to the script didn't feel like Peregrine's forte.

'Afterwards,' I continued, 'I'm going to a club Quinton owns called Papaver.'

'Why?' She knew I hated clubs.

'Honey and the dead boy, Micky Long, both went there, working I presume. I think it's a place where men—'

She held up her hand to stop me. 'Thank you, I know what they do.'

'And someone there may be able to tell me more about Micky. Why he was killed. We don't have much to go on.'

She nodded, her eyes narrowing. 'And?'

I pulled a face. 'And Peregrine implied I wasn't suited to a place like Papaver. He said I wasn't sufficiently … relaxed.'

Rosie's answer didn't come as quickly as I would have preferred. 'Well, I'm sure that's not true at all. But please be careful. Pride can get you into trouble, and I've been thinking about Mr Quinton. He was entirely dishonourable, if you want my opinion, forcing those nice people at the circus to perform tonight when they're grieving for their friend. Not to mention how he bossed around the police. It was him who set them on young Mr Honey.'

I was glad that we were once again communicating, at least on this topic. For us, it was not at all strange to discuss a murder with dispassion, yet be unable to broach why Rosie wanted to keep me apart from her sister.

I realised that Viola, who was a few steps ahead, had been listening to our every word. She spun to face us, a smile on her lips.

'Did you say Papaver?'

'Yes. It's a club.'

I was perplexed. It was unlikely that she knew the place, given what it was, and yet she seemed about to burst with excitement.

'Well, you know what Papaver is, don't you? Oh, Roisin, you must remember. Were you truly more interested in meat than flowers?'

Rosie pursed her lips. 'I had to help Father in the shop. While you were dangling on Mother's knee and making daisy chains, I was slicing ham and selling it by the ounce.'

'Well, perhaps if you'd listened more, you'd know. It's poppies. Papaver means poppies.'

I'd worked for a surgeon of the dead, and I knew all the ways by which a person could ruin themselves. Poppies were used in the making of opium.

The same thought had occurred to Rosie. 'Mr Quinton is a powerful man,' she whispered, as though he might have spies hidden among the pebbles. 'I wonder if he got rich through legal means or some other way.'

I was working through the sequence of events in my mind. 'Honey implied that Quinton knows something about the murders of Micky Long and Natalia La Blanche. Perhaps it has something to do with the sale of opium. Ah, of course! The Blood Flower.'

Rosie and I stared at each other and spoke simultaneously. 'The Blood Flower is opium.'

6

WE PARTED WHERE THE beach met the road. I watched them until they turned the corner, laden with paraphernalia. I had wanted to go at least as far as the house, but Rosie detached Sam from my shoulder and gave me a firm goodbye.

For once I anticipated the walk back with grim pleasure, expecting the grey brickwork, pungent fog and general ambience of decay to suit my mood. But I was to be disappointed. The winding streets were lined with terraced houses of all colours, most with baskets of flowers by the door and laundry in their upstairs windows. It was irritatingly cheery. And the people I was forced to ask for directions were polite and helpful, one fellow offering, with no apparent ill-intent, to walk with me in case I got lost. All in all, I arrived at the theatre in a foul temper.

I wasted an hour in the Clarence Hotel, being served two glasses of ale by a fellow with an impressive moustache who told me everything he knew about Papaver.

'Never been there myself,' he said, in the tone of a man who was thinking he'd like to, 'but I hear it's got all sorts.' He leaned in close and spoke in a low voice, 'Music and *dancing*.'

Well, I thought, that doesn't sound entirely debauched. From what Peregrine had said, you'd think people were fornicating under the tables.

Refreshed and slightly better informed, but no less morose, I found my place in the theatre to watch Peregrine. The audience was meagre, occupying fewer than half of the seats, so I had plenty of elbow room and an excellent view of the stage, which was crowned by two pictures of reclining muses, one comic and one tragic.

The play was *Twelfth Night* and Peregrine was Sir Toby Belch, a part which, as it turned out, didn't place a vast strain on his acting range. Belch lived a life of hedonism and excess, demonstrating an ability to persuade his friends to act against their own best interests. Peregrine strode across the stage like a licentious headmaster, enunciating his lines in a contrived, but very amusing, tenor, and pausing for seconds at a time to stare at his fellow actors in a manner the audience came to anticipate, laughing before he had even done it. And yet, at other points, as when proposing marriage, he was as tender as morning dew on the grass. I never dreamed he could be so affecting. By the end of the first act, I was utterly lost in the play, and as the final curtain fell, I stood and cheered, not simply out of camaraderie with Peregrine, but because the entire performance had been splendid. The actors received three encores and it really did seem as though the applause was warmest for my friend, who bowed low, the feathers in his hat draping down on to the stage.

Afterwards, I waited at the side door, greeting Peregrine with the enthusiasm of a lovesick maiden. 'What a show, Peregrine! You ought to be very proud of yourself. I hadn't the slightest idea you were any good as an actor.'

He gave me a sour look. 'Your acclaim would mean more if it weren't founded on low expectations.'

I shrugged. 'It's not my fault. Your every word and action up to now have led me to believe you'd be awful.'

'I suppose there's that.' He stopped and lit a slim cigar, blowing smoke out of the corner of his mouth. 'Look, Leo, are you sure about going to this club? I'm tired. Why don't we do it tomorrow?'

'Because I took your advice. I'm having dinner at my sister-in-law's house tomorrow and the next day I'm heading back to London, so it has to be tonight if I'm to find out more about Honey and Micky. Why are you hesitating?'

He took another puff, taking an age to roll the smoke around his tongue before replying. But I had already guessed the answer.

'I may or may not owe them a bit of money.'

The club was on a side road not far from the beach. Above ground, it was a wholesale chandlery with stock spilling out on to a covered terrace: rope and chain on rolls, great iron shackles that looked as if they could keep the planet from turning, brass tension gauges and fairleads polished to a shine. One might think such a trove, open to the elements, would be looted in a minute, but the risk was minimal. In amongst this hoard, two armchairs had been set, one of them empty and one occupied by a very large man with short, blond hair and a jacket which, though generous by most standards, was barely up to the task of containing the acreage of his chest. Around him were hung birdcages, seven or eight at least, containing a myriad of finches, parrots and budgerigars, all squawking and chirruping together.

'Don't stare, laddie,' hissed Peregrine. 'Better if he doesn't notice me.'

There was no chance of that. Though sombrely dressed by his own standards, Peregrine was a conspicuous presence. The blond man's eyes followed us as we joined a short queue of people leading around the building and into the darkness. I could just about make out some metal steps down to a basement, and feel, beneath my feet, a rhythmic thrumming.

We shuffled forward behind three gentlemen in high spirits who had clearly spent some time in a pub.

Peregrine was becoming agitated. 'It's a shilling to get in. Each.'

'Good Lord. What do you get for that, aside from bankruptcy?'

'You'll see.' He bit his lip. 'Look, Leo, I owe them one pound four shillings. I wouldn't ask you normally, but we're here at your behest and if they demand it … I mean you've seen Stephan back there and I'm sure you can imagine. I may need you to extend me a loan.'

'How did you build up such a debt?'

I loved Peregrine, but why did he have to get himself into trouble all the time?

He gave me a furtive glance. 'This and that. Will you help me or not?'

I could believe he'd spend such an amount on drink, given enough time, but surely the establishment wouldn't let him run so high a tab. Could it be gambling? I'd never heard him mention cards or horses. I opened my wallet and counted the coins.

'I don't have that much. You can have what I do.' He looked disappointed when I only gave him one shilling. 'For the entrance. I'll give you more if they demand it from you.'

'You're a suspicious man.'

'And one free of debt.'

The entrance was a low door into the basement, where a sallow-looking chap was sitting on a wooden chair. He took our money and supplied us each with a ticket crudely printed with the name 'Papaver' and a picture of a poppy.

Peregrine ducked his head under the lintel and went inside, and after a moment's hesitation I followed him, pushing through a heavy curtain. Instantly, the sound became louder, and we were suffused in thick, sweet smoke.

The place was surprisingly small, perhaps forty feet in length and width, and had a low roof, no more than a few inches above my head. The lamps were easily set to swinging, creating an eerie sense that we were in the bilges of a ship, pitching and tipping with the waves.

It was crowded with men. Some were huddled together in groups near the bar and others stood glumly in the centre, trying to gain the attention of the few women, who were notable for their colourful frocks and exaggerated bashfulness as they flitted from one fellow to the next.

Peregrine leaned down to me and bellowed in my ear, 'If you want to dance with one of the ladies, you have to pay.'

A band was playing on a small stage to one side – fiddle, banjo and drum – and a fellow was standing in front of them, apparently threatening to sing. The performers were flamboyantly dressed in the American style and their faces were coal-tar black. They started up as we pushed through the crowd, but their music was smothered by the babble, reduced to a dull thump and the higher-pitched notes of the fiddle. The singer could hardly be heard at all. He was pulling all sorts of facial expressions, from ebullient to heartbroken, but for all I could hear of him, he might as well have been mouthing the words. As we got closer, I realised the musicians' faces were painted with boot polish, which was dripping as they sweated, creating pale lines on their cheeks and stains on their shirts. Only the singer was truly dark-skinned.

We found the bar and I ordered two pints of ale and two whiskies, which we downed quickly. The whisky was as rough as a cat's tongue, but that was fine by me.

Perhaps it was the effect of the alcohol, but the more I watched, the more I realised that this place was not exactly what I'd expected. The women who were spinning and laughing with their partners were no more physically female than I was physically male. Their hair and powder were perfectly presented, and their corsets and stays were squeezed in, or pushed up, as needed to form a feminine shape, and they'd learned to resist and relent like the most coquettish of maidens. But most of them, I surmised, were not like me. They were playing a game, or giving a performance, rather than correcting a wrong. When the evening was over, much like performers in a music hall, they would wipe their faces, pull off those wigs and be men again.

But a couple of them seemed otherwise. I couldn't be certain, of course, but something in their expressions, in their stance and the way they picked at their sleeves, spoke of another kind of craving. The disguise they wore was during the day, rather than in the evening. I wondered how it was, to be like them: a woman in a man's body. It seemed a harder road than mine, not least legally; the minimum sentence for what the courts called 'the abominable crime of sodomy and buggery' was ten years of penal servitude. How ridiculous that was. The whirling dancers were laughing and shouting, flirting and teasing, leading thoroughly delightful lives. Not as the world would expect, perhaps, but love was still love, and who had the right to deny them?

I nudged Peregrine. 'Do those fellows know who they're dancing with?'

He shrugged. 'Does it make any difference?'

After that, I started to notice more oddities. As well as regular fellows like us, drinking and watching the merriment, there were men sitting on sofas around the edges of the room, holding long pipes filled, I assumed, with opium. Many were slumbering, resembling those cautionary illustrations in magazines, but others were chatting and even swapping pipes, nodding in approval like aficionados. In the furthest corners, pairs were writhing together, hands reaching into jackets or down the fronts of trousers in slow and steady movements. One man was shirtless, his head tipped back as a young fellow in a ringleted wig lay in his lap.

'Are you shocked?' asked Peregrine.

'No,' I lied.

I knew such practices existed. One cannot work as a journalist without hearing of every kind of practice humanity can invent to pleasure itself. And I occasionally spent an evening with the *Chronicle*'s court reporters in a pub near the Inns of Newgate, where lawyers told stories about their clients, few of which were ever aired in front of the magistrates. But even so, to see such acts for myself was a little startling.

On the other hand, I thought, they might be shocked by me too, if they knew the truth.

'Mr Black,' said a voice, and we both turned.

The huge man we had seen outside was looming next to us. He was wearing a smile that might, in one of the sensation novels Rosie was fond of, have been called deceptive, but was not, in fact, deceptive at all. It was intended to be menacing, and it was.

'Stephan,' Peregrine responded in a level tone. I had never seen him looking so nervous.

'Mr Quinton would like a word with you.'

'Of course.'

We followed the giant to an area tucked alongside the bar, where some red velvet armchairs had been placed around a table. Sitting facing us was Quinton, wearing a perfect pinstriped suit, and beside him was a woman. She looked up at us with an enquiring expression, and I recognised her instantly. This was the woman whose portrait Peregrine had in his room. The rendering was uncanny, though not an exact likeness; she was a fraction older and a hair's breadth less pretty than the painting. But it captured her clear eyes and amused, inquisitive mouth to perfection.

Quinton didn't acknowledge us, but pulled out a notebook and ran his finger down a column of figures. 'You owe me four pounds.'

Peregrine smiled warily. 'One pound four shillings, I think you'll find, Mr Quinton.'

The hoodlum checked his ledger, pretended to do some adding up and held up his hands as if to say there was nothing he could do to avoid the inevitable.

'One pound four shillings for the boys, I think. And I paid you two pounds for the portrait of Alice, which you haven't yet delivered. The rest is interest and something for my trouble. Surely, you haven't come here empty-pocketed. That would be very rash, Mr Black. Very rash.'

'The portrait's finished,' insisted Peregrine. 'It's drying in my room. I can give it to you tomorrow.'

The woman, Alice, gave him a smile, tiny lines appearing around her eyes. 'How do I look?'

I couldn't stop myself from answering. 'Beautiful. It's a remarkable piece. You'll love it, truly.'

Quinton puffed out his cheeks, making a note in his ledger. 'That still leaves two pounds.' He pointed a finger at me. 'You're the journalist, aren't you? You were there when Honey was arrested.'

'Stanhope.' I put out a hand which he seemed in two minds whether to shake, eventually deciding there was no harm in maintaining the social niceties. 'Has Mr Honey been charged with the murders?'

He sat back, a smile settling on his face. He liked to be asked things. It recognised his power.

'No,' he said. 'Honey will be let out tomorrow, and by the evening he'll be back at work, where he belongs.'

Alice picked a glass of wine from the table and took a sip, her eyes never leaving me, resting fleetingly on my face, my chest, my hips and my crotch.

'Why are you here, Mr Stanhope?' she asked.

'I'm vouching for Mr Black.' I fished out my wallet, glad of the distraction. 'I have four-and-six. Perhaps it could be considered as a down payment on his debt?'

'I see.' She smiled at Peregrine. 'So, this is your friend, is it? The one you mentioned before?'

It was Peregrine's turn to flush red. 'Yes.'

I realised, with a sudden ache in my stomach, that he'd told her about my affliction. All the agonies I suffered to keep my secret hidden, the sores from the binding, the blisters from my shoes, the endless, endless watching of myself, every word, every gesture rehearsed and then questioned as if I were constantly auditioning myself for a part in the play of my own life – all of that, and Peregrine had told this woman as if it was nothing. I wondered if they'd laughed at me.

It wasn't only a betrayal of our friendship. Divulgence of my secret put me in danger as well. I could be arrested and sent to prison, a women's prison, in a frock and bonnet, denied my gender and made to pick oakum from ropes and weave jute threads into sacks. Or, worse still, I could be sent to an asylum to be cured of my material disjunction and become hollow, a doll, without purpose or thought. And what of Rosie? What would her life be like then? She would be exposed and shunned, a topic of gossip and ridicule. Everyone would know she had married a pretence. Not a man, not a woman: a creature. I would rather die than condemn her to that.

I closed my wallet.

'I was mistaken,' I said. 'I can't spare any money for Mr Black after all.'

Quinton raised his eyebrows. 'A sudden change of mind, Mr Stanhope.'

'Leo, please …' began Peregrine, but he trailed off.

A look passed between Quinton and Stephan.

'Are you sure you've *finished* that portrait, Mr Black?' asked Quinton in a pleasant tone that promised worse to come.

'Oh yes, absolutely. It's finished and ready.'

'Good.' Quinton shut his ledger with a bang. 'In that case, you won't be needing all your fingers.'

'What?'

Peregrine's voice, usually a rich cello, had become a vibrato violin. He reversed two steps, bumping into a fellow behind us, who shoved him back irritably.

Stephan pulled a stubby bone-handled paring knife from his belt. 'Which finger can you afford to lose? Please don't say your little finger. Everyone always does and it's so dull.'

I saw a look settle on Peregrine's face. I recognised it. The Peregrine of the everyday, with his oh-so-genteel manners and velvet frock coats, was melting away, to be replaced by someone else. This version was accustomed to fights and believed they should be won fast and permanently. I had seen him hit a man with a chair, over and over, until it was nothing but blood-soaked splinters. His victim's crime had been to make a quip about a beggar boy in the street.

But Stephan was almost as large as Peregrine, and he was made of muscle rather than fat. He also seemed worryingly relaxed, like a man who didn't expect to lose.

I couldn't let it happen. No matter what he had done to me, I couldn't see my friend risk his safety for the sake of four-and-six.

'Stop,' I said, holding up my wallet once more. 'Please stop. Here's what money I have. We can bring the rest soon.'

Quinton contemplated my offer, working his mouth from side to side, his bald head shining under the lamps. Before he'd made his mind up, Alice whispered in his ear. He shrugged and shook his head at Stephan, who stood back, his eyes still fixed on Peregrine.

'Very well,' said Quinton, taking my four-and-six and making a note in his ledger. 'But I'm a stickler for the numbers. You still owe me one pound, fifteen shillings and sixpence, Mr Black, plus the portrait. And it had better be good.'

He turned away from us and returned to his conversation with Alice. We were dismissed.

We slouched back to the bar.

'Christ almighty,' muttered Peregrine. 'I thought you weren't going to do it, I really did. I need a drink.'

'I haven't any money left,' I said. 'And if I did, I wouldn't buy you anything.'

He wiped his hands down his face and met my eye. 'I know why you're cross, and you're right. It just slipped out. She was sitting for me for two days and you have to talk about *something*. She's interested in certain subjects, curiosities of a particular sort, and I suppose I wanted to impress her. I'm sorry.'

I looked away from him towards the musicians, who were still trying to make themselves heard on the stage. 'I don't want to talk to you, Peregrine.'

'Oh, come on, Leo—'

'No. Not tonight.'

'Very well. But don't forget, I said I was sorry.'

He pushed away from the bar and shoved through the crowd.

I took a deep breath, trying to settle my heart, which seemed to be trying to jump out through my ribcage.

'Would you like a drink?' said a woman's voice, and I was amazed to find Alice perched on a stool beside me, a quizzical look in her eyes.

7

'YOU'RE SOMETHING DIFFERENT,' SHE said, after two whiskies had been placed in front of us on the bar. 'You're not pretending, are you?'

'What would Mr Quinton think of his wife talking to another man like this?'

'I wouldn't worry.' She gave me the smallest of smiles and pulled off her long gloves, showing me her ringless fingers. 'I'm nobody's wife. And you're not exactly a man.'

'What do you want?'

She seemed flustered by my bluntness, and I realised she was less confident than she appeared. I'd been misled by the elegance of her purple polonaise overdress, and her lace underskirt that swished as she crossed her legs. Those clothes must have cost more than Rosie earned in a month.

She touched me lightly on the shoulder. 'Don't think ill of me. I want to know about you, that's all. I'm fascinated by the range of human existences.' She swept a hand across the room. 'All these boys have their foibles. Some of them dress up and do make-believe, some have even convinced themselves. But you, with all this ...' She indicated my jacket and the hat I was holding. 'You're so normal. So commonplace. I could pass you in the street and never imagine what you were.'

'I'm an ordinary man.'

'Exactly. Yet different. That's what's fascinating.' She gazed at me with such frankness I started to blush. 'The extraordinary, hidden beneath the ordinary.'

'No.'

'I mean, *corporeally*. If you were to stand there naked, you'd be like any other woman.'

'I have to go.'

'No, please. I didn't mean to offend you.'

'I've outstayed my intention.'

Such was the thickness of the crowd and opacity of the atmosphere I had some trouble locating the exit. I found myself close to the fellows occupying the sofas, one of whom looked up from his kissing, his eyes at first unfocused and then catching mine. He spoke, but I couldn't hear him in the din. Seeing my confused expression, he leaned forward, detaching himself from the lad he was with.

'Are you a policeman? You look like you don't belong here.'

'No. A journalist.'

He leapt to his feet, straightened his tie and commenced searching about the torso of his somnolent friend, who was now sprawling face down on the sofa.

'Please,' he said, his voice quivering. 'Make no mention of me, I beg you.'

'I'm not planning to write about this place.'

The poor fellow gave up his hunt and swallowed hard.

'It's for amusement, nothing more. A lark. Do you understand?'

'Of course.'

He met my eyes again and seemed at a loss for what more to say. Finally, he came close to me and whispered in my ear. 'The days are so long. Don't you find that? I can hardly bear the hours in between.'

And then he was gone.

The lad he had been with stirred and lifted his face. I recognised him as the same one whom Peregrine had been entertaining in his room. He rolled over on to his back, revealing a squashed felt hat on the sofa.

'You'll have to talk to Stephan.'

'What?'

He waved in the direction of the bar. 'You can't miss him. He's the size of a bull.'

'Why should I do that?'

He sat up. His shirt was open to his navel. 'If you want to spend time with me, or any of the boys, or girls, you have to talk to Stephan. Do you understand?'

'I think I do, yes. He handles the transactions on behalf of Mr Quinton, is that right?'

The lad blinked at me as if was a simpleton. 'Yes, exactly. I don't handle money.'

'I see. Well, I'm not interested, thank you.'

He threw up his hands in mock despair and stretched himself out again. 'Come back if you change your mind.'

The band was still playing, black sweat pouring from all of them except the singer, who was swaying as he sang inaudibly, like someone seen through a distant window.

I couldn't stay in the place a second longer. I blundered around the walls until I found the curtain across the exit, and stumbled out into the night, leaning on the metal railing and sucking in lungfuls of air.

Underneath the metal steps, a fox was lapping at a puddle of puke. My first thoughts weren't of revulsion, but amazement that the city was still here, apparently unchanged. I felt as if I'd been transported to another world altogether, and that on my emergence back into reality, I'd find everything strange and incomprehensible, as if waking and sleeping were reversed.

I was about to climb the steps and make my way home when I realised that I wasn't alone. Alice had come out behind me, now wearing an elegant travelling coat tailored to fit around her bustle.

'I'm glad I caught you,' she said. 'I wanted to apologise.'

'There's no need—'

'And I'd be very grateful if you would walk me home.'

———

She wouldn't take no for an answer. I told her that I didn't know her full name, and she told me it was Alice Morgan, and held out a hand for me to kiss. And now we were introduced, she said, there wasn't any choice, was there? Who knew what dangers lurked on the route between here and her house? And besides, she knew where Peregrine lived, having sat for the portrait, and the detour was half a mile at most. A small price to pay for a lady's safety. And all this while we were strolling along the promenade together, even as I protested that I would be next to useless if she were attacked.

'Well, I know *that*,' she assured me. 'We're like two girls keeping each other company.'

'We are not.'

'I said *like*. And it's true, corporeally speaking.'

'I've found, Miss Morgan, that the corporeal doesn't count for much.'

She pursed her lips, slowing her stride as she was contemplating what I'd said. She appeared quite genuine in her desire to understand me. Eventually, she reached a conclusion.

'Perhaps that's the difference between us. I've found that the corporeal counts for *everything*.'

I supposed she had a point, from her own perspective. She was, presumably, Quinton's mistress, so her body was her livelihood. I didn't know whether he had a wife as well, but even if he didn't, Miss Morgan wasn't likely to get the part. She was, at best, an understudy.

'You were angry with Mr Black before,' she said. 'You didn't want your secret told. I can understand that.'

I didn't reply. My feelings were too complex to express, especially to a stranger. In truth, I felt less anger than despair. First Rosie and now Peregrine had made their feelings clear. They might love me, but when it came to people whose opinions they valued – sisters or clients – my affliction was the only notable characteristic I possessed, overriding everything else: my mind, my soul and my beating, male heart.

I had the urge to run. I'd done it before. By this time tomorrow I could be on a ship to Spain or France, and no one would ever know where I'd gone.

'It's beautiful, isn't it?' she said.

'What?'

'The sea. You were admiring it.'

She was, in literal terms, mistaken. At this late hour, the sea was nothing but a dark strip between the stones on the beach and the starry sky. But I knew what she meant.

She looped her arm in mine. 'It's a warm evening.'

'It is. Would you like me to carry your coat?'

'Thank you.'

She took it off, revealing again her shoulders and slim upper arms.

I had thought we would continue our stroll, but she continued to stand and gaze out at the horizon. 'We should get a closer look. It's glorious at this time of night.'

Without waiting for an answer, she started clambering over the stones between the huts. I had little choice but to go as well.

The beach dropped steeply at the tideline, where the bathing machines were lined up like cannons awaiting enemy fire. She threaded between them, looking back to see that I was following. I was feeling strangely breathless, though the walk was no exertion at all.

When we reached the water, she leaned down and removed both of her shoes, placing them side by side on the stones.

'Come on.'

She picked up her skirts, gathering them tight to her knees, and waddled out, washing her feet in the waves, which were no more than ripples in the stillness of the evening. She gave me a broad grin, her eyes reflecting the lamps on the promenade.

'It's marvellously refreshing,' she said, coming back out of the water.

Perhaps now we would resume our journey home, I thought. But that was not her intention. Instead, she began to undo the buttons of her overdress.

'Miss Morgan, please. I don't know what you're planning, but—'

'I'm planning to swim. Don't you want to join me?'

Always the hardest question. Yes, yes, of course, yes, but it wasn't possible. I could only ever watch from the edge. To *join in* required a wholeness I did not possess. My curvatures would betray me.

I looked each way along the shoreline. The beach appeared deserted.

'We aren't supposed to,' I said. 'And there's no one here to man the bathing machines. I don't think I'm strong enough to move one for you.'

At that, she laughed, covering her mouth like a schoolgirl. 'That won't be necessary. I'm not shy.'

She removed her overdress and laid it on the shingle next to her shoes, and then her flounced skirts and bustle, until she was standing in front of me wearing nothing but a white combination.

'Miss Morgan—'

'It's only swimming,' she said, and walked into the sea.

There were any number of things I could have told myself. I could have wondered at the state of the tide, and whether she was safe out there on her own. I could have remembered that Rosie didn't treat me as a husband, so could hardly complain if I didn't act like one. I could even argue that flirting with other women was exactly what most husbands did anyway, and why should I be any different?

But instead, I acknowledged the truth, no matter how selfish it made me feel. At that moment, on that beach and under that sky, I wanted to do something other than watch from the edge. I wanted to go swimming with Alice. I pulled off my shoes and socks, my suit and my shirt, and whooped as I sprinted into the sea, creating the hugest splash. Alice was already floating on her back, her feet poking above the water, and she clapped as I spluttered and then plunged.

It had been so long. Underwater, all the sounds of the world dulled and, eyes shut, breath held, I was weightless and formless. I kicked and made a stroke with my arms, and then another, feeling my drawers and undershirt pull into my body and float outwards, pull inwards and float out, over and over. More than anything, at that moment, I wanted to leave all the parts of me behind and simply disappear.

When my lungs started to burn, I came up for air. The shore was lit like a diorama, carriage lamps swinging and windows glowing. Against such brilliance, we were the faintest of shadows.

Alice was performing a neat breaststroke, a look of concentration on her face. As she came close, we trod water.

'Thank you,' I said. 'I haven't done this for a very long time.'

'Don't you like it?' she asked, between gasps.

'I do. Very much.'

'You should do it more often.'

My life is more complicated than that, I thought. But why? I would never have swum in the sea if this woman hadn't cajoled me, or coaxed me – or shamed me. Perhaps my life had only become complicated because I'd forgotten it could be otherwise.

After fifteen minutes of joyful splashing, I followed her back to the beach, dripping water on to the shingle. Her underclothes were clinging to her body, revealing the plumpness of her buttocks and the hollowness of her back.

I wondered how I must look to her. I was as spare as a whippet, but I had hips and a waist and small breasts, squashed under my binding. Instinctively, I covered myself, arms across my chest, but she didn't glance back at me. I was grateful for her compassion.

The evening had seemed warm, but now our teeth were chattering. Absent towels, we had no choice but to put our clothes back on over our salt-soaked underwear. It was no easy task, and we giggled and shivered as we hopped to and fro and fiddled with buckles, hardly able to see what we were doing.

Once reclothed, we tiptoed back to the road between the bathing machines and huts. Under the light of the street lamps, anyone would have known what we'd been doing. Our hair was lank and wet, and our clothes were blotchy with seawater. We left two trails like slugs on the paving.

At the formal garden, we headed rightwards, inland, passing an ugly grey obelisk, the kind of thing city officials erect as memorials when they're too mean to pay for a sculptor. The streets were residential, modest but pleasant. She stopped next to a house with a blue door.

'This is where I live. Thank you, I've had a lovely evening.'

Such times as these make a lie of the laws of physics and chemistry. The finest scientists couldn't deny that another energy exists in the universe, an invisible and unmeasurable force that pushes and pulls, both at once. I was cleaved in two by it.

I forced myself to perform a bow.

'Goodnight, Miss Morgan.'

As I turned to go, she produced from her inner coat pocket her door key and an opium pipe.

'Do you smoke?' she asked.

In the past, I'd been guilty of indulging in such temptations, but no longer. I had Rosie and the children to think of.

'No.' I should have left it at that, but more words came into my head, and for some reason, out of my mouth. 'I've heard it called the "Blood Flower".'

The smile faded on her lips. 'The what?'

'The Blood Flower. Opium comes from poppies.'

She narrowed her eyes, and I had the impression she was trying to work out whether I was playing some trick. Fortunately, I had an honest face.

'What do you know of the Blood Flower?'

I shrugged. 'Only that it's in some way connected to two murders, a young man named Micky Long and an acrobat named Natalia La Blanche. Do you know them?'

Alice hugged herself, beginning to shiver again. 'I met Micky once or twice. He worked for Mr Quinton sometimes. I wept when I heard. He had a younger brother, you know. I can't imagine what'll happen to him now. But you're on the wrong track, I assure you.'

'How so?'

'The Blood Flower isn't opium.'

I stared at her. 'Then what is it?'

She looked down at her hands. 'I can't tell you. I truly can't.'

'Miss Morgan, you must. A lad has been arrested.'

'If you mean Honey, everyone knows it wasn't him. He'll be let out tomorrow.'

I was becoming impatient. I couldn't help but remember the faces of the circus troupe when they found out that their friend was dead. They deserved to know the truth of her murder.

'Two deaths, Miss Morgan. Tell me what the Blood Flower is.'

She opened her door and turned back to face me. 'It's the most valuable thing. Beyond price.'

'Why?'

'Because it's dangerous. It contains beauty and parlous magic.'

'What kind of "parlous magic"?'

Her fingers went to her throat. 'I'm speaking plainly. It's cursed. That's all I can say.'

Before I could ask her what on earth she meant, she shut the door, and I was left alone on the step.

8

I SPENT MOST OF the following day in my room. This was of necessity, as I didn't have any dry clothes to wear. Peregrine, eager to show his contrition, had taken my salt-marked suit to the laundry for me.

We had spoken only briefly the previous evening, after I'd been forced to wake him up by throwing shingle and snails up at his window.

I was unfooled by his brimming eyes, especially when he described himself as an ass-head and a coxcomb, insults I was sure I recalled from his play. But of course, I forgave him. If he hadn't betrayed my trust, I would never have had the chance to swim in the sea with Alice.

'Explain again how you got wet last night,' he said.

I wrapped myself closely into the dressing gown he had lent me.

'I fell by the water's edge. I was drunk.'

He raised a disbelieving eyebrow but chose not to start an argument so soon after our reconciliation.

I wasn't sure why I told the lie. I had done nothing wrong. In reality I'd been a perfect gentleman. *In reality*. In my imagination, however, that was not entirely the case. That night, I had lain awake for more than an hour, dwelling upon the vision of Alice leaving the water with her underclothes stuck to her skin so tightly, and so transparently, she might as well have been naked. More than that, at her door, I vividly pictured the softness of her gaze and the amused dimples in her cheeks. What if I had accepted her invitation to go inside? What would have happened then?

But that wasn't the only thing that had kept me awake. What truly stopped my eyes from closing was a simple question: why did I decline? My marriage was a fake, a matter of expedience, designed to protect Rosie from suitors and me from scrutiny. We slept separately. Why shouldn't I have gone into Alice's house?

I wasn't under any illusions. I knew that women didn't swoon over men like me: slim of build, light of voice, overly serious and oddly secretive. Alice was only the second woman I'd ever met who found me attractive and knew what I was, under these clothes, under my binding. Was I expected to remain celibate for the rest of my life?

Mrs Mackay brought us a late lunch on a tray. She was, once again, dressed in a riding blazer, jodhpurs and black boots. Her hair was short and severe, but her face was kindly.

'Chicken-of-the-woods and onions,' she announced. 'Would you like some tea as well?'

Peregrine and I replied at the same time, with equal fervour but opposite answers.

'I would,' I said, at exactly the moment he said: 'No, we won't.'

She looked at each of us in turn and let out a loud 'tut'. 'I'll bring one cup, shall I?'

'Yes, please.'

Mrs Mackay blessed me with a smile and glowered in Peregrine's direction. 'Your young friend is a good deal politer than you, my Thrush. You should listen to him. You might learn something.'

We tucked into the chicken-of-the-woods, which was a touch dry and chewy.

'She's not the finest cook,' Peregrine admitted, toiling through his mouthful. 'Especially compared with what you're used to.'

'Personally, I think she's magnificent in every way. Why did she call you "my Thrush"?'

He swallowed and spent several seconds dabbing his mouth with a napkin. 'A pet name. Like the song, you know. *Thou mellow angel of the air, Sing on, dear Thrush, amid the limes.*'

'I'm not familiar with it.'

'We've already established that you lack a basic knowledge of music.'

My mother had favoured the classics and it was Jane, my older sister, who was considered the musical one. She had learned to play many of the works of Mozart and Chopin with great accuracy, if little feeling, before the age of fifteen. My brother, Oliver, was the sportsman of the family and, as sportsmen often do, he entered the army to inflict his shooting skills upon the natives of Peshawar. I wasn't considered to be anything. I was loved and cherished by my mother, befriended by my sister and tolerated by my brother, but none of them had the slightest idea what to do with me. Perhaps, without being able to name it, they sensed my dislocation.

When Mrs Mackay returned with the pot of tea, she brought with her a telegram addressed to me.

'From Jacob,' I told Peregrine as I read it. 'It's a chess move. Knight to king's bishop six.' I pictured the board in my mind. 'He's threatening my pawn.'

Mrs Mackay widened her eyes. 'Well, aren't you clever, a game like that, and in your head as well.' She gestured at Peregrine with her long, cultured fingers. 'He used to play a bit, didn't you, my Thrush?'

He mumbled something unintelligible, though I thought I made out the words 'idiotic pastime'.

I bestowed upon Mrs Mackay my broadest smile, the one Rosie said reminded her of a Labrador who'd eaten too much custard.

'When did you first meet Mr Black?'

Before she could reply, Peregrine leapt from his chair. 'Now, now, we can't sit here idly. You should go, Mrs Mackay. We have things to get on with.'

She gave him a look and bustled away, trailing a waft of bergamot oil behind her.

In the early evening, I set off on foot for Southsea. Viola and Bill lived on Waverley Road, which was a stone-throw from the sea and consisted of matronly houses set behind prim walls, each with a herringbone path up to the porch.

Rosie answered the door and pulled me into the parlour.

'Please,' she said. 'Make this visit as quick as possible. And try to avoid conversations about ... anything.'

I was getting tired of people telling me I couldn't talk to other people.

A fellow drifted in and introduced himself as Mr Hapsworth, the Broadmans' lodger, shaking my hand with all the firmness of an empty glove. Truly, he seemed so mild that a breath of wind would blow him off his feet.

'I admire Mrs Broadman greatly,' he told me. 'She has a remarkable gift.'

He appeared to think I would know what he was talking about, but Rosie shooed him out before he could explain further.

'Did you learn anything more about the opium trade?' she asked. 'The Blood Flower?'

'The Blood Flower isn't opium.'

'What is it then?'

Again, I pictured Alice on her doorstep, her blue eyes meeting mine: *beauty and parlous magic.*

'I don't know.'

Rosie frowned at me. 'Then how do you know it isn't opium?'

'I just do. Must I explain everything? Would you like a detailed account of all my movements and conversations?'

She stood up with an expression on her face I hadn't seen before. It was, in part, shock, but also something else; something more akin to *recognition.*

'As you wish,' she said.

What had come over me? I knew the answer, of course. I was shot through with guilt at having thought only of Alice for the past several hours. But instead of punishing myself, I had punished Rosie, my wife. And though, for us, that term had only the loosest definition, she was, without any qualification, my friend. She didn't deserve to be snapped at.

'I'm sorry, Rosie. I haven't been myself since we got here.'

She gave the tiniest of shrugs. 'Very well.'

I found the point where my binding met my armpit, where the skin was chafed as raw as minced meat, and dug in my fingernails.

At the corner of my eye, I became aware of a new presence in the room, a white ball hurtling across the rug towards my leg. It moved at such speed that at first I thought it was a rat, but when it buried its teeth into the soft flesh at the back of my ankle, I realised it was a very small dog. I leapt out of my seat, but the blasted creature hung on, growling and setting back its stunted ears as I danced on the spot, squeaking with alarm. I had finally managed to kick the thing off when Viola rushed into the room and swept it up into her arms.

'Don't hurt him. What did you do?'

'The little bastard bit me.'

She clutched the fiend to her bosom, kissing the top of its runtish head. 'You must've scared him.'

I examined the damage, gingerly peeling down my sock. The midget demon's incisors had pierced the skin on either side of my Achilles tendon.

Rosie scowled at her sister. 'Do you have any iodine?'

Viola appeared surprised to be asked. 'You know I don't believe in that sort of thing. We'll call upon the spirits to heal you.'

Perhaps the pain had addled my senses. 'Pardon?'

'You should chain up that animal,' said Rosie, who was usually quite fond of dogs and had been known to accompany young Constance on her walks around Hyde Park with Huffam, who had been my late father's dog and then briefly mine, until Constance grew tired of my well-intentioned ineptitude and took over.

'Jack would never hurt anyone,' Viola insisted. 'Not unless provoked.'

'Jack?'

Rosie pressed her lips together so hard I wondered she didn't break a blood vessel. Her first husband had been called Jack. That her sister had given her vicious rat-beast the same name must have been galling, though not entirely inappropriate.

Rosie fetched a clean cloth and dabbed my ankle with water while Viola responded to my request for a pot of tea. By the time she returned with it, sans my attacker, I was lying on the sofa with my foot elevated on a cushion, one of Rosie's hand-kerchiefs tied tightly around my ankle.

'There must be something wrong,' announced Viola. 'This would never have happened otherwise.'

'Something is definitely wrong,' I agreed, with a degree of heat.

For some reason, I felt she was blaming *me*, though I was the one leaking blood while my persecutor was, from what I could hear, being fed crumbs of cheese in the back room by the traitor Lillian.

'I meant,' said Viola, lifting her chin, 'that there's something wrong in the *spiritual* world. They're trying to communicate with us.'

'Through the medium of a dog?'

In all the fuss and conflict, I had neglected to examine the ornamentation in the parlour. I now realised that the open shelves were crowded with candles, coloured stones, collections of feathers, a pack of cards the size of a bread loaf, a metal compass with a rune inscribed on its face and a wooden board with the letters of the alphabet written around its edge. On the small table was a volume entitled *The History of the Supernatural*.

Oh, good Lord, I thought. I'm in the home of lunatics.

'Jack can always tell when there's an imbalance,' announced Viola. 'He's very sensitive to it. A lot of animals are. They haven't strayed from the natural path, as we humans have.'

'I suppose keeping him on a leash is the answer to that.'

I knew I was being facetious, but if she seriously believed Jack was in touch with a world beyond our knowing, she must have been smoking Quinton's opium.

Rosie clapped her hands together. 'Let's talk about something else, shall we?'

But Viola refused to be distracted. 'There are energies flowing around us that we don't understand. You must agree it's true. We can do unimaginable things, like send telegrams across the country, make a locomotive travel faster than any horse can gallop and send balloons up into the sky with the birds. We can make a lamp light up without burning anything, using electricity.' Her eyes were shining, and I could tell she'd made this speech several times before. 'It's all mystical, isn't it? Why should we assume there's nothing more to life and death than what we can see and touch?'

I sighed deeply. 'Mrs Broadman, I was an assistant to a surgeon for many years, and I've sewn up more dead bodies than I can count. They are … puppets with the strings cut, nothing more. There's no coming and going between the living and the dead. It's a one-way journey.'

'I'll pour, shall I?' offered Rosie.

A look of triumph crossed Viola's face that was the image of my wife's, but for the manic twitching of her lips. 'The body isn't the *person* though, Leo. It's the *spirit* that makes us who we are. And you can't dissect a spirit.'

I opened my mouth to reply, but suddenly found myself flummoxed. Didn't my entire existence rest on exactly that premise?

Bill had come into the room in his shirtsleeves, and he perched on the arm of the sofa. 'You see? She has a talent, my Viola. I'm from near Harlech, you know. Deepest Wales. They don't hold with such stuff round there. But she showed me.' He squeezed his wife's shoulder. 'She truly does speak to the dead.'

Well, I thought, I speak to the dead too. The difference is, I don't expect them to answer.

I rubbed my temples, trying to clear my head. There was a distinction between accepting that the body is separate from the spirit and believing that, after death, our loved ones' spirits remain forever teetering on the edge of our consciousness, waiting to offer us instruction. I didn't get the chance to make this point, however, because Viola chose to press home her advantage.

'You were brought up in a religious home, Roisin told me. Your father was in the clergy.' Her features settled into a serene slackness not unlike some of the opium smokers in Papaver. 'I can see it, actually. There! It's as clear as if it were happening in front of me. A large dining room with a mirror and windows facing the garden. There are trees and a bed of flowers. Hyacinths and roses. It must be summer. And you're there too, Leo. You're a young boy with scraped knees and unruly hair, still quite book-ish. I'd know you anywhere. Your father's talking to you. I can hear him speaking. How hard it must be for you to suffer that voice, day after day, telling you what you ought to believe. The dusty old church and the coffins in the graveyard. How could a young boy like you be expected to keep an open mind?' She blessed me with a benign smile. 'I'm right, aren't I? It's written on your face.'

I honestly had no answer, which she took as affirmation.

'It's being with child that's done it.' She clutched her belly as if she were testing a melon for ripeness. 'The creation of a life within one's womb is a spiritual act. Pregnancy changes a person. You must agree, Roisin?'

Rosie appeared to give the matter some thought. 'It certainly changes a person. I have to use the privy twice as often these days.'

Silence descended as the cups of tea were handed round. I'd rarely felt more in need of one, though it smelled slightly of coffee.

Bill, who had been simmering lightly, now bubbled over. 'I understand your doubts, mate, really I do. But we can prove we're right.' He clenched both fists. 'I'll bet you anything you want that we can solve this murder.'

Viola beamed. 'Yes, of course! A person who dies through violence doesn't settle easily into the afterlife. They remain fractured. Their spirit cries out, if you have the means to hear it. The victims themselves will tell us who did the killing.'

Bill turned to face me, his eyes burning with conviction. 'And then you'll have to believe us, won't you?'

It turned out that contacting the dead required a fair amount of preparation and would be best attempted after dinner, which seemed to me at odds with the spirits' ethereal nature. But still, it meant that Bill, the limp Mr Hapsworth and I were chivvied out for a drink while Rosie put the children to bed and Viola cooked a mutton stew. By the time we reached the pub, my bitten ankle was sending spasms up my calf and I was more than ready for an ale.

Bill knew the establishment well, addressing the barman as 'Ira' and being served in a pewter tankard labelled with his name.

'She really will do it, you know,' he assured me. 'She'll find the killer. She's quite remarkable. A fortnight ago – no, less, ten days – she had a lady whose husband's been dead these fifteen years, and my Viola found him in an instant. She was able to tell the lady her husband's pet name for her, and assure her that, though he'd passed to the other side, he was content. The widow left a handsome gratuity, I can tell you.'

'You make an income from this?'

'Oh yes. More than I make from night soil. People come from all over Portsmouth.' He took a sup, eyeing me over the rim of his tankard. 'When we solve this murder and identify the killer, I suppose that would be noteworthy, wouldn't it? The kind of thing a fellow like you would put in his newspaper.'

'Perhaps.'

I was picturing what Mr Whitford would say to me if I reported that my sister-in-law had solved the case through clair-voyancy. And me, the science reporter.

'Well, I'd hope you would. A bit of fame, a bit of notoriety, is exactly what's needed in this game. Like that bloke who spoke for the dear departed Prince Albert to the Queen. He's prob-ably in high demand now, that bloke. Charges a guinea an hour, I shouldn't wonder.'

The conversation continued along these lines for a further two pints each. At one point, Bill demanded that I should *promise* to include Viola's spiritual gift in my article, and that if I declined, he would withdraw the offer of a séance. I drained my drink and responded that I didn't especially care one way or the other, and he immediately retracted the threat, saying that I was too earnest and didn't know how to take a joke.

Afterwards, we headed back to the house on good enough terms. On the way, he took a long and voluminous piss against a wall, indicating that Mr Hapsworth and I should do the same while urine pooled around his shoes. I replied that I wouldn't want to delay us, and he grinned. 'Bigger the pipe, faster the flow.'

I agreed that he was correct in theory, if not in practice.

On our return, Bill took me through to the back room, which was divided by curtains into three parts. One contained the kitchen, a small dining table and a mattress for Rosie and the children, while Bill and Viola's bedroom took up most of the remainder. Mr Hapsworth had the smallest part, his coffin bed occupying the cupboard under the stairs.

Dinner was a civil affair, the conversation restricted to Viola's plans for a crib and Bill's worries about the dilapidated state of the local cesspools. Viola was no match for Rosie as a cook, but I was feeling quite relaxed, not to say curious, about what was to come. I'd never been to a séance before and was interested to know what one might consist of.

Rosie declined to attend, saying she was tired and had no wish to commune with the dead.

The rest of us went through to the parlour and took our seats around the little table, upon which the alphabet board had been placed. As Viola doused the lights, Bill lit a single candle, which he placed on the mantelpiece. A draught from the chimney unsettled the flame and it wobbled and hissed as if constantly about to go out. In this flickering half-darkness, we sat and waited for the spirits to talk to us.

There was a tiny part of me that wondered if they would. Perhaps the veil between this life and the next was truly so thin that a voice could come through. I pictured Natalia La Blanche as I had seen her on the stones, crumpled and heedless, one arm reaching out and her throat open and raw. If her spirit could find its way here and tell us who had ended her short life, would it croak and wheeze in sympathy with her butchered body or would she be renewed as a whole young woman?

If I were given the chance, I would choose to communicate with my mother. I'd spoken to her only once as my true self, on the very day I left the house, and I never saw her again. I should have written to her, but I did not. If she were able to find her way across the heavenly divide to this small house near the Southsea beach, I would tell her I was sorry.

'Can you talk to *anyone*?' I asked. 'People who died far from here and years ago?'

Viola answered, her voice barely above a whisper and flat in tone, as though her consciousness was already dissolving into the ether. 'If the connection's strong enough. It's a question of the bond, you see. It's love they miss most, I think.' A beatific smile crossed her face. 'Though I must admit that it's *men* I'm best able to talk to. They come more willingly than the ladies. I think it's a sign I have a boy growing inside me.'

That ruled out my mother, I supposed, and I certainly didn't want to hear from my father, cataloguing my failings from the afterlife. I already knew them perfectly well.

'Put your hands on the table,' Viola instructed us. 'Both hands, but lightly. Don't push down. The name of the murderer will be spelled out for us.'

'None of us knew the victims,' I said. 'Let alone loved them.'

'Ah, but they're recently gone, and they'll *want* to be heard, I'm sure.'

She closed her eyes and began to hum and sway. With her back to the candle, her shadow formed a ghostly shade on the board, dancing as the flame wavered and spat. Her voice lowered in tone, becoming a growl like a dog playing tug-o-war, and then a grunt. Without warning, she threw back her head, eyes blinking rapidly, and let out a single long groan.

'Spirits,' she implored. 'Spirits, we beg you, speak to us. Give us your wisdom. We seek ...' She opened one eye and looked at me.

'Micky and Natalia,' I said.

She closed her eye again. 'Micky and Natalia, two young people whose lives were ended unnaturally. If you're there, speak to us now. Tell us who committed these terrible acts.'

For a few seconds, all was silent. And then, as clearly as anything I'd ever heard, a tapping noise came from the table. It was slow and steady, not like a knuckle on a door, but lighter in tone, more metallic, almost a ringing.

My hands, flat on the table, were starting to tremble.

'Good, good, good,' sang Viola, in time with the tapping and matching its note. 'Now, tell us who killed you.'

Under my fingers, the table jerked and began to lift.

9

I HAD ALWAYS PLACED my faith in science. My father's sermons never captured my attention as much as the shape of a wasp's nest or the intricate flight of a flycatcher. The only books of his that interested me were on ornithology or the great work of Mr Darwin, which, in fairness to the Reverend, he read avidly also, desiring to understand what the opposition had to say. I believed in God though. How else could I explain what I was, other than as the butt of some divine joke?

Science, I told myself firmly. Science.

The table was rising and tipping, first in one direction and then another.

'It's a "Q",' announced Bill. 'And an "I".'

The tapping became more irregular and then ceased altogether. The table lurched again.

'The next letter's an "N",' declared Hapsworth, his voice rising to a squeal.

If it was truly a spirit who was attempting to give us the name 'Quinton', the beliefs I'd held for my entire life were wrong. Death was not the end, and I could speak to any number of people whose bodily remains were buried in cemeteries. As well as my mother, I could converse with Miss Maria Milanes who, I once would have said, was more important to me than life itself, little realising how indeterminate that commodity would turn out to be. I felt an unexpected and bitter upsurge of grief.

No, it could not be true. Something more earthly was lifting and moving the table.

Something that wasn't very good at spelling.

'Another "N",' said Bill.

The table itself was circular with a single pedestal leg splaying out into three shorter legs at the bottom. I felt with my foot, and it was indeed suspended several inches from the floor. I could fit my shoe underneath.

I looked down at my hands. They were lightly placed at the table's edge, and likewise Hapsworth's and Viola's, so gentle that only her fingertips were touching it. But Bill's hands were pressed firmly down on the surface, his veins bulging under his skin. He was trying his damnedest not to show it, but he was pushing down hard. Logic put together the pieces. He must have inserted his foot under the table leg on his side, and was lifting it, using his hands to direct the tipping.

'"T",' he announced, his voice shaking with the effort.

Hapsworth could contain himself no longer. 'Quinton!' he yelped. 'That bastard did for them both.'

Viola flopped back in her chair, utterly spent. It was a fine act. I almost applauded.

At that moment, the candle blew out and we were thrown into complete darkness. The table fell away from me, crashing to the floor and setting Jack to yapping in the back room.

I rolled my eyes, though no one could see it. 'May I ask a question of the spirits? Is there a connection between these killings and something called the Blood Flower?'

After thirty seconds of nothing, I stood up.

'I'll relight the candle, shall I?'

Light flared as I struck the match, revealing the table lying on its side and Viola hunched over in her chair with her forehead in her hands.

Hapsworth burst into a fit of clapping. 'Brava, brava! Isn't she a wonder! Two murders solved in a single evening. We must tell the police what we discovered. They need to arrest Mr Quinton immediately.'

I decided to play along with the charade, curious about what they expected to happen next. 'The police will need more than the opinion of the spirits.'

Bill snorted. 'The police are all corrupt anyway. But you can print the truth in your newspaper, can't you?' He seemed very excited by the prospect. 'And make sure you get Viola's name in there, and our address. If she can solve a pair of murders, imagine what else she can do! We'll be the talk of London. Wealthy widows will be begging us to take their money.'

I excused myself to visit the privy, and as I left, I scanned the floorboards. Sure enough, a long piece of cotton was lying there, a loop tied at each end. If Bill had hooked one those loops over the candle and held the other in his hand, it would be the simplest of tasks to give it a tug and extinguish the flame.

When I returned, Hapsworth had left, and Bill was helping Viola to their bed. She was utterly exhausted by her efforts, barely able to lift her feet to walk. All the way, he kept telling his wife what a marvel she was and how famous she would soon become.

I stayed in the parlour alone, until Rosie came through wearing a dressing gown.

'Your sister's a charlatan,' I told her.

She sighed deeply. 'No, she's not.'

'Oh, I assure you—'

'No. She truly thinks she has a gift. I've tried to tell her it's make-believe, but she won't listen.'

'I can show her how it's done, if you wish. Bill faked the whole thing.'

Rosie closed her eyes. 'I guessed as much. He's always had a keen eye for money, that one. And Viola's always been a flibberti-gibbet. But she's not a liar. When she fell pregnant her letters became very peculiar, asking whether I'd like her to contact our father. Can you imagine anything worse?'

'What did you say?'

'I said no, of course. Not because I thought she could do it, but … it's just wrong. I hoped I might be able to persuade her to stop all this nonsense while I was here.'

'You might have told me.'

'While you were being such a brute? You've been awful since we arrived.' She shook her head. 'You shouldn't have come to the beach yesterday. You knew it wasn't what I wanted.'

'I wouldn't have had to come if you hadn't been so deter-mined to keep Viola from meeting me. If you hadn't been ashamed of me.'

'Oh, Leo.' She took a deep breath. 'You are such a fool.'

I must say, I found her attitude incomprehensible. She was adding insult to injury.

When she met my eyes, she had *that* look, the one that spoke of impatience, amusement and a deep well of kindness. 'Leo, did it ever strike you, even for a minute, that it wasn't you I was ashamed of?'

'What do you mean?'

'You're inclined towards science. Such a rational man.' She sighed and rubbed the tops of her shoulders. 'Most of the time, anyway. I couldn't bear the thought that you'd meet her and think her idiotic.'

For a second, I wasn't sure whether to believe her, but Rosie had never lied to me. Always, her opinion of me was higher than my own. *Such a rational man*, she called me, but I didn't feel very rational at that moment. More than anything I felt lost.

I picked up the piece of cotton from the floor and wound it tightly around my finger.

'Viola seems perfectly nice, but ...' I wasn't sure how to finish the sentence.

'But she *is* idiotic,' said Rosie.

'Perhaps. She's being deceived. It's not her fault.'

'I know. Let me talk to her again. Perhaps she'll see sense.' Rosie yawned and I yawned in sympathy. 'It's late. You should go back to Mr Black's lodging.'

I felt a pang of disappointment.

'Very well. But we did learn something from all this. Bill thinks Quinton did the killing. That was the name he spelled out. Or tried to.'

Rosie gathered her dressing gown more closely around herself. 'I doubt he has any idea. He probably heard us mention the name on the way back from the beach yesterday.'

She was right. That was how charlatans worked: telling people what they wanted to hear. A desperate person will readily believe any so-called mystic who tells them that their loved one is safe and well in heaven.

'He doesn't know anything about the Blood Flower. He was silent when I asked about it.'

She smiled. 'For a man who says he wants to go home tomorrow, you seem very intrigued about the mysterious Blood Flower.'

I did want to return to London, of course. I'd told J. T. Whitford to expect me in the office the following morning, and I was already going to miss that deadline. And yet, I found myself inclined to stay a day or two longer. I wanted to know who had taken the lives of two young people for the sake of the Blood Flower, whatever it was.

I limped from Viola's house to the promenade to find a taxi-cab, spending a precious threepence of the newspaper's money to save me from having to hobble all the way back to Peregrine's lodging on foot.

The following morning, a Saturday, I slept until after eight o'clock. A summer rain was pattering on the window, and the soreness from the bite on my ankle had subsided to a dull ache.

I found Peregrine in his room, perching at his dressing table with a mirror, plucking hairs from his nose with tweezers and sporadically sneezing with a screech that sounded like a barn owl coming to a bad end.

'I've only got three shillings fourpence halfpenny left for my expenses,' I said.

'I thought you'd be flush. Top London journalist and all that. Don't you have capital of your own?'

'Twelve shillings, but I was rashly intending to spend that on next week's rent and food.'

He ceased his toilet. 'So, I won't be able to pay Quinton.' His face, usually a florid pink, was becoming increasingly pale.

'Do you have no money at all?'

He sighed and put down the tweezers. 'Four shillings.'

'Is that all?'

'Actors work for love, and live on bread and water.'

'You might have told me that before I offered you a loan.'

He stood up and began pacing the floor, setting the numerous bottles of lotions and creams on his table to clinking. 'He wants one pound, fifteen and six, plus the painting. I'm short almost a pound. He'll have a finger for that at least, maybe two.' He clutched his hands together.

'Peregrine, you're short more than that. I can spare you six shillings of my own money at most.'

I dreaded to think what Rosie would say if she knew I'd promised him that much. She was fond of telling me that her profit on a pie was a single penny. Six shillings was seventy-two pies; more than a day of her labour. And, she would ask me, for what? For Mr Black to sate his lust with molly-lads rather than his sweet, young wife, who was stuck in Holborn with their child.

Peregrine looked down at his hands. 'That'll cost me three fingers, I should think.' He shuddered. 'And possibly a thumb.'

I picked up the portrait of Alice and removed the cloth covering it. Once again, I was struck by how well it captured her wry expression, the merest strokes of white paint making her lips moist and her eyes glint.

'You have a talent.'

'That will avail me nothing with only one hand.'

I ignored his plaintiveness.

'While the portrait was being done, did she ever mention the Blood Flower? She wouldn't tell me what it was, but she said it was dangerous and magical. And very valuable.'

He paused in his pacing and rounded on me. 'When did she tell you that?'

'After you left yesterday.' I moved the topic swiftly onwards. 'What do you think it might mean?'

Peregrine went back to his wringing and pacing, accompanied by the creak of the floorboards and the chinking of his bottles. The room was truly not large enough to accommodate his vexation.

'It probably means nothing at all,' he said. 'Or it's not a thing, but an idea, like "death is the Blood Flower" or "love". Or, I don't know, perhaps it's a polite way of talking about women's monthlies.' He took on a thespian air. 'Young Isabella's Blood Flower has bloomed at last. We must wash the sheets immediately.'

'Perhaps.' If I was honest, I was hardly listening to him. Another thought had occurred to me. 'Fish out your pencil and a piece of paper. In exchange for the loan, you can undertake a task for me. I want you to do another portrait.'

Peregrine, it turned out, had an excellent memory for faces. I found this noteworthy in a man who claimed to be more interesting than anyone else he met. When he'd finished, he held it up, and I applauded.

'That is exactly Natalia La Blanche,' I said. 'I'm certain that's how she would have looked in life.'

I sniffed, and realised I was blinking back tears. I had not expected such a reaction in myself, but those scrapings of charcoal on white paper brought her back to me vividly: the appley youth of her cheeks and slight pout of her mouth contrasting with the powerful sinews of her neck and shoulders. I wished I could have met her.

Peregrine waved away the compliment. 'Will you be meeting your wife today? She's the one with all the brains.'

I swallowed, trying to clear my throat of the lump that had formed there. 'For lunch. Before that, I have to speak to Mr Honey and find out what he knows about the Blood Flower. He's the one who first mentioned it.'

Peregrine glanced at me suspiciously. 'Isn't he at the police station? No, Leo, you mustn't. It's too risky.'

'I'm a journalist, Peregrine. I talk to all kinds of people.'

I was aware that this made my professional life sound a good deal more exciting than it actually was. In truth, I didn't spend any time in whispered conversations around the taverns of the East End or being passed notes by anxious lords in the corridors of power. Most of my articles came from symposiums and announcements, my primary task being to simplify and shorten them to a level at which the subeditors could shorten them further, rendering them virtually senseless, or cut them from the newspaper entirely.

Peregrine raised his eyes to the heavens and mouthed a prayer, though I knew him to be a fervent atheist.

'Not risky for you, you bonehead, for *me*. Quinton knows we're friends. If you go talking to the police, he'll assume I'm trying to evade my debt by getting his club closed. He'll break my knees as well. Or worse.' He sat beside me on the bed and stared into my eyes, resembling more than ever a faithful old hound. 'Really, Leo, I think you should wait for Rosie. She'll tell you not to do it.'

'I won't mention Papaver to the police, if that's what you want.'

'It's not only for me. The clientele require discretion. If the police raid Papaver, a lot of people's lives will be ruined.' He paused, suddenly earnest. 'Promise me, Leo.'

'I promise.' I slid the picture of Natalia La Blanche inside my folio. 'If I can, I'll speak to Mr Honey in the jail, but I won't discuss Papaver with the police.'

'Didn't Quinton say the lad would be freed soon anyway?'

'He did. I'll find out if he was right. Now, tell me how to get to the police station.'

Interviewing Honey wasn't my only reason for going to the police. But the other, I deemed, was too macabre for Peregrine's sensitive constitution.

———————————

The rain had rendered the streets slick and perilous, and once again I missed the well-paved civility of London. By the time I reached the police station, a humble building stuck on a triangle between three roads, my shoes were caked in mud and the hems of my trousers were soaked through.

I loathed police stations: the stench, the clang of doors being slammed and bolted, the constant sense of being watched. I avoided them wherever possible. And yet I wanted to speak to Honey, so I had the choice of going inside or waiting out here in the mud until he came out. The police station had two doors, one to each fork in the road, and with my luck I'd stand outside the wrong one, so, with a heavy heart, I slopped up the steps and through the door.

There were only two people in the modest anteroom, a young constable behind a metal desk and woman in full mourning weeds on one of the benches. I was surprised when she leapt to her feet.

'Mr Stanhope!'

It was Olga Brown. I hadn't recognised her with a veil over her face.

'Miss Brown. What brings you here?'

'I'm here to fetch Timothy Honey, but I've been waiting for two hours and there's no sign of him. They won't even talk to me.'

'Let's see if I can find out what's going on.'

I approached the constable with a determined air. 'I'm a journalist with the *Daily Chronicle* in London. I'd like to speak a man in your custody named Honey.' I gave him my most businesslike expression. 'Sergeant Dorling said he would extend me every assistance in this matter.'

He started rifling through his papers, occasionally looking up nervously under my stern gaze. 'I don't have nothing about that, sir.'

'Please fetch your sergeant. I'm sure you don't want me to print in my newspaper that you refused to help.'

He rushed away and I heard him trip on the stairs in his haste. It was most satisfying.

Miss Brown turned to me. 'Do you know anything more about Natalia's death? I mean, who might've … might've killed her?'

I could see in her face she was afraid of either answer. A 'no' would mean more waiting, more uncertainty. But a 'yes' would bring an almost unbearable end.

'I don't. I'm sorry.'

She pulled back her veil, and her eyes looked red and sore. 'Natalia was a gentle girl. It's unimaginable that anyone would do her harm.'

'I had the impression she was a bit wild as well.'

Miss Brown looked a little torn. I could see that she didn't want to criticise the dead, perhaps mindful of the exasperation she had expressed with Natalia before she'd heard about her murder. Honesty prevailed.

'It's true, she could be ... I don't know how to say it ... easily attracted to something new.'

'Fickle?'

'*Fickle*? Is that a word, truly? Well, then, yes, she was a fickle.' Miss Brown wiped her eyes. 'But only because of her romantic nature. She was always dreaming. An idea would come into her head, and it would be all she could talk about, until the next one. She wanted to see the world, she said, and have adventures. New York. Can you imagine? I told her she was too silly and she would forget about it in a week. But now, I wish ...' She trailed off, but then sniffed and set her shoulders. 'My point, Mr Stanhope, is that everyone loved her. I'm certain she did nothing to deserve death.'

I'd seen the corpses of countless people and more than half of them probably deserved their fate. Wife-killers, rapists, baby farmers and every other kind of vermin found themselves on the slab, to be opened up and emptied out by the surgeon. But what of the others, the innocents, murdered in an alley for sixpence or beaten bloody by their father in a drunken rage? They were equally dead. *Deserving* didn't make a jot of difference.

The clerk returned with Dorling, who was, remarkably, sporting a blue velvet jacket and matching scarf. Rosie had been right; up close, he smelled of sour milk.

He didn't seem pleased to see us and sucked loudly on what was left of his teeth. 'Mr Winthrop.'

Truly, the man was a fool.

'It's Stanhope, and you've met Miss Brown. I'd appreciate your help, Sergeant. It's about Mr Honey. I understand he's due to be let out today.'

'Later this afternoon. He's got alibis for the murders, but I still have some questions for him.'

'Good. We'd like to speak with him now, if possible.'

Dorling raised his eyebrows. 'It's not.'

I'd anticipated that he would require some persuasion. 'Well, that's a shame. Our readers will be very disappointed.' When he didn't respond to that gentle threat, I opted for a more overt approach. 'Perhaps I should speak to your Chief Constable? I'm sure he'll be more cooperative.'

Dorling's expression didn't change. 'I didn't wash up on this morning's tide. If you wish to ask the Chief Constable, then by all means, be my guest.' He glanced at the constable, who was back at his desk. 'If I know Mr Cosser's mind, he'll give you short shrift. The way I see it, you might be a big London journalist, but you've done nothing for us thus far. I don't see a single reason why we should do anything for you. Cooperation runs two ways. Now, if you have nothing more?'

He turned on his heel. As he'd declined my simple request for an interview with Honey, it seemed highly unlikely he would grant my other one. But maybe my trip didn't have to be entirely wasted.

'You said Mr Honey had alibis. Who gave them to him?'

He looked back, and I could see he was considering whether to tell me. I caught something else in his expression too, something sly and calculating. 'An unimpeachable source, or else he'd be going nowhere. It was Mr Thomas Quinton.'

I heard Miss Brown's sharp intake of breath. 'Mr Quinton? He was the one who accused Timothy in the first place!'

Dorling gave a her a look of pure disdain. 'This is how things work in England. When a man like Mr Quinton gives his word, it's as good as if it's from the Bible. Mr Quinton remembered that Honey was at his house framing pictures on the occasions when the murders took place.'

I couldn't tell whether the sergeant actually believed this or not. Why on earth would Quinton accuse Honey of two murders and then give him alibis? It made no sense at all.

'On *both* occasions? That seems rather convenient.'

'Fortunate, certainly. It rules Honey out.'

Miss Brown was glaring at him. 'If he's been given alibis, why is he still here?'

Dorling stuck out his jaw. I could see that he hated answering any question posed by Miss Brown. 'He has information that's of use to my enquiry, so he'll be here for a few more hours at least.'

Miss Brown seemed about to say something heated, but thought better of it and stormed out, slamming the door behind her.

Dorling rolled his eyes. 'Their brains aren't like ours, see? They can't control themselves.'

'You clearly haven't seen her perform.'

His lips curled into a sneer. 'Oh, they're physically strong, no doubt. They have to be. But the primitive brain doesn't have the capacity of yours and mine.' He turned and headed towards the stairs, calling back to me over his shoulder, 'That's just how it is.'

I'd seen no evidence of such a deficiency. Indeed, Miss Brown seemed a good deal more sharp-minded than some I could mention. Dorling believed her to be primitive for the same reason he would think me a woman if, heaven forbid, he ever saw me naked: because he was not truly interested in the truth. It was a terrible trait for a policeman.

'Sergeant, have you heard of something called the Blood Flower?'

He half-stumbled, recovered himself and continued on his way without a word. He knew what the Blood Flower was, I was certain of it.

Outside, I climbed down the steps one at a time, trying not to slide on the mud. There was no sign of Miss Brown.

On the opposite side of the road, a cockle stall was advertising two ounces for a halfpenny, which suited my wallet perfectly. I had just bought a small bag when I heard a voice.

'You, sir. I'd like a word.'

I looked round, and it was the naval-looking gentleman I'd seen outside the Hippodrome. I thought him a little older than me, with a face that might be described as handsome, if rather severe.

He plucked aside his long coat to reveal a pistol in a holster.

MY STOMACH CRAMPED, SENDING a chill across my skin. The street was busy with carts and pedestrians, and all the shops were open. Surely, he couldn't be planning to drag me into an alley and kill me in broad daylight.

'How can I help you?'

He took hold of my wrist. 'You can tell me who you are and what you're doing here.'

'Let go of me, sir. There's no cause to be impolite.'

He snatched away his hand, looking right and left along the pavement. 'My apologies, I allowed my impatience to get the better of me. I'm in a considerable hurry and have been stymied at every turn.' He cast a stern look at the police station. 'I've seen you twice in three days. What's your interest in this?'

I gave him my card and explained that I was a journalist from London and was making enquiries about the recent murders. He listened attentively, weighing my words with the air of a man used to hearing other men talk and, at the end, making a decision.

'Did you meet with Timothy Honey?'

'No. The police wouldn't let me.'

He seemed gratified by that news. 'Do they still have him?'

'They do, but he's not guilty. He'll be allowed to leave tomorrow morning, I understand.'

I wasn't sure why I told the lie. Maybe it was because I didn't trust this man and believed Honey would be best out of his clutches, or maybe I simply lied so often, and so well, that it had become second nature.

'I see.' He checked his pocket watch, tapping his foot with irritation. 'If you discover anything in connection with Honey, you must tell me immediately. Do you understand? I will pay you for *useful* information. My name's Lieutenant Chastain. I'm on the *Colossus*.'

'Is that a ship?'

He looked at me as if I was an imbecile. 'Of course it's a ship. I look forward to hearing from you soon, Mr ...' He checked my card. 'Mr Stanhope.'

He marched away, and I resisted the urge to ask him what he knew about the Blood Flower. He was the type who might turn and shoot me, probably with great accuracy.

Instead, I made the short journey to the telegraph office, still shivering at the encounter and slurping cockles from their shells. I sent two telegrams.

The first was to Jacob: pawn to king's bishop three, which defended my central pawn from his knight and allowed me to move out my queen if I wished to. Of our hundreds of matches, he'd won perhaps ten per cent, so I was feeling confident. Yet I also had the niggling sense that on every previous occasion he'd consumed a fair amount of ale and whisky and that, when sober, his game might improve.

The second telegram was to J. T. Whitford at the newspaper, apologising for the delay in my return to the office and asking permission to spend a further five shillings on account. Having given him no choice in the first matter, I had no doubt of his refusal of the second. I was dreading what Rosie would have to say regarding my improvidence. A great deal, I imagined.

I wound my way through the side streets towards Southsea beach in the blustery wind, picking cockles out of my teeth. They'd been soaked in vinegar and were as chewy as old leather. I turned right at the ugly obelisk, retracing my steps from the night before last. The rain was starting up again, dancing in puddles and hammering on shop awnings. I hurried through the mud, recognising a milliner's and an overflowing window-box on the corner, and finally the place I was searching for: Alice Morgan's house.

I needed to know more about the connection between Micky, Natalia and the mystical Blood Flower, and I was running out of threads to pull. There was no other reason for my visit, I told myself. No other reason at all.

I paused at her front door. Should I bang on it with confidence, rat-tat-tat, like a man sure of himself? Or should I tap gently and stand back, as if I'd been passing by and wasn't certain this was the right house?

It didn't matter. A voice called down from the window above.

'You, sir. Go away immediately.' A woman was looking down at me, her face scrunched into a hostile snarl. 'You've no business here. We're respectable people.'

'I don't doubt it. I'm calling on Miss Morgan. Is she at home?'

I gave her my broadest smile, and she recoiled slightly. 'You mayn't come in.'

'As you wish. I can speak with her on the doorstep.'

Quite honestly, this woman's insistence on matters of propriety seemed a mite redundant given Alice's relationship with Quinton. I wondered whether she was Alice's mother or her landlady.

There was a sound of muttering from within, and the woman's head retracted, to be replaced by Alice's.

'Leo! I'll come down.'

Moments later, the door opened, and Alice was there, wearing a simple cotton dress and an apron, holding out her hand. I wasn't sure whether to shake it or kiss it, so I did neither, feeling as awkward as it's possible to feel.

'Miss Morgan, I was wondering if you'd be able to help me.'

The rain was gathering pace, and water was cascading from the brim of my hat.

'At least stand in the doorway,' she said. 'Out of this awful weather. I'm sorry about your welcome. Mother's rather old-fashioned.'

I did as she bade me, standing just inside the house, even though my shoes were heavy with mud, my jacket was saturated with rainwater and my breath stank of cockles and vinegar.

The front room was plainly furnished: two chairs facing the fireplace and a sideboard laden with statuettes, finger bowls and an earthenware vase of the type one can buy for sixpence at Covent Garden Market.

Mrs Morgan stood watching us with her arms folded. I supposed she had good cause to supervise her daughter, given how little Alice seemed to care for modesty.

'When we last spoke, you said you didn't know Natalia La Blanche.'

She looked surprised at my question. 'Yes, quite true.'

I produced the picture from my folio. 'Have you ever seen this woman?'

She took the piece of paper and examined it. 'This is Mr Black's work. I recognise his style. And yes, she does seem familiar. I believe the boys brought her to Papaver once. Her name was …' She clenched her fists, trying to remember. 'Her name was Miss White, I think.'

'That's a translation. Her real name was La Blanche.'

Although that was almost certainly a stage name, I thought. Like Olga Brown, like me and even, it turned out, like Rosie. Natalia had worn her name in the manner one might wear a hat, to be put on or taken off at will.

'Oh.' Alice's fingers went to her throat. 'Is she the one who was … ? Oh, that's awful, isn't it?' She took a deep breath and lowered her voice. 'I only saw her once that I can remember. It would be two or three weeks ago. Micky Long brought her to Papaver and introduced her to us. I think he hoped she'd start *working* for Thomas. Mr Quinton, that is.' Her emphasis indicated the kind of work Quinton might have wanted the girl to do. 'She was pretty enough and quite charming, but she didn't want to stay. She was only there for an hour. Maybe less.'

'Thank you.' I retrieved the picture and spoke in a low voice. 'You must tell me everything you know. This young woman deserves your honesty. Was she murdered in connection with the Blood Flower?'

'This again? I've told you all I can.'

Behind her, her mother sniffed loudly. 'No whispering. I won't have you two making *arrangements*.' I half expected her to produce an ear trumpet.

Alice rolled her eyes. 'If the weather weren't utterly dreadful, I'd suggest going for a walk. Look, Leo, I know you're a compassionate person and it does you great credit.' She gave me a brief, conspiratorial smile. 'I've never met anyone quite like you. But there are things I can't talk about, and the Blood Flower is one of them.'

'Does Quinton threaten you?' I whispered.

Her face, normally so lively, lost all expression, as if a blossom had been suddenly blighted, its perfume lost, its colour faded.

'No.'

'Are you trapped?'

'Few people have your freedom.'

I felt both anger and pity, so thoroughly mingled that I couldn't tell which was which. She had known Micky Long and had met Natalia, if only briefly, and yet was withholding information that might help bring their killer to justice. Her recalcitrance was unforgivable. Surely, it could only be the result of a power Quinton was exercising over her.

'Alice, if you need to escape, please tell me. I may be able to help you.'

She gave me a desolate smile. 'It's not that simple, Leo. One can't escape oneself.'

When I got back to Peregrine's lodging, Mrs Mackay opened the door to me. 'Ah, at last. Your wife's been waiting for you.'

I felt a shiver in my stomach. I'd completely forgotten I was supposed to meet Rosie for lunch, and it was after three o'clock.

She stood up as I entered the front room. 'I thought something must've happened to you.'

'I'm sorry.'

Her face was tense, and her hands were fisted in front of her.

'Mr Black said you'd gone to the police station. I was starting to think they'd locked you up.'

'No. I was accosted by the man we saw before. His name's Chastain and he's a Navy lieutenant.'

I told her about that meeting, and she listened agog. I didn't mention my visit to Alice's house. Rosie and I never discussed the physical aspects of our marriage. We'd kissed on our wedding day like two children playing husband and wife, and that was that. We slept in separate beds, and I had never seen her naked. And it hadn't mattered, until now. Until Alice.

But Rosie was not easily fooled, least of all by me. She could tell whether the day's newspaper carried one of my articles or not simply from the way I was holding it. She had a knack. Her eyes narrowed. 'And that's what delayed you?'

'Exactly. It's not too late for us to get a *late* lunch. I'll explain on the way.'

She took a deep breath. 'We've had lunch, thank you.'

Her 'thank you' was the prick of a pin.

Mrs Mackay thrust her hands into her pockets. 'Made it specially. Mutton pie.'

I thought I saw Rosie wince at the memory.

'Very well,' I said, anxious to move the conversation along. 'Where's Peregrine?'

Rosie pointed up towards the ceiling. 'He said he needed his "restoration", whatever that is.'

'Right. I'll go and wake him up. He'll know Mr Honey's address. Sergeant Dorling told me they'd release him this afternoon and I want to ask him some questions. Will you come?'

'I don't know.'

'Please say yes.'

For a few seconds she stood motionless, caught in a dilemma, and then her shoulders sagged.

'You're soaked through,' she said.

———

Rosie was silent for most of the walk, except briefly to turn to me with a frown.

'That *thing* Mrs Mackay has in her parlour ...'

'The horse? It's for art.'

'But—'

'I know. Don't ask.'

The address Peregrine gave me was a house backing on to the railway. In that part of town, the track was below the level of the street, and the thundering of the trains came as much from under our feet as through the air.

Rosie peered over the metal railing at a set of wooden steps down to the front door. 'That could give way any minute.'

Several of the steps were missing, and those remaining were half-chewed with rot. I clutched hard at the banister as I climbed down. At the bottom, I looked back at Rosie's silhouette. 'Is this really the right address?'

'I think so,' she said.

The door was slightly open, and inside I could see only darkness. I pushed on the handle and was met by the stench of excrement, urine and stale sweat.

I had lived in such places myself, after I'd run away from Mrs Castle's shop on Kentish Town Road with eight shillings and sixpence in my pocket. That fortune lasted less than three hours. I made easy prey.

'Shall I come down?' called Rosie.

'No.'

But of course, she came anyway. It wasn't in her nature to let me take risks alone.

I took off my hat and ducked through the door, immediately bumping my head as I straightened up. This was a coal cellar, barely five feet from floor to ceiling. As my eyes grew accustomed to the dimness, I could see it was crammed with people sleeping in rows, some wrapped in blankets, most just in their clothes. One or two looked up briefly and closed their eyes again, finding me of no interest. All were boys and none looked older than eighteen.

'Mother of God,' whispered Rosie behind me. 'Do you think he's here?'

I cleared my throat and addressed the room. 'I'm looking for Timothy Honey.' I grubbed in my pocket for some coins. 'I can pay.'

There was a stirring in the far corner. 'I'm Honey. Where do you want to go?'

I watched my step, hunching to avoid banging my head again.

'You misunderstand. I only want to talk, nothing more.'

He was sitting on the floor, leaning against the wall under the only window, which was shuttered. I pulled one side open, releasing a wedge of sunlight and a welcome breeze into the room. There was some grumbling at this from the sleepers, one insisting I should shut it again and go to hell, but none took more action than turning away or wriggling into the shadows.

In the light, I could see Honey's face. Around his eye, a purple bruise was forming.

'Did the police do that to you?'

He gave a bitter laugh. 'Not this time. Some men like to punish us for existing.' He put out his hand. 'Even talking will cost you money.'

I placed two shillings into his palm. His expression told me that I'd overpaid.

'You were at the Hippodrome when Dorling came for me.' His voice was as light as a cloud. Again, I had the impression he was not so much speaking to us as offering a commentary from within his own mind, ordering his thoughts in their expression.

'It wasn't us who brought him.'

'I know. You were surprised, I could see that. You tried to help.'

Rosie put her hand on his shoulder, an act which, I must admit, surprised me. While I knew her to be a person of the deepest compassion, Honey was virtually a stranger. He might have stuck her in the ribs with a blade. I moved closer, so I could grab him if necessary. No one would hurt Rosie while I had breath.

'Natalia was your friend,' she said. 'You must be very sad that she's dead.'

His eyes were welling up. 'She was kind. And fun. She didn't care what we were. We used to meet up each afternoon at the pier before we started work. She bought us pastries.'

'You lost two friends within a few days,' I said. 'I'm very sorry.'

His expression hardened and he brought his voice down to a whisper. I had to strain to hear him. 'Micky brought it on himself. What did he expect? He had no business taking such liberties. He had responsibilities.'

Honey's eyes strayed upwards, to a pencil drawing pinned on the wall above his head. I opened the window shutter wider, ignoring the objections from the room, and examined the picture. It was of a lad, from his chest upwards, apparently naked. I had no doubt of the artist.

'Is that Micky?'

He reached up and pulled it off the wall, tearing it into small pieces and hurling them on to the floor.

'I'm sorry,' he mumbled, lowering his forehead on to his knees, his shoulders shaking. Rosie moved closer and put her arms around him. He angled his head towards her.

This was the truth of death, I thought. The worst of it was for the dead, but those left behind were little better off. For Honey, for Olga Brown, there was a gap in the world where someone they loved had once been. Rosie's sister believed she had the ability to bridge that divide, but she was credulous and conceited. The dead were for ever gone from us.

After the events of the previous year, I had dwelled much upon the afterlife. My late father believed everyone was either wheat or chaff, destined for heaven or hell, but I had good reason to hope he was wrong. Was it not possible that a single husk of chaff might be lost among the wheat, and find its way into heaven?

Honey recovered and detached himself from Rosie. 'We worked together on the ships, me and Micky. It was well enough paid, and safer than some, as long as you keep their secrets.'

'What secrets?'

'What do you think? The Royal Navy doesn't like to admit that some of its officers prefer lads to ladies.'

'Only the officers?'

'For the likes of Micky and me, yes.' He lifted his chin with a tinge of pride. 'High class, us. We were rowed across the harbour at night and smuggled on to the ships.'

Rosie's brow furrowed; I could almost hear her mind clicking, 'Did you tell the police all of this?'

A smile lit up his features. For such a wan creature, he had pretty teeth. In another life, and with some feeding up, he could have been an actor on the stage. Ladies would have wept in the stalls at the sight of him, and young girls would keep flyers of his portrait under their pillows.

'There's nothing I can tell the sergeant he doesn't already know.'

Rosie and I exchanged a look. If the police knew that Quinton was selling these boys as prostitutes, they were complicit. How could anyone be convicted of a crime if the machinery of justice was broken?

'Why did Quinton accuse you and then give you alibis?' I asked. 'I assume you weren't really framing pictures.'

He pulled his knees up to his chest and wrapped his arms around them. 'If Mr Quinton says I was, then I was.'

Rosie gave him an assessing look. I could see what she was thinking. The lad's life depended on his ability to dissemble, to lie, to deny. I knew how he felt.

'Natalia is dead,' she said. 'If you know anything that might help catch the killer—'

'I don't.'

She leaned forward. 'Do you suppose you're safe, Timothy? Micky and Natalia were murdered, and you could be next. Why did Quinton give you an alibi? Was it because he wanted the Blood Flower?'

I had to admire her. Truly, there was no one to compare.

He paused as a train clattered by, sending a haze of black dust down from the ceiling. 'Yes, but I don't have it. I don't even know what it is, and I don't want to.'

Rosie gave a sigh and straightened up, which, at her height, she could do. 'It's not opium, then?'

He looked at each of us in turn, half-despairing and half-amused. 'Why do people think there's fortunes to be made in opium, which you can buy on any street corner from here to Penzance for a shilling? It's cheaper than beer. And pharmacies will sell laudanum to anyone who walks in.'

He had a point. Prior to being married to Rosie, I'd lived with my good friend Alfie Smith and his daughter, Constance, above Alfie's pharmacy. He was a decent man, but he made a reasonable profit on bottles of laudanum, sold to cure all manner of ills from women's monthly pains to childhood sleeplessness. And judging from how often some of his customers required the stuff, they must have had a very large number of insomniac children indeed.

'I was told the Blood Flower is magical in some way,' I said.

'Magical, how?' asked Rosie.

'I don't know.' I remembered Peregrine's ideas. 'Perhaps it refers to something abstract, like death or love?' I ignored Rosie's dumbfounded expression, but Honey seemed equally nonplussed. 'Or could it be a *person*?'

He rolled his eyes. 'This isn't game of twenty. I told you, I don't know what it is.'

A sound came from outside and the door was shoved roughly open. A figure in a long coat loomed against the light, immediately banging his head on the ceiling.

'Bloody hell.'

I stared at Rosie and mouthed: 'Chastain.'

I pulled her to me and down, lying on the floor like the boys, hiding our faces in an embrace.

Honey didn't hesitate. Eel-quick, he slid out through the window and was gone before I had time to blink.

Sunlight from the doorway filled the cellar. I could hear Chastain's boots echoing on the floor and more grumbling from the sleepers, quickly subsiding. Chastain approached the window. Taking a step back, he thrust his boot against the wooden bar that went across it, splintering the thing instantly. He clambered through after Honey, and we heard his footsteps in the back yard. We all remained silent and motionless.

After half a minute, he came back through into the cellar, tearing his sleeve on the shards of the window frame and swearing loudly. I lost sight of him because Rosie's hair was blocking my view, but I could hear his heavy breaths.

'Where's he gone?' he demanded of the room. 'I have sixpence here. If any of you can tell me where Honey has scarpered to, it's yours.'

Still, there was no reply.

Then I heard a sound I was dreading; a pistol being pulled from its holster and cocked.

'Alternatively, I can start shooting parts off you. Parts you wouldn't want to lose, I imagine.'

I was shivering and could feel Rosie shivering also. Her hand found mine, gripping it tightly.

Chastain's boots scraped the floor as he turned. I imagined him pointing the pistol at each of us in turn.

His footsteps grew louder as he came closer to where we were lying.

'You, there! No use hiding your face, I recognise it. You're going to tell me where Honey's disappeared to right now.'

I GAVE ROSIE A single kiss on her forehead and started to turn.

But before I could open my mouth, another voice spoke, quavering and still unbroken. 'I don't know, Mr Ch—'

'Don't use my name, boy.'

'I'm sorry, sir. Timothy was here, and now he's gone.'

'I can see that.'

Chastain approached the boy and leaned down, so close I could feel the air as he moved. His boot was no more than eighteen inches from my face.

'Jake, isn't it?'

'Jonathan, sir.'

'Ah yes. Well, Jonathan, you're going to tell me where I can find Honey. And don't tell me you don't know.'

I could hear rustling. The boy was shrinking away from the lieutenant, his back against the wall.

'He goes to the Hippodrome, sir.'

'But he won't go there any more, will he? Not now the girl's dead. Where else?'

Jonathan was weeping. 'I don't know, sir. He was here, sir, and now he's not. I was asleep.'

I released Rosie's hand and she grabbed it again, holding it tighter. 'Don't,' she whispered.

There was a sudden noise and rapid footsteps. The boy had made a dash for it. Chastain caught up to him in the doorway, and I risked raising my head to see. They were bathed in light, and Chastain had Jonathan by the shoulder. A man like him – a Royal Navy lieutenant, a gentleman – could throttle any of these lads and never be held to account.

As silently as I could, I pushed myself up to a crouching position, every muscle screaming at the agonising slowness. Rosie's eyes were wide, but she didn't try to stop me. Faces in the room turned in my direction, and I put my finger to my lips.

Jonathan was whimpering and begging, and his legs were wilting under him. 'I know of one place, sir. One place he might've gone. There's an artist. He does pictures of people. Him and Micky went there a couple of times. I don't know the address, but I can take you.'

I contemplated rushing at Chastain, but I knew he was too strong for me, and he had that pistol. I would have to use a bit of cleverness instead. As another train came past, drowning out all the other sounds, I turned to the window and stepped through.

I found myself in a dank back yard containing nothing but a rotting scuttle. Low wooden fences divided it from its neighbours on either side, and along the back, not four paces away, a wall higher than my head hid the railway. The train was still clattering past, smoke and steam billowing up as if the house backed on to a chasm down to hell.

I had to be quick.

I vaulted over the fence into the next-door yard and then the next, hoping I wouldn't be spotted. I found what I was looking for: steps up to the road. I sprang up them two at a time and took a single deep breath at the top. I straightened my coat, brushed down my trousers and lifted my chin.

A smart black brougham was waiting on the street, facing away from me. I couldn't see the driver, but I would've bet every farthing I possessed that the carriage was owned by the Royal Navy.

I could hear Chastain's voice. 'Are you lying to me, lad?'

He was dragging Jonathan up the steps by the collar. The boy was wearing boots split at the toes where he'd outgrown them, a ragged shirt and a jacket of indeterminate original colour, made grey by the dirt. Atop his head, he had a too-small cap balanced on a sprout of black hair. At most, he was twelve years old.

'Lieutenant Chastain!' I exclaimed, as though we were met by chance at our gentleman's club. 'Did you get my note?'

'What?'

'I sent a message to you at the *Colossus*.' I wagered that he hadn't come straight from his ship. By the time he discovered the truth, the boy would be safely out of his clutches. 'My investigation led me here. Who's this?'

Realising his position was somewhat compromising, Chastain loosened his grip on Jonathan and gave him a pat on the back. 'He's helping me. Honey isn't here, but this lad here knows where he's gone. Something about an artist.'

'Oh.' I smiled in a convivial manner; just two fellows discussing business. 'Well, I can save you a trip. It was the artist who gave me this address and he hasn't any idea where Mr Honey is.'

'Well, that's as—'

'This young man may as well go about his business, don't you think?' I gave Jonathan a severe look and he stared back, goggle-eyed. 'I'm sure he shouldn't be wasting any more of your time, Lieutenant.'

The boy needed no further encouragement. He dashed past me and along the road.

Chastain watched him go, his mouth drawn back into a grimace. 'Where's your hat, Mr Stanhope?'

I put my hand to my head, like an idiot. My bowler was still in the cellar. And it was my favourite too, a gift from Jacob.

'How foolish of me. I seem to have come out without one.'

Chastain raised his eyebrows. Truly, he seemed more offended by my naked head than by the sight of young boys sleeping in a dank coal cellar prior to returning to selling themselves on the street.

'And this artist? Where is he?'

'He doesn't know anything, I assure you.'

'I insist you tell me.'

'I regret, I cannot.'

Chastain glanced towards the waiting brougham. I could see him weighing up his options. Kidnapping street urchins was one thing, but I was a gentleman, and a journalist at that. The tension in him was injurious to watch.

'Mr Honey has something that belongs to me.' He was speaking slowly, pushing out each word as if he was disgusted to have it in his mouth. 'Or he knows where it is. I wish to get it back.'

'Oh? What is it?'

He didn't reply but, quite unconsciously, he positioned his finger and thumb as though he were holding something between them; something about the size of a hazelnut. And then it came to me, what the Blood Flower must be. I wasn't certain. But if I was right, it was indeed beyond price.

Chastain worked his mouth. 'Keep me informed, will you?'

He marched away towards the brougham and climbed inside. I watched until it reached the end of the road and disappeared. Not five minutes later, Rosie had ushered all of the boys out of the cellar and on to the pavement. Some were taller than her, almost young men with fuzz around their chins, and some were kids, rubbing sleep from their eyes.

She handed me my hat.

'Look at them.' She pointed to the smallest. 'He's hardly older than Robbie. It breaks my heart. Where are their mothers?'

I collected all my change together and Rosie went among them, handing a precious coin to each one, a penny for the older ones and a farthing for the younger. They gathered close to her, some clutching her skirt or sleeve, eager grins lighting up their faces. As she paid them, she touched them, a squeeze of the shoulder, a ruffle of the hair, and I could tell she wanted nothing more than to take them home and give them a square meal and a place to sleep. But this city wasn't our home, and these boys were only a few among hundreds or thousands. No one could feed them all.

As we were about to leave, I noticed a movement in one of the doorways, a frightened face peeking out. Jonathan had returned. I beckoned him over and shook his hand, which was scarred and rough despite his tender age.

'You're safe now, young man.'

He whipped off his cap. 'Thank you, sir.'

'I don't have any coinage left for you, I'm afraid. I do have this.' I gave him my empty wallet. 'It's a nice one. Leather. Might fetch ninepence, if you're lucky.'

He bobbed his head. 'Thank you very much, sir.'

'That gentleman – did you meet him on his ship?'

'Yes, sir.'

The boy had a solemn face, not prone to smiling. I was uncomfortably reminded of Lillian.

'You …' I struggled for the right words. 'You provided a service for him, did you?'

'No, sir. My brother, sir. I waited outside.'

'Oh, I see.' I realised who this boy must be. 'Your brother was Micky Long.'

Jonathan swallowed hard. 'Half-brother strictly, sir, yes. He died.'

I had the strong urge to put my arm around him, and he must have sensed it because he leaned slightly towards me. But I was unpractised at physical contact and the moment passed.

'I'm sorry this happened to you,' I said. 'I hope whoever did it is brought to swift justice. I'm sure they will be.'

He didn't argue or agree. I wasn't sure he was capable. He was like a pigeon I'd once seen, caught by a cat, unable to flap its wings. I will never forget its black and yellow eye blinking at me as it waited for death.

'Will you want anything else, sir?'

'Only one thing. The artist you mentioned to Mr Chastain. You should forget about him, all right? Don't mention him to anyone again.'

'I won't.' He shoved my wallet down his shirt. I could see its outline bulging through the cotton.

Without another word, he went back down to the cellar, his bare feet almost soundless on the rotten steps. The other boys went as well, bar a couple of the oldest, who set off towards the city. I wondered what kind of life any of them would have. I couldn't imagine they would survive into their twenties.

———

As Rosie and I started back towards Viola's house, she turned to me. 'Poor child,' she said. 'Now he has no one. What'll happen to him?'

'I don't know.'

I didn't want to tell her what I really thought: that the boy would most likely follow in his brother's footsteps, and sooner rather than later. He would end up dead of disease or cold or violence before his voice had broken. What a brief and terrible life.

'That awful man,' said Rosie.

I nodded, but I also noted that Chastain hadn't harmed the boy. Lots of threats and demands, but no actual harm. But perhaps I'd interrupted him just in time.

'I think we can assume Chastain was one of Micky Long's customers on the ships,' I said.

'That makes sense. And Micky brought his brother along to ... what, keep him safe?'

'Perhaps. Or to show him the ropes.' I winced at the thought of it. 'Chastain has lost something that belonged to him: the Blood Flower. My guess is, Micky stole it. And Chastain thinks Timothy Honey knows where it is. The two lads were friends, sleeping in that cellar in the day and visiting the ships at night.'

'And they knew Natalia too.'

'Yes.'

Rosie's mouth twitched, not quite a smile. 'But you have doubts. I can see it in your face.'

I did, but I was struggling to articulate them. Some of the pieces simply didn't fit.

'It doesn't feel quite right. Micky was killed because he was the thief, but he clearly didn't have the Blood Flower in his possession when he died. Chastain indicated it was an object. Something small.' I couldn't explain the rest of my theory about the Blood Flower; she would want to know where I came by it.

'All right,' she said. 'So that'd be why that horrid man is hunting Timothy Honey, and perhaps why that poor girl was killed too, if someone thought she had it. So, what are your doubts?'

'None of that explains why Quinton accused Honey and then gave him an alibi, does it? Nor who has the Blood Flower now.'

She squeezed my elbow. 'Nor one other thing, Leo, I'm afraid: it's obvious to me that Mr Black knows more than he's saying.

He's your friend, but you have to consider he might be involved in some way.'

She was right, yet I couldn't believe it. Peregrine was many things: oversensitive, rash, bombastic, careless of others and, I was forced to admit, violent when provoked. But always in the service of his own sense of justice. A crime like this … it wasn't in his nature. But, when I thought about it, how much of his nature did I really know? We'd only been friends for two years or thereabouts and for more than half of that time he'd been away with the theatre company.

Neither of us spoke for a while, lost in our thoughts. I knew what I had to do next, but it involved a betrayal.

'How bad would it be to break a promise to someone, if the reason for the promise, the justification, no longer applies?'

She looked up at me, her green eyes reflecting the afternoon sun. 'I suppose it depends. You could ask the person you made the promise to whether they see things the same way.' She slowed slightly and detached her arm from mine. 'Is it me?'

'No, of course not. It's Peregrine.'

'Oh.' She took my arm again. 'You've seemed a tad distant over the last day or two. I wondered if that was the reason.'

'Not at all.' I felt a wash of heat in my chest. 'I've been distracted by the investigation, that's all.'

'Is that what it is now? An investigation?'

I supposed it was, though I'd surprised myself by calling it that. Of course, discovering the truth wouldn't change anything for Natalia and Micky. Justice was a footnote for them, nothing more. But what else was there, now? Better a footnote than being forgotten completely.

'There's more I want to know, yes.'

'So, where are we going?'

'To see Sergeant Dorling. I need something from him, but he'll want something in return.'

When we reached the police station, I was once again struck by how small it was compared with those in London. Rosie paused at the entrance.

'You don't need me,' she said. 'I'll go and relieve Viola. She doesn't like looking after the kids for too long. She says they discourage the spirits from speaking to her.'

I suppressed a laugh. 'Of course.'

As ever, we were incapable of parting sensibly. With every other person I knew, a cheery wave would be sufficient. Rosie deserved more, and yet I couldn't embrace her or kiss her cheek. That wasn't how we were. So, we did what we always did, hopping on each foot and smiling, without ever quite turning away, until one of us did, or we both did, and the spell was broken.

———————

Dorling met me in the foyer, this time wearing full police uniform and a medal on his chest.

'What is it now, Winthrop?'

'Stanhope. You said before that you wouldn't help me unless I gave you something in return. Well, I have a proposal for you.'

He pulled out his pocket watch and glowered at it. 'All right, make it quick.'

'I want to examine the bodies of Micky Long and Natalia La Blanche.'

'Why?'

'I have good reason. And I have experience. I used to work for a surgeon of the dead.' I held out my hands in a manner I hoped was reassuring. 'The corpses will be left exactly as I found them. I assume they're still in the mortuary?'

'I believe the girl's been claimed by the circus people for burial.'

'But Micky Long is still there?'

The lines on Dorling's his face grew darker and more pronounced. 'No one cares about *him*. Why would they?'

Unclaimed and penniless, he would get a pauper's funeral. I needed to see him before that happened.

'Very well. I'd like to examine him. Today.'

Dorling folded his arms. 'You said you had something to offer in return.'

'I have. It's about a club owned by Mr Quinton. But first, do I have your agreement?'

I felt a prick of guilt. I'd promised Peregrine that I wouldn't mention Papaver to the police, and I was breaking my word. But Honey had told us that Sergeant Dorling already knew everything, so I wasn't giving him any information he didn't already have. It was a betrayal, but only in the narrowest sense. I wasn't hurting anyone.

Dorling glanced at the constable at the desk, who was pretending to read some papers, and gave me a brisk nod. I spent two minutes telling him about the dance partners for hire at the club and the illegal opium trade. Through it all, he remained impassive. Not a flicker of interest.

'Anything else?' he said, when I'd drawn to a close.

In for a penny, I thought. 'Yes. There's a lieutenant on the HMS *Colossus* named Chastain. You should question him. I believe he was one of Micky Long's … customers. I saw him earlier on Cumberland Road. He's searching for something he claims was stolen from him.'

Dorling, who, up to that moment, had looked utterly bored, suddenly stood up straight. 'Really? That's very interesting. Thank you, Mr Stanhope.'

'You're welcome. Can I assume you'll—'

'But not enough for me to grant you access to the mortuary.'

'What? But you agreed. I've told you everything I know.'

I couldn't bear the thought that I'd broken my promise to Peregrine for nothing. And yet Dorling wasn't leaving. He remained looking down at me, his moustache trembling with anticipation. 'Which is what any subject of Her Majesty should do if they have information regarding criminal activity. You've done your duty and for that you deserve my thanks. Which I've given.'

'And that's all?'

'What else could there be?'

I was tiring of his sanctimony, especially as it was clearly a preamble to a negotiation.

'What else do you want?'

He rubbed his hands together. 'Ah, well, that's the question, isn't it? What do we want, here on the south coast, miles and miles from London? See, Mr Stanhope, we toil away without the benefit of recognition from the powers that be, and lacking adequate resources to hold back the tide of—'

'I take it you want me to write a favourable article about the police in Portsmouth. Very well, I'll do it.' I didn't mention that such blandishments would never get past the subeditors.

'Thank you, Mr Stanhope. And if my name were to be—'

'Agreed. Leader of men, unsung hero, worthy of the highest commendation. Is that it, or would you like me to propose you for a knighthood?'

He drew himself up, feigning disgust at my impudence. 'It's nothing more than what's deserved.'

'If you say so. I'll need a letter from you giving me permission to enter the mortuary. And directions for how to get there.'

He leaned on the constable's desk to scribble out a note, virtually stabbing the paper with the final dot of his signature. The haggling over, he was impatient to be leaving.

'If they refuse to let you in, there's nothing I can do about it.'

12

THE TAXICAB HEADED NORTH and west, over the railway bridge and through a tangle of dour residential streets. All the colourful paintwork and gay shops near the beach were left behind, replaced by brown brick and hardened dirt. We took a lane alongside the mudflats stretching across the harbour, and the stink twice made me gag. I'd grown used to the smell of this city, but no one could tolerate this. The entire harbour was a pool of silt and sewage, picked over by noisy gulls and a host of plague-doctor oystercatchers, with pied plumage and crimson bills.

We pulled up behind a queue of carriages. I had spent all the money J. T. Whitford had allowed me for expenses, so I had to dip into my personal capital for the threepenny fare. Rosie would not be happy.

But the driver didn't put out his palm. 'Leave it on the bench, mate.'

'I'm not sick, just visiting someone.'

No need to tell him the *someone* was dead.

'I ain't taking no chances.'

The path up to the hospital was sunken and muddy, and the front wall was scarred by cracks in the brickwork I could have put my hand through. One of them was so wide, an entire section of the building seemed on the brink of sliding away into the harbour.

My scribbled note from Dorling won me a meeting with Miss Squires, the mortuary assistant, who was a cheerful woman despite her ghoulish position. In fact, she reminded me of a younger version of Flossie, whom I had known at the Westminster Hospital; it seemed a hundred years ago.

'I can show you the body, but I'll have to stay with you.' She reread Dorling's note, her lips mouthing the words. 'It says here no touching it neither. So.'

I followed her to the furthest-flung tentacle of the hospital, windowless and cold. The corridors were lined with cracked tiles and lit intermittently by sputtering gas lamps, and the smell was, impossibly, worse than ever, the stink of the harbour being rivalled by the nauseating reek of lye.

All in all, I began to feel quite at home.

'Take this,' she said, and handed me a muslin bag filled with dried leaves and berries.

'I don't need it,' I told her, as I stuffed it in my pocket. 'I used to assist a surgeon of the dead in London.'

She shrugged and pushed open the door. 'Your choice.'

Inside, the mortuary was large and surprisingly full. Twelve bodies were lined up in two rows, each covered with a sheet. Most were men, but at the end, under the skylight, were two women and, worse still, a single corpse on a very short table, its shrouds trailing down on to the floor.

'This city's more violent than I thought.'

'Ships are dangerous.' She pointed down the line on the left side. 'Micky Long's number ten.'

'Thank you. I understand Natalia La Blanche has been taken already.'

'Yesterday. A Negress claimed the body.' She checked her book, running her finger down the page. 'Here we are. Olga Brown, she said her name was. The coroner gave his permission. I'm praying Mr Long leaves soon too as he's been here ten days already, and that's more than enough, if you get my drift.'

Micky Long's sheet was damply glistening, a stain coming through in the shape of a man, a ghost trapped inside the cotton.

I pulled it back.

One can become accustomed to looking at cadavers: the bloated torso, mottled skin, teeth shrunken in their gums, nails loosened from their sockets – none of this bothered me. Always, I tried to imagine them as they had been in life, with their bodies whole and their laughter strong. Micky's hair was black, like his brother's, and he had a straight nose and a firm jaw, but the skin of his face was pocked and torn, and his eyelids missing altogether, giving him a startling, mask-like mien. But these injuries were posthumous, the actions of greedy seagulls. In life, he would have been a handsome fellow, though in a different way from his friend Honey, whose delicate features exuded a tenderness certain to set romantic hearts aflutter. Micky Long's face was larger and more prominent, with the beginnings of a beard, full lips and high cheekbones.

His neck had a one-inch incision right above his Adam's apple.

When looking upon death, I'd known people to bow their heads in prayer or cross themselves, even surgeons with years of experience. I didn't know why. The object lying on the table was nothing but a mechanism, a collection of bones and joints and muscles, absent the spark that made it human. The soul: that was somewhere else. Upon my own death, I had to believe that my male soul would continue while my female body rotted in the ground. None of which explained why I talked to corpses. I just did.

'I'll bet you were quite the rogue.'

I tried to imagine the scene; Micky, sitting on the beach, watching night fall on the sea, perhaps lobbing pebbles into the surf, until he feels the chill of metal on his skin, sharp and hard, and falls backwards into the arms of his killer as the world turns black.

To creep up behind someone and drive a knife through their throat was relatively easy, but the result would be messy and irregular. This was as neat as any butcher could achieve. Controlling a victim sufficiently to make such a perfect cut demanded considerable strength and determination. His killer must have held him tightly as he died, and then posed his corpse, displaying him like a specimen. I shivered at the thought of a killer with such discipline.

But, of course, that perfect display hid a devastation within. If had put my finger into the cut, I would have felt the ruptured tube of Micky's windpipe, which, in his last moments, would have been clogged with blood, drowning him on dry land.

'I'm sorry this happened to you.'

Miss Squires, who was sitting at her desk by the door, looked up. I gave her a brief, apologetic smile.

'It's no matter,' she said. 'I do the same thing, talking to 'em. I lack for better company, if I'm honest.'

I peeled the sheet further down. It had become attached to him in places, tearing away the stratum corneum, the topmost layer of his skin, exposing the grey and pink flesh beneath. It was stretched taut by the expansion of his internal gases.

The part of him I wanted to see was the nape of his neck. Forbidden from touching him, I was forced to lean close and squint. The stench became notably worse. The muslin bag was still in my pocket, but I was too proud to pull it out and hold it under my nose, so after another moment of almost retching, I opted to hold my breath.

Sure enough, there was a line, a faint weal which, if it had continued, would lead over his clavicles and down towards his sternum. It was exactly the mark that would be left if someone had ripped a chain from around his neck – the kind of chain from which a jewel the size of a hazelnut might hang.

Before I pulled the sheet over his face again, I gave his forehead the briefest of strokes and smoothed his hair. Miss Squires was too distracted by her papers to notice. It was all I could do for the lad, except one thing.

I leaned down and whispered close to his ear, 'I will find out who did this to you.'

———

'Do you still have that portrait of Alice Morgan?' I demanded of Peregrine, back at his lodging.

He was lying in his bed, the covers pulled up to his chin.

'Why do you want it?'

My tone was sharp. 'Do you have it or not?'

He disappeared further underneath his blankets, so his voice was muffled. 'There are two telegrams for you. I'll save you the trouble of reading them. Your editor says you can stay but there's no more money and you must return to the office on Tuesday without fail. The other's from Jacob Kleiner.'

I glanced at Jacob's move: pawn to king's bishop five. I imagined the board and couldn't work out his intention. He was allowing me to take his pawn without losing a piece. But for now, I had more urgent things to think about than my friend's poor chess strategy.

'The picture, Peregrine.'

'In the corner.'

I picked it up, admiring the fine brushwork. Examined from an inch or two away, it consisted of nothing more than smears of coloured paint on canvas. But at arm's length it came to life: Alice in the flesh. I felt a tremble run across my skin. Those blue eyes. Those inviting lips.

Around her neck, a jewel was hanging on a chain, oval in shape, blood red, its facets glinting in the light. That jewel was the Blood Flower. I was certain of it.

'Was she wearing this when you painted her?'

He didn't look. 'What are you talking about? Who cares now?'

'What's wrong with you?'

His substantial bulk shifted under the blanket. 'I can't pay Quinton. I gave him your six shillings and my four, but he wants the rest tonight. I don't have it, Leo.'

'Please, Peregrine, concentrate for a moment.' I held the picture in front of his face and pointed. 'Was she wearing this jewel when you painted her?'

He peered at his own handiwork. 'No. She gave me a description.'

'How detailed was it?'

He rolled over, facing away from me. 'Very. She said it was exactly the length of my thumbnail. She knew how many facets it had.'

'I have to talk to Rosie.'

Always, Rosie was my confidante, my first thought whenever I had news to share.

'What about me?'

He sounded so plaintive I had the urge to cuddle him, the way I did with little Sam whenever he had the flu. I once stayed up all night with the boy, lying on the floor next to the bed he shared with Robbie, unable to sleep for fear his coughing and gasping would peter out.

But Peregrine wasn't five years old.

'Pull yourself together. I won't let Quinton hurt you.' I ripped a piece of paper from my folio and scrawled a note on it. 'Give him the painting and this. It's a promissory note from me for the rest of your debt. I'll pay him on your behalf.'

He sat up, revealing a blue- and green-striped undershirt. 'Truly? You'd do this for me?' His eyes were wet, lending him an even more doleful air. 'He'll add interest, you know.'

'Go and see him this evening, Peregrine, directly after the theatre. It'll only get worse if you don't.'

———

I was tempted to run to Viola's house, but I generally found more gratification in the anticipation of exertion than in the performance of it, so I settled for a brisk walk in the late-afternoon sunshine.

Bill opened the door and threw it wide. 'Leo, old man. We were beginning to think you didn't like us.'

'Not at all, Mr Broadman. I've been busy, that's all.'

He looked surprised when I put out a hand for him to shake. I wondered whether night-soil men didn't often get their hands shaken.

Viola came through from the back room with a cigarette in her mouth and her heinous dog in her arms. 'Has Mr Quinton been arrested yet?'

'No.'

She took a deep draw. 'Weren't you able to convince the police?' Her tone suggested disappointment at their paucity of faith in the spirits.

'I didn't try.'

She flinched backwards and I immediately felt guilty. I shouldn't have been so blunt with her. She was deluded, but well intentioned.

'I'm sorry, Viola. I agree that Mr Quinton may well be involved, and I'll speak to the police again soon, I promise. Now, where's Rosie?'

Viola showed me rather stiffly through to the parlour. Rosie was doing her knitting, which was going to be a hat for her new niece or nephew, though at the speed she was going the child would be born and have celebrated a birthday or two before it was finished.

She scowled when she saw Jack, whom she'd taken to calling Jack-the-bloody-dog when Viola wasn't within earshot.

'You look out of breath,' she said to me, her voice low because Lillian was asleep on the sofa next to her.

'I rushed here.'

I looked at Viola, who got the hint.

'I'll carry on with the potatoes,' she said, withdrawing and taking Jack-the-bloody-dog with her.

I could hardly wait for the door to shut.

'I've worked it out, Rosie. I believe the Blood Flower is a jewel. It's bright red and the size of a hazelnut.'

She examined her wedding ring, which was unadorned. Jacob had fashioned it in his workshop, complaining all the while that pinchbeck was a crude alloy and unworthy of our marriage. She told him that she'd rather have a crude ring and a good husband than the other way round.

'What kind of jewel could be that large?'

'One valuable enough to kill for. I believe Lieutenant Chastain obtained it while abroad.'

She pulled a face. 'By foul means, no doubt.'

'Quite. Micky Long stole the Blood Flower while he was on the ship. I believe Quinton had him killed and took it for himself.'

'Why Mr Quinton?'

I paced around the room, too full of energy to sit down. 'He's involved somehow.'

Rosie put her knitting to one side on the sofa and placed her hand protectively on Lillian's head.

'Assuming you're right, two lives have been taken for a rock dug out of the earth. What a terrible and ridiculous thing.'

'I know. Even if it's …'

'What?'

Beyond price, Alice had told me. But still, I hardly dared say the words.

'I think it's a ruby.'

Rosie looked doubtful. 'How big did you say it was?'

I showed her with my forefinger and thumb. 'It's oval-shaped and cut with facets.'

A ruby of that size would be worth more than either of us could imagine. Men would kill for a hundredth as much. A thousandth.

'How do you know what it looks like?'

'From a painting Peregrine did.' I hoped she wouldn't see the blush on my cheeks. 'It showed the jewel, though it was done from a description. Peregrine didn't realise what it was.'

'It may be much smaller in reality.'

'I suppose so.'

'And didn't you say before that it was *magical*?'

Her expression suggested that she didn't believe that for a second, and she was right, of course. Rubies were of enormous value, but to my knowledge, they couldn't do magic. This was why I needed Rosie in these moments; she never lost sight of those small details. She was my metronome, keeping me to time.

'Perhaps it's more a turn of phrase,' I said. 'A ruby that size is worth a fortune and might seem supernatural to some.'

Though, if I was honest, Alice didn't seem the type to entertain such a notion. Nor to overestimate the size of the stone for her portrait.

Rosie resumed her knitting. 'So, what now, Leo Stanhope?'

'I'm not sure. The police won't arrest Quinton without a lot more evidence. When I told Dorling about Papaver, he hardly reacted at all.'

Rosie looked up, a frown forming on her face. 'That was the promise you broke, was it? Not to tell the police about the club.'

'Yes, I promised Peregrine I wouldn't. But it didn't make any difference as the sergeant obviously knew all about it already.'

Her frown deepened, and I had that feeling when you realise your queen is about to be taken. You thought you had all the moves planned out, but you'd missed one thing.

'But there's knowing, Leo, and there's *knowing*. You're a journalist at a London newspaper and he thinks you're a man of importance. You've given him information about a criminal club in his own town. Even if he's fully aware of it, what do you suppose he'll do now?'

I could feel the colour leaving my face. 'You mean the police will raid the club?'

'They'll have to, won't they? A sergeant in the police can't risk you writing in your newspaper that you told him about it, and he did nothing.'

I remembered the men in that underground room, spinning and laughing on the dance floor, clinching in the darker corners.

Ten years of penal servitude.

'I have to go. I need to warn them. I'll be back tomorrow morning.'

As I entered the hall, still looking back at Rosie, I cannoned into Bill, who leapt backwards with a cry.

'Good grief, mate, what are you doing?'

'I'm sorry. I was—'

Mr Hapsworth appeared holding a candle, a worried look on his face. 'What's happening? I heard a shout.'

Bill glowered at him. 'Go back to your room, it's no business of yours.'

Hapsworth retreated so quickly the flame went out. I heard his involuntary squeak.

'I apologise, Mr Broadman,' I said.

Bill rubbed his shoulder. 'Leaving without saying goodbye again, are you, Leo? Seems to be your habit.'

'I have to be somewhere urgently.'

He sidled close to me, and I could see him deciding whether to ask me something. Whatever it was, I didn't have the time. I put on my hat and coat and was about to pull open the door when he cleared his throat.

'A quandary, I suppose.'

I sighed, my desire to exit being held back by a cotton-thread-thin anchor of politeness.

'What is?'

He squinted, one eye almost closed, as though he could only bear to half look at me.

'The Blood Flower.' When I didn't immediately reply, he continued. 'You mentioned it in the séance. I was curious.'

'It's nothing. I was ...' I threw out my hands, a picture of honesty. 'I was mistaken.'

His eye closed completely, his mouth twisting into a lop-sided smirk. I had the feeling he thought he was sharing some great secret that no one else should overhear.

'Opium, I thought. A red flower, see?'

'I have no idea. Goodnight, Mr Broadman.'

I arrived at Papaver as it was opening for the evening. Indeed, I was the first customer across the threshold. The barman was putting bottles on the shelves and two of the musicians were on the dais, tuning the strings on their instruments.

The place looked very different empty of its clientele: the ceiling was smoke-stained yellow, the walls were rank with beer and the plush sofas at the edges of the room were not a fiery red, as I had thought, but a patchy puce, bleached in spots by substances I had no inclination to guess at.

I sat on a stool; not my favoured furniture, but my coat hung down behind me, obscuring my hips.

'You need to close for the evening,' I said to the barman, a young fellow who was prematurely bald, lending him a trust-worthy air.

'Do we?'

'Yes.'

He didn't hurry to shut the place up. In fact, he seemed to be carrying on as normal, wiping each glass with a cloth and lining them up precisely in rows.

'I said you need to close. I have reason to believe the police are coming here.'

'Is that right?' He was taking no more interest than before.

'Aren't you going to do anything?'

'Possibly.'

I sighed. Clearly, the man lacked the authority, or inclination, to take action.

'Are you expecting Mr Quinton to be here this evening?'

'Maybe.'

'And Alice Morgan?'

'You never know. Will you be wanting a drink?'

Might as well, I thought. I felt nervous knowing the police could arrive at any minute, but they could hardly arrest the person who advised them about the club in the first place. And what choice did I have, but to wait?

'An ale, please. And a chess set, if you have such a thing.'

He produced one from behind the bar, and while I waited for my irritation to subside, I played out my game against Jacob. For the life of me, I couldn't work out why he'd moved his pawn into danger.

The barman was watching me, resting his chin on his knuckles. 'Bit daft, that.'

'I know.'

'Do you want a game?'

I interlaced my fingers. 'Certainly. And if I win, will you tell me what I want to know?'

He examined me with a mild expression. 'If I win, will you endanger your livelihood and risk your health in exchange?'

'Probably not.'

'Well then. Shall I be white?'

I eased my impatience by concentrating on the game as the club filled up with people. The barman's name turned out to be Louis, after his French grandfather, he said, who'd taught him to play. He turned out to be very competent, and I was glad to win our second game after losing the first, though he was handicapped by having to plan his moves and serve customers at the same time. During his absences, I kept an eye out for Quinton and, I must confess, for Alice. The thought of her sent flutters across my skin.

'Is Mr Quinton married?' I asked Louis, as we started our third game, the decider.

He grinned and moved a pawn. 'Might be.'

I heard a voice beside me, a familiar and unwelcome Welsh growl. 'Pale ale, mate.'

Bill was leaning on the bar, a shilling in his hand. He grinned at me in a conspiratorial manner.

'Quite a place this, isn't it?'

'Why are you here, Mr Broadman?' I thought for a second, putting together the sequence of events. 'Ah, of course. You followed me.'

'I was intrigued.'

The way he extended the second syllable of the word 'intrigued' made me think this was no momentary curiosity. He received his ale from Louis and took a sip, closing his eyes as though every waking hour without alcohol was a waste.

'Do you know what your wife said about you, Leo?'

'No.'

And I genuinely didn't. Probably that I was an idiot, her usual opinion.

'That you were the finest man she'd ever met. What do you think of that?'

Honestly, I didn't know what to say. It seemed quite unlike her. I mumbled that I was certain she had a lot of respect for him too, but he scrunched up his face, which was arguably already quite scrunched up, even in its resting state.

'She thinks I'm a scallywag, and I am. Or I was. And she thinks I'm bad for Viola too, but she's wrong about that. I'm what Viola needs. She's not like you and me. Her feet don't touch the ground, you know?'

'Perhaps the spirits keep her aloft.' I was unable to stop myself.

'Very good.' He took another sip. 'Roisin told me you'd worked out my little ruse.'

He didn't seem the slightest bit ashamed. He was leering as though he'd played a minor prank on me, much as my colleague Harry was prone to do, putting a red ink ribbon into my typewriter or sugar into the salt cellar.

'It's fraudulent. Not to mention, you're deceiving your wife.'

'Not really. Viola truly does have a gift. But it's unreliable, is the thing. If you've got some rich old widow sitting there with a pound note in her handbag, you can't say "I'm sorry, but your late husband's feeling a bit shy today." People expect a result. We're doing them a kindness, giving them comfort in their time of grief.'

'You're taking their money at their most vulnerable moment. It's dishonest.'

'It's commerce.' He cast an eye over the chessboard. Our conversation had interrupted the game. 'Never played, myself. Is this why you're here?'

'Yes.'

He gave me that squinting leer again. 'Ah, you see, mate? You're not above a bit of dishonesty yourself.'

I spun round on my stool, facing the room, hoping this fool would leave before Quinton and Alice arrived. I recognised a familiar face. Peregrine was pushing through the crowd towards us. At the very second that he saw me, the musicians started playing, rather giving the impression they were accompanying his entrance.

Under his arm, he had the portrait of Alice half-covered with a cloth. I'd completely forgotten he would be coming to the club this evening and cursed myself doubly. I couldn't bear the thought that he might be arrested, especially as it would be my fault.

He gave me an odd look and bellowed above the noise. 'Leo, I wasn't expecting you. Are you here for the entertainment?' Before I could answer, he clicked his fingers at Louis. 'A beer. And will Mr Quinton be in later?'

Louis and I exchanged a glance and I answered for him. 'Might be.'

Peregrine pulled up a stool and lowered himself on to it, enveloping the thing completely with his substantial behind.

I pointed at the portrait. 'I thought I'd take over for you. Speak to Quinton on your behalf. I'm concerned that he might not believe my promissory note if I don't deliver it to him personally.'

He scratched his head under his bowler, which was a ridiculous item, made from some kind of green corduroy.

'That would be very kind. But what if he doesn't accept it from you either? I'll stay in case I need to soothe any trouble.'

I patted his shoulder, not something I would normally choose to do. 'My dear Peregrine, when have you ever soothed trouble? You're far more often the cause of it. Anyway, I'm a journalist and there are witnesses. Leave it with me and I'll handle everything. He can't break your fingers if you're not here.'

My friend's eyes strayed towards two fellows whirling around on the dance floor. 'I'll think about it. Let's have a drink first.'

I glanced at the chessboard and wondered how it would be if, like people, the pieces constantly raised objections and complaints when they were required to move from square to square.

Peregrine frowned at Bill, realising he was listening to our conversation. 'And who are you?'

Bill introduced himself as my brother-in-law, which I supposed was true, technically.

Peregrine raised his eyebrows at me. 'You brought the family, did you? Is Rosie here as well? And the kids?'

I had the feeling Peregrine didn't much like the idea of socialising with Bill. When his ale arrived, he downed it in successive gulps.

'All right,' he said. 'I'll leave you two to your cosy chat.' He handed me the picture and my promissory note and headed for the door.

Bill leaned towards me with his one-eyed leer. 'Why did you really want him out of here?'

'The police are likely to be raiding the club this evening.'

He grinned lopsidedly. 'And you didn't want the big guy to know that.'

'For his protection. He's been in prison before. You should go home too.'

At that moment Quinton entered, locked in conversation with a drab-looking fellow in a grey suit. Stephan loomed behind them, on guard as ever, and behind him, I caught sight of a pink silk hat.

My heart started pounding in my chest.

Alice smiled as she passed people, polite but disengaged, for all the world like a duchess amidst the proletariat. Around her neck, a vivid red jewel was hanging from a gold chain.

The Blood Flower.

13

THE RUBY LAY ON her skin like a drop of blood. I couldn't tear my eyes away from it, nor believe that everyone in the room didn't immediately turn to look.

I pushed through the crowd towards Quinton. Towards Alice. She was laughing with a man to her left, the jewel moving on her breast, glinting in the light. It was a far deeper red than in Peregrine's painting. Every other colour in the room seemed grey in comparison – at least, until Alice looked up and saw me. The blue of her irises was undimmable.

Her eyes slid away. I understood. She didn't want to talk to me in front of her ... whatever Quinton was. Her owner.

Quinton himself was occupied with the drab fellow, a banker if I was any judge, speaking earnestly and making boxes in the air with his hands.

I cleared my throat. 'Here you are, Mr Quinton. Your portrait of Miss Morgan.'

His lip curled when he saw me. 'You again? All right. Let's see what my two quid has bought.'

He took the canvas and pulled off the cover, giving it a quick up and down with the air of a critic, turning it to catch the light in different ways.

'It'll do,' he said, and passed it to Alice.

Where did she meet him, I wondered? How did she end up sitting thigh to thigh with him in a place like this?

She held up the portrait, a smile forming on her face.

'Mr Black is very talented,' she said. 'Don't you agree? He's made me look far more beautiful than I am in reality.'

I blushed a little. 'I wouldn't say that.'

Quinton jutted his jaw in my direction. 'Black still owes me the balance. I'm a stickler for the numbers.'

'I have a promissory note.'

It had seemed a good idea when I wrote it, but now I was standing there, with Quinton half turned towards me, an irritated expression on his face, and Stephan watching us with his dead eyes, I wondered if I would be the next to be deposited by the bridge like a piece of flotsam. Quinton examined my note in the same manner he'd examined the picture. It was all the same to him.

'Why are you doing this, anyway? I suppose you're in love with Black, are you? Or some other damn fool nonsense?'

'What? No. I'm his friend, nothing more.'

Quite honestly, I was shocked that anyone would think such a thing. Did I give that impression? Surely not. I felt no attraction to my own sex.

Quinton gave a one-shouldered shrug. 'Everyone's someone's friend in this place.'

'I'm a married man, Mr Quinton.'

A smile twitched at the corners of his mouth. 'Well, if you're *married*, then it's out of the question, isn't it?'

The banker honked out a laugh like a startled donkey.

I thought of Miranda Black, stuck with a baby in London while Peregrine lived a bachelor's life on the south coast. I imagined her in their single room, weeping away her evenings. But what did I know? Quite likely, she found her own entertainments in his absence. She might be grateful he was gone.

Quinton tossed my note on the table and sat back in his seat, arms folded.

'No. I don't accept this.'

I was confused. I had thought him to be, at heart, a straight-forward man. He was surely better off taking a promise from me than getting nothing but fingers from Peregrine.

'Why?'

'First, I don't like people changing the terms of a deal. My arrangement was with Black, not you.'

'I see. Well, let me assure you—'

He held up his hand and I stopped talking. 'I said, "first", Stanhope. That implies there's a "second" at least, doesn't it?'

'Yes. I'm sorry.'

He gave the merest nod, acknowledging my apology and, by extension, my acceptance of his authority.

'Second, I want a down payment to show good faith. Ten shillings to start with. We'll talk about the balance later.'

'I don't have that much.'

He raised his eyebrows. Like many rich men, he had trouble conceiving of the idea of poverty.

'What do you have?'

I searched through my pockets. 'Five shillings and some pennies.' It was the last of my money.

'I'll take the five shillings.' He piled the coins neatly on the table in front of him and produced his ledger from his pocket, inscribing the amount before looking up. 'Finally, to clear your balance, there's something I want you to do for me. You're a journalist, aren't you?'

'Yes.' I could feel my stomach tightening at his mention of my profession.

'There's a man named Chastain. A Navy man. He has a secret.' He waggled his hand towards the dancers. 'He likes mollys. Has them sent to his ship. One of them was the lad who died. My lad, as it happens; worked for me. Michael Long.'

'I see,' I said, trying to act as if I didn't already know all this.

'It would make a good article, don't you think? A grand article. He'd be arrested for sodomy and murder, and the general public would be shocked.' He leaned forward and pointed his finger at my chest. 'You'd sell lots of newspapers.'

I supposed he was right. I imagined what Harry would make of such a story: *Depravity on the Waves* probably, or *HMS Deviant*. But I had vowed never again to write such tattle.

'I can't imply that Chastain killed Micky Long without proof of—'

'I'm sure you'll work out the details.' He screwed up my promissory note in his hand. 'If you don't print that article, I'll take it out on Black twofold.' He thumbed towards his vast bodyguard. 'Stephan's been looking forward to it. He's an artist too, in his own way.'

'That won't be necessary.' We had strayed from the most urgent point. 'And I didn't only come to talk about Mr Black's debt. You must evacuate the club. I have reason to believe the police will be visiting, probably tonight.'

He nudged the banker with his elbow. 'As long as they buy their own drinks, why should I care?'

They both guffawed, rocking together red-faced as if Quinton was the greatest comedian ever to grace the stage.

I waited for them to finish. 'I'm serious.'

I glanced towards Alice, who was gazing at the portrait as if it was a mirror, mimicking her pose, her fingertips touching the Blood Flower. I couldn't help but stare at it, hanging at her breast. Was it truly magical? Its proximity was making me feel giddy.

Quinton was wiping his eyes. 'The police only do what I tell them, Stanhope. We're quite secure, believe me. These fellows, these *married* fellows, don't want people prying into their affairs. They buy my expensive drinks and my expensive girls and boys, and I pass on a modest percentage to our hard-working policemen. That's how it works. They're quite happy, believe me. Better to keep everything in here where it's private than let it spill on to the street and worry the good people of Portsmouth.'

'You aren't worried I might print *that* in my newspaper?'

He turned fully towards me, resting his elbows on his knees. 'You're a grub. You'll print what I tell you about Chastain and Long, and nothing else. If I read a single word about me in your stinking rag, I'll send Stephan up to London to pull out your lungs through your mouth. Is that clear?'

Stephan pushed himself away from the wall and came towards me, his face blank: no pleasure, no regret. Just another chore he had to perform.

Alice stood up. 'Please, Thomas, let's not be unkind to Mr ... Stanhope, is it? I'm sure he means well.'

Her eyes flicked towards mine and I had a sudden urge to take her hand and run away from this place, from Quinton, from this city, and never look back. In that second, I was two people; one who cared for Rosie, who let little Sam ride on his back around the floor, who read stories to Lillian and helped Robert with his times tables. And another, more primitive being, who wanted to feel that someone might caress him, kiss him, *desire* him. That creature was kept in check, but only just.

Quinton gave Alice a look, and I realised that I had under-estimated his feelings for her. He cared what she thought.

'All right,' he said. 'Go away, Stanhope, before I change my mind.'

I didn't know what to do. The room was full of people, the musicians were playing and the drinks were flowing. If Quinton was wrong and the police did come here tonight, all these men would be in danger.

Back at the bar, I was disappointed to find Bill still there, leering and sweaty. He drained his ale and signalled to Louis for two whisky chasers.

'Well?' he said.

'Quinton won't evacuate the bar.'

'Hmm. No surprises there.' He looked around the room, his lips pressed together. 'I imagine the police will take a dim view of men in dresses and such. Seems a shame. They're a bit peculiar but they're not doing any harm, are they?' He threw his whisky down his throat and climbed to his feet. 'Leave it to me.'

He straightened his shoulders and headed towards the little dais, bouncing off a pair of spinning dancers but somehow keeping his feet. I watched in horror as he shoved aside the singer, waving at the musicians to stop playing.

The crowd looked considerably irritated at the interruption, one of them yelling, 'Get down, you horse's arse!'

I guessed Bill wasn't the first drunk to consider this the perfect place to make an announcement.

He put his finger to his lips and, miraculously, the room fell quiet.

'I have some bad news for you,' he said. 'We have good reason to think the police are on their way.' He held up both hands to mollify their fears. 'Now, let's face it, most of you are deviants, perverts and addicts, so you'll most likely be sent off to the clink. Some might say that's right and proper, and you need to be locked away for the good of society. But not me.'

Stephan was pushing towards him, but found his path obstructed by the static nature of the crowd. One or two were looking towards the exit, perhaps wondering if the risk of staying was too great.

Bill raised his voice. 'It may surprise you to hear that I've some experience of the police myself, a matter connected with goods they found about my person, which turned out to be stolen through no fault of mine. But they never bloody listen, do they? So, here's my advice. Anyone smoking something they shouldn't, get rid of it now, because if it's not on you at the time, there's nothing they can do. And as for you guys wearing ladies' clothes ...' He paused and, remarkably, his audience continued to listen attentively. 'Well, there's only one thing for it. When they catch you, tell them you're putting on a play. A bit of theatre, you see. They can't touch you for that. And it's for the best if you all say the same thing, for credibility.' He waggled his fingers, trying to think of something suitable. 'How about *Little Women*? That's got lots of ladies in it, I should think. If you all say you're in *Little Women*, you'll be home and dry, I reckon.'

There was about ten seconds of silence. Then, one of the smokers tossed his pipe under a chair, and the clattering noise reverberated around the room. Another followed suit, and before long, the club was filled with men buttoning their shirts and looking for their hats. Those in dresses were pulling bags from under the sofas and rifling through them, tugging on jackets and trousers even as their crinolines bumped against their ankles.

Bill hopped down from the stage just as Stephan arrived there, and things might have gone ill for him.

But the main door banged open, and all hell broke loose.

Three policemen rushed in with billy clubs raised.

The first constable grabbed a fellow in a blonde curly wig and hurled him on to the floor. He lay prostrate while one of the other constables started kicking him. I lost sight of them as the world filled with people running in all directions, barging into one another, wide-eyed and open-mouthed.

I heard Quinton bark an instruction over the din, but no one was listening, not even the banker, who was crouched behind the table, squealing, 'I was invited.'

I felt a hand in mine. 'Come on. Quickly. There's a back door.'

Alice wasn't the only one with that idea. A minor crush was developing, people squeezing to get through the narrow gate that led behind the counter. I was squashed together with a small fellow, wriggling and elbowing to get ahead of me, urgently looking back over his shoulder and wriggling some more.

'Be patient,' I said to him. 'It'll be quicker if we don't all push.'

'I don't really come here,' he muttered, perspiration shining on his forehead. 'It's not fair, do you see? I don't really come here.'

The lights went out. Someone had cut the gas.

I could feel limbs and shoulders all around me, knees and hands, quickly becoming less polite, reaching and pulling, clawing towards the bar. I felt detached, as though I was watching someone else stuck in this mass of people, hearing blows, kicks and screams behind me.

Still, Alice's hand was in mine.

My eyes grew accustomed to the thin light coming in through the back door. We reached the counter and Louis the barman was there, perched on one of the stools.

'We never got the chance to finish that game,' he said. 'Perhaps next time.'

'You should leave,' I told him. 'It's not safe.'

He shrugged, apparently indifferent to his fate. 'Can't.'

There was something odd about how he was sitting, his coat wrapped closely around his knees. He seemed too high, somehow.

'You're on the cash box,' I said, struggling for breath. 'Staying with the money.'

He inclined his head, his eyes flicking towards Alice. 'You too, apparently.'

I lost sight of him as we were squeezed peristaltically through the gate and deposited on the other side.

'Come on, Leo,' Alice shouted, and we ran.

We emerged into a stable yard, watched by the horses in their stalls. The rancid air of Portsmouth seemed fresh after the sweat, smoke and terror of the club, and I sucked in lungfuls of it. The small fellow who'd been beside me in the crush brushed past, puffing and panting as he scurried towards the side alley that must lead to the road.

I followed Alice, our pace slowing as we reached the pavement. Running would draw unwanted attention, but walking, we were the same as any other couple, enjoying the warmth of the evening and the sunset.

She linked her arm in mine.

I looked back along the pavement towards the club, and for a moment, was certain I saw Viola. Her face was angled towards me, her mouth open as she remonstrated with a police constable. I could guess why she was there. Rosie must have told her the club would be raided, and she'd come to drag Bill home before it happened.

I turned away immediately. If she saw me with Alice, she might tell Rosie. That was unthinkable.

A bolt of shame ran through me, top to toe. Why was I doing anything I wouldn't want Rosie to know about?

I glanced back again and wasn't certain it had even been Viola. Probably, I'd imagined her. Whoever it was, she was now obscured from view.

'Are you all right?' asked Alice.

'Yes, of course.'

If it *had* been Viola, I thought, she was safe enough. She'd done nothing illegal, and anyway, the police would never arrest a pregnant woman.

I took a breath and settled into our stroll. The evening was pleasantly humid, and we ambled our way through the back streets towards the sea. I could hear it, washing on to the beach and sucking on the shingle as it retreated. I wondered if we'd go swimming again. I would like that.

But as we reached the formal garden, Alice stopped, her hands to her chest. She stared at me.

There was no gold chain around her neck.

The Blood Flower was missing.

14

'WE CAN GO BACK,' I said. 'It must have fallen off as we were leaving.'

'You don't understand, Leo. It's—'

'The Blood Flower. I know.'

She was turning in small circles, groping at her own throat as though the stone would magically reappear if she wished for it hard enough. 'I had it when we were sitting down. Thomas was talking with Mr Edgar, and I remember it was there. You were staring.'

I was about to protest, but of course, she was right.

'It was probably kicked under something,' I said. 'A chair or a table. I'll go back and talk to the police. I'll say we're looking for clues.'

She took my face between her hands. 'Leo, the Blood Flower is a ruby. Do you understand? It's worth more than this street, probably more than the whole city. When he finds out I've lost it, he'll kill me. We can't go back. Not now.'

'Mr Quinton will be in jail.'

She gave my face a squeeze. 'You are silly. Thomas will be having a nice chat with the superintendent soon, and he'll be tucked up in bed with his fat wife before midnight.'

We walked on, passing the obelisk, and turned north towards her street. As we approached her door, I detached my arm from hers.

'What will you do?'

'I'll go back to the club in the morning. Stephan will let me in. I'll tell him I lost a purse or something.'

'And if you can't find it?'

She forced a smile and opened out her arms. 'Then you'll find me on the beach tomorrow night with my throat cut.'

'I can help you.'

'How? Do you mean I should run away? With you? Tut, tut, Mr Stanhope. You're a married man.'

'No, I wasn't thinking—'

'I'm only playing with you, Leo. It's a bad habit I have. Would you like to come in?'

She unlocked her door and went through, leaving it open. I was alone in the street.

Oh, but who are you, at this moment? Are you the man who doffs his hat and strolls away, back to his wife and family, remembering that moment when you were tempted, but resisted? Or are you another kind of man altogether, one who removes his hat and goes inside? And afterwards, do you carry an icy shard in your heart for ever, the shame of that night, the secret you keep? You can never be certain until you're given the choice.

I stood on the threshold for a full minute before removing my hat and going inside.

Alice put her finger to her lips. 'Quietly,' she whispered. 'Mother's upstairs.'

She took my coat and bade me sit in one of the armchairs facing the unlit fire, remaining standing herself.

'Where does your mother think you go every evening?' I asked.

'She knows full well where I go. Thomas pays the rent here. I think she loves him more than she loves me, or his money anyway.' She fluttered her eyelids, acting the innocent. 'But as long as nothing happens under her roof, she can tell herself I'm still a maiden and one day some fine gentleman will come along and marry me. But I'm twenty-nine now, and any man who shows an interest gets his fingers broken.'

She said this with no apparent concern for *my* fingers.

'I shouldn't be here,' I said.

'But you are here, and I shall probably be dead tomorrow.'

She removed her coat and gloves and unpinned her bonnet from her hair. I felt a tightening from my chest directly to my groin.

'What are we to do?' she asked.

I kept my eyes on the grate. A spider was building a cobweb between two brushes, diligently spinning his silk.

'If you can't find the stone tomorrow, you should come to Mr Black's lodging, where you had the portrait done. You can hide with us there.'

She brushed my cheek with her fingertips, sending explosive charges through my body. 'I meant right now.'

I thought she'd take the other armchair, but instead, she slid her arms around my neck and coiled herself on to my lap.

Briefly, Rosie's face came into my mind – the children, our rooms at home, the outside of the shop. The feeling of coming home at the end of the day. Rosie didn't smile much, but I always knew she was glad to see me. Other thoughts pushed them aside: my narrow bed, my cold feet at night, the single hook on the back of my door.

Alice put her head on my shoulder. 'I've been with women before.'

'I'm not a woman.'

'I know. I meant something else.' She nuzzled into my neck. 'Men and women, but never anyone quite like you. You're special.'

'I've always thought I was rather ordinary.'

'Not ordinary,' she whispered, touching my cheek where my skin was burnished to a leathery hardness.

I closed my eyes and felt her warm lips on mine.

The ceiling above us squeaked, the sound of feet on floorboard. Alice froze, her eyes darting towards the doorway. Truly, she seemed more afraid of her mother than she had been of the police.

After a pause, we heard the metallic ring of a stream of urine hitting an empty chamber pot. Neither of us moved a muscle. The noise seemed to continue for ever, eventually reducing in tone and volume as the pressure waned to mere dribs and drabs.

And then the squeak again and the sound of someone climbing into bed.

Alice giggled quietly, sighed once and kissed me again. Her lips were soft and wet, and I felt her tongue probe gently into my mouth.

One of my hands was around her shoulder and the other was hovering in the air. It didn't know where to go. She took it in hers and lowered it down to her waist, shifting her weight, pulling up her knees and curling on me, round me, pressing up against me.

I pulled back. 'Please, can we stop.'

She pouted and brushed her fingers through my hair. 'Why should we? These could be my last hours alive. I want to enjoy them.'

She ran her finger down my forehead to my nose and lips, and onwards to my chin and my collar. She undid my top button, and I didn't stop her. She undid another button and a third, slipping her hand inside my shirt. She closed her eyes, and I could smell the sweetness of whisky on her breath. Her fingers met my binding and she pushed underneath, nails scratching against my flesh.

'It's all right,' she whispered. 'Truly, it is. I know what to do.'

She released the rest of my shirt buttons, one at a time. Down, down, down her fingers went, fluttering gently against my belly, until they were pulling at the belt of my trousers.

I gasped.

When I was six years old, I found a dead badger in the park.

It was the twins' birthday. Oliver always chose for both of them, and he wanted a picnic, so we walked down from our house and sat away from everyone else on our yellow blanket. Mummy spread out the sandwiches and cakes, while Father showed Oliver how to use his birthday present: a bow and ten arrows with red feathers.

Not long after that, the trouble started. Oliver had promised me I could have a go if I ran around and picked up all the arrows he'd loosed, but my turn never seemed to come. When I got cross and took a swing at him, he jumped out of the way, laughing, holding out the bow towards me and snatching it away at the last second. He was four years older and there was nothing I could do but scream with frustration and run away into a copse full of jackdaws. That's where I found the badger.

At first, I didn't know what it was. I'd seen badgers before, lumbering along on their stumpy legs in the woods at the bottom of our road, but those were whole and cuddly, not bags of offal that could be ripped open and emptied out, strewn across the grass as if someone had been in a hurry to find something inside. I crouched down and touched the top of his head with my fingers, tracing the coarse fur around his ears.

'Why are you dead?'

The jackdaws were lining up in the branches above my head, fretting and waiting for me to leave, but I didn't think they could kill a badger. More likely foxes, or one of the dogs tearing up and down on the grass, off their leashes. Father always said that an untrained dog was like a wolf.

I still had one of Oliver's arrows, and I prodded it under a flap of skin, leaning down to peer inside. A fly flew out and landed again, sucking at a cream-rimmed eye. Another was investigating the badger's lips, crawling along its oily tongue and into its throat. I touched my teeth with my tongue, and my tummy felt funny.

I was wiping the arrow on the grass when I heard a voice. 'Don't touch it, will you?' I looked round and there was Jane, with Oliver behind her. 'Dead things give you diseases. And we have to go now anyway. Mummy sent us to find you.'

I sneaked a glance at my arm. A white hair was sticking to my sleeve. It didn't *seem* diseased, but I brushed it off anyway and shoved my hand into the pocket of my apron dress.

Oliver took the arrow from me and pushed it under the badger's body, tipping him over on to his other side and revealing flat, wet grass where he'd lain.

He grinned up at Jane. 'Still hungry?'

'Don't be disgusting.'

'He's only little,' I said, looking around the copse. 'I wonder where his mummy is.'

Oliver shrugged. 'Maybe she's dead too.'

He didn't seem very upset. But he'd cried himself to sleep when Pilgrim died, and that was of old age. This was much sadder.

'We have to go back,' said Jane. 'Both of you. Or I'll tell Father you wouldn't.'

'You go.' Oliver stood up and took the bow off his back. 'I'm going to hunt some more badgers. I'll hang their heads on the wall as trophies.'

The thought of it terrified me. This one might have younger brothers and sisters who wouldn't know to run away. I could picture their trusting faces as he took aim.

'No, you mustn't,' I shouted, but neither of them cared.

Jane stamped her foot. 'You have to come *now*.'

Oliver shrugged. 'I'll be home later.'

'Well, we're going back anyway. Come on, Lottie. My goodness, look at your knees! After everything Mummy told you.'

'I don't care about my knees,' I protested. 'I want to go with Oliver.'

I was desperate to protect those other little badgers. I'd forgotten that my brother's arrows weren't nearly sharp enough to kill anything. He'd already shot me twice that morning and Father had told him off severely, but I wasn't *dead*.

'You'll care when Mummy sees that dress.'

'Anyway, you can't.' Oliver was looking up at the trees, shielding his eyes from the sun. 'Ladies don't hunt.'

'I'm not a lady.'

'You will be.'

Jane set her mouth and tugged on the cuffs of her coat. 'Come *on*, Lottie.'

'I don't want to,' I screamed, but she grabbed my wrist and pulled me away.

The last I saw of the badger, Oliver was stepping over him, notching an arrow into his bow, ducking under a branch and disappearing into the copse. The jackdaws were already dropping down on to the body.

It's not fair, I thought. Why can't I go with Oliver? I'm never, ever going to be a lady.

And that was when I knew.

Alice's fingers were pushing underneath my trouser belt.

'No,' I said, my voice sounding thin and distant.

She stopped kissing me, but her lips still brushed mine as she spoke. 'You'll enjoy it, I promise. Trust me.'

My red raw sense: my sore tooth, my hangnail, the splinter in my palm that always catches. How I wished I didn't possess it. It heard what she said, and it knew what she meant.

I put my hand on hers.

'I'm not a woman, Alice.'

She pushed down further. 'Well, you are. I mean, you are really. Corporeally speaking.'

'But I'm more than just corporeal. I'm also …'

Also what, I thought? A man's soul? A man's desires? It had been four years since a woman truly wanted me for who and what I was. And even then, Maria had played so many parts, how could I be certain?

Alice nuzzled my cheek. 'Just relax and let it happen.'

'No. Please. I have to go.'

She tipped her head back to see me clearly, doubting I was serious. When she saw that I was, she uncoiled herself and went to sit on the other armchair. Her lips – her slightly sore-looking lips – were pushed into a pout. 'You can't help what you are, Leo. None of us can.'

I was doing up my shirt, my fingers shaking so hard I could scarcely push the button through the hole. Why had I come here? I should never have stepped inside this house.

I found my coat and hat and was almost at the door when I stopped. In my haste, in my lust, I'd forgotten the danger she was in.

'Don't go back to Papaver tomorrow,' I said. 'Don't take the risk. Pack your bag and take the train. Or a ship. Go far away. Be anywhere but here.'

She looked around the wing of the armchair. 'If I did that, he'd punish Mother. That's how he works. He insisted I should wear it, even though I told him.'

'Told him what?'

She gave me a melancholy smile. 'I told him it thought I was unworthy.'

I frowned, my critical faculties returning from wherever they'd been. '"It" thought you weren't worthy of wearing it? You mean, the stone itself thought that? It may be a ruby, Alice, but it's still just a stone.'

She turned away from me, now completely hidden, so I was talking to the back of the armchair. 'The Blood Flower was made in the midst of war, Leo, and it can do things no normal jewel can do. Pull things towards itself and push them away. It broke the chain that held it.'

Of course, that was nonsense. And hardly the point.

'Don't be here tomorrow, Alice.'

But she didn't reply.

I opened the front door, stepped out in the street and breathed deeply. How could it still be dark? I felt as if I'd been out all night.

My footsteps echoed in the narrow street. I pulled my coat closely around myself and fixed my bowler on my head. I was exactly like any other gentleman who'd stayed out too late and was yearning for home.

We had only kissed, I told myself. Nothing more. We'd been carried away by the drama of the moment: the police raid, the lost ruby, Alice's fears. No one could blame us.

In which case, said a small voice at the back of my head, you won't mind telling Rosie about it, will you? Surely, she couldn't expect real fidelity to a sham marriage.

But, I asked myself, how would I feel if our positions were reversed? If one day Rosie told me candidly that she'd been tempted by another man and had almost indulged that temptation, then ... well, in truth, I couldn't imagine it happening. But if it did happen, against every trait in her character, I would feel utterly untethered. But that was because she had told me the sham was what she wanted, and she had no interest in anything more.

I'd never said I had no interest in anything more.

15

IN MY DREAMS, THE church bells were ringing, and when I woke up, they truly were, demanding our attendance for the worship of God, who cared so little for us. They hammered through my head with a toneless clang, holding none of the charm of St Paul's.

Ten minutes after I'd woken up, Peregrine barged through my door with a tray. 'Mrs Mackay's done you fried eggs.'

I remained underneath my covers with only my face poking out.

'Thank you, that's very kind of her.'

'I heard there was a raid on the club last night,' he said. 'Those poor boys. I wish I'd stayed. I might have been able to help them. Did you get caught up in it?'

'Not really.'

I should probably have left it at that. But to omit the truth was self-serving and wrong. He was my friend and I had to tell him what I'd done.

'It was my fault, Peregrine. I broke my promise to you. I needed a favour from Dorling, and he already knew everything anyway, and I thought it wouldn't make any difference. I told him about Papaver.'

Peregrine looked at me squarely. For all his jovial flamboyance, he could be as stern as a judge. 'What favour?'

'It doesn't matter. Rosie said Dorling would have to take action because I was a journalist, and he wouldn't have any choice. And she was right.'

Peregrine said nothing for several seconds and then closed his eyes. 'That's why you were keen for me not to stay last night.'

'Yes. I didn't want you involved.'

'I see.'

I had expected him to shout and stamp and call me every name he could think of. I had expected him to fling Shakespeare at me and leave in a spectacular fury, and then come back and fling some more. This calm self-possession was new to me, and quite terrifying.

'Was it revenge for my telling Miss Morgan about you?'

'No, of course not—'

'Because if so, it was a pretty poor show.' He lowered himself on to the bed, stiff and upright like a man with back pain. 'There are few enough places where we can be ourselves.'

'I know. And I'm sorry.'

'You always think you know best, Leo. You take charge and everyone has to accommodate whatever it is that you decide. Rosie, Jacob, me, we all have to play to your rules, right or wrong.' He looked away from me. 'Quite frankly, I've had enough of it.'

'Do you want me to leave?'

'It might be for the best, yes.'

He stood up and left the room.

I pulled on my clothes, gathered my essentials into my hessian tater sack and headed down the stairs, feeling as awful as I could remember. Peregrine was my friend and I had hurt him. I couldn't bear the thought of it. And he was correct; I had chosen my own judgement over my promise to him. And my judgement had been wrong. Even had it been right, that still didn't justify my actions. A promise was a promise.

Sometimes, I got so focused on one thing, I couldn't see anything else. My only thought was to tell Rosie about it. She always knew what to do.

As I left the lodging, I caught sight of Mrs Mackay in the parlour, helping a portly gentleman on to the half-horse.

'Did you enjoy the eggs?' she called out.

'No, I'm sorry ... I'm not feeling very hungry.'

When I reached Viola's house, the front door was wide open and Jack-the-bloody-dog was barking furiously.

'Rosie?' I called. 'Are you here?'

Viola appeared from the parlour and rushed towards me, her face red.

'Have you seen them? Are they with you?'

'Who?'

She took the lapels of my jacket in her fists.

'Bill and Roisin, of course. They've disappeared.'

'What?'

I could feel a coldness rushing up from my feet.

Viola let go of me, struggling to avoid tears. 'I hoped they were with you. But if not … oh, God. What could have happened?'

'When did you last see them?'

'I asked the spirits, Leo. I asked them where my sister and husband have gone. But they wouldn't tell me. They've fallen silent.'

'Listen.' I took her shoulders and looked into her eyes, uncannily like Rosie's though they were nothing alike in temperament. 'Mr Broadman left the house shortly after me last night. What about Rosie? When did she leave?'

Viola seemed to be disintegrating. 'It's not my fault. I was worried about Bill. You rushed out and then he did. I didn't know where he'd gone. Roisin was doing her knitting and she jumped up and said she could guess exactly where he was, and off she went as well. I tried to stop her, but you know how she is.'

The coldness in my veins expanded into my stomach, as if I'd drunk from a tap in winter.

'Viola, did you go to the club last night? Answer me honestly.'

'No, I didn't go anywhere. I waited at home for them. What club? What do you mean?'

I felt a tension across my chest as if my binding was contracting, trying to squeeze me in two.

It wasn't Viola I'd seen outside the club: it was Rosie. And she hadn't returned home, which meant she'd been arrested by the police.

While I'd been kissing Alice, Rosie had been in jail.

'I know where they are. I have to go right now.'

'Please, Leo.' She sagged, her hands reaching out as if she might collapse on me in tears. 'Everyone keeps going away and they don't come back.'

'I will. I'll bring them home.'

I was about to leave when two faces appeared from round the parlour door: Lillian and Sam.

Viola leaned down to speak to them. 'You have to go with Mr Stanhope now.'

I shook my head. 'No, please, Viola. Look after them for a little longer.'

She wrapped her arms around herself, her eyes darting from side to side as if a hornet had found its way in.

'They can't stay here, Leo, not now. The spirits are confused by their presence. Ever since I became pregnant, they've spoken to me as clear as a bell, but now, when I need them most, complete silence. It's the children distracting them, I'm sure of it. I can't think of another explanation.'

I rubbed my forehead with my palm, feeling a headache starting to form above my left eye.

'I can't take them with me.'

'Of course you can. You must. Once they're out of here, the spirits will talk to me again. They'll know where Bill and Roisin have gone.'

Her tone suggested I was an idiot for arguing. Perhaps I was. The only way I would win this was by telling her the truth about her séances, and that seemed cruel – and unlikely to work. Anyone who believed such nonsense wouldn't be swayed by mere facts.

'Very well. Lillian and Sam, get your coats and shoes on. Viola, you'll have to lend me some money. Rosie can repay you when she gets back.'

Getting them ready took an age. Sam couldn't find one of his shoes and Lillian was determined to bring her book and gloves, and ribbon, and Lord knew what else, each time returning to the back room and promising she'd only be a minute.

By the time we left, I was shaking with exasperation. I couldn't bear the thought of Rosie in a jail cell. I knew exactly how she would react to incarceration. She would take her fury and fashion it into armour. She wouldn't sleep at night or even lie down. She would be rigidly polite and endlessly patient. And she wouldn't despair because she would know that I was coming for her.

By the time I'd found a cab, the bells were ringing for one o'clock and Sam was starting to grizzle.

'He's hungry,' said Lillian. 'We didn't get breakfast. Auntie Viola said we were a barrier to the spirits and made us sit in the yard.'

I rolled my eyes. 'Your aunt's a good woman, but she thinks some things which aren't true.'

'Where are we going?'

'To the police station to get your mother out.' It struck me that I could have phrased that more delicately. 'A mistake has been made.'

Sam's grizzles became louder as we bounced along. My usual trick of putting him on my lap and distracting him with a set of keys didn't work, and even his favourite game of who-can-spot-a-doggie, failed to interrupt the flow. By the time we reached the police station, he was red-faced and covered in mucus. We certainly made a strange rescue party.

The driver gave me my change.

'Discipline,' he said. 'That's what they need. Otherwise, they turn into devils, the lot of 'em. Couple of whacks with a paddle and he'll be right as rain.'

I didn't give him a tip. Nor did I explain that their father had begun hitting Sam when he was a babe in arms and had once hit Lillian so hard with a bottle, she'd suffered a concussion. Rosie told me how she ran through the streets, cradling her daughter in her arms, believing she was dead. I couldn't imagine the pain of that, nor the relief when the child opened her eyes.

All the tea shops were shut, but I spotted a muffin stall along the road and paid fourpence for two; extortion, perhaps, but it was a seller's market.

Truly, I didn't know how anyone could look after kids and get anything else done at the same time.

It must have been half past one at the earliest when we climbed up the steps and entered the police station. The clerk told us he didn't have anyone named Rosie Stanhope in the cells, but he would make further enquiries.

We waited in the foyer with a young wife who was hoping her husband would be freed soon. He was an assistant at the customs house, she told me, and a good man, though he hadn't taken well to fatherhood. But he would adapt in time, she was sure of it. She had no idea why he'd been arrested. Most likely drunkenness or some ridiculous jape like stealing a bicycle. I listened quietly, hearing the anxiety beneath her garrulousness. Eventually, the clerk summoned her to the desk and explained that her husband would be released shortly.

'But what did he do?' she asked.

'Good question, ma'am. A bit of a kerfuffle last night. Some arrests were made in error. Him and some of his friends were acting in a play, apparently.'

'A play?' She blinked several times. 'What play?'

'It was *Little Women*, so I'm told. He's the last of 'em to be released.'

'Why would he … I don't understand.' She looked utterly confused. 'And isn't *Little Women* a novel?'

'I couldn't say, ma'am. I'm not much for these things.'

When her husband appeared, he still had the remains of powder on his face, though it didn't disguise his bruised cheek and fat lip. I caught his eye, and he looked away. His wife was in tears as they left.

Sam, who had been playing on the floor with Lillian, came and sat next to me on the bench, fidgeting and picking at the leather despite my entreaties to stop. After ten minutes, he put his head on my lap and was soon snoring gently.

At half past two, the clerk approached me.

'I've worked it out,' he said. 'People give false names, you see. Your wife said her surname was Flowers, not Stanhope. She was brought in last night with the others. The sergeant said to take anyone in a dress and not assume they were a real woman just 'cause they looked like one.'

I closed my eyes and took a breath.

'Is she here?'

'No, we've let her go already. Soon after lunch, it was.'

At least she was safely out of the cells.

'And what about Bill Broadman? He's shorter than me, Welsh, red in the face.'

'Yeah, we brought him in too. We know that one of old. Always mixed up in something. Never thought of 'im as the type who'd be in a place like that though.'

I gave the clerk my most genial smile, the one Rosie said made me look like a jack-o'-lantern carved by a ten-year-old. 'I can vouch for Mr Broadman. It was me who told Sergeant Dorling about Papaver. Mr Broadman was doing under-cover work on my behalf. He hasn't committed any crime, I assure you.'

The clerk went away to confer with his superiors, and we had to wait a further twenty minutes until he returned, this time with Bill, who didn't seem at all contrite.

'Leo,' he said. 'I'm surprised you came, if I'm honest. You're a life-saver.'

'Mrs Broadman is worried about you. I promised to bring you home.'

'Well, that's wonderful, isn't it? You know Rosie's here too, don't you?'

'They've released her already.'

He slapped me on the back. 'Perhaps now you'll be less inclined to lecture me about marriage, eh? I may have my faults, but I've never abandoned my wife to a jail overnight.'

Lillian looked up sharply.

'I didn't *abandon* her,' I insisted. 'I didn't know she was here.'

As we were leaving, the clerk caught my sleeve. 'He's a nasty piece of work, that one. You should watch 'im.'

I could believe it. And yet, without Bill, the events at the club might have turned out far worse.

Bill seemed in a good mood as we walked back. He hoisted Sam on to his shoulders and capered down the pavement, kicking up his heels and making wild circles, as if he was about to topple over, while Sam giggled, and Lillian clutched hard at my hand.

They ran into the house together and I heard Jack-the-bloody-dog barking, followed by Viola's delighted cry. I could picture her throwing her arms around her husband.

I walked up the path with my hands in my pockets.

In the hall, Viola gave me a look of such gratitude I feared she would attempt to kiss my cheek. I kept my distance.

'Where's Rosie?' I asked.

Her face fell. 'She's in there. She got back an hour ago. I'm afraid she's not very happy.'

Rosie was sitting on her mattress with Lillian.

'Is Sam all right?' she asked.

'Of course. I'm sorry, Rosie. I didn't realise you'd come to the club. I'd never have let them take you if I'd known.'

She nodded to Lillian, who gave me such a look as she left that a shiver ran through me.

Rosie's own expression was unreadable. Her face seemed slack, devoid of all thoughts and feelings.

'I saw you,' she said, in a flat voice. 'You were coming out. I called to you, but you were too far away, and the police took me.'

'I didn't hear. I'm sorry.'

I went to sit next to her, but she flinched away as if I was a stranger.

No, no, I wanted to say, I'd never do anything to hurt you. Meet my eye and you'll see that I'm still your Leo. Nothing's changed.

'Did the police mistreat you?'

She shook her head and spoke without inflection, as though she were talking about a trip to the market. 'A constable told me to get in the cart with those other poor souls. They stuck us in the cells overnight, but they couldn't prove anything, so they let us all out. I'm tired, that's all.'

I wanted desperately to protect her, but what if the thing she needed protecting from was me?

'All right. You should get some sleep.'

Finally, she raised her eyes to mine. 'You were leaving with a woman. Holding hands. I saw you.'

I felt my face flushing pink. 'She was scared, that's all. I hardly know her. What was I supposed to do?'

Rosie gave a little laugh, but there was no humour in it. 'You looked back, and I'm certain you saw me. I thought to myself: "Now, Leo will find a way to free me. He always finds a way." But you didn't.'

'Rosie, it was hectic, and I thought ...'

My sentence petered out. What could I say? That I had thought she was Viola? Suddenly, it didn't seem like a very good excuse.

'I thought our marriage, our arrangement, would be simple, Leo. I thought we'd be friends, you and me. No fuss and no pain. But I suppose it's never like that, is it?' She stood up. 'I'm going back to London tomorrow with Lillian and Sam.'

'We'll go together.'

She took my hand and pressed something into it. 'No. I need time to myself.'

'Rosie, please. I would never ...'

'Don't,' she said.

She left the room and closed the door behind her.

When I opened my palm, it contained her pinchbeck wedding ring.

16

I COULDN'T STAY AT Viola's house, but I had nowhere else to go. I stumbled down to the promenade and spent twopence on a small bottle of gin, which I drank sitting on a bench overlooking the sea for the rest of the afternoon.

As darkness fell, I knew I was drunk. Gratefully drunk. Passers-by gave me pitying glances and mothers guided their children in an arc around me. I lay down on the bench and for a while, my mind roamed unchecked. I was examining a dead badger in the park, and then I was the badger, trapped in an attic room with a slanting roof, two men gazing down at me with flies buzzing around their faces.

No, I would not conceive of that. I'd locked it in a box and sunk that box into deep, black water where I could no longer find it.

I tried to think of something else: all the names I'd ever had, from the first, the one I was born with, to the last, my own. But what of Rosie? Would she ever be Rosie Stanhope again?

During most of the twenty-eight years of my life, I had been waiting to leave, and at any minute during the last decade or so, I expected to be uncovered and *forced* to flee, to change my name and live among strangers once again. Mentally, my bag was always packed. Until Rosie. Wherever Rosie was, was home.

And I had thrown it away. I wept; for Rosie, for myself, for an unhappy child in an apron dress.

And finally, I slept, clutching Rosie's wedding ring in my hand.

I was awoken by a seagull, its cry penetrating my head like an industrial lathe. I was lying on the paving stones, my head resting on my tater sack and my hat over my face. I had a vague memory of being evicted from the bench the previous evening by an older gentleman who seemed to think it was his. He was still there, curled up and snoring, a cotton bag cuddled in his arms.

I relieved myself under the pier, crouching down behind some concrete boulders, and then brushed down my jacket and trousers as best I could. Only one thought was in my head: to catch Rosie before she boarded the train back to London. If I could only talk to her, she might forgive me, and everything would be as it was.

I strode at some speed towards the railway station, ignoring the rumblings of my stomach. Dishevelled as I was, I fitted in well amidst the clamour and chaos of Monday morning. Men were crowding the streets, rushing to their offices and factories, sucking on cigarettes and queueing at the crabmeat stalls. Somewhere, a clock chimed eight times, and the rushing men increased their pace.

I reached the station and pushed my way into the forecourt.

Of course, I had no idea what time she would be here. It might be in ten minutes or ten hours. I hoped it would be soon. She was an early bird by nature, and once she'd decided to do something, she liked to get it over with. I waited by one of the columns in the foyer, scanning from left to right. But there was no sign of her.

The crowd thinned as the morning wore on. I wandered out to the forecourt again, where an air of torpidity had taken over from the previous bustle. The salesmen were sitting on chairs by their stalls, taking a rest from shouting, and the horses were noses down, sweating in the heat or noisily lapping water from half-barrels set alongside the taxi rank. To my right, Quinton's New Hippodrome loomed, its frontage despoiled by those gaudy letters and lights. The last time I was there, I had been with Rosie. It seemed like a different life.

The crowd ebbed and flowed with the timetable. Those who were in good time sauntered in and joined the short queue for coffee, and those who were overdue hurtled towards the ticket office with their hands on their hats. Noon came and went, and then the afternoon.

Still, I waited.

The sun began to dip, and my stomach began to ache.

It was after six o'clock in the evening when I saw her and the children. They must have emerged from a taxicab on the other side of the forecourt because she already had a ticket in her hand. I dashed after her, but as bad luck would have it, a train had disgorged its passengers a moment before, and I had to wade through them.

'Rosie!'

If she heard me, she showed no indication of it. I caught her up at the barrier.

'Rosie.'

She turned and took me in with an expression which chilled my bowels. 'I told you. I need time to think. Time away from you.'

And with that, she herded Lillian and Sam on to the platform and was gone.

––––––

I stumbled out and sat in the shade of the Hippodrome awning, my head in my hands. I had been foolish to come to the station. She'd told me she wanted time to think. I would have to be patient. I had no choice.

'Mr Stanhope? I thought it was you.' I looked up and was surprised to see Olga Brown peering down at me. 'Are you waiting for me?' That wisp of an accent floated between her words.

'No. I mean, I'm not waiting for anyone. I just happen to be here.'

'I see.' She frowned, angling her bonnet to keep her face in the shade. 'Is your wife here too? I'd like to speak with her.'

I wiped my eyes on my sleeve. 'Just me.'

'Oh, that's a shame.' She tapped her foot, reminding me of Rosie. I could have wept again, truly I could. 'It's quite important. Perhaps you'd be kind enough to spare me a few minutes?'

'No, I'm actually ...'

'Have you had dinner? There's a café along the street over there. The owner gives me free food in exchange for the odd spare ticket. She's a fan of the circus.'

I hadn't eaten in more than a day and was starving.

'Of course. It would be a pleasure.'

The café was tiny, squeezed between a cobbler and a wheel-wright in a dismal alleyway. It didn't seem to have a name, just a door and a few tables, every one of them occupied by Negro men, hunched over their plates and conversing in low voices. They turned to look at me as I sat down, and I felt even more out of place than usual.

The owner and – as she explained with a resigned air – cook, waitress and washer-up, was an elderly lady who treated Miss Brown with a mixture of motherliness and awe. She reminded me of Jacob, but while his skin was the colour of raw cod, hers was like the bark of an ancient tree. The only item on the menu was rabbit stew.

I cleared the bowl in two minutes flat before addressing my host. 'How can I help you, Miss Brown?'

'It's about Natalia.' I could hear the falter in her voice as she spoke the girl's name. 'I've been piecing together things she told me. I believe she once visited a club owned by Mr Quinton. A disreputable place. Honey and Micky Long took her.'

'It's called Papaver,' I volunteered. 'When did this happen?'

'She mentioned it perhaps a fortnight before she died, so I suppose the visit was a few days before that.'

I knew I should ask her some more questions, like why Natalia had gone to such a place and what had happened there. But later, I wouldn't be able to discuss my deductions with Rosie, wouldn't be able to watch her turn the details over in her mind and touch upon the very thing I had missed.

Why was I even here? I cared about the deaths of Micky and Natalia, I truly did. I abhorred the thought of their young lives being taken from them. But I also wanted to curl up on one of the benches on the promenade and be picked apart by the seagulls.

Fortunately, Miss Brown did not need prompting. 'Natalia told me she met a woman at the club. Micky seemed quite enamoured with her, apparently. The woman was very persuasive and was cajoling Micky to do something. To break the law, Natalia thought. She didn't like it, so she left. I don't know the woman's name. If I did, I'd find her and ...' She trailed off, her eyes filling with tears.

The mysterious woman could only be Alice. She'd started this whole fiasco by encouraging Micky to steal the Blood Flower, and by now she might have died for it.

So many lives lost for that damned stone.

I took a deep breath. Despite my own grief and guilt, I should at least fill in some of the gaps in Miss Brown's knowledge.

'I believe Micky did break the law,' I said. 'He stole an object of considerable value from a Navy lieutenant named Chastain. But Micky didn't have it when he was killed. It was pulled off him beforehand.'

'What was it, this valuable object?'

'Believe me, it's better if you don't know. Two people have already died for it.'

Possibly three, by now.

Miss Brown looked as though she might insist, but then thought better of it. 'Very well. But regardless of what the object is, I'm certain Micky wouldn't have taken such a risk if he hadn't fallen under that woman's spell. He has a younger brother, you know. Jonathan.'

'Yes, we've met.'

I wished I could do more to help to her, but I felt drained of all sense and feeling.

She glanced at my hessian sack. 'If I may make an observation, Mr Stanhope, you seem troubled. I don't know what the problem is, but your wife seems like a wise woman who would give you good counsel if you asked her.'

Now it was my turn to blink back tears.

'I would, but I don't have money for a ticket to London.'

'I see.' She hesitated, and then reached a decision. 'Perhaps I can help you with that.' She dug in her purse and produced a shilling. 'Consider it a loan. You can repay me when you return.'

'Thank you, but I don't know if I will return.'

'I think you will. You're the kind of man who cares about the truth, and I very much want to know who killed Natalia. I'm afraid you've missed the last train though.'

'You know the timetable?'

'My friend Mr Woodson is in London at present, and I like to visit.'

'Oh. So, you and Miss La Blanche were not … I mean, I had thought perhaps—'

'No. We were like sisters, nothing more.' She must have noticed my embarrassed blush because she put her hand on my forearm. 'It's all right, I'm not offended. In the circus, love takes all forms.' She smiled damply. 'If you wish, you can come and see us perform this evening. You can be my guest.'

───────────

The curtain was not yet raised. Miss Brown put me on a folding chair in the wings of the stage, alongside an elderly gentleman with impressively trimmed whiskers. He introduced himself as Lau.

'I'm a surgeon,' he confided in me. 'I put them back together when they fall.'

'How often does that happen?'

'More than you might think. Clavicles, carpals, a femur or two. An ilium once.' He seemed thrilled by the rich variety of injuries he'd been required to mend. He nodded towards Miss Brown, who was now on the stage stretching, dressed in her stage outfit of a sleeved corset and striped bloomers. 'Never Miss La La, of course. She doesn't make mistakes.'

'And Miss La Blanche?'

'Hmm. Bad business, that. Tragic. No, she never fell either, though that was more to do with Miss La La than any skill of her own. She never misses, you see. Caught her every time. On and off stage, you might say.' He made a motion with his hand like a fish swimming. 'Natalia was prone to going her own way. Only turned up half the time. Olga, Miss La La that is, kept having to find her and bring her back.'

'I dare say that annoyed the rest of the performers.'

He considered this for a second. 'You'd think so, but no. They were fond of the girl. It annoyed the management though. Thomas Quinton was livid.'

I was going to ask him what he meant by that, but the curtain went up and the audience burst into anticipatory applause.

The show was quite magnificent. First, the burly fellow lifted a woman above his head with one hand and proceeded to lift another with the other hand. The two women sat up there as neatly as if on a park bench, and then fell backwards into flips, causing the audience to gasp, but they landed on their feet, arms outstretched. Then a fellow swung from the trapezes, somer-saulting from one to the next, and another fellow juggled with knives. As he came off stage, dashing past Lau and me, I saw that the edges of the blades were filed down to bluntness.

The audience welcomed each act with a decent amount of enthusiasm, but when Miss La La appeared, they became positively enthralled. All eyes were on her, including mine. First, she walked on a piece of rope strung taut and high between two pillars. The audience shuddered as she wobbled and recovered. Then she did it again, this time juggling the knives, and then a third time, juggling lit torches. I could only watch between my fingers, so sure was I that she would fall or burn herself, and yet she did not. The flames whirled so fast between her hands they became a circle of fire, and I found myself shrinking back in my chair.

Lau leaned towards me. 'Are you all right?'

'Yes, of course.'

Next, Miss La La repeated the act I'd seen before, being pulled up by her teeth, and finally, what they had all been waiting for. A cannon was wheeled on to the stage. I could tell from the effort required of the burly fellow and the rumbling from the wheels that it was truly a heavy thing, made from cast iron. A harness was fixed around it and a member of the audience, a young fellow in a flat cap, was invited to come on to the lime-lit stage and test its authenticity.

Up until that moment, the audience had seemed like a single, many-headed creature sprawling in the dimness. But now I looked more closely, my eyes fell upon Thomas Quinton and Alice Morgan in front-row seats. He was as dapperly dressed as ever, and she was a vision in a sky-blue frock and matching feather fascinator. The two of them were talking, occasionally smiling, their faces so close together that if they'd each turned a little further, they would be kissing.

I couldn't believe it. Alice was not dead, nor apparently had she been punished for losing a gem worth more than this entire auditorium and all the jewellery and wallets within it. She appeared utterly forgiven. But why?

Once the young man had averred that the cannon was genuine, Miss Brown bit down on to a piece of leather attached to the harness, and dangled upside down from a trapeze by her knees. The trapeze was slowly raised on two ropes by no less than six men, while the cannon first tipped up and then left the stage altogether, hanging freely, held aloft only by the grip of Miss Brown's teeth. Still, she ascended, until the cannon was the height of a man above the stage, demonstrated by the juggler fellow, who was brave enough to stand below it and even lie down, so if her bite had failed, he would have been crushed.

The audience stood and clapped as one, while Miss Brown unhooked one knee from the trapeze and extended her free leg and arms, hanging from just the other knee. It was remarkable, unfeasible, and yet my attention remained fixed on Alice and Quinton. I was certain she had genuinely lost the Blood Flower and had feared for her life. Or was that simply what I wanted to think? Was I afraid that if she had lied about that, then she might have lied about other things as well? She might never have been interested in me at all.

And then, without meaning to, I caught her eye. She blinked several times, unsure it was me, hovering at the edge of the stage. She nodded a fraction, still looking, so we were, for those few seconds, locked together, communicating ... something. I didn't know what. Regret, maybe, and a hint of fear? Perhaps we both saw what we wanted to see.

Quinton followed her gaze. He squinted at me and back at her, and then clenched his jaw.

Miss Brown started her descent, and the spell was broken. The cannon was guided down to the stage, and she slipped off the trapeze and performed an elegant curtsy to rapturous applause.

The curtain came down.

When it was raised again for the troupe's bow, Alice and Quinton were already leaving. He was pulling her by the hand up the aisle.

'Well, that was splendid,' said Mr Lau, attempting to hide his disappointment.

I waited for Miss Brown to return but saw her only briefly. She seemed exhausted and said little to me before she left, only reiterating the well-meant, if unnecessary, advice that Rosie was a wise woman, and I should do my best to stick with her.

Afterwards, having nowhere else to sleep, I wandered out to the station and lay down on one of the benches. I was alone until a fellow from the railways approached me with hostile intent, declaring that I could only stay if I bought a ticket right there and then. He looked astonished when I agreed.

And so, after a fitful night, I was awoken when the platform started filling with yawning commuters for the seven-fifteen train to London.

17

AS I STRODE OUT of Waterloo Station and into the familiar tumult of London, I couldn't remember a time I had felt less uplifted about coming home. I loitered on the corner by the church, watching smoke rise from a tray of chestnuts, wishing I had a penny to spend on lunch.

Above me on the wall, a poster read: *Visit Sunny Southsea and be Amazed. Miss La La at Quinton's New Hippodrome.* The picture was of Miss Brown hanging upside down from a trapeze, holding a rope in her mouth from which another woman was dangling, her arms balletically outstretched. Natalia La Blanche, I presumed. *Born to fly.*

I felt a surge of pity for her. I should be there, solving her murder, instead of here, trying to repair what I had broken. I slung my sack over my shoulder and set off.

I imagined ripping out my heart and laying it, still beating, on Rosie's doorstep. How ridiculous that was. How *romantically* ridiculous. No more self-indulgence. I scraped the sack against the soft skin of my neck as punishment.

Rosie, Rosie, Rosie.

What had I been before I met her? I looked back on that man with a kind of shame. He was a woodlouse on its back, legs in the air, wiggling and curling, unable to right itself.

I wouldn't be alive if I hadn't met Rosie.

I stopped on Waterloo Bridge, watching the river churn below me, imagining the rush of cold through my skin as I hit it, pouring between my bones, soaking into my organs, dispersing my cells and atoms until I was part of the current and then the sea. My name waited for me still, scratched into the paintwork beneath the guard rail, a promise I had made to myself. Jump, if you need to, if you choose to. You can always jump.

More self-indulgence. This wasn't even the same bridge.

I crossed over and looked south along the river, and there it was, grey and hazy in the smoke and steam: Westminster Bridge, where I had once spent half a night in the rain, wondering if I wanted to live or die.

But then: Rosie.

She never had any time for such nonsense. Morbid thoughts don't get the kids up in the morning or the pastry rolled out, do they? She made me forget about my name scratched into the paintwork. I'd crossed over the river a hundred times since and had rarely given it a thought.

Without her, would I be that man again?

I turned right at the Strand, around St Clement's church, which hulked in the middle of the thoroughfare like a frigate caught at low tide, and onwards to Fleet Street. My first stop was my newspaper office. I'd written a letter to my editor, J. T. Whitford, explaining that I needed another day or two before returning and was prepared to take it unpaid, which was the equivalent of stealing something from him and then offering it back as a gift.

I pushed the envelope through the letterbox, wishing I had time for a beer with Harry. His irrepressible bonhomie would pass the time quite nicely. But instead, I hurried away with my face kept low, almost in my collar, hoping no one would take a second look at a hangdog fellow with a half-filled sack over one shoulder.

I was not far from our home. Just a little further, and I would almost see it. But she'd asked for time, hadn't she? She could have all time in the world, but I wished I knew whether, at the end of that time, she anticipated an outcome in my favour. What she saw as the odds, either way. The pros and cons of me.

I also wished that Peregrine was in London, and that we were on speaking terms. I missed my friend and his terrible advice. On an occasion of a previous argument with Rosie, he had advised me not to be too hasty. Take your time, he said. Send her a letter first, that she can read and reread, clutching it to her breast as the tears fall. Can she ever forgive you? She will, of course, moved by your abjectness and your pathetic entreaties. Later, you go to her saying you can stay away no longer and must have her answer. Does she still love you as you love her? Of course she does. A smile, a kiss and the curtain falls. The audience leaps to their feet in wild applause.

But Rosie was not the heartsick heroine of one of Peregrine's plays. She was, at heart, a practical person. What would move her would be … something else. An apology. An explanation. A way to fit what I had done into a future we could share.

I pinched myself hard under my armpit where my binding met the weals on my skin. The pain shot through me. The balls of my fingers and the soles of my feet throbbed with it. Thus refreshed, I took a deep breath, straightened my hat and walked back the way I'd come.

The nearest of my two friends' houses was Jacob's. He and Lilya lived above his jewellery repair shop, not ten minutes' walk away on Shoe Lane. He would welcome me with a glass of some foul brew, and Lilya would make us a late lunch, slicing mutton and mashing swede as expertly as any chef, though she was blind. It was a tempting option. But they would ask questions, and questions and more questions, and make a fuss, and give me counsel that was well meant but ill aimed. And anyway, though I cared for them greatly, their house had never been my home.

No, I needed somewhere less bothersome.

My old landlord Alfie Smith had moved his pharmacy business to Hanover Square since I lodged with him, but I knew he'd find a space for me to sleep. Better still, he'd pour us a couple of glasses of decent whisky and sit beside me in silence. I set off for Hanover Square, almost sniffing the whisky in the air like a dog.

Of course, there was still one impediment to be dealt with: Alfie's daughter, Constance.

'Good afternoon, Leo,' said Constance. She had taken to calling me by my Christian name since turning fourteen, and it still sounded strange to my ears. 'I thought you were on holiday by the sea. I've never seen the sea.'

She was standing behind the main counter of the pharmacy, which was busy with five customers, one of whom, a lady with a grand hat, was looking at me fiercely, clearly surmising I was about to jump the queue.

'I was working, young Constance. Investigating two murders.'

The lady looked aghast, but Constance digested the information with equanimity. 'Did you solve them?'

'Not yet.'

I confess, my own answer surprised me.

'I see you have a sack.'

'I have. You are as observant as ever. I believe it was once used to hold potatoes. Where's Alfie?'

Anyone overhearing us could be excused for thinking Constance and I disliked each other, that we were enemies or harboured simmering resentments, but nothing could be further from the truth. She was like a favourite niece to me. But neither of us was inclined towards outbursts of sentiment, so this verbal fencing was our only means of showing affection.

She blinked at me twice and cocked her head the merest fraction, all the while continuing to serve her customer, a rotund fellow in severe need of a salve.

'How is Mrs Stanhope? I would love to see her.'

'Rosie's not here.'

She glanced briefly at the sack and raised her eyebrows. 'Well, please give her my regards. Tell her I've been practising making hop yeast like she told me, and I'm improving with every batch.'

I doubted this very much. Constance cooked food the way surgeons sawed off limbs: hastily and with unpleasant results.

'Constance, I beg of you please, tell me where your father is.'

She thumbed over her shoulder. 'Stock room, avoiding Edith.'

Alfie and Edith had married the previous year. I didn't doubt that he was enjoying some time alone, but Constance's assessment of his motivation was biased. She maintained a persistent mistrust of her stepmother for no other reason, as far as I could tell, than habit. Poor Alfie suffered the sporadic battles between his wife and daughter like a hillock which is of strategic importance but possesses no armaments of its own.

He was indeed in the stock room, sitting on a pile of crates and smoking a cigar.

'Leo! Weren't you on holiday somewhere? Brighton, was it?'

'Portsmouth, and I was working. Why does everyone think I was on holiday? Anyway, I'm back now.'

'Yes, I can see that. What's in the sack? If you have a couple of Rosie's pies in there, I may fall at your feet in gratitude.'

When I'd first met Alfie, he was as lean as a weasel, but of late he'd grown somewhat portly, perhaps because his new wife's cooking was less unappetising than Constance's. Whatever the reason, the crates were bowing and creaking under his weight.

'No pies, I'm afraid. I was wondering if I could stay with you?'

'Oh? … Oh.' He gave me a sympathetic expression. 'Sorry, old man. Would you like a glass of whisky?'

That was the marvellous thing about Alfie: he would neither pry nor dwell. I had long since reached the conclusion that the loss of his beloved first wife and, before that, his time in the army had dulled his fears and anxieties on any topic, save one.

'Did Constance seem well to you?' he asked, leading the way up the stairs.

'Yes, I think so. Do you have cause for concern?'

He paused and half turned. 'I'm the father of a daughter.'

Their sitting room faced over the Square. I took a seat by the hearth while Alfie poured the drinks. The familiarity made me feel peculiar, as if the past year hadn't been real, and I was still living with Alfie and Constance. I might go to Rosie's shop tomorrow and she would welcome me with a frown, give me a pie in a paper bag and tell me about her day. For all the intervening months, I would have said our lives were better now than then: to be married, to spend time together, to read stories to the children at night. Nothing had ever made me happier. And yet today, I would give anything for all of that to have been a dream.

We drank in silence, dusk falling outside. Edith came in with some much-needed bread and cheese, and she and I talked about the martins that had nested under the eaves at the back of the building. All the chicks had hatched and flown. When she bustled out, her hand brushed Alfie's shoulder.

'You two seem very happy,' I told him.

He nodded, narrowing his eyes. 'We have our arguments as well. Marriages can be difficult. Go to Rosie tomorrow and apologise.'

'What makes you think I did something wrong?'

He drained his whisky. 'It's obvious.' He chuckled at my expression. 'Your wife's no fool, Leo, and she adores you. If you're here rather than there, she has good reason to be annoyed.' He poured two more large glasses. 'We have a lodger, but there are two beds in his room. You can take the other.'

I was almost certain he thought of me exactly as I appeared: a slim fellow with a strong inclination towards privacy. *Almost* certain. I'd wanted to tell him the truth more often than I could count, but how does one drop such a thing into the conversation? Especially now, after, what, five years or more? No, it was too late.

'That won't be necessary. I'll sleep in the stock room, if you don't mind. I hope this will only be short term.'

That night, I slept badly. Alfie had dragged a straw mattress downstairs and Edith provided blankets, but the room was a lean-to at the back of the shop, so was draughty and filled with strange noises: whistling wind, scratching rats and lamps creaking on their chains. The crates were stacked high, and in the half light, I imagined them to be all sorts of horrors; at one moment an old woman holding a douche, and at another a door being pushed from the other side, and at yet another, Stephan sitting in an armchair amidst a cacophony of birds.

I awoke to the rattle of the shutters being raised on the shop windows. Such a familiar noise, I could almost think I was home, except Rosie's pie shop had only one window and Alfie's grander establishment had two, one either side of the central door.

I dimly recalled making a rush outside the previous night as my stomach contents lurched upwards. It was as well the door to the back yard was close by.

In the shop, Constance was polishing the counter while Huffam the dog ate noisily from his bowl.

'Salicin,' I growled, my throat like sandpaper.

She rolled her eyes. 'Father is similarly afflicted,' she said.

When she had mixed the medicine, and I'd thrown it down my throat to avoid tasting it, she sat on the stool opposite me and folded her arms.

'Would you like breakfast?'

'My goodness, no.' I doubted my stomach would take any further abuse. 'Constance, are you aware of the effects of opium?'

This may sound a strange question to ask a young woman of fourteen, but she had an ambition to be a surgeon and was often to be found with her nose in a book about physiology or chemistry, such that Alfie had ceased trying to dissuade her. She knew more about the workings of the male anatomy than I did, and a few weeks previously had confided to me that she was exchanging correspondence with Mrs Garrett Anderson at the women's hospital, who had been most encouraging.

'It's a sedative,' she said, without hesitation. 'It relaxes the bowels. Is that why you need it?'

'No. My question isn't on my own behalf.'

'Oh. A newspaper article? How interesting.' She started ticking off the points with her fingers. 'It's an anaesthetic and, taken externally, an anodyne. And an intoxicant, of course. What more do you wish to know?'

'Would it have any permanent effect? Would it make an otherwise rational person believe something that wasn't true?'

'Such as?'

'That an object, a very valuable object, has magical powers.'

She raised her eyebrows. 'While intoxicated, a patient may have severe dreams, including grotesque and impossible things.

But these effects are temporary. They quickly give way to depressive thoughts and sopor.'

I sensed that she was quoting one of her books. She knew them off by heart.

I stood up, moving my head as minimally as possible.

'Thank you, Constance.'

'Good luck with Mrs Stanhope, Leo.'

My feet wanted to go to Rosie's shop, but I would not let them. She had asked for time, and knew I had to provide it. And yet I could not stop thinking about her. I needed a distraction.

Consider the Blood Flower, I thought.

If it wasn't the effects of opium that had made Alice think the Blood Flower possessed magical properties, then perhaps the stone itself held the solution. Not magic, obviously, but something. And I knew a man who was an expert on jewels, though extracting information from him often came at a price.

The walk was long, and my binding, still damp from the previous night's terrors, quickly set about scouring my flesh, sending trickles of blood down the inside of my shirt. I would need to find a way to do my laundry. I thanked the Lord I was still two weeks away from my monthly curse, though in truth, such thanks were ill-deserved. It was His fault I had to endure it at all.

I reached Shoe Lane and knocked on Jacob's door. It was Jacob himself who answered, which I took to be an encouraging sign. It meant he had risen from his bed.

'Ah, Leo, I wasn't expecting you. I thought you were on holiday. Is it Thursday already?'

That was our regular day for chess.

'No. I was passing.'

He beckoned me inside and we picked our way through his workshop. I was sure most men in his profession were fastidious, keeping their tools in neat cases and drawers, but that had never been Jacob's way. His benches were covered with the apparatus and particulars of his jewellery trade: tweezers, pliers, brass wire and settings, all manner of hooks and rings.

He led me up the stairs, one sparrow-claw hand gripping the banister and the other on his cane.

'What's the news? Are the Irish blowing things up again? Not that I blame them.'

'How can you say that?'

'They're young. When I was their age, we fought for weeks on end, rebelling against the *Pale*. The settlements, you know.' He waggled his beard, a straggly thing that hung from his chin like cobwebs. 'We pushed the *Politsiya* out of the docks with nothing but our fists and the bricks we pulled out of the pavement.'

I was never certain whether his stories of youthful daring and heroism in Nicolaev were true or not.

'Perhaps you had good cause to fight.'

'We wanted freedom, like all young men.' As he spoke, his eyes became vague, as though he were seeing the events all over again in his mind. These days, he lived more in the past than the present. 'Many of us died. Too many. And all for nothing. Going to war to gain freedom is like leaping off a building to gain flight.'

Even for him, it was too early for alcohol. Lilya made a pot of mint tea and brought it to us, feeling her way with the expertise of a cat in the dark.

'For your head,' she said, though I had not told her I was feeling poorly. 'Why do you visit us, Leo? Always, you're welcome, but today, in the morning, it is unusual, no?'

'I have a question for Jacob. And I wanted to check on our chess game. The one we've been playing by telegram.'

His board was laid out on the table, but the pieces were not in positions corresponding to the moves we'd made. The white queen had been advanced and black had two knights on threatening squares.

Jacob licked his lips. 'I'm winning, I think.'

'But this isn't our game.'

'Of course it is.'

'No, it isn't. Look here, the sides have made several moves each. Six or seven at least. But I've only sent you four telegrams.'

Jacob frowned and I could see he was at risk of losing his temper. When I'd first met him, that was a rare occurrence. He would harangue and argue, but always with a glint of mischief in his eye. Now, the slightest thing would send him into a rage.

'You hate to lose, don't you? And to an old man too. The shame of it.'

I sat back, feeling tears well up in my eyes. First Peregrine, then Rosie and now Jacob? It was too much.

'Of course not. I'm mistaken. I apologise. We can play from here.'

I searched in my pocket for my notebook, so I could make a note of the board. One of my knights was about to be taken by a white bishop and at least two of my pawns were vulnerable.

'No, no, if you accuse me of cheating, I concede.' He flicked a forefinger, knocking over his king. 'There. You've won. Congratulations. I hope you're happy.'

Lilya rapped her knuckles on the table. 'You foolish man. We have spoken of this.' She rattled off a number of sentences in Russian which I didn't understand, but seemed very likely, from her tone and demeanour, to be an expansion on the theme of his foolishness. When she'd finished, she nodded firmly. 'I explained to my husband. I do dusting and maybe I move around the pieces. I don't know. I don't understand what they do, the horse and the castle and all the little ones. I put them back wrong.'

I sipped my tea in silence, certain that it wasn't Lilya who had ruined our game. I could imagine Jacob examining the board and playing a few moves ahead, seeing what would happen, and getting sidetracked or starting on another bottle, and forgetting what he'd done.

Truly, he was not the man he had once been.

Lilya poured me another cup of tea. 'Rosie was here.'

I closed my eyes. Of course, how could I have been this stupid? Lilya and Jacob had been looking after Robbie while we were in away, so the boy could continue his schooling.

'How did she seem?'

Lilya moved her head from side to side. 'She did not stay. She came for Robert, and they left. Two minutes, no longer.'

'I see.'

Lilya gazed towards me with her blank eyes. 'What was your question?'

'What?'

'You said you had a question for Jacob.'

'Ah yes.' I leaned forward. 'Rubies are very valuable, aren't they?'

Jacob shrugged, still simmering. 'Of course. And snow is cold, and acorns fall in the autumn. What of it?'

'If a ruby was very large, say the size of a nut ...' At his expression, I paused. 'I know that would make it immensely rare, but if it *were* that size, would it be able to attract things and people? Or repel them? For example, could a ruby that size break a gold chain due to, I don't know, a build-up of static electricity? Something of that nature.'

He snorted, and I saw that glint reappear in his eye. 'Ah, Leo, you ask this only to amuse me. Having offered insult you wish to return to my ... what it is? My *good books*, as if I'm one of your priests keeping a record of your sins.'

'So, the answer is no.'

'Can a ruby repel itself from a chain? This is what you're asking? Of course it is no. Rubies are stones. They are inert.'

'You're certain of this?'

He banged his cane on the floor. 'You don't believe me? I work with these materials all my life.'

'Of course I believe you. Thank you, Jacob.'

As I was leaving, Lilya caught my wrist. 'What did you do, Leo? All this with rubies and science, and yet you ask us how is your wife? This is a question we should be asking you.'

'I know. I'll try to ... make it better with Rosie.'

She uttered something in Russian and clouted me on the shoulder. 'You are also a very foolish man.'

'Thank you.'

'You don't know what is in your own hand.' She took my palm and opened it up. 'My sweet, silly boy. Always you reach for the thing you cannot get, that is too far away. And you miss what is right here. Right *here*. It is the whole world. Everything.'

Back at the pharmacy, Constance was spinning on a stool while their new lodger leaned on the counter and talked about declensions, whatever they were. He was a handsome young fellow with a well-groomed accent, the very quintessence of a student at the University College.

Constance didn't so much as glance in my direction. 'There are eggs if you're hungry.'

'Thank you.'

Since I had moved out a year previously, she'd generally treated me as a favoured uncle and my visits as something akin to an event. She would follow me upstairs and remain until her father insisted that she should leave, whereupon she would reappear at intervals to offer refreshments, each time remaining until told, with increasing firmness, to go to her room. I didn't seek out such attention – indeed, I was glad she was growing up and becoming more independent – but I hadn't expected it to happen this quickly. I felt oddly displaced.

Huffam followed me into the kitchen and watched as I cooked and ate three scrambled eggs, his hungry eyes following my spoon to my mouth and back to my plate as if he hadn't eaten for a month. When I cut myself two pieces of bread and smeared them with dripping, he started to whimper.

'Don't give him any,' said Alfie, coming in. 'He's getting fat. And don't look at me that way either.' He patted his own stomach. 'I'm not fat, I'm *comfortable*.'

'*Very* comfortable, some might say.'

He grinned, rolling up his shirtsleeves. 'I hope you're enjoying *our* eggs. Look, if you want to make yourself useful, in lieu of rent and board, you can sort out the stock room. It's getting out of control.'

'Certainly. Some manual labour would suit me very well. Will you show me what you want where?'

He gave me a glum expression. 'Not really. I have a customer any minute who wants six teeth taken out, and the truth is, we've never had a system. Just make of it what you can.'

In the light of day, the stock room was chaotic. Crates and boxes were piled up with their labels facing every which way, bicarb on top of face powder, pessaries muddled with linctuses. I set about creating some form of order, opting for an alphabetical approach, starting with arsenic.

The lean-to had become greenhouse-hot, and I was sweating like a navvy when I came across a square box containing four brown bottles. I checked the label: laudanum. My first thought was that it should go next to the iodine, but then I stopped.

The principal ingredient of laudanum was opium. I held one of the bottles up to the light, watching the liquid inside twinkle and dance.

One quick sniff, what harm could it do?

It was a wild, bitter smell, reminding me of dandelion leaves broken between my fingers. Such power in this little bottle. I sniffed it again, finding this time a tenderness, a memory of our kitchen long ago in the vicarage: our maid Bridget bustling from stove to pantry, talking and talking, to me, to the food, to her apron. 'Look at you! Covered in flour! I shall have to launder you all over again.' Broccoli boiling on the hob. I could never stand the stuff; it stank of old boots. And yet now, I would give anything to taste Bridget's food and hear her voice again. Perhaps if I drank this, I would.

I held the bottle to my lips, feeling a reckless despair. Whatever I'd once had to lose, was already gone. But what next? Some of the opium smokers at Papaver had been insensible, scattered across the floor like jellyfish at low tide. Would I want Alfie or Constance to find me in such a state?

I replaced the stopper and put the bottle back in its box.

That evening, after a dinner of mutton and potatoes, Alfie told me he was feeling too delicate to stay up with me again, adding that he was out of practice at drinking and these days was usually in bed early. This implication – that he had been the innocent victim of my malign influence – was for the benefit of Edith, who smiled approvingly. I noticed she'd left a pamphlet for the Temperance Society next to our empty bottle. Not half an hour later, I heard his snores rumbling through the shop like the bilge pump of an especially leaky barge.

I sat on my own in the pharmacy, listening to the rattle of traffic in the Square and watching the patterns of light form and fade in the gaps between the shutters. The lives of other people, hurrying along the pavement, calling across the street, pushing a handcart with a squeaky wheel. I generally thought of myself as a man with a secret, but their lives were as closed to me as mine was to them. What do any of us know of the mind of another?

The lamp had been turned down to its lowest level, almost guttering, and I could scarcely see the liquid in the laudanum bottle. I unscrewed the top again, breathing it in. This time, I was not returned to my childhood, but to a more recent time, a descent into black water teeming with fishes with bright eyes, silver carapaces and teeth like fork tines. Two men with wolves' heads were staring down at me from above, flies circling and landing in their fur. Their faces wavered on the surface of the water, and I could hear the muffled sound of someone humming. And that noise – jangle, thump, jangle, thump, jangle, thump – like a dog pulling its chain, like a child being pushed on a swing, like metal shutters blowing in the wind. The taste of salt on my tongue, the light slanting against an attic ceiling. Would I never be rid of it?

Rosie had saved me before, but she wasn't here now.

I put the bottle to my lips and closed my eyes.

A knock on the front door interrupted me: bang, bang, bang. I almost ignored it. A visitor for Alfie was no business of mine, and I didn't want to go through the whole rigmarole with the bottle again. I was set on my path and wanted no distractions. But there was something about that knock. It was neither loud nor quiet, neither hurried nor languid. It contained a firmness, a determination. I recognised it.

I put down the bottle and ran to the door, feeling my fingers shaking with excitement as I pulled it open.

'Rosie!'

My smile quickly faded.

She was standing in the doorway with her hands clutched in front of her and a look on her face of utter blankness, as though she was feeling every emotion at once and they'd cancelled each other out.

'Leo,' she said. 'You have to come with me tomorrow morning.'

'To where?'

'To Portsmouth. Bill's been murdered and the house ransacked. Viola's lost her mind with grief. There's no choice now. We have to go back.'

18

THE FOLLOWING MORNING, I arrived at Waterloo Station before seven in the morning. Rosie was standing on the steps holding a cotton bag and two tickets.

'I wasn't sure you'd come,' she said.

'Of course I've come. But I'm going to need at least a shilling for the fare. And another to repay a loan.'

The previous evening, Rosie had declined to explain further nor even come inside. Afterwards, as I was bolting the door, I wondered whether I had drunk from the bottle after all and was suffering an hallucination. It seemed impossible that Bill had been murdered. I'd seen him only four days previously and he'd been hale and mischievous, frolicking down the pavement with Sam on his shoulders. Why on earth would anyone want to kill him?

Rosie walked almost the length of the train before finding an empty compartment. Another fellow looked as if he might try to follow us in, but she slammed the door and gave him such a fierce glare through the window he blanched and hurried away. She sat down and opened her copy of *Molly Bawn*, which I knew for a fact she'd read several times before.

The guard blew his whistle and the train lurched forward. The platform was quickly bathed in smoke and steam, and I daydreamed that, when it cleared, we might magically be thrown back to our first trip down to Portsmouth and the last week would never have happened. Bill would be alive, and I would be about to attempt an explanation of the working of the tides to little Lillian.

'Where are the children?' I asked.

Rosie didn't look up. 'With Lilya and Jacob. Lilya told me you were lodging at the pharmacy, though I would've guessed that anyway.'

She went back to her book, and we were about an hour into the journey, pulling out of the station at Guildford, before I made another attempt at conversation.

'What do you know of what happened to Bill?'

She removed her spectacles.

'Not much. Viola sent me a telegram. She said Bill was dead, murdered and left on the beach like the others.'

'Was his throat slit as well?'

She flinched, and I ground the heel of my right shoe down my left shin. Asking questions too bluntly was a malady I seemed unable to cure. Normally, Rosie was the one who softened my indelicacies.

'I don't know.'

She opened her bag and extracted a handkerchief – one of a set I had given her for Christmas – and dabbed her eyes. For the next few minutes, she faced the window, though I sensed there was something else she wished to say as her breathing was increasingly uneven. Eventually, she spoke so quietly I could hardly hear her.

'Who was that woman you were with?'

I had already decided to be completely candid.

'Alice Morgan. She's Mr Quinton's mistress.' I waited for Rosie to meet my eyes. 'I didn't think it was you, after the police raid. If I'd known, I would've gone straight back. I would never have let you be arrested and spend a minute in jail, let alone a whole night.'

It was the honest truth.

She stared down at the cover of her book and I feared she would open it again and resume reading. But instead, she raised it to her face and began rapping it against her forehead with growing force.

'I hate this. I do. I want to trust you, but I know you looked back and saw me. And still you walked away with that other woman.'

'I thought ...' I put my head in my hands. 'This is the truth. I thought you were Viola.'

Rosie ceased beating herself with the book. 'And you think that's a good excuse?'

'Probably not. But she's not my responsibility. Bill was there to look after her.'

'Mother of God, Leo. She's pregnant.'

'I know, but I had no idea they'd arrest her ... I mean, *you*. Why were you there anyway?'

'Viola told me Bill had followed you. She was upset. Bill's been in trouble with the police before, apparently. I went to warn him, but too late.' She sat back, hugging her book to her chest. 'Tell me about this Alice Morgan. I've never heard of her.'

'Quinton gave her the Blood Flower as a pendant, but she lost it. It came off when we were leaving the club. She was afraid Quinton would kill her in retaliation, although ...' I pushed my fingers through my hair, knowing how feeble this would sound. 'Although he didn't.'

Rosie gave me a harsh look. 'It was good of you to hold her hand. Very comforting, I'm sure. You're a sap for a damsel in distress.'

I took a deep breath and sat back. 'Rosie, what do you expect of me? We're husband and wife, but we don't share a bed. You've always made clear this was a convenient arrangement, nothing more. Am I supposed to lead the life of a priest?'

She closed her eyes, and when she opened them again, I could see some part of my Rosie again, the merest flicker of compassion behind the glare.

'We should've talked about that, I suppose.'

'We should.'

'But, Leo, are you sure this woman truly lost the ruby? Isn't it more likely she still has it, and her fright was an act to play on your sympathies?'

'No.'

'Why not?'

I couldn't explain my reason: that if Rosie was right, then the evening Alice and I had spent together was nothing more than a charade.

'She was genuine. I'm sure of it.'

Rosie gave me a look that said: *are you truly that gullible?*

'Who then?' she said. 'Let's go through the list of possible murderers. I'll start. Alice Morgan.'

'Very well, if you insist.' I didn't want to prolong the argument. 'Next, the Navy man, Chastain. He brought the Blood Flower to England in the first place. Micky Long stole it and ended up dead.'

'And Mr Quinton.'

'Yes.' I pictured the hoodlum, and the brute that shadowed him. 'He would've instructed his man, Stephan, to do the actual killing. A very scary fellow indeed.'

'And that young lad, Timothy Honey, who was arrested. He was Micky's friend. And Natalia's. Perhaps he wanted the ruby as well.'

This was all I had hoped for: Rosie and I together again, trying to solve a crime, spreading out the suspects in front of us like ingredients.

'We must consider Olga Brown too.' I remembered her being lifted on the rope by her teeth. 'She knew Micky and Natalia, and she has the strength of any man.'

Rosie scoffed. 'More, I would say. But I don't think it was her. She was distraught at Natalia's death.'

It was my turn to give her the look. 'Is your judgement of people so much better than mine?'

'Yes. And I'm sure it wasn't her.'

'She said she likes you as well.'

Rosie looked pleased despite her frostiness. 'Truly, what did she say?'

'That you were wise.'

'Hmm.' She gave me a sour look. 'I don't always feel very wise.'

'Perhaps truly wise people don't.'

She rolled her eyes. 'What nonsense. Of course truly wise people know they're wise, otherwise they wouldn't be wise, would they?' She contemplated this for a second. 'But I can see why you'd make that mistake. Idiots don't always know they're idiots.'

I suppressed a grin. Being insulted by Rosie was an honour.

The guard came down the corridor, staggering from side to side as the train rattled and jerked.

'Next stop Liss!' he shouted. 'Ten minutes.'

'Who else?' said Rosie. 'We have to be quick.'

I couldn't think of anyone but didn't want her to go back to her book.

'Miss Morgan told me the Blood Flower has magical proper-ties. She said it has the power to pull things towards itself or push them away. She thinks that's how it detached itself at the club.'

Rosie pursed her lips so hard I thought she might burst a vein. 'Does Miss Morgan smoke opium by any chance?' When I said nothing, she folded her arms.

I was tempted to tell her that Constance had assured me the effects of opium were short-lived and no permanent derange-ment could ensue from its use, but I had already determined that nothing would shift my wife from her low opinion of Miss Morgan. And, if I was utterly honest, I rather liked that Rosie felt ill-disposed towards her; no one had ever been jealous about me before.

'When all this is done,' I said, 'will I be able to come home? Will we be as we were before?'

Rosie returned to gazing out of the window. 'I don't know. All I can think about at the moment is Viola.'

At Liss, a young couple joined us in the compartment, talking avidly of their plans for the seaside, and we couldn't continue our conversation. But still, Rosie fetched her cotton bag down and produced a pasty wrapped in waxed paper.

'I got it at the station,' she said, handing it to me. 'I'm not hungry now. Lord knows, I can't afford for it to go to waste.'

We reached Portsmouth shortly after nine o'clock. As we exited the station forecourt, I found a messenger boy and handed him a note with an address.

'Take this,' I said. 'For Mr Black. Do you understand?'

Rosie gave me a curious look. 'Are you sure? He should be added to our list of suspects.'

'Peregrine?'

'Of course. He has a terrible temper, and he mixes in dubious company. And like you said before, you really know nothing about him.'

'But I know *him*. And we need his help.'

Rosie sniffed. 'We can't rule him out.'

I chose not to risk another frost so soon after the thaw. But inside, I discounted my friend. He wouldn't murder a person. Or, more accurately, he wouldn't murder a person *in that way*. A victim of Peregrine's wrath wouldn't be left on the beach, pristine but for a cut to the throat. They would be hacked into tiny pieces or beaten with furniture, and Peregrine himself would be roaring in the street, bathed in their blood.

We reached Viola's house shortly after ten o'clock. The door was open, but before I could go inside, Rosie stopped me.

'Wait, Leo. Remember that she's newly widowed in the worst way. I know you think she's half-mad, but please be sensitive.'

I saw in her face that she was frightened for her sister. Rosie was a resourceful person, and she didn't like problems she wasn't able to fix. She would mend the whole world, if she could.

Sergeant Dorling was in the hallway, smoking a cigar and paging through a notebook. He looked up as we came in.

'Stanhope. And Mrs Stanhope. Terrible business, this.'

Rosie tensed beside me and didn't reply, which was unlike her. I couldn't blame her though. A night in the police cells probably deserved a little discourtesy.

'Do you have any suspects?' I asked.

He peered at me from under his grey eyebrows, more resembling a stern grandfather than a policeman.

'We have a number of avenues we're exploring.' I took this to mean 'no', an inference which visibly annoyed the sergeant. 'How's that article of yours coming along? I hope it's as supportive of our efforts as you promised.'

'Of course,' I lied, not having started it. 'Is Mrs Broadman at home?'

'Well, that is a question.' His face took on an ugly sort of smirk. 'She's present *in person*. But her mind is somewhere else as far as I can tell. She's at home, but she's also *not* at home. In the head, do you see?'

I refused to acknowledge what he presumably thought was a joke.

The parlour was a mess. Every drawer had been opened and on the floor were scattered candles, crystals, books, feathers and broken glass.

Viola was sitting by the pedestal table we had used for the séance, with Jack-the-bloody-dog on her lap. She turned as we came in and her face was as pale as ash. Rosie put her arms around her sister, holding her tightly.

'I'm sorry,' she said. 'I shouldn't have left.'

Viola slightly pulled away. 'It's all right. Truly.'

'I'll ask you again, when did you last see your husband?' said Dorling, who had come in behind us.

'I've answered all your questions,' she replied, with a hint of tartness.

I realised there was something strange about her appearance, which was that there was nothing strange about her appearance. I had expected her to be dishevelled and distraught, possibly in weeds, but she was wearing a simple green frock, and her hair was neatly tied. Aside from the paleness of her skin and the redness around her eyes, she appeared exactly as before.

'You haven't answered *any* of my questions,' said Dorling. 'Do you have the slightest clue why your husband was killed? Anything at all?'

'He'll tell us soon,' she replied, giving us a knowing smile. 'Can you imagine how furious he is at this moment? Absolutely livid, I'd imagine.'

I exchanged a look with Rosie, but she was as lost for words as me.

The door opened and their lodger came in carrying a tray with the air of a man who believed he alone knew what ought to be done. He placed the tray on the table and proceeded to pour a dash of milk into the two cups from a patterned jug, and swirl around the tea in the pot, which was covered with a knitted cosy.

'I'm sorry, gentlemen,' he said. 'And Mrs Stanhope, of course. I didn't realise you'd be here.'

He poured the tea, spooned three sugars into each cup, pushed one towards Viola and retired to the sofa with the other.

Dorling frowned at his notebook. 'What was your name again?'

'Edward Hapsworth. I'm sure you'll want to know when we last saw Bill. It was two evenings ago at approximately eight-fifteen. He was on his way to the pub. He often stops – stopped there before he began his evening's work. He was a night-soil man.'

'And how did he seem?'

'Excited. Elated. Brimming with *joie de vivre*.'

Dorling raised his eyebrows and smoothed out his moustache. 'Why was he like that?'

'He said he'd soon be rich.' Hapsworth pulled his mouth into a brittle smile that didn't reach his cheeks, let alone his eyes. 'He said they wouldn't need to take in a poltroon like me as a lodger any longer.'

Viola reached out and squeezed his wrist. 'He didn't mean it, Eddie.'

I saw Rosie glance from her sister's fecund belly to Mr Hapsworth and back again.

'What made him think he'd soon be rich?' asked Dorling.

Hapsworth took a sip of his tea. 'I have no idea. Some scheme, I should think. He wasn't what you'd call an honest man.'

I cleared my throat, and he looked in my direction as mildly as if I'd interrupted him watching a game of cricket on the green.

'Mr Hapsworth, someone has clearly searched this house. Presumably, it was the same person or people who murdered Bill Broadman. Where were you when that happened?'

'I was at my place of work. I'm a post office clerk.' He indicated Viola. 'Mrs Broadman wasn't here either. She was taking her morning walk with the dog. It's good for the baby, you see. When she came back, the house was … well, like this.' He cast around the room in a disinterested fashion. 'I suppose someone ought to tidy it up.'

I got the impression it wouldn't be him.

'Is every room like this?'

'Yes. Or worse. Disgusting, some of it.'

'If they'd found what they were looking for, they would've stopped looking,' I said. 'So, unless it happened to be in the very last place they searched, it's reasonable to suppose they didn't find it.'

Of course, I knew what *it* was. There was only one sensible explanation. Bill had been at Papaver when Alice lost the Blood Flower. He must have got close to us in the crush and pulled it from her neck. It was worth more money than he could imagine, and he would have no way to sell such a treasure, but still, fool that he was, he'd bragged about his new wealth to Mr Hapsworth and, most likely, every dubious character in half the pubs in Southsea. His stupidity had got him killed.

I turned to Sergeant Dorling. 'Where was Bill's body found?'

He seemed to toss up in his mind whether to tell me, eventually deciding it would do no harm. 'Same as the others. Throat slit and left on the beach.'

'Clearly, Bill didn't have the … whatever it was … on his person when they killed him, and they came here to search for it. Do you have no suspects *at all*?'

Dorling ran his tongue over his blackened teeth. 'Honey's gone missing. That Negress has been nagging at us to find him but I'm not wasting our time hunting for some molly-boy.'

'There's no need for any of this,' said Viola. 'The spirits will give us all the answers we seek.'

Rosie crouched down in front of her sister. 'You can't stay here, Viola,' she said. 'Whoever did this might come back and hurt you. They might think you know where it is.'

Viola put her hands lightly on the table as if about to play the piano.

'I have to stay,' she said. 'The spirits know to come here.'

Rosie closed her eyes. I had the feeling she had expected that answer.

'Very well,' she said. 'Then we'll stay with you.'

19

THAT EVENING, MR HAPSWORTH didn't answer when called for dinner. I went to his paltry space in the back room, and it was empty, no clothes on the hooks or books on the shelf.

'I suppose we can't blame him,' I said to Rosie. 'He was just a lodger. No reason for him to stay and risk his safety.'

'Just a lodger?' she said. 'Is that what you think?'

'What do you mean?'

She pursed her lips. 'Strange that Viola's pregnant now, after she was married to Bill for eight years.'

I goggled at her. 'You can't think ... Mr Hapsworth?'

'It's common enough.'

'Why would he leave?'

Rosie gave me a look, as only she could: a mixture of impatience and forbearance. 'Also, common enough.'

Viola took the news of Mr Hapsworth's disappearance with equanimity. Nothing could hurt her further. 'My concern isn't with the living.'

It was well after ten o'clock when she turned down the lamps and asked us to join her in the parlour, where she took a seat at the little table with the alphabet board in front of her. Once again, Rosie pleaded that she was too tired to converse with the dead.

'That means it'll just be Viola and me,' I whispered to her. 'The two of us. At a séance.'

'That's right.'

Her expression left me in no doubt that I shouldn't upset her grieving sister with petty concerns such as science or rationality.

I righted a chair and sat opposite Viola, our hands on the table like last time. I was unused to being in a house on such a quiet street, and the silence was oppressive. The blood was rushing in my ears.

She closed her eyes and started making low groans in the back of her throat, rising in tone and volume to a peculiar, closed-mouthed scream, as though she'd been unwillingly gagged. Abruptly, she became silent and flopped forward, almost touching the board with her forehead, and then jerked upright again. I flinched, and immediately she opened her eyes wide and clutched my hand.

'Don't move from the table.'

I was shivering. 'I won't.'

She went back to her groaning, her face full of twitches and grimaces. Finally, after a queasy convulsion, she started to speak, as though bringing up the words from her stomach. 'Spirits, we beg for your help in all humility. We seek Bill Broadman, my husband, newly taken from this world. We need to know who committed such an awful crime.' She straightened her shoulders. 'Allow him to speak to us, please.'

Of course, it had been Bill who had communicated on behalf of the dead last time. And now he was one of them. She was waiting for a message that would never come.

The silence seemed to stretch for hours.

Tears were forming in her eyes. 'Please,' she begged. 'I want to speak to my Bill. He's a good man, though he wasn't himself at the end.'

Again, there was no reply.

She stood up and started walking in small circles on the rug. 'I don't understand. Why won't they let me? Why can I speak to other people's husbands, but not my own?'

'I'm very sorry. Maybe they can't. Or perhaps Bill doesn't *know* who killed him.' I stood in front of her to interrupt her circum-ambulations. 'What did you mean when you said Bill wasn't himself near the end? Did his behaviour change in some way?'

She tapped her foot on the ground, exactly as Rosie would have done. 'It's not fair,' she said, wringing her hands and scratching pink lines down her wrists. 'They've abandoned me is what it is. I'm alone, utterly. No Bill, no Eddie, no spirits, and Roisin will be going back to London soon. What am I to do?'

'All right.' I pulled out her chair for her to sit. 'Let's have one more attempt.'

She was so pitiable; what else could I do?

I replaced my fingers on the board, and once again she started to groan. So lost was she in her own mind, she didn't notice that I had moved my chair so that my foot was now next to one of the tripod legs.

'Spirits,' she began. 'I beg you to speak to me. Is Bill in a better place?'

I tipped the table forward and slid my foot underneath. Then, pressing down hard with my hands, I lifted it a few inches from the floor on my shoe. It was devilishly difficult to keep it steady without being obvious. Bill must have had muscles like a stevedore.

Viola inhaled loudly. 'Bill? Is that you? Where are you, my love?'

I tipped the table towards the 'H' and the 'E' and the 'A', which were fairly easy as those letters were roughly on the other side of the table from me. But the next was a 'V', which was to one side, meaning I had to keep hold of the table between my hands and my shoe while leaning it to the right. I barely managed, accidentally producing a 'T' and a 'Z'.

'It's a "V",' I announced hastily. 'He's in heaven, Viola.'

Her shoulders relaxed and she fell back in her chair, facing the ceiling as though basking in sunlight.

'Spirits, we thank you,' she said, her voice breathy and hoarse. 'Now, tell us who committed—'

At that moment, there was a tap at the window. Viola shrieked with shock, and I nearly fell off my chair. My foot slipped out from under the table leg and the table itself rocked to one side, tipping the alphabet board on to the floor.

My heart was fluttering like a starling's wings. I peered out through a crack in the curtain, and there was Peregrine's giant face peering back at me.

'What the hell are you doing?' he bellowed through the glass. 'Have you completely lost your mind?'

I opened the front door, still shaking. He wasn't alone.

'Mr Honey,' I said to his companion. 'Sergeant Dorling told us you were missing. We were worried.'

Peregrine ushered Honey into the hall and they made quite the contrast: Peregrine's profligate bulk, wrapped in a fur-collared coat and topped with a velvet opera hat, beside Honey's skinny frame and gentle prettiness. His skin was so pallid it was almost translucent. I found it hard to believe the two men were of the same species.

Peregrine took off his hat and scowled at me. 'What on earth was all that?'

'A séance.' Before he could ask anything more, I held up my hand. 'Not now, please. I'm glad you're here.'

His scowl deepened. 'It doesn't mean you're forgiven. I came for Rosie, not you.'

Honey turned his pale blue eyes in my direction. Truly, he seemed so removed from the earth and its torrid concerns that this brief attention carried disproportionate weight. 'I hope you don't mind that I'm here too.'

'Not at all. Any friend of Peregrine is welcome.'

'Mr Black is the best of men. He was kind enough to take me in, and he asks for nothing in return.'

Peregrine coughed into his fist. 'Well, let's not exaggerate. That Navy fellow, Chastain, has been looking for him. Anyone would've done the same.'

'An act of philanthropy,' I said, sounding, even to myself, half-way between flattery and sarcasm.

Viola came into the hall, and I introduced them.

'Mrs Broadman is a …' I wasn't sure what to call her. A spiritualist? A mystic? A fantasist? 'She's my sister-in-law. I'd like to ask Mr Black to stay here for a day or two, Viola. He can help keep everyone safe in case whoever did this comes back.'

While Honey and Peregrine made themselves at home in the sitting room, I took Viola aside.

'What you said earlier about Bill, that he was acting out of character at the end. In what way?'

She gave me the smile of someone who has forgotten what a smile is supposed to mean. 'Nothing at all.'

I looked her in the eyes, attempting to reach the woman inside this swaddle of delusion.

'Viola. It's important.'

She sighed. 'Bill was always very neat and tidy. He took care of things.'

'But he changed?'

'He was proud of that privy. Professional pride, I suppose, him being a night-soil man. He always kept an eye on it and was ready with his spade when needed. He hated the chamber pot for … anything solid. Despised it, never used it, not even in the coldest weather. He said our privy was good enough for a king on his throne.'

I admit this wasn't the direction I'd expected the conversation to take. The exactitudes of Bill's toilet habits didn't seem likely to lead to a killer. But I had asked her, so I couldn't abruptly exit the conversation now.

She lowered her face and I noticed something in her expression I hadn't anticipated: shame.

'You mustn't tell people, Leo. I don't want it ending up in that newspaper of yours. He was a good man and deserves to be remembered well.'

'Of course. This is just between ourselves.'

She sighed deeply and winced a couple of times, trying to persuade her mouth to force out the words. 'The last day or two, I think he lost his mind. He started using the chamber pot and was fascinated by its … you know, by its contents. Staring at his own … discharge.'

'He examined his own faeces? Why?'

'I haven't a clue.' She shook herself, casting these horrors from her mind. 'Will your Mr Black and the other one be wanting some tea, do you think?'

I didn't answer. My brain had already skipped onwards.

I pulled open the door to the sitting room and called to Peregrine. 'I know I have no right to ask, but please keep an ear open. I have to go out.'

'Very well.' He withdrew something from his pocket, but I couldn't make out what it was in the dimness. 'If anyone comes, I have this.'

I squinted more closely, and realised it was a gun.

The night was pleasantly warm as I headed north towards the main road. I kept up a good pace. The hospital was an hour away at least.

I couldn't help but feel pity for poor Viola, wondering whether Bill had gone mad before his death. What a memory to have of him, staring at his own faeces in a chamber pot.

As I reached the junction, the streets became more crowded: women smoking on their doorsteps, men in groups on their way to the pub, children chasing each other and stray dogs sniffing round empty stalls. I wasn't certain of the route and had stopped to consider whether I should go left or straight on when I heard a voice.

'Would you care to have a go, mister? I can tell you your future. Only a penny.'

She was sitting at a table in a doorway with a pack of cards in front of her. She had a round face and large eyes, and was no more than fifteen years of age. Behind her on the step, two babies were fast asleep in a basket.

'Thank you, no.'

'No need to be squirmish. I'll tell you one thing, and if you like it, you can pay for the next.' Without waiting for a reply, she started shuffling her cards. 'What brings you here today?'

'I'm visiting someone. Out for a stroll.'

She deftly cut the pack and turned four cards over on the table. I didn't notice what they were, nor could I imagine what difference it would make. My fate lay in my hands and Rosie's, not in cartomancy.

'Two hearts, but at either end,' she said. 'You're divided.'

'I'm not divided.'

She looked me up and down, her eyes sharp. 'Is it a matter of love, mister? One's a queen and the other a five. You know which of 'em you want. How am I doing?'

I produced a penny from my pocket and tossed it on the table. 'You're very good. Very observant. You see a single man in the evening approaching from a residential street, pensive expression, suit and ascot, no coat. You ask a question, make a suggestion, then another. It's a deception, but it's clever. You've earned your fee.'

I turned to go, but she called after me: 'Mister! The other two cards are both knaves. Neither love will last. But you know that already, don't you?'

I stopped, briefly perturbed, but it was all nonsense. She was a Mr Jingle, a teller of stories, nothing more. I was allowing the moist evening and unfamiliar roads to unsettle me. I hastened onwards, growing impatient with the pair of sailors staggering in front of me, arms around one another, leaning in to keep themselves from falling. On the main road near Peregrine's theatre, there was a rank of hansom cabs. The first fellow in the line was asleep, as was his horse. At such moments, I dearly wished Jacob was with me; one of his favourite games was poking sleeping cabbies with his stick.

'Excuse me, I want to go to the Royal Hospital.'

He opened one eye. 'What's wrong with you?'

'Nothing. I'm visiting.'

He closed his eye again. 'It's shut at this time of night.'

I had to think of a lie. 'I'm visiting near there. I want to look at the harbour.'

'The harbour? Christ almighty. Have you lost your sense of smell?'

'Will you take me or not?'

Once he'd woken his horse, we set off, winding northwards and westwards, the stink rising with every turn of the carriage wheel. We reached the street alongside the harbour, and the stench became almost overwhelming. The tide was out, and the shore beyond made a twinkling stripe between the inky black sky above and the dull grey mudflats below.

'This will do.'

The cabbie pulled on his reins. 'Your loss.'

I made the walk of two hundred yards to the hospital wishing I had a scarf to wrap around my mouth.

The lamps were lit inside, but the main door was locked. I sloshed round the side of the hospital, marvelling that the building had not yet fallen into the sea. The crack in the front wall was matched by one at the back, and the ground under my feet was sodden, seeping into my shoes.

I tried every window and door. The fifth window was unlocked; indeed, it was unlockable because the frame had twisted and split as the brickwork surrounding it sank inch-by-inch into the mire. The misaligned hinges creaked as I pushed it open. The sill was low, and I was able to get a knee on top and alight with passable grace on the other side.

I was in a women's ward. On each side, a dozen or so beds were lined up, and some of the occupants were awake, their white faces peering above their blankets.

A hand reached out. 'Is that you? Are you here?' The voice sounded constricted, as if she had little breath left in her lungs.

'I'm sorry, no.'

I hurried out into the corridor. Last time I was there, I'd been following the mortuary assistant, Miss Squires, and had not expected to have to remember the way. Hospitals differ greatly in their designs, except in one respect: you will find the mortuary in the furthest, deepest, coldest corner. No one wants to pass it on the way to somewhere else, so it's always the last stop on the line.

The door was locked. I ran my fingers along the sill above, and sure enough, a key fell down. All mortuary assistants were the same, too.

I lit the lamp, keeping it low. It huffed softly like an old man on his pipe.

Nine corpses, each covered with a sheet.

The trolley where Micky had lain was empty now. Presumably, he'd been carted off, literally, for his funeral, probably far from here in a big cemetery with a small chapel. No cross would mark his place; no gravestone would stand at his head. Paupers' graves were dug deep and their coffins stacked to save space. Pine boxes rot and flesh is eaten away, so their bones intermingle at the lowest point. You can look across a paupers' graveyard and spot the divots every few yards where the ground has fallen in.

The first two corpses were women.

'I'm sorry,' I said to each of them, keeping my voice low, though there was no living person in the room to hear me.

The third was Bill.

His face wasn't the beery russet it had been. Now it was grey. His lips too. I pulled his covering down further; his throat had been cut. It was thorough and certainly fatal, but lacked the precision of those slashes administered to poor Natalia and Micky. This was ragged and crooked, ripping the skin beneath his jaw.

'Who killed you?'

I was sounding like Viola at her séance, but I didn't care. People talk to themselves, to their dogs and cats and chickens, to wooden icons on the wall. How was this any different? Rosie had been known to hold entire discussions with her knitting, arguing with it about dropped stitches and poorly dyed yarn.

I checked Bill's limbs and torso for any damage and was glad to see nothing unusual there. He had died quickly.

Now, it was time for the real work to begin.

Had this been the mortuary at the Westminster Hospital, where I had previously worked, the tools would be hung on a rack in strict order. But here, they were not, and I had to search the room, finding a somewhat rusty scalpel in a drawer along with a collection of other disused tools: broken needles, jammed calipers and blunted bone saws. In the cupboard underneath, I found a metal bowl and some thread.

'I'm truly sorry for what I'm about to do, Bill. But it's for the best, I promise.'

I fixed a spot a couple of inches to the right of his belly button, took the scalpel in my fist and stabbed him as hard as I could.

20

THEY ARE MUSCULAR THINGS, bowels, and the blade was not sharp. It was hard work. And afterwards, when everything had been stuffed back inside Bill and his skin sewn up, as best I could, no amount of scrubbing would remove the smell from my hands; half-digested food and beer rendered yet more sour by bile and time.

The Blood Flower was bloody indeed, resting in the metal bowl like a clot, like a cancer, squeezed out through a cut I'd made in his lower intestine. Such a small thing. I polished it and held it next to the lamp, watching the facets shine in deepest red, burgundy and almost purple.

I thought of Olga Brown, weeping for her friend Natalia La Blanche. And Micky Long's brother Jonathan, alone in the world with no one to look after him. And Viola, pleading with the spirits, willing to accept my obvious charade rather than the truth that she would never speak to her husband again.

The stone was beautiful, but it wasn't worth a life, let alone three.

'Oh, Bill,' I said. 'You were an idiot.'

My supposition had been proven right. He'd noticed the jewel at Papaver, hanging on its slim chain around Alice's neck, and greed had conquered good sense. In the rush to escape from the club, he got close to Alice and tugged it free. And then what? Anticipating that he would be captured by the police and searched, he did the only thing he could think of. He swallowed it.

But before the Blood Flower could complete its journey through his guts and into his chamber pot, he couldn't resist boasting of his good fortune. Word spread and someone killed him, greedy for the stone, probably the same someone who'd killed Natalia and Micky.

Those pretty reflections were a poor exchange indeed.

Even in such a short time, I'd come to hate looking at the thing. I wrapped it inside my handkerchief and put it into my jacket pocket, retracing my steps to the women's ward and out of the window. Outside, I crouched against the wall amidst the sludge and filth, and wept all the tears my eyes could make.

I didn't pass a single hansom cab on my way back through the city, and it was three in the morning or later by the time I reached Viola's house. I was exhausted but I didn't have a key. I peeked through a gap in the curtain and could see Peregrine asleep on the sofa, but I didn't want to disturb him. There was a wooden bench in the back yard, and I curled up on it, falling asleep almost instantly.

In the morning, I awoke with the dawn. My first thought was of the stone, searching for it in a panic before I felt it nestling inside my handkerchief. This was the burden of possessing such a thing: the constant fear of losing it. It was like the queen in a chess match, holding the greatest power and therefore the greatest risk. Any other piece must be sacrificed to preserve your queen.

A little later, Rosie spotted me through the window. She beckoned me inside before immediately shushing me out again, holding her nose.

'My goodness, what have you been doing? I'll heat some water and you can bathe in here. When did you last wash?'

It had been some days. But I had more important things to discuss.

'I have the Blood Flower, Rosie. Bill stole it and swallowed it.'

'How did you … ? Oh.' She wasn't a squeamish person. Her father had been a butcher and her first husband a slaughterer at Smithfield Market, so she knew how flesh and bone were constructed.'No wonder you stink. How did you get permission?'

'I didn't, but it had to be done. We need to know the truth.'

She sat at the other end of the bench. 'Let's see it.'

I unwrapped my handkerchief, and we both examined the red stone as though it might leap up at us or burn a hole through the cloth.

'Very nice,' she said. 'Now what?'

'Well, no one knows we have it, do they? Right now, we're probably the richest people in the county. We could buy anything we want.'

She looked thoughtful. 'You should buy a bath,' she suggested.

'I could buy one made of gold.'

'A bit heavy to move around.'

'I could hire servants to carry it for me.'

She laughed. 'Much as I would like to see you being carried on the shoulders of servants in your solid gold bath, I was hoping for something more immediate. The Blood Flower was stolen from its rightful owner, and none of us are safe while we have it. We'll be arrested or murdered. Or both.'

———

Ten kettles later, I took my first bath since I was fifteen years old.

Rosie stood guard on the other side of the door while I stepped out of my clothes and stood shivering and naked. I was so accustomed to using a bowl and flannel in my bedroom, I'd forgotten how bathing felt.

And oh, but the water was soft and warm. I sank into it with a sigh of delight. My knees stuck up like two pink, bony islands, and I swished them to and fro, creating waves that washed up towards my chin. Below the surface, the world sounded dull and hollow, but the lights above me glittered. I could have stayed there for hours.

But I didn't have time.

I took the pumice and soap, and cleaned myself thoroughly, every nook and crevice. I'd never felt so clean. And then, I dried myself and put on a tweed suit of Bill's. It was too short and too broad, but that didn't worry me. I was more concerned by the absence of the roll of cloth I'd sewn into the crotch of my own trousers. It was my illusion, my sleight of hand, but also my truth. It represented what I would've had, if my inside and outside had been made the same.

When I emerged, Rosie looked me up and down. 'Well, it's not your usual style, but at least now no one will mistake you for something the tide brought in.'

'Do I look … as I should?'

She inspected me again. 'Close enough. And thank you, by the way.'

'For what?'

'For allowing Viola to speak to Bill.' When I looked askance, she rolled her eyes. 'I know she can't speak to the spirits, Leo. It was a kind thing you did. She's calmer now, though she's hardly said a word. Wandering about like a ghost herself.'

'She'll find out it's not real eventually.'

'But not today.'

Rosie tied up my clothes in a sack and persuaded Peregrine, against his inclination, to take them to the launderer on the main road on his way to the theatre. The director of his play had called a meeting.

'I'm sure they're closing us,' he grumbled. 'This city was always full of dullards.' He sniffed at the sack. 'Jesus, Rosie, what's in this thing, a dead cat?'

When he'd gone, Rosie sat at the table while I made us a pot of tea.

'The Blood Flower is too valuable to leave lying around, so I've found this,' she said.

She picked up a slim wooden cigar box from the table and gave it a shake. I could hear a rattling sound inside.

'Good,' I said. 'Only you and I should know about it, just in case.'

I was suddenly reminded of the Artful Dodger and his silver snuffbox. I hoped not to share his fate of transportation to the colonies.

Rosie was eyeing me curiously. 'What do you suggest we do now?'

I only had one idea, and I knew she wouldn't like it. We debated for twenty minutes, and she harrumphed and complained, but she couldn't think of a better one. In the end, I composed a note and went out to the main road to find a messenger boy.

Not an hour later there was a knock at the door. But it was not who I was expecting.

Olga Brown was standing there.

'Mr Stanhope,' she said. 'Your wife sent me a message. She told me Mr Honey is here, safe and sound. I've been worrying about him.'

'Yes, of course. Come in.'

I should have thought of it. I should have sent a message to her myself, so she would know her friend wasn't missing any more. But it hadn't occurred to me. Truly, Rosie had the better heart.

I fumbled in my pocket. 'I have your shilling. Thank you for the loan, and for your kindness.'

She angled her head. 'That's quite all right. I'm glad you were able to return here. I have no faith in the police solving Natalia's murder.'

Honey was in the sitting room, fast asleep. Rosie roused him, and he was instantly awake, shrinking away from us, until he saw Miss Brown. He leapt up and gave her an embrace.

It was a curious gathering: Rosie and me, an acrobat, a mystic in weeds and a molly-boy. We didn't have enough chairs, so Honey curled up on the floor in front of the hearth, for all the world like an alabaster ornament.

Viola seemed perturbed. After casting a number of glances in Miss Brown's direction, she spoke to her slowly, as if to a child, 'Do you drink tea, like we do?'

Miss Brown blinked a couple of times. 'I do, but I'm not thirsty at the moment.' I sensed she was making an effort to remain polite. 'We have tea shops at home. It's imported over-land from China.'

Viola frowned, glancing at Rosie and me in turn. 'I see,' she said, though she clearly did not. 'Is there anything you'd prefer?'

Miss Brown shook her head. 'No, thank you. It's very kind of you to see me at all, especially after your own loss. We have that in common, I suppose. Our grief, I mean. It's an ache, isn't it? Like love unrequited. We yearn for something we can't have.'

'True,' Viola agreed, relieved to be on more solid ground. 'But I've spoken to my Bill since he died. The spirits allowed it. I may be able to do the same for you, for your friend.' She stared at her hands, her voice breaking. 'Though I admit I've never tried for someone like you, so I don't know if it'd work. And I've been better able to speak to men than ladies. It's because of my son, I think, in my belly. I'm partly male and partly female, for the time being.'

Miss Brown nodded, accepting this as plausible, though in general she seemed quite a sensible person. Honestly, I despaired of my fellow humans.

'Thank you, but I'd rather let Natalia rest. She was never peaceful in life, so perhaps ...' Her voice trailed away, and she wiped her eyes. 'I know I should get over it and carry on without her. But I don't seem to be able.'

'I'm sorry.' I felt as though we were a sort of Greek chorus, observing her private grief. 'We'll do our best to find whoever killed her.'

She inclined her head towards Honey. 'I was hoping Timothy here would be willing to help.'

He looked up, surprised to have become the focus of our attention. 'I don't know anything.'

She fixed him with a look. 'I think you do,' she said.

'Mr Black said—'

'He's not here.' Rosie gave him her warmest smile. Anyone who knew her could've told him how dangerous that was. If she truly loved you, you got amusement, impatience and an occasional eye-roll. Her smiles were reserved for other purposes. 'You're under our roof, for now. It's in your interest to tell us what you know.'

Honey looked at Miss Brown.

'Go on, Timothy,' she said.

He bit his lip and I caught sight of the boy he had so recently been. 'What do you want to know?'

'You told me before that Quinton wanted the Blood Flower, but you didn't know what it was,' I said. 'But that was a lie.'

He bowed his head and twitched as if the truth was alien to him and he wasn't sure how to form the words.

'Micky, he was a risk-taker. I'm careful, but he never was, even though he had responsibilities. He put us all in danger, nicking stuff from a customer like that. I told him so, but he wouldn't listen.'

'You fought with him,' I said. 'You pulled it from his neck. I saw the mark on his body.'

Miss Brown looked perplexed. 'The Blood Flower? What's that?'

'A ruby,' said Rosie. 'The cause of all this.'

I pointed at Honey. 'Then someone killed Micky—'

'Not *someone*,' he said. 'Mr Quinton.'

'But you don't actually *know* that.'

He gazed at us in mild surprise. 'Of course I do. He told me himself.'

The room went quiet. Rosie looked at me and back at Honey, who seemed almost amused at our puzzlement.

'I thought you knew,' he said. 'You seemed so clever.'

I shook my head, more confused than ever. This boy, this ghostly boy; I didn't know whether to believe him. Why would a man like Quinton risk making a confession to anyone, let alone a lad in Honey's line of work? And yet, I didn't think he was lying.

It occurred to me that he probably didn't expect to survive all this.

'If you knew Quinton was guilty,' I said, 'then why didn't you tell the police?'

He laughed. 'They wouldn't take my word against his, would they? Me, a molly-lad and him a fine gentleman.'

He was right, of course. No one would believe him. If justice was a pair of scales, men like Quinton had their thumbs firmly pressed down on one side.

'You could have left the city and taken the Blood Flower with you.'

'I was planning to. I heard America is a good place to start again. Catch a ship to New York. Nat was my friend and I thought she'd come too, but she couldn't make up her mind. She loved the circus. Then Mr Quinton killed her.'

'Why did he do that?'

'To accuse me. He said if I didn't give him the Blood Flower, I'd hang for her killing, and Micky's too. Or I could give it to him and live. He'd give me alibis, he said.'

If Honey was telling the truth, then Natalia had been murdered for no other reason than to gain leverage. Was that possible? Could a man be so callous? Perhaps Quinton had also been angry with her for considering leaving the circus. He didn't strike me as a man who would deal well with one of the Flying Sisters flying away.

'Didn't you have a real alibi? A witness to your whereabouts?'

Honey rolled his eyes. 'Who'd admit they were with me?'

'You were working, then,' I said. 'Were you on the ships?'

'Not the ships. No one asked for me. I went to Sailortown to find a customer.'

'Sailortown?'

'The streets around the docks, where the Navy is. And when Nat was … when that happened, I was in the cellar, asleep.'

'So, you did what Mr Quinton wanted. You gave him the Blood Flower.'

'I had no choice, did I? I told him where it was. Now he has it and all the money in the world, and Micky and Nat are dead.' His chin started to wobble, but he gathered himself and took a deep breath. 'Nat didn't deserve it. She wasn't like us, she was *good*. She thought the clouds were puppies and when it rains it's them crying.' Tears were running down his cheeks, any hint of his previous reticence gone. Once the floodgates had opened, he couldn't close them again.

Rosie gave him a handkerchief.

I spoke slowly, gathering my thoughts. 'Even if we assume that Quinton did murder Micky and Natalia, we still don't have any proof.'

'My Bill as well?' asked Viola.

I nodded, but in truth there were details I couldn't reconcile. Bill's wound was different from the first two, more hurried and desperate. My first thought was that he'd fought back, but if so, there would have been signs of defensive lacerations on his arms and hands. It made no sense.

Another knock came at the door, and I almost leapt out of my chair.

'I'll answer it,' I said.

Standing on the doorstep was Alice Morgan. She was sporting a black eye, poorly covered up with powder.

'Hello, Leo,' she said. 'I was delighted to get your note. It's a lovely day, shall we go for a walk?'

I couldn't afford to let Rosie meet Alice, so I called, 'I'm going out for a while,' over my shoulder and guided Miss Morgan back down the path and along the street.

The sun was bright, and I felt the weight of Bill's tweed suit. Another man might have taken off his jacket and slung it over his shoulder, sauntering in braces and rolled-up shirtsleeves. But I was not that man.

Besides, I liked the reassuring feel of the cigar box in my jacket pocket.

We wandered south through the side roads towards the beach, seagulls swooping and diving around us. I felt peculiar, walking beside her. Occasionally our hands would touch, or I would feel the brush of her sleeve, sending flutters across my skin. And yet, I found I could experience it with equanimity, almost like a scientist watching it from outside of myself. I allowed my fingers to brush hers and felt the reaction, as when bicarbonate of soda is mixed with vinegar: a pause before the bubbling up.

'I saw you at the circus,' she said. 'I was surprised. Where on earth did you find that suit?'

'I've borrowed it. Did Mr Quinton do that to you?'

She put a hand to her eye as if surprised I had perceived the bruise. 'He does love me, you know. He shows it in strange ways, but it's true. If he didn't, I'd be dead.'

'That's the truest sign of love: not killing someone.'

'Don't be *ordinary*, Leo. Passion has its price.' She shivered as if the sun had gone behind a cloud. 'And he may kill me yet if he doesn't recover the Blood Flower soon.'

'You must surely run away now, after he's been violent towards you.' I turned to her, very nearly taking her hands, but not quite. 'I know of a refuge in London where—'

'Are you trying to rescue me, Leo?' She cocked her head in mock innocence. 'I'm not worth it, you know. Honestly, I'm not.'

'I'm sure that's not true.'

She smiled, but it was sad, as if she was remembering a loved one long dead. 'If I ran away, Thomas would think I had it, wouldn't he? He'd be certain of my betrayal. I'd be running for ever.'

She bought two pastries and we sat on the wall by the colourful beach huts. Above us, the pier loomed. Up on the deck, people were enjoying the end of a pleasant afternoon, looking over the railings or trying their luck at games, but beneath them, the great metal struts holding up the whole edifice were white with bird droppings, and in the shadows, the swell of the sea echoed and rang.

She clutched her bag on her lap and shifted close to me, thigh to thigh, not caring that her frock was getting grubby on the wall.

'You said in your note you wanted to ask me something.'

I took a bite of my apple turnover, which was overly sweet.

'Yes,' I said. 'How well did you know Micky Long?'

'The boy who was killed? Not well. I met him a couple of times.'

'At the club?'

'Yes. What's this about?'

She pulled down the brim of her hat to shield her eyes from the sun and in that moment, in her pale blue frock, her eyes alight with curiosity, she had the beauty of a theatre star, equal to Kate Vaughan or any of the girls of the Gaiety. I could scarcely pull my eyes away from her. And yet, could she truly be called beautiful if she had coaxed a lad to risk his life for a red pebble? The better part of me said no, but there was a small minority that insisted: *yes, truly, yes.*

I swallowed hard and tossed the rest of my pastry on to the stones, where it was set upon by a fat, angry seagull.

'I was told that someone persuaded Micky Long to steal the jewel from the ship. I was told it was that person's idea.'

'Told by who?'

I noticed she wasn't denying it.

'It doesn't matter who. He would still be alive if it hadn't happened. Natalia La Blanche and Bill Broadman, too.'

She took a breath and stared out to sea. The day was clear, and the ships were sharp on the horizon like tiny shades, as though I could pick one up between my forefinger and thumb and put it into my pocket.

'I do regret that,' she said. 'But I never for a second thought he'd actually steal it. I was being playful with him, that's all. It's a fault I have, to dally and gush, and forget that others take me seriously.'

'I see. But it wasn't just playfulness, was it? You told Mr Quinton about the jewel and that's when he became interested in it. This whole thing started at that moment.'

'I thought he'd be pleased with me.' She tutted under her breath. 'You really are being no fun. I thought we were going to have a merry time. I'm truly sorry for what happened between us that night. I was scared and you were being kind, and I suppose I thought—'

'It's the jewel that concerns me, Alice. It's caused too much death already.'

'That's not my fault.' She clenched her fists in a tiny rage. 'The Blood Flower was born in war and destruction, and it carries death with it.'

I put my head in my hands, tired of these vague metaphors. 'You said as much before, that it's cursed with magic. What can that possibly mean? An artefact dug out of the ground cannot contain any more than physical properties. You're telling yourself it's magic to lessen your guilt.'

She sighed and didn't speak for a while. When she started, she didn't seem to be addressing me at all. 'Micky told me an officer on the ship showed it to him. Pillow talk, I suppose, trying to appear impressive. I can understand it. Micky was terribly handsome.' A smile twitched at the edges of her mouth. 'The officer said it was found in Madagascar. Such a romantic name, don't you think? Mad-a-gas-car.' She almost sang each syllable. 'Anyway, Thomas – Mr Quinton, that is – told me there'd been war and conflict there, and the Royal Navy had fled from it. So, you, see, the Blood Flower doesn't belong to that officer at all. He stole it the same as Micky did. The jewel itself decides whether to stay or go.'

I looked at her squarely. 'I've also been told that Mr Quinton murdered Micky Long.'

She swallowed hard. 'I don't know anything about that. I can believe it though. Not that he did it himself, but that he instructed Stephan. Thomas is a powerful man, and he wants the Blood Flower very much. Very much indeed. He believes he was *meant* to have it.' She looked at me closely, her mouth twitching. 'Do *you* have it? Is that what this is about?'

'Perhaps.'

Her eyes widened. I realised that her question had been a kind of joke and she hadn't expected that answer.

'But you didn't steal it from me.'

'Of course not. I … obtained it from the person who did.'

She licked her lips, and I could feel her desperation. The Blood Flower could save her life.

'Either way, you'd do best to get rid of it, Leo. He won't stop until he has it back.'

'I do want to return it to him,' I said. 'But with certain conditions. First, my family and me, and Mrs Broadman, must remain safe and unharmed. Is that understood? No more violence.'

'Are you asking me to tell him this?' She dusted off her hands and stood up. 'Is that why you wanted to see me? You want to *negotiate*?'

'Yes.' I allowed her to digest that while I organised my thoughts. 'Secondly, Mrs Broadman has lost her husband, thanks to Mr Quinton. She's a widow now, and without an income. She hasn't the means to pay her rent. I suggest a sum of two hundred pounds, by way of recompense for her.'

Alice's mouth turned down at the corners. 'Do you understand that he may slit my throat too?'

I was feeling shaky, but I had to stick to my plan.

'You said that he wanted it back. Well, I'm offering it to him for a very small price, considering. It could save both our lives.'

She straightened her hat, gazing out at the bathing machines. Almost all of them were empty now, and a fellow was going round to each one, checking the doors and sweeping the steps.

'You're not the person I thought you were.'

I stood up and looked her in the eye. 'I'm not the *man* you thought I was. Do we have a deal?'

'Will you cease your investigation and not mention Thomas in your newspaper?'

'Yes.'

'Then I'm certain he'll agree. Do you have the jewel with you?'

She asked the question in a relaxed fashion, but she was gripping the clasp of her bag so tightly her knuckles were white.

'It's safe.'

Without meaning to, I patted my jacket pocket, and her eyes followed my hand.

'Show me.'

'It's not necessary. I wouldn't lie to you.'

Of course, that was itself a lie. I was an expert at deception. I had concocted an entire boyhood for the benefit of Alfie and Constance.

'Even so. Show it to me.'

I pulled the cigar box out of my pocket, and she extended her hand as if I would give it to her without hesitation. I opened up the box and tipped the Blood Flower into my palm.

Except it wasn't the Blood Flower. It was a piece of shingle, like a million others on the beach.

She stood up and took a step away. 'Is this a jape? Are you mocking me?'

'No.' I realised I was gazing at the thing as if it might change into a ruby before my eyes. 'I'm sorry, it was here ...' My mind was a blank. Where could it be? Ah, I thought, of course. Rosie. 'I suspect that my wife didn't trust me with it.'

'She's probably halfway to France by now.'

'No, she wouldn't do that.' I took off my hat and wiped my brow with my sleeve, feeling suddenly too hot.

Alice slung her bag on to her shoulder. 'Well, you do seem genuinely surprised.' A forlorn smile crossed her face, making a dimple in her cheek. 'Your wife is a wise woman.'

'That she is. But I do have the ruby so please convey my offer to Mr Quinton.'

'You can tell him yourself. Papaver will be reopening after the unfortunate events of the other night. Free entry before ten all this week.'

'I hardly think that would be safe, Alice. No, we'll meet back here tomorrow. In this spot, at this time. Just you and Quinton, not Stephan.'

'Very well. But I must warn you, Leo, the Blood Flower will betray you. It's made of death, and it pulls or repels as it wishes.'

And with that, she stalked away and didn't once glance back.

For a time, I sat on the beach, musing. It was madness to think that an inanimate object could have magical powers. And yet, Rosie took Communion every Sunday, consuming the Host as the blood and body of a man who had died more than eighteen and a half centuries ago. Was that any more reasonable? Even I, the son of a vicar and therefore ill-disposed towards any form of religion, could feel the touch of God. How else could I explain the dichotomy of my body and soul? Someone had to take the blame.

But a ruby was nothing more than a stone. You could cut it and set it and give it an exotic name, but it was still an object, no more capable of choosing to stay or go, to pull or repel, than the piece of shingle in my hand.

Pull or repel. Something about that phrase intrigued me. These myths and rumours always had a source of some kind, however distant.

I walked swiftly north, following the main road until I came to the telegraph office. I scribbled my question to Jacob. He was a jeweller and would know the answer.

Can a ruby be magnetic?

That done, I hurried on to my next destination: the police station. For my plan to work I needed the help of Sergeant Dorling.

I was damned if I'd let Quinton get away with three murders.

21

I ARRIVED AT THE police station as Dorling was coming out. A black carriage had drawn up in the street and he began giving the driver instructions.

'Sergeant!' I called as I approached him. 'I need to speak with you.'

He opened the carriage door and indicated I should get inside. 'Very well. You can keep me company.'

This seemed uncharacteristically genial, but I was glad to have the conversation in private.

The carriage was plain and dark, with two wooden benches facing one another. Dorling indicated the bench opposite him, which meant I would be travelling backwards, never my preference.

'What do you want?' he asked. 'Did the widow Broadman finally say something useful about her husband's death?'

'No, she hasn't said anything, but—'

'I knew Bill Broadman from years back, you know. He was trouble from the off. Petty larceny, moving stolen goods, you name it. Wasn't above a bit of stealing neither. The world's better off without him, some might say.'

I hope this didn't mean he would be making even less effort to catch Bill's killer. Not that his efforts had yielded any results so far.

'I may have some useful information for you, Sergeant. I have good reason to think Mr Quinton ordered the three killings.'

As I was saying the words out loud, I knew they weren't strictly true. Honey had told us a great deal about the deaths of Natalia and Micky, but nothing about Bill.

'And what is this reason?'

'I will tell you, but—'

'Hmm.' He stared out of the window. We were passing the railway station, heading north. 'Are you about to propose another deal, Stanhope? Seems to me that our previous arrangements haven't work out very well, at least for me. I still haven't seen any sign of an article praising our work here, and when we went to that club, no crime was being committed. Some damn fool story about rehearsing a play. You live and learn, I suppose. I'm not buying this time.'

'Mr Quinton ordered their murders for the Blood Flower, Sergeant.'

He scoffed. 'Ah, the rumoured ruby, more valuable than a barrel of gold. And magical, to boot.' He fluttered his fingers in front of him, presumably to indicate something supernatural, and then laughed. 'A lot of nonsense. I doubt it's real.'

'It is real. And Quinton killed Micky Long and Natalia La Blanche for it. I need your help in proving his guilt. I'm not proposing a deal; I'm giving you an opportunity to catch a murderer.'

'And for you to get a good story, I'm sure.'

Out of the window, I could pick out the masts and anchor lines of the ships in the harbour, and beyond them, the grey smear of Gosport on the other side. The familiar stink was growing.

'Where are we going, Sergeant?'

His mouth split into a smile, like a lemon being broken open.

'Finally, a sensible question. See, there was a break-in at the hospital last night. Sad to say, someone desecrated a body. Can you guess which one?'

My heart started thumping so hard I thought it must be audible.

'How would I know?'

'It was your own brother-in-law. Someone cut him up.'

'What? That's awful.' I did my best to look shocked. 'Body snatchers, I suppose.'

'No bodies were taken. Seems more like someone was *rummaging* inside of him. I remember you told me you'd been an assistant to a surgeon of the dead, Mr Stanhope.'

'So?'

'You'd know all about a man's guts, wouldn't you? How the parts fit together.'

In the half-dark of the carriage, I hoped he couldn't see the redness blossoming on my cheeks. I swallowed hard and raised my chin.

'Are you accusing me, Sergeant? Why on earth would I break into a hospital to search through Bill's organs?'

He raised his eyebrows. 'See, there's the thing. Up until a minute ago, I wouldn't've been able to hazard a guess at that. But you mentioning the ruby, the Blood Flower, well, it's given me an inkling.'

I had wondered why he'd been willing to let me ride with him in the carriage, and now I knew. He wasn't a complete fool, this sergeant. There was at least one detective inspector in London I could name who couldn't match his wits.

'You said you didn't believe it was real.'

He interlocked his fingers and pointed both forefingers at me. 'And you said it definitely is.'

'I had nothing to do with what happened to Bill. I'm a respectable journalist and I'm more interested in who killed him than who cut him open after he was dead. And what about Natalia La Blanche and Micky Long? Don't you want to arrest their killer?'

Dorling sighed deeply. 'I suppose you'd better tell me what you have in mind.'

———

Having explained my plan to the sergeant and gained his reluctant agreement, I was not anxious to remain in his company. The feeling appeared to be mutual. As we reached the queues heading for the hospital, he opened the carriage door and indicated I should exit.

The sun was setting by the time I got back to Viola's house. Rosie opened the door before I could knock, alerted by Jack-the-bloody-dog's barking. I was assailed by the unmistakeable aroma of fish pie.

Rosie's expression was grim. 'The landlord heard about Bill,' she said. 'He came round. Luckily, we'd finished cleaning up.'

'How long does she have?'

'Six weeks, and that's every penny she owned. After that, she's out. She'll be giving birth homeless and broke.'

I had the urge to put my arm around my wife's shoulders, but I couldn't. That wasn't how we were.

'We won't let that happen.'

She led me through to the back room. The fish pie was on the table, mostly eaten but with a good helping still left in the bowl.

Viola was staring out of the window at the yard. 'Mr Black's at the theatre,' she murmured. 'He said he'd be back later in case anyone comes to murder us. I've made up Eddie's bed for him.'

'What about Mr Honey?'

'He left with that ... with Miss Brown. She said they had space at their lodging. Mr Black came back before they left and there was an argument. I think she has a poor opinion of Mr Black.'

I glanced in Rosie's direction. 'I'm sure you did nothing to dissuade her from that view.'

She inclined her head in affirmation. 'I don't think well of a man who brings a gun into the house.'

'Oh, you saw that, did you? I shouldn't worry. I'm sure it's a theatre prop, not real.'

'Even a fake gun can be dangerous if someone *thinks* it's real.' She pushed the remains of the pie in my direction. 'Codling and apple, and there's a bowl of kale on the dresser.'

She spoke casually, almost apologetically, but it was the best news a person could receive. If I hadn't missed her remarkable cooking while we were apart, it was only because I'd missed Rosie herself so much more.

I explained that my afternoon had been a success.

'Quinton will meet us at the pier tomorrow evening at nine o'clock. Alice – Miss Morgan – will come too.'

Rosie looked nauseated. 'And the sergeant?'

'Dorling agreed. He'll get there early and hide under the pier.'

Rosie looked vaguely surprised, but also impressed. 'You'll have to persuade Mr Quinton to confess to the murders,' she said. 'It won't be easy.'

'I know. And there's something else too, something I need to test.' I turned to my sister-in-law. 'Viola, did Bill own a compass?'

She stirred as if reaching wakefulness after a nap. 'No, but I do.'

'*You* have one?'

A compass seemed an entirely practical item. I couldn't imagine Viola having such a need.

'Of course. Haven't you heard of the Vegvisir? The Viking rune of a compass. It keeps you safe when you can't find your way.' She clutched her hands together on the table, her knuckles white. 'Though I confess my own way is still unclear to me.'

I was trying very hard to remain patient. 'I need an actual proper compass that points north, not a rune. Do you have one of those?'

'Yes. I mean, I think it points north.'

Pull and repel.

When Viola had left the room, I exchanged a look with Rosie, or I attempted to, which is to say I gave her a look which she correctly interpreted as scepticism and chose not to return.

'You removed the stone from the box,' I said to her. 'You don't trust me.'

Her expression didn't change. She had no qualms. 'It seemed prudent. I trust your honesty absolutely, but this woman … she's manipulative, Leo, and you have a tendency to be soft-hearted.'

'I'm not a fool. I would never have given it to her.'

'Probably not, but why take the chance? You're not a fool, but you do believe you can save people. You think it's heroic. You think that's what it is to be a man.'

'Isn't it?'

She gave me a wan smile. 'Not in my experience.'

243

Viola returned with a metal compass the size of a small clock, its face inscribed with a symbol. I thought it rather elegant and pretty, and somewhat regretted having doubted her before.

'Thank you,' I said. 'Rosie, would you fetch the jewel please?'

She reached into her apron pocket and produced it, as if it was something she'd picked off the floor and hitherto forgotten about.

Viola gazed at it. 'What a beautiful thing,' she said. 'But also evil. I can see that. It's made from blood.'

The compass needle was pointing at the dresser.

'Due north,' I said, nodding in that direction. 'And south is that way, towards the sea.'

I took the stone and placed it directly next to the needle, and then moved it a quarter of an inch around the perimeter, still touching the metal body of the compass. The needle went with it.

Rosie watched, open-mouthed.

'That's not possible,' she said.

I moved it further, so the stone was at the north-west point, and then west and all the way round to the south. Each time, the needle followed. I found that if I went too fast, the connection was lost and the needle swung back towards the dresser. But if I was careful, moving the stone a tiny distance each time, I could rotate the needle through a full 360 degrees.

Viola shivered and backed away from the table. 'I told you that thing is evil.'

That evening, I remained alone in the sitting room with a glass of Bill's unpleasant whisky, wondering why Jacob hadn't replied to my telegram. I chose a book from the bookshelf to distract myself, a copy of *Oliver Twist*, which, as far as I could tell, had never been opened. I had just settled down in an armchair when Peregrine came back from the theatre, the blush of his stage make-up still colouring his cheeks.

'They're closing us down,' he declared, sprawling on the sofa. 'Hardly anyone was in again tonight. The locals don't appreciate true art. They'd rather watch people dangling cannons from their teeth.'

'Yes, I heard you didn't get on well with Miss Brown.'

'She believes her talent is the equal of Shakespeare's.' He lit one of his sweet cigarettes and eyed me through the smoke. 'Half her audience is only there to see a woman in her underclothes. Oh, don't look at me like that. I wasn't unkind to her, I promise.'

'And Mr Honey left with her.'

He gave a plaintive shrug. 'He does as he pleases.'

I sensed that my friend's feelings had been hurt, so I poured him a glass of whisky and topped up my own.

'Well, I'm sorry about your play. I'm sorry about everything, Peregrine.'

A smile lit up his doleful face. 'Oh, that's all right. You're forgiven. And as for the play, it's for the best. The director wants us to go back to London with *The Merry Wives*.' He lifted his chin dramatically. 'I am to be his Falstaff. So, you see, it's an ill wind which blows no man to good.'

'Well, that is welcome news. Congratulations.' We clinked glasses. 'The whisky is ghastly, I warn you.'

'Excellent. I much prefer bad whisky to good. You know where you stand with a truly terrible whisky. It asks nothing of you.'

'You realise that's completely meaningless, don't you?'

'Yes, but I prefer bad conversation too. And bad clothes, though not as bad as what you're wearing.'

His exuberance, often an irritating feature of his personality, was oddly comforting when faced with the possibility of imminent death. My plan had seemed flawless when I'd devised it, but with every passing minute I was less and less convinced.

'Thank you for being here,' I said. 'We need all the help we can muster.' My voice was hoarse. The whisky was burning the skin from the back of my throat.

'I couldn't leave you to your own devices, could I? Especially after you got Quinton and Stephan off my back. Anyway, I quite like a scrap. It's been a while.'

'It might be worse than a scrap. Quinton knows we have the stone. I wouldn't be surprised if he comes here tonight to take it.'

Peregrine considered the prospect. 'Why would he, when you've agreed to give it to him tomorrow?'

'To save himself two hundred pounds, which was my price. He wouldn't have believed me if I'd offered to hand over a jewel of such value for nothing. But now, we're at risk, and if something happens—'

'We'll be ready.' Peregrine gulped his whisky and pulled a face. 'Christ, what awful stuff. If Quinton doesn't kill us, this will.'

I swirled the alcohol around in the glass. As it stilled, sediment drifted down to the bottom.

'Are you ever going to tell me your story, Peregrine?'

He surveyed me. 'What story?'

'Yours. All right, let me guess. I think you know this town better than you claim.'

He shrugged. 'I know lots of places. I've toured all over England.'

'No, it's more than that. You were brought up here, weren't you?'

He sat back in the sofa. 'I wasn't *brought up* anywhere.'

The way he said it was laced with bitterness, but also pride. He had created himself, much as I had.

'I see. An orphanage then?'

'For a while.' He grimaced at my expression. 'Don't pity me, Leo. It was perfectly fine. They did their best with what they had.' He nodded towards my book. 'You read too much Dickens.'

I could see he was growing annoyed at my intrusiveness, but I was feeling reckless. My dread of the next day was diluting my usual reserve. I supposed this was how Alice had felt when she lost the Blood Flower; all the normal boundaries collapsed, and nothing meant anything any more.

'And after that, you were on the street, I dare say. Honey said something about you I thought was interesting. He said you asked for nothing in return. That's what set me thinking. You look after these lads, give them somewhere to stay and some money, because you were one of them once. Am I right?'

'It was a long time ago. I was a child.'

'But you haven't forgotten. You're giving them the helping hand you didn't get. That's why you were in debt to Quinton.'

'Don't be romantic. These lads aren't saintly, sickly Oliver Twist and I'm not Mr bloody Brownlow. A few pennies and a night of safety, that's all they get.' He downed his whisky. 'Not everyone's like you.'

'No one's like me.'

'I'm not talking about *that*.' He waggled a finger up and down to indicate my physical self. 'That's all very difficult, I'm sure, but you were *brought up* in a nice, safe home with food on the table, weren't you? No doubt your mother made you say your prayers before she tucked you in. You left because you *chose* to.'

I sensed that his anger with me hadn't altogether drained away.

'I had to leave.'

'You probably thought so, but it was a choice you were able to make. You might consider, just occasionally, that you're not actually the most unfortunate person on the planet. It's pure arrogance to think that God has singled you out.'

I didn't reply, stewing in my resentment and imagining that he was doing the same.

Eventually, he held out his glass and I poured him another tot.

'Mrs Mackay called you her Thrush.'

He sighed deeply. 'You don't bloody give up, do you? Very well. The orphanage gave me a name, but I never used it after I left. The girls called me Thrush because they thought I had a nice singing voice. I was Thrush for years.'

I had a vision of a small boy entertaining the girls between their appointments; moments of simple delight for them to hold on to.

'Why did you change it?'

'Thrushes are little birds, aren't they? They get eaten by bigger birds. So, I chose to be Peregrine. Seemed like a good idea when I was sixteen, as with so many things.'

My recklessness was fading as quickly as it had come, replaced by a feeling of exhaustion. I yawned, and Peregrine yawned in sympathy.

'Your sister-in-law put my things in the back room,' he said. 'The bed vacated by that drip Hapsworth. Still smells of his pomade. You can take it if you'd rather.'

'No, I'll sleep on the sofa.'

At least, I thought, it was more comfortable than the bench outside.

Peregrine heaved himself up and bade me goodnight.

As he left the room, I called after him, 'Goodnight, Thrush,' and relished his roar of laughter.

I had managed to get myself comfortable on the sofa when I heard another noise. I leapt up, about to rush to the window and look outside, when I realised it was Rosie, coming in from the back room in her dressing gown.

'You can't sleep there,' she said.

Her voice was croaky, as if she'd recently awoken, and her hair was like wild grass.

'I'll be all right. I'll get up before Viola. She won't know we didn't sleep in the same bed.'

Rosie shook her head. 'No, and I'm too tired to argue. You're going into danger tomorrow and you need a proper night's sleep. Come along.'

And so, for the first time, after more than a year of marriage, I was able to join my wife in bed; or, more accurately, on a straw mattress so narrow we were pressed together, our shoulders and feet touching. We stared up at the cracks in the ceiling plaster, and I was reminded of being back at the vicarage. My favourite times were when my sister allowed me to share her bed, reading me stories before Mother came up to insist that we said our prayers. Peregrine had been right about that.

I blew out the candle and within ten minutes, Rosie was gently snoring.

The night was damp and sweaty, and I found myself overly warm beneath the blanket. I stuck a leg out into the cooler air and then shoved the blanket aside completely, lying in my drawers and undershirt, having removed my binding. The skin under my arms had been scoured to callouses and needed this respite.

I realised that I didn't feel exposed, though I wasn't alone. Rosie was different. There was nothing of me I wouldn't allow her to see.

Finally, I went to sleep.

I was jolted awake by sounds outside. I went to the parlour window, but it was only some drunken fellows coming back from somewhere, two of them towing a third along the street in a handcart.

I returned to bed, and Rosie stirred and turned over, facing away from me.

I hadn't intended to look. I held Rosie in the highest esteem and wouldn't dream of prying and peeking while she was asleep. But as I pulled back the covers to get in, I couldn't help but see her skin under her nightdress. From one shoulder blade to the other, scars criss-crossed, some an inch long and some seven or eight times that length. My scientific mind told me they were old and long-healed, but another part, the feral part, wanted to take the throat of the man who did this to her and squeeze until his face went blue. But I could not. Jack Flowers was long dead.

'What is it?' she mumbled.

I must have inadvertently gasped, or perhaps she'd been disturbed by my getting up. Neither of us was used to sharing a bed these days.

'Go back to sleep,' I whispered.

She turned to face me, her cheek squashed by the pillow and her hair straggling across her forehead. Our faces were no more than eight inches apart.

'Are you worrying about tomorrow?'

'No.' It was only partially a lie. 'Do you regret us marrying?'

'I don't know, Leo. We didn't really think everything through, did we?'

'Not everything, no.'

She closed her eyes again, but I sensed that she was still awake. The rattle of the handcart in the street grew quieter and faded to nothing.

'Is it because of Jack? What he did to you?'

She stiffened. 'That's in the past. You're not him. I wouldn't've married you if I'd thought for a second—'

'I know, but you must remember what happened. We carry our hardest times with us, don't we, no matter what we do? Anyone bitten by a dog must afterwards be a bit more nervous of dogs.'

'You're not like other dogs.'

'Maybe I am.'

She put her palm to my cheek, a rare gesture. 'Oh, Leo. It's not only your fault: I haven't been fair to you.'

I smiled and closed my eyes. 'We're in an unusual situation.'

'That we are. Now go to sleep.'

———

In the morning, I dozed, listening to Rosie's singing. She was always up at six; you could set your clock by her. Viola was still in bed, where she'd been for much of the last two days, and Peregrine was rarely up before ten. So, when I heard a noise outside, I was alert in an instant.

I ran into the parlour and peeked out between the curtains. I could hear voices and caught sight of someone going round to the back of the house. Jack-the-bloody-dog started barking and then, cutting through the racket, a scream – it was Rosie.

I reached the door in one second flat, before realising that her scream was one of delight.

And a voice: 'Bah! This whole town smells worse than a cesspit.'

Jacob! I couldn't imagine what he was doing here.

I didn't want to greet him in my drawers and undershirt. Fortunately, my clothes were still in the parlour, so I was able to get dressed in private, using an onyx pyramid as a mirror to tie my ascot.

In the back room, Rosie was frying eggs, and Jacob was seated at the table with his back to me, his hat in one hand and his cane in the other. What little hair he had left was every which way, and I could see his pink scalp beneath it, blotchy and scabbed where he'd bumped into things. Facing him at the table was Constance.

'Mr Stanhope,' she said, forgetting that she was now calling me 'Leo'. 'I was just hearing how a man tried to sell you a partridge that was really a crow.'

'Oh, yes. On the train.'

It seemed like a decade ago.

'Crow meat is perfectly edible,' said Rosie. 'I simply objected to him lying about it.'

Jacob tapped his cane on the floor. 'Why are we talking about damned crows?'

Outside of his home, he was prone to irritability. In fact, it was true inside his home as well, but was worse when he was out.

I squeezed his shoulder. 'It's good to see you, Jacob. What would you rather talk about?'

He looked up at me, and I could see in his face that he regretted his outburst. Sometimes, he was like two people, one of them constantly frustrated by the other.

'I don't … I mean, I don't mind. We could talk about …' He clicked his fingers.

'Rubies,' offered Constance. 'That's why we came. Mr Kleiner was telling me all about them on the way. It was most interesting.'

I doubted that very much, but I admired her diplomacy.

'Yes!' barked Jacob, suddenly animated. 'Rubies. You sent me a telegram. I came immediately. Miss …' he clicked his fingers again, harder this time, as if the louder sound would force his memory to bend to his will. It didn't work. 'She wanted to come also, and I was happy to allow it.'

'Does your father know you're here, Constance?'

Her eyes slid away towards the yard. 'I may have forgotten to mention it to him.'

I was about to commence an avuncular lecture on the topic of responsibility but caught Rosie's brisk shake of the head.

'Constance told me that *Mrs* Kleiner suggested she might like to accompany Mr Kleiner on the journey,' she said. 'They took the early train and will be back by late afternoon.' She gave Constance a pointed look. 'Won't you?'

I understood. Jacob had insisted on coming and Lilya, concerned he might get lost, had asked Constance to go as well. It suited Jacob to think he'd brought Constance, but the truth was that she'd brought him.

'Ah, yes, the train,' said Jacob. 'That was a duel. The *pridurok* at the ticket office refused to sell me a second-class ticket. Can you believe it?'

'We encountered some problems,' Constance said, a flicker of anguish crossing her face. 'But third class was perfectly all right.'

'He called me a name,' said Jacob. 'A bad word for a Jew. I won't repeat it. I almost turned back. Nearly, but not quite. I had to come.'

'Because of the ruby?'

'Yes, of course. Why else? You think I want to sit on the beach?'

'It might help your complexion.'

He laughed, and his sour mood was broken. Indeed, he was positively cheerful as we ate our fried eggs and bread, and he told us a story about a customer of his who'd bought a ring for the woman he hoped would become his wife. The poor sap had tried it on his sister's finger first, only to find it couldn't be removed.

'I told the sister I would cut it off with a saw,' he said, his whiskers twitching. 'And she screamed. She thought I meant her finger.'

He hooted with laughter, and we all laughed along, though I had heard the story several times before. The details changed depending upon his audience. Sometimes, as now, it was a customer's sister who tried on the ring, but if Constance hadn't been present, the same role would have been taken by the customer's former wife. Had Jacob and I been alone, it would have been a prostitute the customer had visited. This was the way with him; lots of bluster, but he really just wanted to make people happy.

When we had finished breakfast and I'd enjoyed my second cup of tea, Rosie left the room and came back with the cigar box. She tipped out the Blood Flower on to the table.

'My goodness,' exclaimed Constance. 'It's beautiful. Is it real?'

Jacob peered at it down his nose and waved a hand towards Constance. 'Fetch my case from the hall.'

She was so captivated, she did as she was told without a murmur. Jacob rummaged through his case and produced a loupe and two cloths. He polished the stone thoroughly with one of the cloths and placed it in the centre of the other. Against the white cotton, it shone blood red.

'A fine colour,' he said, looking at me over the top of his spectacles. 'And nicely cut too. Excellent workmanship. And you think it is … *magnetic*, yes? That it has the ability to leap from its own chain.'

'Yes. I mean, I know it can't leap from its chain, but it truly is magnetic. I tested it with a compass. But rubies can't be magnetic. They're not made of metal.'

'Hmm. You're right. And you're wrong.' He sniffed and sat back in his chair. 'Mostly wrong.'

I wasn't going to rise to his bait. Constance was less patient.

'What do you mean?'

'First, you are wrong that things have to be metal to be magnetic. Ask Mr Clerk Maxwell, he will tell you.'

I saw no point in informing him that the acclaimed physicist had been dead for three or four years. Jacob tended to treat such demises as personal affronts.

'What am I right about?'

'You're right that rubies are not magnetic.'

'This one is.'

He grinned, enjoying the attention. 'Yes, but that's because you're wrong about something else. This is not a ruby.'

I stared at him. 'What? Then what is it?'

He placed the stone under his loupe. 'I will tell you in a moment. But certainly not a ruby. Can you imagine if it was? It's, what, twelve carats? Fifteen? A ruby of this size would be worth a fortune. It would belong in your Queen's crown jewels.'

He removed his spectacles and put his eye to the lens, taking on a stillness I was familiar with. When working, he was utterly engrossed.

In the silence that followed, I could hear Jack-the-bloody-dog wheezing in his sleep in the next room.

After a few seconds, Jacob looked up. 'Red tourmaline,' he said. 'Some call it rubellite.'

Rosie folded her arms. 'So, it's not valuable?'

'Oh, it is. You or I could not afford it.'

'How much?'

'Hmm.' He moved his hands up and down like a pair of scales. 'Twenty guineas, perhaps. Or twenty-five, depending on the weight. You're lucky, actually. I thought at first it was a garnet, which would have been less. But it's a tourmaline, I'm sure of it. A lovely colour, but not exactly like a ruby.'

I put my head in my hands. All those secrets, deceptions and deaths for a misunderstanding. Twenty guineas? Six months of my salary. I almost wished it had been made of glass, completely worthless, the kind of thing you could buy at a stall on the seafront. But twenty guineas? That was God laughing at us.

'People have died for this stone,' I said.

He picked it up and squinted at it, so from my perspective he appeared to have a bright red eye. 'People have died for less, my friend, believe me. Much less.'

'And one of these – what did you call it – a tourmaline? They're magnetic, are they?'

'They can be. Manganese and iron in the crystal. Unusual in a red one, but not unknown. It's a lovely piece. What will you do with it?'

I exchanged a look with Rosie. 'As of this minute, I really have no idea.'

She picked up the Blood Flower and dropped it back into the cigar case. 'We don't have a choice. We must continue with the plan.'

'How can we? I've asked Quinton for two hundred pounds, which I thought was a fraction of its worth. But now we know it's far too much.'

'But he doesn't know that, does he?' Rosie started pacing up and down. 'And by the time he finds out, he'll be in prison.'

'What plan?' asked Constance, her face lighting up.

'Nothing you need be concerned about,' I said.

I tried to imagine myself handing over the Blood Flower to Quinton, acting as though it was worth tens of thousands of pounds when in fact it was worth twenty guineas, maybe twenty-five, depending on its weight. If I'd been scared before, now I was truly terrified.

Rosie was still pacing, her heels clicking on the floor. 'More than that, you've arranged to meet him. So, if you don't give him the jewel, he'll think you've kept it for yourself, and then we're really in trouble.'

Jacob was looking from one of us to the other. 'If you can sell this gemstone, this tourmaline, for two hundred pounds, then do it. Otherwise, I know people in the trade who'll buy it for a fair price. Very fair.'

'What trouble?' asked Constance, leaning forward.

She'd been known to complain that her life was tedious and lacked excitement, and I fully intended to keep it that way. In fact, her questions had decided me on my first course of action. I would dearly love to have spent the afternoon playing chess with Jacob and taking Constance to one of the tea-rooms on the seafront for cakes. I yearned to listen to them talk and watch them breathe and know that they were whole and well.

But the risk was too great.

'How's Lilya?' I asked Jacob. 'I hope she's quite safe without you there to care for her.'

'Hmm,' he muttered. 'Yes, quite safe. She's less clumsy than me. She finds her way by sense of smell, I think.' He pondered for a moment. I could always tell his moods from the way his whiskers twitched. 'But still, perhaps we should go back. She will be worried for me.'

'This soon?' Constance looked aghast. 'I thought we'd spend most of the day. I want to see the sea, at least.'

Jack-the-bloody-dog trotted in, his tail wagging, and before I could stop her, Constance leaned down to stroke him. I was certain she'd be bitten, but instead the evil monster started licking her hand. It was infuriating.

'I'll go with you to get a cab,' I said. 'We can go via the beach.'

The weather was delightful, neither too cold nor too humid, with bright sunshine and a gentle breeze coming off the sea. We walked along the promenade at Jacob's speed, and I listened to his griping with peculiar joy. This was true magic: the familiar, the day-to-day, the expected. Alice had called me *ordinary* and meant it as an insult, but ordinariness was all I desired.

'How's that new lodger at the pharmacy?' I asked Constance. 'What was his name?'

She quickened her pace. 'I'm sure he's quite well.'

'You seemed … struck by him when I was there.'

She raised her eyebrows unconvincingly. 'Would you prefer I was rude to him?'

I made a play of considering the question. 'Your father probably would.'

'Father didn't like him initially but has warmed to him since he expressed certain views. My opinion has gone in the opposite direction.'

'Oh? What views did he express?'

Her face hardened. 'That a woman has no place in the medical profession. Or any profession. He believes we're not capable of rational thought and should restrict our ambitions to mothering babies and housekeeping.'

'I see. Well, it's certainly been a bad week for lodgers.'

Jacob had caught up to us. He could still make a reasonable pace on the downhill slopes. 'What nonsense!' he exclaimed, winning a rare look of approval from Constance. 'I know of at least one woman who's been an assistant to a surgeon in a hospital and is now a journalist. A poor one, but that has nothing to do with her sex.'

Truly, I would suffer this treatment from no one else in the world. I directed a filthy look at him, and he gave me a broad wink. Fortunately, Constance was pondering his point and didn't notice.

'She's followed a similar path to yours, Mr Stanhope. How amusing. Though of course, you're a *fine* journalist.'

'Well, thank you. I do my best. Shall we go on to the beach?'

Jacob said he'd seen more than enough of the sea in his youth and had no wish to examine it further, so Constance and I were alone as we picked over the shingle, avoiding the horse dung and half-clad bathers coming and going from the beach huts and bathing machines. When we reached the water's edge, she crouched down, not minding her damp hems.

'I'm glad you've apologised to Mrs Stanhope. She truly is a most admirable lady, and the two of you are a perfect match. But I also wish ...' She swished her fingers in the sea. 'When you lived with us in Little Pulteney Street, it was the best of times, wasn't it? Just you and Father and me.'

'Indeed, it was. The best of times.'

After a few minutes, she'd seen enough. We walked back and found a cab on the promenade, and I watched them climb inside.

'I hope you get a second-class ticket for the train this time.'

Jacob scowled. 'Bah! Let them try and stop me.'

Constance leaned out the window as they pulled away. 'And we won't buy any crows!'

I watched them go, feeling that part of my heart was leaving with them.

I walked slowly back to Viola's house, lost in my own morbid imaginings about what might happen that evening. A carriage was waiting in the street and a man was standing beside it. As I pushed open the gate, he tapped me on the shoulder.

'Mr Stanhope, is it?'

'Yes.'

I turned, and he punched me in the stomach.

22

MY VISION WENT BLACK, and I had to crouch down, struggling to regain my breath. The pain was spreading outwards from my stomach to my chest and bowels. I didn't dare look up at the fellow. His heavy boots were scuffing the paving, as though he wanted nothing more than for me to stand, so he could punch me again.

A voice came from the direction of the carriage.

'Was that necessary, Fenny? He wasn't going to be any trouble.'

The fellow who had hit me spat on the ground. 'Never does any harm to make sure.'

I held up one hand. 'What do you want?'

'You, mate.' He hauled me to my feet and looked into my eyes. 'Are you all right?' He patted my cheek. "Course you are.'

I had never seen him before. He was my height, but heavier, dressed plainly, with lavish sideburns decorating a face you would otherwise forget.

My intakes of breath were causing sharp pains in my chest, and I was having trouble straightening to my full height.

The driver rapped his knuckles on the wooden seat. 'Let's go.'

My assailant rubbed his hands together and a smell wafted into my nostrils: the silt of the harbour. 'You've got a choice now, Mr Stanhope. Or may I call you Leo? Leo, it is.' He indicated the carriage as if inviting me into his parlour. 'You can get in now, like a good boy, or I can hit you again first. Either way, you're coming with us.'

I had no idea what would happen if I got into that carriage. I had a vision of lying on the beach by the bridge, my throat neatly cut.

Viola's house was agonisingly close, and Peregrine was probably inside. I took a shallow breath, testing the contractions of my stomach muscles.

I was quick, but was I quick enough to reach the front door before they caught me? Probably not. And the house was hardly a castle. Being trapped inside with these two circling like hungry dogs wasn't a pleasant prospect. And no matter what came next, I couldn't allow them anywhere near Rosie.

Which left only one choice.

I started towards the carriage, allowing the fellow to get half a step ahead of me. I braced myself, took one agonising lungful of air and elbowed him hard and sharp in the kidney. He let out the smallest groan and tried to twist away, but these days I knew how to win a fight: don't talk, don't think, don't hold back and don't stop until it's over. I punched him hard in the back of his neck with my right fist and he staggered forward with an 'oof'. I brought up my left towards his face.

I would not be taken. The last few years had exhausted my patience with ruffians and bullies. I'd been burned, beaten and half-drowned, and had decided with absolute conviction: never again.

So much for that.

He turned, slapped my fist out of the way, grabbed my jacket and slammed his head into the bridge of my nose. A blinding pain shot across my cheeks and up into my forehead.

I made one last attempt to swing at him, but I could hardly see, and he dodged it easily. I heard him laugh. He was enjoying this. He danced around behind me, grabbing me around the neck with his forearm, and pulled me sharply backwards so I was right at the point of falling. He held me there, perfectly balanced, neither quite dropping nor able to stand upright.

'Last chance, Leo. Get in the carriage or I'll be tempted to get nasty.'

I nodded, and this time I meant it. He shoved me forwards, and I climbed inside. He followed me in and sat on the bench opposite, so we were knee to knee like old mates on our way to the pub.

The driver flicked his whip and, as we were leaving, I heard a shout. I looked back through the rear window and a figure was running after us, waving both hands. My eyes were watering liberally, and I couldn't properly see who it was. She shouted again, and I knew it was Rosie. But she was too late.

We reached the junction and turned westwards into the city.

My assailant put out his hand, but I declined to shake it. My mother always told me that politeness is never wasted, but of late I'd begun to wonder whether she'd acquired enough experience in her life to make that determination with certainty.

'Fenwick,' he said. 'Nice to make your acquaintance.' He thumbed towards the driver. 'And that's Mr Hall.'

He handed me a rag and I put it to my face. My nose was bleeding and sore as hell, but the bone appeared to be intact.

'Why are you doing this? I've arranged to meet Mr Quinton later anyway. There was no need for violence.'

Fenwick stretched out his back, twisting left and right, wincing a little. 'Cuts both ways, Leo. Nice shot you got in there. Didn't think you had it in you.'

'What does he want with me? I don't have the ... object with me. I won't renege. Tell him that and let me out.'

His mouth formed a sneer. 'Renege? *Renege?*' He tapped on the roof of the carriage. 'Hey, Hallsy, what does *renege* mean?'

A voice came down from the front. 'It means to back out or default, usually on a deal. It's the kinds of behaviour that gets a bloke into trouble. Like *renegade*, you see?'

'Oh.' Fenwick seemed to process this information and then called up to his friend. 'You ever reneged on a deal, Hallsy?'

'Can't say I have.'

'Good man. Seems like a pretty low thing to do.'

I wasn't impressed by this double act. 'I spoke with Alice Morgan yesterday. I asked her to tell Mr Quinton he could have it. All of this is pointless.'

A chill was creeping into my chest. Why was this happening if Alice had passed on my message? And then an icier feeling still. What if she hadn't?

We had already passed the turn-off for Papaver, so we weren't going to meet Quinton there. And we couldn't be headed to the New Hippodrome either as that was far behind us. He must have an office somewhere, I thought; a lair where he counted his money.

Fenwick was biting his nails, a contrarily boyish act.

'I have a question,' he said. 'It's been eating away at me for the last couple of minutes. I'm a man of curiosity. Not educated, I grant you, but keen as mustard to learn.'

I watched his eyes, wondering whether I should refuse to play this man's game. But I could still feel the ache where he'd hit me. Better wits than fists.

'What's your question?'

'It's this. Who's this *Mr Quinton* you keep talking about? I've no idea who he is.'

My skin seemed to shrink on my bones. If Quinton hadn't sent them, then who had? And where did these men come from? Every single other person I'd met in this ghastly town had recognised his name. I realised I'd already given them an awful lot of information on the assumption they came from Quinton. I would have to be more careful from now on.

'He's an important man and I've arranged to meet him later. You must let me out.'

If I didn't attend the meeting as planned, Quinton would certainly go to Viola's house and take the Blood Flower by force.

Fenwick patted me on the knee. 'Sorry, Leo, no can do. Looks like you're going to have to *renege* after all.'

We took the main road, passing the police station, and veered north through a maze of shaded side streets. We emerged next to the railway bridge, and I feared he would force me out and on to a train, and then what? Where would we go?

But we continued, around a park dotted with trees and a Navy barracks, and into a residential area; narrow lanes with houses tightly packed on either side, each one coordinated with its neighbours, the same black doors and white window frames. Even the brass knockers and numbers matched, as if someone had measured them with a ruler. But the buildings weren't the only things that were identical. Everywhere I looked, there were sailors dressed in loose blue trousers and shirts, white scarves tied around their necks.

Fenwick pulled down the window and exchanged friendly words with one of them about a recent fracas at a pub they called The Nut. I had the impression the two men had been on opposite sides, and yet they seemed quite affable now, treating the event more like a sports fixture than a battle.

Afterwards, we turned north and progressed at a slower pace, obstructed by the sheer volume of people, mostly sailors, spilling off the pavement and into the road, so close we could have leaned out of the window and prodded their caps from their heads.

'You're in the Navy,' I said.

Fenwick gave me a sarcastic clap. 'Very good, Leo. I'm Petty Officer Fenwick and my friend there is Hall. He's a civilian.' He spread his arms as if showing off his own estate. 'Welcome to Sailortown.'

'Mr Chastain sent you.'

'You mean *Lieutenant* Chastain. Show due respect to the Royal Navy. That's the way of it.'

'Where are we going?'

'You'll find out soon.' He grinned. 'I hope you don't get seasick.'

We pulled up by a stable next to a vast quay, milling with people. Two huge ships were groaning and aching, attached to the dock with ropes thicker than my waist.

Hall left the carriage with a rating who looked about twelve years old, and the three of us went down a ramp to a wooden pontoon. As we dropped below the quay, the noise changed, from the hubbub of people and creaking of ships to the slapping of waves against the concrete wall and clinking of halyards on masts.

They led me to a substantial clinker rowing boat, perhaps sixteen feet long, with three rowlocks either side, but only two oars.

'Get in,' said Fenwick.

I had very little experience of the sea, having been brought up about as far inland as it was possible to get. I suffered a pang of unease, lowering my foot on to the wooden seat, feeling it rise and fall with the movement of the water. The last time I had been on a boat, I'd thrown myself off it and almost drowned.

'Hurry up,' said Hall. He was a pinch-faced fellow with a restless manner.

I sat down gingerly. The two men untied the boat, fore and aft, and jumped in. They picked up an oar each and used them to push us away from the pontoon. Then they settled in to row, with me facing them like a lady being courted on the Serpentine.

I kept my expression neutral and tried not to shiver in the chill wind. No need for them to see how nervous I was. After ten minutes, I broke the silence. 'How did you know where I was staying?'

Fenwick was red-faced, speaking only as he leaned forward and groaning with effort as he pulled back.

'Mr Honey was kind enough ... ugh ... to tell us when we found him ... ugh ... at the circus place.'

'Did you hurt him or Miss Brown?'

'Only a little, and ... ugh ... no Miss Brown with him ... ugh ... just some darky bobtail was all.'

It didn't seem worth continuing the conversation, and anyway, the boat was starting to get buffeted by the chop in the harbour. The waves were small, but when they hit us at a particular angle, they slopped over the gunwales, soaking my captors and puddling around my shoes. It wasn't long before I had to pull my feet up on to the seat to keep my trousers dry.

We skirted a couple of single-masted ships and headed across the harbour towards Gosport on the other side. But gradually, the hazy grey cranes started to slip away to our left, and I realised the tide was sucking us into the harbour along a sort of channel between the mudflats.

An hour into our journey, the patches of glistening mud shrank away, and we were in open water, surrounded by craft of all sizes and types. Some were not much bigger than our rowing boat, while others were proud sailing vessels with portholes and colourful paintwork. A couple were stocky steamships, the noise of their engines throbbing across the water. Almost all were anchored, though we did pass a schooner making slow progress towards the open sea, its sails barely filling. Fenwick saluted, and a sailor at the prow returned the gesture.

Not long later, both men stowed their oars and started bailing out water, now seven or eight inches deep. The boat spun slowly, still being pulled by the tide, sliding into the lee of a hulking iron barge which blotted out the light.

As we emerged from its shadow, Fenwick looked up and pointed. 'Ain't she a beauty.'

I looked over my shoulder, and there was the sleekest ship I'd ever seen. Nothing on the Thames could compare. She was the length of a football pitch, red at the waterline, black on the hull and a shining white on the rails. At the centre was a giant steam funnel that spoke of speed, and either side of that, circular shapes like giant hat boxes.

From where we were, still several hundred feet away, I could hear the sound of hammering.

Fenwick was watching my reaction like a proud father. 'The *Colossus*. Newest in the fleet, not yet finished. Still waiting for her artillery. Hall here is working on the engines, aren't you, mate?'

Hall emptied the last dregs of water over the side from his pail. 'Engineer, see.'

A thought occurred to me, and I felt a shiver run across my skin. These men were surprisingly free with their names and positions. I wondered whether they were intending to kill me.

Of course, my thoughts strayed back to Rosie, her voice crying out as the carriage pulled away. If I die here, I thought, I hope she doesn't try to find out what happened to me. Better she goes home and forgets all about this place.

I still had her ring in my pocket. I touched the circle of metal through the cloth and felt myself calmed.

The two men went back to their oars and, as we neared the *Colossus*, Fenwick threw a couple of fenders over the side and hurled a rope up to a sailor on the deck. The fellow dropped us back along the hull towards a ladder, the pitch and roll of the sea becoming more violent, throwing us against the side of the ship with a metallic clank.

'Up you go, Leo,' said Fenwick.

I caught hold of the ladder and tried to lift my foot to the bottom rung, but our boat was lurching and bucking, and I was forced to let go. I tried again, getting one foot on to it, but found my weight neither fully on the ladder nor fully on the rowing boat, and the gap between the two getting larger. Another second, and I would be in the water, in danger of being crushed between the hulls. I felt a shove on my behind and managed to pull myself on to the bottom rung. Behind me, I could hear Fenwick's jeering laughter.

'Ain't got your sea legs yet.'

I reached the top and clambered on to the deck. The racket was deafening. Half a dozen men were on their knees hammering rivets into the decking. None took any notice of me.

Fenwick came up the ladder behind me and pointed towards a door. 'This way.'

He clapped Hall on the back by way of a cheerio and ducked under the lintel, leading me down some steps and into the bowels of the ship. The corridor below was too narrow for two men to walk side by side, so I had to follow him, our shoes ringing on the floor and my nostrils filling with the smell of new paint. The sound of hammering became hollow and echoic, and I was reminded of being in the iron bath at Viola's house. What a moment that had been.

Fenwick knocked on a door and Chastain himself opened it. He was wearing a naval uniform, but compared with the last time I'd seen him, he was dishevelled. He hadn't shaved or brushed his hair, and his face was pasty and shining with sweat.

'Mr Stanhope. You're very welcome here. Please come in.' He turned to Fenwick. 'You can go.'

Fenwick stuck his hands in his pockets. 'Payment of half a crown was mentioned, sir, and sixpence for Mr Hall. I'm sure you wouldn't *renege* on that, as Mr Stanhope here would say.'

The man simply wouldn't let go of an idea, once it had entered his head.

Chastain's expression grew colder. 'Later, Petty Officer. This isn't the time.'

There was something about how he said it that made me suspicious. I wasn't the only one. Fenwick eyed his superior for a few seconds.

'Your debt is growing, sir. These trips to fetch gentlemen on your behalf do add up.'

Chastain glared at him. 'We have an arrangement, you and me. I will keep my part of it, and you keep yours.'

Fenwick angled his head in acquiescence. 'I'll be very keen to see that you do, sir, as will Mr Hall, I'm sure. Keen as mustard, we'll be.'

He stalked away down the corridor.

Chastain indicated I should sit on one of the three hard chairs. The room was as plain as the inside of a biscuit tin.

He looked at me up and down, and left the room, returning with a dripping flannel. 'Wipe your face,' he said. 'You have blood on it. I'm sorry for the manner of your arrival. The petty officer isn't as gentle as I'd prefer. I can't offer you anything, I'm afraid.'

I admit that even in this place, shivering mostly with cold, but a little with fear, I was disappointed not to get a pot of tea.

'What do you want, Lieutenant?'

He sat down, his elbows on his knees and his foot tapping on the metal floor. Despite his efforts to appear calm, his fidgetiness gave him away.

'An object was stolen from me, as you know. An object of great value.'

'A jewel,' I said. 'The Blood Flower.'

He nodded. 'So, you already know. Good. That makes this easier. I would like it back.'

'How did you come by it?'

'We were in Africa. Madagascar. Our government, in their wisdom, decided to abandon the island to the French. I was on the *Dragon* at the time, and we had to ship out at short notice.

The locals hated us for leaving, and they were right. We followed orders, but it was a betrayal of trust. An act of cowardice.'

Though he was speaking calmly, I sensed an anger boiling below the surface. He talked about the 'locals', but I was certain he was referring to a single person. A lover, perhaps.

'And you decided to take a prize with you.'

'They called it the *Voninkazo Ra*. The Blood Flower. But it wasn't plunder.' His mouth twitched into an unconvincing smile. 'Why leave such a treasure to the French?'

The noise from the deck shifted in tone and volume; someone was hammering right above our heads.

'I want your agreement to something.' He had to speak loudly to make himself heard over the din. 'I represent the Royal Navy. You're a journalist, and you know things that I've done, things my superiors would frown upon.'

'Frown upon? Three people have been murdered.'

He looked at me in surprise. 'Not the *murders*, Mr Stanhope. Those people were of no importance to the Royal Navy. No, it's something else altogether that would concern them. That's where I'd like some assurances from you.'

'Oh, I see. You're referring to the visits of Micky Long and Timothy Honey to this ship. And others, I'm sure.'

He blinked, struggling to maintain his composure. 'Quite. I propose a business arrangement. In exchange for your discretion, I will share one tenth of the ruby's value with you. Furthermore, if you ensure its safe return to me, I will pay you another tenth. That's a considerable amount of money.'

I had no desire to write tittle-tattle about a naval officer's liaisons with young men. I cared about Natalia, Micky and Bill, their lives snuffed out like tallow candles. And I cared about the people they'd left behind. But even so, my mind was whirring. He still believed the Blood Flower was immensely valuable. I wondered how he'd react if I told him that it was worth about six months of my meagre wages.

The hammering changed again, moving further down the deck like thunder rolling along a valley.

'You may be assured of my discretion,' I said.

'Good. But keep in mind, if avarice starts to influence your judgement, that the Royal Navy has considerable resources at its disposal. They don't like to be embarrassed. It would be very much in your interests to keep your word.'

'I understand.'

He looked relieved. 'Now, as to the gem itself, I know that Mr Honey is no longer in possession of it. The outstanding question is, where is it now? He's been in the company of a man named Black, I believe. An *artist* and an *actor*.' His manner suggested he thought of these as depraved occupations. 'My belief is that Honey has given the ruby to this fellow Black. Furthermore, I believe that you know the man. Last time we met you were very keen to dissuade me from approaching him.' He steepled his fingers. 'Of course, you can see how this implicates you.'

'Not really.'

'It suggests you've been party to a deception, a plot to keep me from my property. But now, with our arrangement, your interests and mine have aligned. You stand to earn twenty per cent. You will give me the fellow's address as a token of good faith.'

Of course, I couldn't do that. And besides, as soon as Chastain had the stone, or knew where to find it, I would probably be tipped into the harbour with deck rivets tied to my feet.

'Mr Black doesn't have it, Lieutenant.'

'How can you be certain?'

When I didn't immediately reply, Chastain leaned back in his chair. Gradually, he smiled.

'Ah, I see. That is a surprise. It's you. You have the Blood Flower.'

I could feel the balls of my fingers itching.

'Not with me, but yes, I know where it is.'

'In that case—'

'You're probably thinking you can hold me here and search for it at my sister-in-law's house. Or that you can torture me until I give you the location. But there's no need.'

He rubbed his chin, still staring at me.

'Why?'

'I've arranged to meet Mr Quinton at nine o'clock tonight. I'm going to give the Blood Flower to him.'

Chastain raised his eyebrows. 'I don't understand. How does that help me?'

'I also have an agreement with Sergeant Dorling, the policeman who's investigating the murders of Miss La Blanche, Mr Long and Mr Broadman. He will lie in wait under the pier, within earshot. I shall coax Mr Quinton into admitting that he's guilty and the sergeant will arrest him and retrieve the gem. Then the police will restore it to its rightful owner. You.'

Chastain weighed up my proposal, finally shaking his head. 'That all seems rather complicated.'

I had to agree. As I was explaining my plan, I couldn't help but conclude it was destined for failure.

'Perhaps, but what are your choices, Lieutenant? My wife saw me leave with your men earlier. There are lots of people on this ship. Keeping me here will be a gamble at best.' I sat back with my hands behind my head, a posture I couldn't remember attempting before. 'I'm giving you a chance to get your property back with the least possible risk, recovered for you by the police, no less. You can pay me my twenty per cent and keep the balance. And Mr Quinton won't be able to threaten you because he'll be in prison. It's the perfect solution for you.'

He narrowed his eyes. 'You're a clever man, Mr Stanhope.'

My goodness, I thought, I do hope so.

It took a further fifteen minutes to persuade Chastain that he shouldn't accompany me to my appointment with Quinton. But eventually he sent for Fenwick, who arrived eating a baked potato wrapped in paper, and instructed him to take me safely ashore. Fenwick wasn't keen, but after some discussion, they seemed to reach a financial accommodation.

'Time for another trip, Leo,' he growled at me. 'Hallsy ain't going to like it though. Not one bit.'

The journey back was hellish. The tide was still coming in, so the two men had to work twice as hard as on the trip out. If they stopped pulling on the oars to take a breath, the boat started to spin and drift back the way we'd come. Fortunately, the wind and waves had dropped almost to nothing, so we remained dry, but a thick fog was descending on to the water, meaning we were reliant on Fenwick's handheld compass to know in which direction we were heading. The needle kept sticking, prompting him to curse and shake it vigorously, once slamming it against the thwart. I feared he would break it, and we would be lost completely.

They rowed for an eternity. Hall was as relentless as a steam-pump, but Fenwick was soon red-faced and puffing. Eventually, he begged for a pause.

The stench of the fog was sickening, sulphurous, like the Bermondsey tanneries on a still summer day, except this fog was cold and damp, sticking to my skin and clogging up my lungs.

'This is far enough,' he said. 'Let's do it.'

They stowed their oars and Fenwick stood up, setting the boat to rocking. I backed away to the furthest point of the bow.

'What are you doing? Far enough for what?'

He came towards me, rubbing his hands together. 'Can you swim, Leo?'

'Listen,' I said. 'I won't tell anyone who you are, I promise. I don't remember your names. Please take me to the shore.'

He grabbed my collar and pulled me to my feet. 'We don't care if you know our names, Leo. We're the Royal bloody Navy.'

The boat tipped alarmingly as he dragged me towards the edge.

'No,' I pleaded. 'Stop this minute. Lieutenant Chastain is an officer. You must respect his rank, remember? That's what you said. And he told you to take me back safely, didn't he? Didn't he?'

'I said *you* had to respect his rank, not me.' He patted me on the cheek. 'Every trip I take for 'im, I raise the price. Started at sixpence and now it's half a crown. One day soon he'll stop paying and I'll wring the buggerer's neck and sink him. A person like that on the *Colossus*, and an officer to boot? It ain't right.'

I tried to struggle, but he was too strong and far steadier on his feet. It was all over in a second. He gave me a shove backwards and I flailed briefly, whirling my arms, before crashing into the water. The last thing I saw before it closed over me was Fenwick and Hall looking down, huge grins on their faces.

The water was freezing and all I could see was grey as I floundered, trying to bring myself up to the surface despite the weight of my clothing. The water had seemed calm from the boat, but now it was chaotic, slapping against my face and filling my throat. I managed to take a breath but couldn't inhale enough air to raise a shout. The cold had stolen all the strength from my lungs.

And then, my feet touched the mud. I stood up. The water only came to my chest.

Fenwick pointed behind me. 'The shore's that way.'

I turned to half-wade, half-swim in the direction he was pointing, hearing their laughter ringing across the water. The mud sucked on my feet, and I feared I might get stuck, but Fenwick and Hall kept an eye on me, circling in the boat, until a low quay emerged from the fog. I climbed up on to it and turned, intending to yell a few obscenities in their direction, but they were already pulling on their oars, heading back to the *Colossus*.

I squeezed as much water as I could from my clothing, but even so, goosebumps were rising on my arms and thighs. Wet footprints followed me alongside the harbour.

I had no idea where I was, but I knew the city was on a peninsula, so if I headed south I must eventually end up somewhere I recognised. There was no pavement, and the road wasn't much more than a mud track, so I didn't pass anyone on foot. But several carts went by, splashing dirt on to my clothing. Finally, I reached somewhere familiar: the hospital. It was the last place I wanted to be as I could ill-afford someone to recognise me from my last visit. But at least now I knew where I was.

I headed inland, reaching a paved road lined with tenements, shops and guest houses. It was crammed with people, eyeing me and talking behind their hands. One lad asked with a snigger if

I'd been for a swim. I didn't reply. A sort of fatalism had engulfed me. I cared not a jot what anyone said or thought.

The church bell chimed for eight o'clock and I quickened my pace. I had less than an hour until I was supposed to meet Quinton by the pier.

I passed the train station and the barracks near Sailortown and the common next to the beach. My stomach was growling, my feet were sore and I was as filthy as any mudlark. I made the final mile on sheer determination, pounding one foot in front of the other like a boy stamping on ants. By the time I was in sight of Viola's house, my teeth were clamped together so hard, my jaw ached.

The lamps were lit inside. Rosie opened the door to me.

'Leo! Thank God. Who were those—'

'I'm all right. What's the time?'

'Almost nine. But Leo—'

'I mustn't keep Quinton waiting. Please fetch the Blood Flower.'

She didn't move and for a moment I thought she was reluctant to let me have it. But then I noticed her flushed cheeks and wet eyes.

'What is it, Rosie? What's wrong?'

'Viola's gone. And she's taken the Blood Flower with her.'

23

'WHERE DID SHE GO?'

'I don't know.' Rosie flapped her arms like a fledging sparrow. 'She told me she needed to consult the spirits and it might take a while. I thought she meant an hour. Later, I realised she'd taken the Blood Flower with her. We've looked everywhere I could think of. Mr Black's still searching.'

'I don't understand. Is she intending to sell it?'

I was thinking of my sister-in-law's impending eviction. Twenty guineas would pay her rent for the next couple of years at least.

'No, she wouldn't do that,' said Rosie. 'She has no head for money, and she believes the thing's evil. I'm starting to wonder if she's right.'

'What are we to do now?'

I was feeling dizzy, so I sat on the bottom step of the stairs, leaning with my back against the door to the upstairs neighbours' rooms. My suit was grey with dried mud, my cilice had rubbed my skin to a pulp, my hair was stiff with salt and I'd lost my favourite hat in the harbour.

Rosie sat beside me and examined the bridge of my nose where Fenwick had butted me.

'Hold still. This will hurt.' She tested the cartilage while I clenched my teeth and fists. 'It's not broken. I'll get some Calvert's.'

She went into the back room, came back with a bottle and a cloth and sat beside me.

'This will hurt more.' She dabbed the cut, and I almost cried out. When she'd finished, the cloth was pink.

I took a deep breath.

'Do you still have that box with the pebble inside?'

Rosie blinked three times. 'You can't be thinking of going ahead with your plan? Without the Blood Flower?'

'What choice do we have? If I can coax Quinton into confessing to the murders before he realises I don't have it, then Sergeant Dorling can arrest him. He'll never realise he was being fooled.'

'But what if he doesn't confess? What if he demands to see it?'

'I'll run.' I had no other consolation for her. 'This was always going to be a bluff. He thinks the stone's worth a fortune when it isn't. Now, it's a bigger bluff, that's all.'

'That's all? You're going to get yourself killed and I won't be close enough to stop it.'

We were still sitting side by side. Once again, I was reminded of being a child at the vicarage. On the rare occasions when my sister had committed a misdeed – sitting with her knees not pressed together or feeding Pilgrim from the table – she was made to sit on the step, and I, four years her junior and her supporter in all things, would sit beside her. I would not be gainsaid and screamed and hurled myself on the floor if denied. I could comprehend no other way to be; if she must suffer, so must I.

'Not this time, Rosie. But if I don't meet Quinton, we'll never know for sure who committed those murders and he'll go free. Plus, he'll assume we've stolen his precious property and come after us. You, me and the children. I have to do this.'

She took my hand, which showed how much danger she thought I was in. 'Do you have my ring with you, Leo?'

For a moment I feared it might have been lost in the water, but then I felt it in my jacket pocket. I pulled it out and cleaned it with my sleeve before handing it to Rosie. She held it up briefly, turning it in the light, and then popped it on to her finger.

'Thank you. I missed it when it wasn't there.' She twisted it round and round. 'I made a mutton and date pie for us. We can have it together later.'

I didn't know what to say. My heart was too full.

Peregrine burst in through the front door, whipping off his hat and drawing in a huge breath as if he were on stage and about to deliver a grand speech. Rosie and I leaned forward expectantly, but he sagged against the wall.

'No sign, I'm afraid. I tried everywhere. Knocked up all the neighbours, but no one's seen her. The fellow over the road suggested she might have gone through the veil to the spirits, but I think he was joking.' He wiped his brow on the curtain. 'What happened to you, laddie?'

'Nothing of consequence. I have to go and meet Quinton now. Alone.'

He cracked his knuckles. 'It doesn't sit well with me, to stay out of things. But all right, I'll watch from the road.'

Rosie stood up. 'And me.'

'Very well,' I said. 'But no closer than that. And regardless of what happens, you cannot intervene.'

———

At the roadside, Peregrine clapped me on the shoulder and Rosie gave me that rarest of things: a brief hug. She pressed the cigar box into my hand. I opened it, and it contained what looked like a bone. I looked closer, and it was a tooth, or a pair of teeth bonded together. She gave me a what-did-you-expect look.

'I tried a pebble, a nut and a cotton reel, but they didn't sound like a precious jewel rattling about. And I'd bought a sheep's head from the butcher this morning, so ...'

I closed the box and put it into my jacket pocket. 'Very well. I'll try to sell a sheep's tooth to a murderer for two hundred pounds. Why not?'

I didn't look back at them as I took the concrete steps down to the beach. If I had, I wouldn't have been able to continue. This might be it, I thought. This might be the end of me. After fire and water and beatings, and all the sorrows and elations in between, these might be my last minutes. I felt as I had only felt once before: knowing that death was coming and yet prepared to face it. Every other time, it had chased me and almost caught me, but somehow I had wriggled free. But now I was walking towards it.

One last breath.

The pier loomed above me, a black shadow leading into the sea. Up there, another world was thriving, brightly lit and noisy with music and stallholders entreating their customers to come and play. *Dice, dice*, I could hear. *Why not try your luck?* Young couples were leaning over the railing, throwing bread into the air for seagulls to catch. I doubted they could see me. I was one more shadow amidst all the others: beach huts drained of their colour by the dusk, bathing machines hauled up above the tide-line and fishermen's dinghies upside down on the shingle, their chains trailing across the groynes.

I was about halfway down the beach when I saw two figures ahead of me, lit by the orange lights of the pier against the blue-grey expanse of the sea. One of them was a woman in a long frock, the hems of her skirts pulled clear of the wet ground, and the other was a stout gentleman in a bowler hat, who was turning from side to side, the very embodiment of impatience. I kept to the gloom, my eyes searching under the pier for the sergeant. He was there somewhere, I thought, waiting to spring out from between the metal struts and lumps of concrete.

Behind me, I heard a sound, a crunch of boots on the shingle. I turned, fearing Peregrine or Rosie had followed me against my instructions, but it was the beggar who'd stolen my bench a few nights before. He was wearing a mould-stained sweater reaching almost to his knees.

'Can you spare a farthing, sir? I'd dearly like a bite to eat.'

I dug in my pocket and pulled out a twopenny bit. 'It's not safe here. Take this and go home, please.'

How ridiculous that sounded. His home was a bench. He skulked away towards the road, relieved, I supposed, to have an evening not battling with the seagulls for scraps.

I was within hailing distance of the two figures at the shore-line when I heard more footsteps behind me. I turned, ready to command the old boy to go back the way he'd come, when I realised it wasn't him. It was Stephan.

'Keep going,' he said.

At the shoreline, Alice gave me the briefest of bows, holding my eyes long enough to prompt a fluttering in my chest. Quinton went to tip his hat but stopped, frowning at my appearance. Indeed, I was a mess, my suit stained grey and white with mud and salt, and my nose bruised and grown to the size of a bread roll. And I was exuding a stinking miasma that would embarrass Jack-the-bloody-dog. Quinton was, naturally, dressed immaculately in black boots, a pinstriped suit, a silk cravat and a bowler of exacting proportions. I felt like a scruffy jackdaw between a pair of elegant jays.

'You're late,' he said, looking me up and down. 'What the hell happened to you? Have you been swimming?'

I ignored his questions. 'I told you this should just be the three of us. I was quite explicit about that.'

He was looking bored. 'I don't take instructions from anyone, least of all someone like you.'

'I know you don't trust journalists, but I'm very competent, I assure you. I do my research. I know you're a killer.' I glanced at Stephan, who had sauntered into the darker shadows under the pier and was perching on an iron crossbeam. 'My friends know I'm here and who I'm meeting. You can't hurt me.'

As I said it, I could feel the cigar box in my pocket, and imagined the sheep's tooth inside. No, no, I told myself, you can't do that. You have to believe it's a ruby that could buy an army or a fleet of ships. If you don't believe it, they won't.

Quinton shrugged. 'Don't need to hurt you, do I?' He pointed his finger at me. 'You're going to give me the Blood Flower anyway. Let's get on with it and we can all get off this damned beach. I'm due a large whisky at the club.'

I couldn't stop myself from peering into the blackness for a sign of Dorling. I knew he was a former military man. Perhaps he was more adept at camouflage than he was at police work. I had no choice but to assume he was.

'There was a price, Mr Quinton. I explained it to Alice ... to Miss Morgan.'

He turned towards her as if needing a reminder, though I was certain no such detail would have escaped him.

'I did tell you, Thomas,' she said, playing along. 'Safety for him and Mrs Stanhope. And her sister ...' She clicked her fingers. 'I don't recall her name. And a sum of money. I think it was two hundred pounds.' She smiled in my direction, but it was a hollow thing, a bell with no ringer. 'Was that everything, Leo?'

'It was. A small price to pay for a ruby of this size.'

Quinton sniggered. 'Two hundred pounds, a small price? It's more than a year of your wages, I'll warrant.'

Considerably more, but I wasn't going to tell him that.

'My sister-in-law has lost a husband,' I said. 'You took him from her. She's penniless now and I think two hundred pounds is the very least you should do.'

He blew out his cheeks and looked up at the rapidly darkening sky. 'I knew I shouldn't have come here. You were right, Stephan. I should've gone straight to the club and let you deal with this. My inquisitiveness got the better of me, I confess. I had to see it with my own eyes.'

Stephan said nothing and I waited, feeling the thump of my heartbeat and listening to the gentle wash of the sea. This conversation wasn't going as I'd expected. Why was Quinton quibbling over the money?

'Do we have a deal, Mr Quinton?'

'Miss Morgan here told me something very interesting about you. Unexpected, you might say, but definitely interesting.' He looked at Alice. 'Didn't you, sweetheart?'

She kept her gaze out to sea, not meeting my eye. I couldn't believe it of her. Surely, she hadn't told him my secret.

'I'm sorry, Leo,' she said, hardly loudly enough to hear. 'I didn't have a choice. Mother told him you'd visited my house. It's why ...' She pointed to her bruised eye.

Quinton rubbed his hands together. 'I don't like my property being messed with, see. Another man enjoying the meal I've bought and paid for. That ain't right. So, when I saw you mooning after Alice at the Hippodrome, well ... I may have lost my temper. But then she tells me you're really a female, and that's altogether different. Girls will be girls.' He examined me, top to toe and back again. 'Wouldn't have believed it before, but now ... yes, maybe. Under that bloody awful suit there's a cunny and a pair of dugs.' He licked his lips, and I felt a shiver run between my shoulder blades.

'Do we have a deal?' I said again. I could hear my voice shaking.

'No, we do not. See, there are a couple of problems with your proposal. First, a ruby that size would certainly be worth a lot more than two hundred pounds. But it's not a ruby.' His expression turned almost to one of pity. 'I'm sorry, but did you seriously think I'd let Miss Morgan wear it around her neck in public if it was a real ruby? Not a chance. Christ, if she'd lost something of that value, I'd have left her by the bridge to bleach.'

I felt a creature clawing inside me, climbing up into my throat.

Alice's mouth was hanging open, not, I suspected, because of his threat – she must have long ago become accustomed to his violent nature – but because he hadn't thought her worthy of his confidence. He hadn't told her the Blood Flower wasn't a ruby.

'You had it checked,' I said.

'Of course I did, as soon as I got my hands on it. I'm a businessman, not an idiot. That was a big disappointment, I can tell you. It's a pretty thing, but it ain't worth two hundred pounds.'

For some reason, my mouth felt so dry I could hardly force out any words.

'You killed three people for it.'

He pointed his finger again. It was a habit with him.

'Ah, you see, that's the second thing. It was two people, not three. I'm a stickler for the numbers. I didn't do nothing to your brother-in-law. If I'd found him, I'd have gutted him like a fish, much like I'm guessing you did – except I'd've done it while he was still alive. Then I'd have the Blood Flower in my possession, and we wouldn't be having this conversation. But I didn't find him or kill him, so I don't owe his widow a farthing.'

The problem was that I believed him; not because I thought he was in any way trustworthy, but because it made sense. Of course he wouldn't have let Alice wear the Blood Flower at the Hippodrome if he'd thought it was a real ruby. And that meant he'd known what it was worth when Bill was killed. Why would a man in Quinton's position risk the noose for twenty-five guineas?

'And Micky Long?'

Quinton shrugged. 'I wanted the stone. I thought it was worth something then, didn't know it was fake. But he didn't have it. That molly-boy Honey had nicked it off him.'

'You didn't need to kill him.'

'Well, I was in two minds, but my friend here gets pleasure from that kind of thing.' He nodded at Stephan, who was as still as statuary. 'He's an artist. He's got what you might call *finesse*.'

I shuddered. 'And you killed Natalia La Blanche to get leverage over Honey. He would be hanged for her murder without your alibis.'

He angled his head in acknowledgement. 'Very good, but not the only reason. Natalia La Blanche was a wastrel. Unreliable. She was talking about going to America of all places. I overheard her discussing it with Miss La La. *She's* the real star and I didn't want La Blanche putting ideas in her head. I'm planning to do the whole show about Miss La La and get rid of most of the others, the hangers-on.' He spread out his hands, picturing the poster. 'The African Princess! Jungle theme, with snakes and monkeys and such. There's a lot of interest in that kind of thing these days.'

'She's not from Africa.'

'Eh? Truly?' His mouth twitched into a brief smile as if he thought I was joking. When he realised I wasn't, his expression returned to its previous sourness. 'Well, it doesn't matter. Now you know it all and can't prove any of it.'

I glanced in the direction of the pier. Where was Dorling? Surely, Quinton's confession was sufficient, and about now, the sergeant should be springing out to capture his man. What the hell was he waiting for?

I had no choice but to stall for more time.

'I still don't know who murdered Bill Broadman.'

He sighed and gazed up at the blackening night sky. 'This again? Damned if I know. Or care. Give me the Blood Flower.'

I pulled the box from my pocket and rattled it. His eyes followed the box. He hated to lose anything he considered his own.

'It's worth twenty-five guineas,' I said. 'But I'll forgo a monetary price in exchange for the truth.'

'Stanhope! I'm impressed. You knew what it was all along, and still attempted to con me out of two hundred pounds. Bravo.'

He started clapping, and Stephan joined in, his huge hands making a sound like gunfire on the empty beach. Alice seemed lost in thought, watching the distant dots of light on the horizon.

I thought I heard a sound from under the pier, a movement of stones. It could have been a bird or that old fellow again, but my better sense told me the tread was heavier and more deliberate: finally, Dorling was getting ready to pounce. Stephan heard it too and looked round, seeming uneasy for a moment before settling back into his previous serenity.

And yet, the sergeant did not appear.

Quinton held out his hand. 'No more chit-chat.'

I could feel panic pinching at the soles of my feet and palms. A dash straight up the beach, I thought. That was my only chance. Take the steepest slope to make a disadvantage of Stephan's extra weight and height. I swallowed and took another breath, shoving the cigar case into my pocket. Now or never.

Quick as lightning, I was gone.

I heard Quinton's exclamation of rage and felt the swish of Stephan's lunge as his fingers brushed my jacket. I pushed against the stones and felt them slip and slide under my shoes, until I fell forwards on to my hands, half-running, half-crawling up the beach towards the lights of the road.

I would have made it. I very nearly did. But I was unlucky. As Stephan dived forwards, his fingers grasped the very hem of my trouser leg. I fell, scrabbling with my hands against the shifting pebbles, unable to get any purchase. Stephan clawed over my body on his hands and knees, finally sitting astride me.

Quinton leaned down and pulled the cigar box from my jacket pocket. 'That's enough of that,' he said.

I didn't have much breath under Stephan's weight, but I managed to gather enough for one last shout: 'Dorling! Dorling!'

There was no reply.

Quinton peered at my face. 'Oh dear, are you still hoping the brave policeman's going to come and save you? The sergeant told me of your little plan right after you proposed it to him. He ain't coming.'

24

STEPHAN CLIMBED OFF ME, and I rolled to a seated position. He took hold of my lapels with his right hand and, with his left, reached into his pocket and produced a bone-handled paring knife of the kind Rosie kept in her kitchen at home.

Oh, Rosie, Rosie, Rosie. What madness came upon me that night? And what wouldn't I give to be at home with you now, in our rooms behind the shop, reading my book by the fire and listening to the clicking and clacking of your knitting needles.

Alice was wringing her hands. 'Please, Thomas,' she said. 'Let's go home. I'm cold. We've got what we came for.'

He didn't look at her. 'Have we? I'm thinking some punishment is due for all the inconvenience I've suffered in the recovery of my property.'

'Didn't you say you're a businessman, Mr Quinton?' I said. 'How would hurting me help you?'

He chuckled. 'I'm in business the same way you're a man, Stanhope. Only for appearances.'

Stephan moved the knife to my throat, his eyes slightly narrowed, focused on the blade as it gently scratched me, cold against my skin. Instantly, I knew it must be the weapon that had killed Natalia and Micky. It had cut into their necks and through their windpipes, and those eyes had followed it with a surgeon's care, making precise incisions, not a quarter-inch too deep or too shallow.

But not Bill. Whoever had killed him had imitated Stephan's work, but the result was ragged and slanted, lacking his exactitude.

I shrank away from the blade and heard Stephan's 'tut' of frustration. He had an exact point on my neck in mind and was impatient to be getting on with it. He was just waiting for Quinton's permission.

I felt a serenity settle over me. Sometimes, it was that way. Amidst all the turmoil and panic, there was always a part of me that wasn't caught up. It was my soul, I had concluded. Having spent so long observing my physical self for the slightest slip, the wrong gesture or an unwanted lightness in my tone of voice, my soul had become disconnected from the rest of me, a thing apart, untouchable.

Rosie had a different explanation. She claimed my mind was made of honeycomb, each tiny hexagon containing its own drop of sweetness, independent of every other.

Again, I heard a sound from under the pier. And this time, I saw something too, just for a couple of seconds: a black shoe catching the shine of the lamps on the promenade. If it wasn't Dorling, then who was it?

Quinton pulled a face. 'Not here.' He pointed a finger at me. 'Bring her with us.'

'"Him",' I said, through gritted teeth, but no one was listening.

Stephan pulled me upright, and a noise came from the direction of the road, a rush of stones like an avalanche. It leapt towards us with an ursine roar, and I threw myself out of its way. Peregrine was in full flight, head forward, fists tight against his body. He hammered into Stephan, who was thrown backwards into the rubble under the pier, landing with an awful crack.

Quinton backed away towards the sea, keeping Alice behind him. Peregrine took a step towards them, teeth bared.

'Mr Black, please,' said Alice. 'I wouldn't have let them hurt Mr Stanhope, I promise you.'

He was puffing hard. He cast a look at Stephan, who was lying awkwardly on his back, his arm twisted behind him. I feared the giant might be dead, but his chest was rising and falling.

Behind Peregrine, at a more sedate pace, Rosie was picking her way down the beach. 'Are you all right?' she said to me.

'I am.'

'What should we do with *them*?' She threw a look at Alice which would have sent any dog to its basket.

A voice came from under the pier. 'I have an idea.' We all turned, and Lieutenant Chastain stepped into the light. 'I'd like my property back.'

He was holding a pistol, shaking so hard he needed both of his hands to keep it steady. His face was drawn tight.

Quinton held up his hands. 'I'm unarmed, Lieutenant.'

'We all are,' I said. 'What are you doing here?'

He gave the tiniest shrug. 'Your plan seemed overly complicated and relied on the truthfulness of a man like Thomas Quinton, which is rarely wise. But from what I could hear, you, at least, were honest in your endeavours. You tried, Mr Stanhope, and I thank you for that.' He tilted his head towards Quinton. 'My property, please.'

Quinton squared his shoulders and handed him the cigar box. 'You'll regret this, I promise you.'

'I won't.'

Chastain shook the box, and the sheep's tooth rattled about inside. He slid the box open, and his eyes flicked down to view the contents. He frowned and took another, longer look, and tipped the sheep's tooth into his palm. 'Is this a joke?'

Quinton tipped his head back and addressed the night sky. 'Jesus Christ, Stanhope. Did you never actually have the bloody thing?'

'We did,' I stammered. 'I mean, we do. Just not here.'

Chastain pointed the gun at my head. He was no more than five feet away. 'Not honest after all. Where is it?'

His voice was quavering, and in the light of the pier, I could see sweat shining on his forehead. He seemed like a man with nothing more to lose. I watched the end of the barrel, as though I might spot the bullet emerging and dodge out of its path. Absurd, of course. But I held on to the hope of life, if not for me, then for Peregrine and Rosie. If Chastain shot me here, he would certainly shoot them as well, and I couldn't bear the thought of that.

'I'll get your property for you, Lieutenant,' said Rosie. 'Let's all calm ourselves and go back up to the town.'

Chastain stuck out his jaw. 'No. Fetch it now. We'll wait for you.'

She kept her eyes fixed on him. 'I can't. It will take some time. Give me until tomorrow morning to retrieve it.'

He took several steps closer, so the gun was pressed against my temple. This close, I could see that his eyes were bloodshot and wet, flicking from side to side.

'It must be now. Do you understand?'

She smiled, doing everything she could to reassure him. 'Of course. But I can't fetch it immediately. I'm not deceiving you, sir. My sister has it and I need to go to her and get it back. Come to the house tomorrow morning and we'll give it to you. I can tell you the address.'

My clever wife, I thought. She'd parley with the devil if she had to.

Chastain pulled a watch from his pocket. 'It's almost ten o'clock now. You have until midnight. No later. Return with the Blood Flower during that time or I'll shoot your husband in the head. Do you understand?' He pointed at a bathing machine standing on its own like an abandoned carriage. 'We'll be in there.' He nodded towards Peregrine. 'And don't bring him with you. Come alone. I'm a man of my word. Bring the ruby and no one will get hurt.'

Rosie's eyes flicked towards me. 'I'll be back with the Blood Flower, Leo. I promise.'

Quinton straightened his hat. 'Well, this is none of my concern. My man Stephan is injured and needs help. I'm going to fetch him a doctor. Come along, Miss Morgan.'

Chastain stepped back, keeping them both within an easy angle to shoot. 'No. If I let you leave, you'll return with a dozen men. You come with me.' He indicated Stephan, who had begun to emit low groans. 'Bring him as well.'

'He's badly injured,' I said. 'We shouldn't move him.'

Chastain barely gave him a glance. 'I've seen men worse injured than that and some of them lived. Bring him.' He gestured towards Alice. 'You too, miss.'

She blanched. 'I can't see why you think ...'

'Now, please. I won't ask again.'

Stephan was lying against an ugly concrete boulder, whimpering and cursing, his pale hair soaked in blood and his arm hanging at an unnatural angle. He wasn't able to stand, so Peregrine and Quinton hauled him across the shingle, and I helped them carry him up the steps and into the bathing machine.

It was nothing more than a hut on four wheels. One of the four was missing, so the thing lay crookedly against a groyne wall like a drunk against a lamp post.

Peregrine squeezed my shoulder. 'I don't like to leave you here, Leo. I should stay.'

'No, go with Rosie. Keep her safe. Don't let her do anything stupid. That's the most use you can be.'

He nodded and raised an arm as if to give me a hug, but then thought better of the idea. 'You'll get out of this, laddie. Don't worry.'

He climbed down the steps and stood next to Rosie. She looked terrified – I could tell from her face that she had no idea how to find Viola and return with the Blood Flower in time.

Chastain shoved Alice in through the door and closed it behind us all, so we were in semi-darkness. There was an open sliding panel in the roof, but the sun had set an hour before and the only light coming in was from the illuminations on the pier and the pinprick stars over our heads.

'Sit down, all of you,' said Chastain.

We crammed together on the bench, Quinton nearest the door, Alice in the middle and then me. With Stephan taking up all of the floor, we had nowhere to put our feet, and had to crouch on the bench like gargoyles, tipped forward by the hobbled stance of our temporary prison. My suit was still damp from the harbour and the salt stung the grazes under my armpits.

'What now?' asked Quinton.

Chastain peered at his watch, trying to see the time. 'We wait.'

———

For about ten minutes, the only person to speak was Stephan, and the only intelligible words he uttered were curses of the worst type.

'I should help him,' I said. 'He's in agony.'

Chastain gave him a look of distaste. 'Good.'

'Have you ever killed anyone, Lieutenant?'

'I've never murdered anyone, if that's what you're asking.'

'I understand, but a life is a life. An enemy soldier, perhaps?'

He winced, as if from a physical pain. 'I'm an officer in the Royal Navy. I've given orders and taken them. That's the nature of command.'

'Of course. But if you let Stephan die here, it won't be an order, will it? It'll be your own doing.'

I confess that I wasn't only motivated by morality. It was Peregrine who had buffeted Stephan on to the rocks, and I didn't want my friend to be made a killer.

Again, Chastain pondered, before nodding. 'Very well. Stop him dying if you can. But there's no need to be overly gentle. I won't worry if he screams. He killed Micky Long. He deserves all the agony in the world.'

'Did you like Micky?' asked Alice. She was the only one of us who might be described as presentable: Chastain was bilious and sickish, Quinton was covered in Stephan's blood from helping to carry him and I was in an even worse state than before, which one would hardly have thought possible. Somehow, through it all, Alice had remained unruffled.

Chastain thought about her question. He was a man who considered things, weighed them up, not unlike myself. I might have enjoyed his company, had our circumstances been different.

'Well enough, until he stole from me. He was an impetuous, but engaging fellow.'

I squatted on the floor next to Stephan, hardly able to see a thing. The whispering of the waves became hollow and the revelries on the pier sounded tuneless and warped.

He grabbed my sleeve and pulled me close. 'Thank you.'

'Try to relax.'

I tipped his head forward and examined the cut. It was deep, but the bleeding had almost stopped, and I didn't think his skull had been cracked. I eased his jacket off him and rolled up his right shirtsleeve, which was soaked in blood. His arm had been snapped at the humerus, the jagged shard of its lower part emerging through his skin as if a crayfish was trying to claw its way out.

I was feeling queasy, but swallowed it down. 'This needs to be bound. It will hurt.' I nudged Quinton. 'Please steady his shoulders. Keep him from writhing around.'

He gave me a brief, flat smile, and took a deep breath. 'All right,' he said to his bodyguard. 'I've got you. Safe hands, mate. Safe hands.'

Alice turned away and covered her eyes.

I ripped the sleeve from Stephan's jacket and rolled it up for him to bite on. Then I took a lace from his boot and tied it tightly around his arm above the wound.

'Are you ready?'

The bone wasn't easy to manipulate. The frayed edges wouldn't smoothly move over one another, and I had to twist and pull to fit his arm back together. He growled and snorted, hammering his other fist on the floor so hard I thought he would burst through the wood and we'd fall through to the beach beneath. When I had finished, I tightened the binding further and removed the rolled cloth from his mouth. He'd bitten clean through it.

I took my seat again.

'He has a concussion and a badly broken arm, but he'll live.'

Chastain acknowledged this without interest, checking his watch, holding it up to catch the jaundiced light. I wondered whether I could charge at him and knock the gun from his grasp. But what then? If Quinton picked up the weapon, I would be in the same situation as before.

Outside, I heard a muttering and shuffling of feet on the stones.

A voice shouted: 'I can hear you in there. What are you doing?'

The old man had returned, drunken on my twopence and curious about the noise. We all remained silent until he staggered away.

'Half an hour gone,' said Chastain.

I shivered. The temperature was falling, and a light wind had started to blow in through the open panel in the roof. I looked up at the stars, not wistfully or pensively. I wasn't drawn to astronomy and was free of fantasies about our fates being determined in the celestial realm. Rather, I was tired of looking at the wooden slats of the wall opposite or watching the aperture of the gun barrel, wondering whether a twitch of Chastain's finger might blast a hole in one of us.

'Why are you doing this?' I asked him.

'Why do you think? The Blood Flower is mine.'

Alice stirred. 'Can't you see that it's betrayed you, Lieutenant. That's what it does.'

'A ludicrous superstition.'

A smile flickered across her face. I had once thought her beautiful, but no longer. Now, she seemed more like Peregrine's portrait of her: delightful from a distance, but close up, the artifice was clear.

'Perhaps,' she said. 'Yet every one of us has held it in our hand, and none of us possesses it now. And here we are.'

'Because of men's avarice,' said Chastain, 'not the ruby.'

Quinton snorted. 'You must've overheard our conversation earlier. It's not a *ruby*. It's a common … what's the word again?'

'A tourmaline,' I said. 'It's worth about twenty or twenty-five guineas. Will that be enough to pay off your debt to Petty Officer Fenwick and Mr Hall?'

Chastain narrowed his eyes at me. 'You're lying.'

'He'll kill you, you know. Fenwick, I mean. He despises what you are, and he'll keep raising the price for rowing over to fetch lads for you. Up and up and up until you can't afford to pay him any more, and then he'll tie weights to your feet and sink you in the harbour.'

Chastain took a deep, quivering breath. 'You think I don't know that? It's nothing less than what I'd expect. Men like me aren't permitted the smallest happiness without a price being exacted.' He waved his gun towards Quinton, who shrank back. 'We love and we suffer, while others profit.'

'I don't judge,' the hoodlum said. 'I provide a service, that's all. Lads and lasses alike, makes no difference to me.'

Chastain's eyes met mine. 'You would know, I suppose. Was it true, what he said earlier, that you're a woman?'

'No,' I said.

Alice took my hand and squeezed it. 'Only corporeally speaking.'

I snatched my hand away.

Chastain looked mildly impressed. 'I see. Does your wife know? I suppose she must. Well, you've nothing to fear from me, anyway.'

'Except the gun.'

He looked down as if surprised to find it in his hand. 'You should pray she brings me the Blood Flower in time. She has less than an hour.'

If she can find Viola, I thought. And if Viola hasn't done something daft, like throw it into the harbour or bury it as an offering to the spirits. Who knew what she might have done? She thought the thing was evil.

'And if she doesn't bring it?'

Chastain pushed the barrel of the pistol against my brow, so I could see it twice, once with each eye, forming a V against my forehead. I leaned back, gripping the bench, watching his finger trembling on the trigger.

'I know exactly how you feel, Lieutenant,' said Alice. 'I'm as much a victim as anyone.'

'What are you talking about?'

'I have no place among these people. I'm their plaything, nothing more. I love and I suffer, the same as you.'

'You want me to let you out, I suppose,' said Chastain, moving the gun away from me.

I sagged, breathing hard. I couldn't abide the thought of dying here, in this hut on three wheels, in a city I loathed. I wanted to see Peregrine play Falstaff, and to take care of Jacob in his dotage, and watch the children grow up, and see Constance become a doctor. I wanted Rosie and me to argue our way into old age together. I had no right to wish for these things, but I did it anyway. What else did I have, but wishes?

Alice gazed at Chastain through her eyelashes. 'I haven't hurt anyone, Lieutenant.' She was using his title often, appealing to his vanity. 'I am a … I don't know … a *courtesan* you might say, if you were being polite. I know the more accurate term. I'm the same as Micky Long, do you see? We're alike, him and me; we've both suffered because of men's avarice.'

She was clever, I had to acknowledge that. Employing Chastain's own words and using his sympathy for Micky Long to her advantage.

Could it be Alice, I thought? Might she have murdered Bill? I hadn't previously considered her as a suspect, not seriously. She had seemed more inclined to ingratiate and charm than to stab a man in the neck. Yet it wasn't impossible. She'd believed the Blood Flower was valuable beyond measure – enough to buy her freedom. Perhaps she'd realised who it was that had ripped the jewel from her neck. Perhaps she found Bill and slit his throat as best she could and then laid him out on the beach like the others.

Many in the police thought a woman incapable of a violent murder. A woman might poison her husband or toss a sickly baby from a bridge, but to hold another person still and cut his throat with a knife? To them, that didn't seem like a woman's crime. But I knew better. To be sure, it was unusual, but I'd seen it done with my own eyes.

Chastain examined Alice, his expression blank. I doubted he'd given her a second thought until that moment. 'I don't know you,' he said.

'Alice Morgan.' She held out her hands, a picture of innocence. 'I am as you see me. Nothing more.'

'Hmm. Be that as it may, you're staying here.' He angled his watch to see the face. 'It's a quarter to twelve. Almost out of time.'

I could feel my own heartbeat and started counting the thud of it against my chest, losing track at a hundred or so. One might think I would want time to move more slowly, eking out every second, but I just wanted all this over with. Whatever happens, I thought, for goodness' sake, let it be soon.

Minutes ticked away.

And then, outside, I heard footsteps on the stones. Quinton looked up, cocking his head.

Rosie's voice called out: 'I'm back, Lieutenant. I have the Blood Flower. You can let my husband go now.'

Alice and Quinton exchanged a relieved smile, but my heart sank. I knew Rosie too well. She was trying her best to sound convincing, but her voice was edgy and tense.

I was in no doubt that she was lying.

25

'LISTEN TO ME, LEO,' shouted Rosie. 'Don't do anything ridiculous, do you understand? Nothing heroic. Just wait where you are. Viola came home with the Blood Flower. I'll give it to the lieutenant and we can be on our way.'

She knew me well also. She knew that if I thought her endangered, I would throw myself at whatever was threatening her: no hesitation, no equivocation. But still, I was glad to hear her voice.

Chastain was trying to peek through a crack in the door, but I doubted he could see much in the darkness.

'Well done, Mrs Stanhope,' he called. 'We're all glad you're back. Put the Blood Flower on the steps of this bathing machine.'

There was a silence from outside, and then: 'How do I know my husband's still alive?'

Chastain nodded to me, and I called out: 'Rosie, I'm unhurt. Honestly.'

'Oh, Leo,' she said, and I could hear her relief.

'Enough talking,' called Chastain. 'Put my property on the steps and leave. When I've got it in my hand, I'll let Mr Stanhope go. Not before.'

'What about the rest of us?' demanded Quinton.

'No,' said Rosie, sounding very close to where I was sitting, though of course there was a wall between us. 'Send out my husband first.'

Chastain gave me a long look.

'You can trust her,' I said. 'She truly doesn't care about the jewel. It will be returned to you, I promise.'

'Very well,' Chastain called to her. 'I'll come out with your husband and check that what you say is true. If it isn't, I'll put a bullet in his head.'

He waggled his pistol at me. 'Get up.' He gripped my shoulder and put the gun to the back of my skull. I could feel him shaking. 'Open the door.'

'I wasn't lying before,' I said. 'It's not a ruby. It has value, but ...'

'Not enough, that's what you're saying. I understand. All I wanted was enough capital to ... to live as I wish to live. Is that so much to ask?'

I turned to face him, and he let me. His skin was sallow and damp, and his eyes were darting from side to side as if he'd lost control of them.

'I don't believe you're a killer,' I said.

He smiled, though he was almost weeping at the same time. His face was a battleground of emotions. 'Madagascar is quite beautiful, you know. The sea is warm, and they have trees like parasols, and huge squirrels called *babakotos* that sit outside your window and sing to each other. We used to listen to them in the evenings. Sometimes, we sang along with them, hooting and howling like children.'

I looked into his eyes. 'What's your Christian name, Lieutenant?'

'James.'

'Well, James, you can go back there, if you choose. You can have the life you crave. As long as you don't hurt anyone.'

He turned away from me, wiping his eyes, and at that moment I felt a hand on my collar. Two hands. Before I had a chance to cry out, I was lifted bodily upwards, hoisted up through the sliding panel in the roof. I heard the tiniest grunt of effort, and then my head emerged into the night air. I put my hands on the wood frame and tried to push myself up so I could stand.

'Quick!' said a voice. 'Roll off. Now!'

The hands threw me sideways with surprising strength and I found myself slipping and falling down the sloping roof. It all happened so quickly, I only heard Chastain's cry of anger as I hit the beach, knocking the wind out of me. Looking up, I could just about make out a face staring down from atop the bathing machine.

'Miss Brown?' I asked stupidly. 'Is that you?'

Who else could have crept up on to the roof without anyone hearing, and then had the muscular power to lift me out?

'Shh. This is a rescue.'

She leapt down, landing on her feet as neatly as a cat, and this while wearing a full-length frock and bonnet.

And then another, more familiar presence. 'Get moving, you idiot. We can't stay here.' Rosie pulled me upright and put a hand to my face. 'You're bleeding.'

'Not my blood.'

I had the urge to hug her. I resisted.

Inside the bathing machine, I heard Alice say: 'There's no need for you to keep us here any more, Lieutenant. Your leverage has gone.'

Chastain cursed, and I had a vision of him bursting out with his gun or, almost worse, randomly shooting through the walls. Rosie could be hit. As we clambered away over the stones, I stayed between her and the bathing machine, just in case.

Miss Brown was already ten yards ahead of us. 'Thank you,' I called after her. 'You saved me.'

She turned. 'Your wife said you needed help, and that you'd be able to prove who killed Natalia. And now you have.'

'Yes, but it wasn't Lieutenant Chastain. It was Stephan on Mr Quinton's orders.'

She remained still for several seconds, but I could see the tension in her face. 'So, Timothy Honey was telling the truth.'

'He was. Natalia's death was a meaningless bargaining chip.'

I chose not to mention that Quinton had also feared Natalia would tempt Miss Brown away to America. I didn't want her to have to carry the burden of that guilt.

'He should be punished,' she said, taking a step back towards the bathing machine.

Rosie held up her hand. 'He will be,' she said. 'They'll all be arrested now. I've brought the police.'

I stared at her. 'You've what?'

Rosie beckoned in the direction of the pier, and a figure appeared, striding towards us. He raised his hand as he grew closer.

'Sergeant Dorling!' Rosie called to him. 'Mr Stanhope is unharmed, as you can see.'

He was holding a pistol, a stubby thing with a barrel no longer than my thumb.

We were lit by the illuminations on the pier, and Miss Brown stepped a little away from us into the shadow. I could see the unease in her stance. She had no reason to trust the police. I gave her a brief nod of thanks, and she hurried away towards the promenade.

'You were supposed to be here at nine o'clock,' I said to Dorling, keeping my voice low. 'That was our agreement.'

'As I told Mrs Stanhope, I was called away.' His eyes were fixed ahead of him. 'This isn't my only case. Where's Chastain?'

'Inside that bathing machine with Quinton, Stephan and Miss Morgan. I'm sure he won't hurt anyone.'

Dorling took a deep breath and raised his pistol again. 'Stand aside, Mrs Stanhope.' And, as an afterthought. 'You too, Mr Stanhope. That's a Royal Navy officer in there. A dangerous man. And he's already murdered three people.'

I stood in front of him. 'No, Sergeant, he hasn't. Quinton ordered Stephan to kill Micky Long and Natalia La Blanche. He admitted it. Lieutenant Chastain is homesick and lonely, that's all. Let me try to persuade him to come out peacefully. Please.'

Dorling's moustache twitched a couple of times and then he shrugged. 'Very well. Can't do any harm.'

I went to the front of the bathing machine and raised my voice. 'Lieutenant!' I called out. 'James! The police are here. You can't escape. Come out peacefully and you won't be hurt.'

I heard a shuffling from inside and then Chastain's voice. 'How do I know?'

'You haven't murdered anyone, James. I've told them that. You'll be treated fairly.'

After a pause, he opened the door and tossed something out. I heard it land with a soft thud on the shingle.

'There's my gun,' he called. 'I'm coming out. I'm surrendering. Here I come.'

He stepped out, his hands in the air. He didn't have time to cry out. The shot rang out so loudly I thought it must burst my eardrums. He lurched against the frame of the door and fell sideways on to the beach.

I turned away and fell into a crouch as a waft of smoke emerged from the barrel of Dorling's pistol.

'What did you do?' I shouted. 'He was surrendering. He threw out his gun.'

The sergeant shrugged. 'He might've had another. I wasn't to know. Couldn't take the chance.'

I heard Quinton's voice from inside: 'Is that you, Dorling? Good man. Now let's get out of here.'

'Wait there, sir,' said Dorling, cocking the hammer of his pistol. 'I'm coming in.' He climbed up the steps and entered the bathing machine.

Rosie was sitting on the shingle, her hands clutched to her chest. Her face was as pale as a goose's egg. I put my arms around her and pulled her close. 'We need to go,' I said. 'We're still in danger. The sergeant's in the pay of Quinton.'

'What?' She stared at me, aghast. 'But I brought him here.'

Then another gunshot tore through the silence from within the bathing machine. I looked back, and a further shot rang out, accompanied by a flash which lit up every crack and knot in the wood.

'Quickly,' said Rosie, and took my hand.

But making progress over the loose stones was hard and Rosie was further hampered by her skirts and the canvas bag she was carrying. We hadn't gone ten yards before we heard Dorling's voice behind us.

'Come back, both of you. You're suspects in a crime.' He held out his hands. 'It'd be best if you gave me the Blood Flower now. It's evidence. I'll take it to the police station.'

I turned and stared him. 'You shot them.'

'I had no choice. They rushed at me. I was in fear of my life. Stephan's a dangerous man.'

I felt my insides turn to liquid. There was no possible way that Stephan could have rushed at anyone, and Quinton had thought the sergeant was under his command. And what about poor Alice, killed as she had lived, in thrall to powerful men? I knew that in time I would weep for her, for the memory of her soft skin and quizzical smile. But for now, my brain was jangling. Why had Dorling shot them?

Dorling himself was pacing up and down, fumbling with his gun, reloading it. I considered taking this opportunity to charge at him, but it wasn't worth the risk. We had what he wanted anyway.

And suddenly I realised why he'd killed Quinton.

I leaned close to Rosie and spoke quietly. 'He'll kill us too. He wants the Blood Flower for himself. Our only choice is to give it to him.'

She looked up at me with a glum expression.

'Good grief,' I said. 'You don't have it, do you?'

'I couldn't find Viola. Mr Black's still looking for her.

'But you came anyway, with nothing but a bluff? Oh, Rosie.'

That made the decision for me. I had to keep her safe. I had no choice but to run at Dorling and kill him, or at least postpone my own death long enough for her to escape. I set my jaw and prepared for the leap.

She gripped my hand tighter. 'Don't be stupid,' she whispered. 'You're not going to die, not here. And you won't kill anyone either. I won't have it. I won't have you tainted that way.'

'Rosie—'

She whirled to face me, hissing through clenched teeth. 'No, Leo. It's not a debate. You *will* trust me on this. I know what I'm doing.'

Dorling had finished reloading his gun. 'The Blood Flower, Mrs Stanhope, if you wouldn't mind. I'll take it for safekeeping. It's caused enough trouble.'

'Of course, Sergeant.' She held up the canvas bag. 'It's in here. I'm always happy to help the police.'

He licked his lips. 'Very good.'

She crouched down, searching through her bag. 'Would you mind putting away the gun, Sergeant? All that noise and destruction is bad for my nerves.'

He tucked it back into his belt. I had no clue what she was thinking. He could easily pull it out again and shoot us both. After all, he'd just killed four people without so much as a flinch. And then I realised the truth. How could I have been so stupid?

'Ah!' said Rosie. 'Here it is.'

She pulled her hand out from the bag, and she was holding a gun of her own. As close as I was, I could see it wasn't real. It was Peregrine's theatrical prop, carved in wood and painted black, no more lethal than a stick. She stood up straight and pointed it at Dorling.

'We'll be leaving now,' she said. 'Don't try to stop us.'

My goodness, I thought, she had some nerve. She didn't have the Blood Flower and she didn't have a real gun, yet here she was, facing down an armed policeman whom she knew to be a killer.

She took a step backwards, her eyes fixed on Dorling.

He froze in place. 'It's a crime to threaten a policeman, Mrs Stanhope.'

'You can't claim the protection of the law now,' I said. 'You wanted the Blood Flower for yourself, and you murdered Bill Broadman to get it.'

Dorling scoffed. 'He was a thief and a fool. A waste of breath. He stole a jewel worth more than he could earn in a thousand years, ten thousand, and was stupid enough to brag about it down the pub. Word gets round. No shortage of lowlifes who want a favour from the police.' He thumbed back at the bathing machine. 'And those three were worse. Stephan killed the two kids on Mr Quinton's orders and Chastain was a filthy pervert. I've worked all my life to bring men like them to justice. Why shouldn't I be the one to benefit for once?'

'And what about Miss Morgan? What did she do to deserve death?'

He frowned and cast a nervous glance back at the bathing machine. My brain stirred into life. He had only fired two shots inside.

Rosie took another step backwards, and I followed her.

Dorling held out his hands. 'You're not going to shoot me, Mrs Stanhope. It's not in a woman's nature.' He was right and wrong respectively, but she was selling the ruse as best she could. She renewed her grip, lifting the prop gun with both hands and looking straight along the barrel at him.

'I don't want to,' she said. 'But I will.'

I was almost convinced. I had to take another look at the thing to be certain it wasn't real.

Dorling was watching her, his hand moving towards his own revolver.

'Don't,' she said.

His fingers touched the hilt, his eyes fixed on hers.

'She'll kill you, Sergeant,' I said. 'If you want to live, you'll let us walk away.'

His eyes flicked to me and back to her. 'I'll take my chances.'

He slowly pulled his revolver out from his belt and raised it until it was pointing at Rosie.

'Best to put that down,' he said.

She had no choice. She dropped the prop gun on to the stones.

'You see?' he said. 'Ladies can't shoot people. Now, no more delays. The Blood Flower, if you please.'

I ran all the moves in my head, like a game of chess, trying each of them in turn, holding them up in front of me and measuring their worth. Every possible option was a mad gamble, but gambling was all we had.

I stood in front of Rosie. She tried to push me aside, but I refused to let her.

'We don't have the jewel,' I said.

Dorling jerked as if he'd touched something hot. 'What do you mean?'

'We don't have it. We never had it in our possession. The whole thing was a bluff from start to finish.'

Rosie gave an angry tug on my jacket. 'Leo, what are you doing? You will *not* sacrifice yourself for me.'

I continued to block his view of her, having to dodge from side to side as she tried to evade me.

'You see, Sergeant, if we did have the Blood Flower, a ruby of such value, you'd have to shoot us. You wouldn't want any witnesses, and with that much money, you could run away and live like a king on his throne. America, perhaps, or Madagascar. I hear it's delightful. They have singing squirrels, so I'm told.'

'What are you blathering about?'

Rosie went left, trying to stop me from standing in front of her, and I went left too. Behind Dorling, the pier was still illuminated. People were dotted along it, late-night revellers and couples stealing kisses before they headed home.

Something glinted on the stones.

'If we had a thing of such value, do you think for one second, we'd still be in Portsmouth? We'd have left days ago.'

He frowned. 'You truly don't have it?'

'No. You'll get nothing. There's no Blood Flower here. If it ever existed at all.'

'Why would you pretend to have it if you don't?'

I forced my face into a confident smile. 'Isn't it obvious? For money. We knew Quinton and Chastain would pay handsomely for a ruby like that. Things didn't work out as we planned.' I gave a theatrical sigh, all shoulders and pout. 'Too bad for us and too bad for you too. You're stuck here, Sergeant, in this city. No throne for you, no singing squirrels.'

He lifted the revolver towards my face. 'You always have a deal, don't you, Stanhope? Some crafty proposal that'll get you what you want. But you know what I've done, and I'm better off with you dead than alive.'

I held up my hands, keeping myself in front of Rosie, who was kicking the backs of my ankles. 'Don't be hasty, Sergeant. All the deaths so far, you can explain. Saving civilians from danger, self-defence, a policeman's loyal duty, I'm sure you can find the appropriate words for a story like that. But you can't explain killing us. We're not criminals and we didn't take any hostages.'

Again, I caught a glimmer of light among the stones, a reflection from the lamps on the pier.

Rosie veered right, and this time I stayed where I was. She kept moving, making an arc around Dorling, away from me. Now, he could shoot one of us, and the other might get far enough away not to be shot as well. He took a step back, swivelling to aim the gun at each of us in turn.

'I may not be a clever London man like yourself, but I know this city. Every nook and corner of it. I can dispose of your bodies easily enough. I'll put you where no one will ever look.'

Rosie picked up a rock and heaved it at him. It fell six feet short. 'You should be ashamed,' she said. 'You're a terrible policeman. A disgrace. People trust you, but you're nothing more than a common criminal.'

She was goading him, trying to give me a chance to escape.

I took a step forward. But as I moved, my angle to the lamps on the pier changed, and the glint on the stones disappeared. I stepped back again, and there it was.

Dorling was facing away from me, fully occupied with Rosie. She caught my eye, and I could see her willing me to go the other way, to turn and run. But I could not. I had to reach that metallic glint. I took another step forward and it went out again, but this time I kept my eyes locked on the exact spot. I couldn't afford to miss it.

'What are you waiting for?' Rosie demanded. 'You say that a woman can't shoot a man, but I've beaten one to death with a chain. What do you think of that?'

I almost missed it in the darkness. In fact, I trod on it.

'You've been brave, Mrs Stanhope,' said Dorling, 'but your time is up.'

He pulled back the hammer of his revolver.

I crouched down and there it was: Chastain's gun, right where it had landed after he threw it out of the bathing machine.

I picked it up and aimed it at Dorling.

I pulled the trigger.

26

ONE'S BRAIN CAN RUN at surprising speed. An entire idea can spring into life in a single second. Rosie had been known to foment a new worry about one of her children in the time it takes to blink. In the smallest possible division of time, with the gun in my hand, my finger pulling the trigger, a number of thoughts hurtled through my mind and arrayed themselves. Perhaps Rosie was right after all, and my brain was like a honey-comb, each individual thought occupying its own tiny hexagon.

I wondered if Chastain's gun was actually loaded. What a fine joke God would be making if it wasn't. One of His best. If the gun wasn't loaded, and Chastain had been bluffing all along, much as we had, then the entire night's bloodshed was a tragic farce.

Rosie would be dead. Rosie, gone from the world. There were no words for such a loss. My brain absorbed it and put in away in that locked box with the wolves and the jangle and thump and that awful, tender humming.

And shortly after that, I supposed I would be dead too. It seemed the lesser price. I couldn't place much value on something I had once sought to throw away.

Dorling would survive and suffer no punishment for his crimes. And, sooner or later, he would wonder whether I'd been truthful about never having possessed the Blood Flower, and he would go to Viola's house in search of it a second time – because it was certainly he who'd ransacked it before. That was obvious now. Who but the police would make such an awful mess? This time he might find the damned thing, if Viola hadn't already tossed it into the sea. He would believe himself wealthy beyond imagining, until he discovered the truth. A small part of me laughed at that.

All these thoughts as my finger closed on the trigger.

The gun was loaded.

The report was enormous, like a thunderclap. The bullet hit Dorling squarely in the back, and he jerked forward, staggering as his body lost contact with his brain. His legs gave way and he crumpled on to the beach.

Rosie fell too, and I had a clutch of panic that the bullet had been diverted on its way through him to hit her as well. But she immediately scrambled back to her feet.

She stared at me for a full ten seconds before putting out her hand. 'Give me the gun, Leo,' she said. 'Now.'

'Why? He's dead. I killed him. A police officer.'

'I know. Give me the gun.'

I did as she instructed. 'I'll be hanged.'

She shook her head. 'No, you won't. Not if we're quick.'

I followed her to the bathing machine. She pulled open the door and, as our eyes adjusted to the dimness, we gasped at the carnage. Quinton had fallen forward into a strange crouch, his head against the opposite wall like the most pious of suppliants. Blood was pooling at his knees. Beyond him, Stephan was half-sitting, half-lying on the floor, as if he'd tried to raise himself when Dorling entered and had got no further. One of his eyes was open and the other a messy hole.

'Where's Alice? She was in here too.'

Stephan began to move, his torso shifting and lifting in an unearthly contortion, his head lolling to one side as if to examine us with his one unblinking eye. Rosie raised the gun, her hand shaking. The corpse listed to one side and seemed to subside as something emerged from beneath him. It crawled out, almost unrecognisable as Alice. Her hat was gone, her sleeve was torn and her face, hair and bodice were soaked in blood.

'Please don't shoot,' she said, her voice hoarse and weak. 'I'm unarmed.'

'Are you hurt?' I asked.

'No. I hid beneath Stephan when I heard Sergeant Dorling's voice. Thomas thought him his man, but I never trusted him. I'm glad you're safe.'

Rosie did not lower the gun. 'You made no attempt to help us though, did you?'

Alice wiped her mouth with her sleeve, smearing Stephan's blood across her cheeks. 'What could I have done? I have no weapon, no physical strength, no clever way to disarm a killer.' She spread her hands wide. 'I'm like you, Mrs Stanhope: a woman trying to survive in a world made by men.'

She was admirable, in a certain way: relentless in her calculation.

Rosie's eyebrows tilted upwards about a tenth of an inch.

'I'll make you an offer, Miss Morgan,' she said icily. 'I ought to shoot you, but I won't. Leave this beach and go home, and never mention what happened here to a soul. If you do, I'll take retribution. Do you understand? As far as the police know, Sergeant Dorling confronted these men, and they were all killed in the crossfire. Is that clear?'

Alice raised her chin as if she was about to speak, but something in Rosie's demeanour deterred her. Seeing them this way, facing one another, my attraction to Alice seemed no more real than a cloud that looks for a moment like a face or an outstretched hand but blows away into nothing.

'Very well,' she said.

I followed Alice outside. She waded a few steps into the sea and washed the blood from her face, wringing out her hair and twisting it expertly into a bun. I was taken briefly back to our swim in the moonlight, and my elation at such freedom. I silently vowed not to lose that feeling again.

'How do I look?' she asked.

Her efforts had made some difference, but still, her clothes were soaked through and stained pink, as if she'd spent the day gutting fish.

'Perfect,' I said. 'Goodbye, Alice.'

'Goodbye, Leo.'

She left the sea and walked slowly up the beach. I watched until I could no longer pick her out against the lights of the city.

Two figures were hurrying towards me, one toiling over the stones and the other small and nimble.

'Miss Brown,' I said, as she came near. 'I really must thank you again.'

'Not at all.' She thumbed back towards the other figure. 'He insisted on coming also.'

'Leo!' called Peregrine. 'Are you all right? And Rosie?'

I assured him we were safe, and he clapped me on both shoulders.

'That ridiculous plan actually worked?' He beamed at me. 'Good Lord. I was certain you'd both be dead without me here.'

Miss Brown gave him a look. 'Could *you* have climbed up there without anyone knowing, and pulled Mr Stanhope to safety?'

He tapped a knuckle on the dry, fragile structure. 'Of course. I have an actor's finesse.'

Miss Brown opened her mouth, but was saved from having to reply by Rosie. She came out of the bathing machine with her arms folded. 'Mr Black, did you find Viola?'

He nodded. 'Just now. She was on the common. And I have the stone.'

Rosie blew out her cheeks. 'Good. That's a relief. You can give me a hand, please, getting Mr Quinton's body out of here and on to the beach. We need to make it look as if he was killed in a gun fight with Sergeant Dorling.'

She explained the events of the evening while they tugged and hauled Quinton's remains out of the bathing machine and laid him out, his arm extended in the direction of Dorling's corpse. She placed Chastain's gun next to him, as if it had dropped there when he died.

Miss Brown and I went to do the same for Chastain himself, but when I got to the spot where he'd fallen, he wasn't there. I found him leaning against the broken wheel of the bathing machine. I crouched down beside him.

'Is he still alive?' asked Miss Brown.

Before I could check his pulse, a rasping sound emerged from his mouth, and a bubble of spit formed and burst on his lips. I pulled aside his blood-soaked jacket and shirt and found a bullet hole below the eighth rib on his right side. It must have somehow missed his vital organs and blood vessels. His eyes flickered open. 'Christ,' he muttered. 'It bloody hurts.'

I beckoned to Miss Brown. 'I'll need your help.'

We pulled him to his feet, supporting him between us. Rosie watched in amazement, and Peregrine fished in his pocket for his flask and held it out.

'Whisky?'

'He'll need more than that,' I said. 'We'll have to take him to the hospital.'

'Perhaps,' said Peregrine, taking a swig himself. 'But I imagine they'll have some awkward questions for us.'

'The barracks then,' said Rosie. 'The Navy must have doctors.'

Chastain lolled close and whispered into my ear. 'No, please. Not the Navy.'

'I know,' said Miss Brown. 'I'll take him to Mr Lau, our surgeon. He'll mend him. You should leave here before somebody sees you.'

'Thank you, Miss Brown,' I said. 'For everything.'

She gave us a rare smile. 'No, thank you. You found Natalia's killer and he's dead. That's good enough for me.'

She took the lieutenant's weight and half-supported, half-carried him up the beach towards the promenade.

'Well,' said Peregrine. 'All's well that ends well.' He ignored our expressions and drained his flask 'What we need now is a lot more terrible whisky.'

———

The following morning, I took another bath, asking Rosie to stand guard again.

Through the door, I could hear her exasperated remonstrations with Viola.

'But why?' she was saying. 'Where did you go?'

'I knew the Blood Flower was evil,' said Viola. 'It carried death with it.'

'What did you do?'

'I went and sat on the common. You know, by the beach. It was terrifying for a while. There were flashes and bangs like thunder and lightning coming from the direction of the sea. I was sure it was the spirits angry with me for having such a thing in my possession.'

There was a pause in the conversation. I could imagine Rosie struggling to form words.

'How far were you from the beach?' she asked eventually.

'No more than a hundred yards. I daren't go any closer. There were monstrous shadows dancing there.'

'But you're pregnant.'

'I was quite safe. It was quite warm, and after a time, there was peace. The noises and the dancers went away, so I decided to go home, and met Mr Black on the way. I knew the spirits had taken all the evil from the jewel. They made it good again, Roisin. It's not the Blood Flower any more. Now, I'm calling it the Gift.'

When I'd finished my bath, I put on Bill's awful suit and found Rosie and Peregrine in the parlour. Our bag was packed.

'Viola will have to come with us,' said Rosie. 'She can't stay here with no income.'

'Plus, she's mad as a spinning top,' added Peregrine, earning a filthy glance from the madwoman's sister.

I found that I'd hardly spoken since the previous night. Words weren't springing easily into my mouth. I knew Rosie had noticed my reticence, as she'd exchanged a couple of concerned looks with Peregrine. But what I lacked in speech I made up for in the written word. I'd already drafted my article about the murders of Natalia La Blanche and Micky Long, the innocent victims of Thomas Quinton, a celebrated local businessman who was killed in a gunfight with the police. With insinuations of opium-smoking and sins of the flesh, the story had all the lurid elements J. T. could wish for.

I didn't mention Dorling by name, but I was certain he'd be heralded as a hero. It stuck in my throat, but what else could

I do? That was the tableau we'd created on the beach. And I didn't mention Bill Broadman either, as I would've had to include the fact that he'd stolen the Blood Flower, and Viola didn't deserve that. And finally, after much deliberation, I left out James Chastain as well. I was certain he wouldn't return to his ship and the Royal Navy. He was desperate to get back to those singing squirrels and the lover he'd left in Madagascar. I hoped he would.

'Leo,' said Rosie. 'Are you listening to me? I said Viola should stay with us until she's had the baby. And for a while afterwards, I'm sure. All this ...' She waved at the room. 'This *stuff* can go into storage. Or be burned.'

Jack-the-bloody-dog came in and jumped up on the sofa beside me. I prepared myself to be bitten, but instead he curled up against my leg and emitted a deep sigh. Perhaps it was the suit. He thought I was Bill. Oh, good Lord, I thought. I suppose he'll have to come too.

'Are you sure about the Blood Flower?' asked Peregrine. 'Or the *Gift*, as I should call it now.'

'Yes,' replied Rosie. 'Mr Kleiner can sell it as he suggested. Twenty-five guineas, hopefully. We'll send you the money to help these poor boys. Find little Jonathan for me, will you? And Mr Honey and all the others. Give them somewhere to stay that's warm and put some proper food in their bellies.'

'I shall,' he said. 'But I'll have to hand over to Mrs Mackay soon. I'll be at home in London with Miranda, receiving rave reviews for my Falstaff.'

'Do you trust Mrs Mackay?'

He smiled. 'Absolutely. She's the nearest thing I have to family. And talking of which ...' I could see from his twinkling expression he was about to start some mischief. 'Where will Mrs Broadman be sleeping at the Stanhope residence?'

Rosie raised an imperious eyebrow. 'Viola will stay in the box room. Leo and I will take the main bedroom. We are husband and wife, after all.'

She gave me a quick look, checking I was happy with this allocation, and I gave her a nod in return. It meant no more than what it was: a new arrangement for sleeping. Yet I knew that she loved me. Not in any simple way, not as the world would expect perhaps, but love was still love, and it was more than I deserved. Such a strange pair we made, oddly shaped and ill-fitting, except with each other.

Whatever we were, we were it together.

I watched her alternately rolling her eyes and laughing at Peregrine's good-natured teasing and could not care for her more. All that mattered was that she was happy, and I would soon be carrying her bag to the station, and she would confront with ferocity any dishonest crow salesmen who happened to cross our path.

And we would remain silent on the subject of love. It was like the pies she gave me that she said were left over from the day before, or the newspapers I brought home for her that I claimed were offprints from the presses. We both knew the truth, but neither of us wanted to talk about it.

Strange, I supposed.

But it was how we were.

Historical (and Geological) Notes

A TOURMALINE IS A gemstone found in a wide variety of colours. Red ones, sometimes known as rubellites, can be confused with rubies to the untrained eye; for example, Caesar's Ruby, a 255-carat stone which has, at various times, been part of the French, Swedish and Russian crown jewels is, in fact, a rubellite tourmaline. In the absence of sophisticated equipment, such mistakes were easily made. Indeed, the British crown jewels include the Black Prince's Ruby, which we now know isn't a ruby either, but a red spinel. One way to tell the difference is that tourmalines can be magnetic, but rubies cannot. It would be unusual for a rubellite tourmaline to display as strong a magnetic force as the Blood Flower, but not unknown.

Both rubies and tourmalines were imported to the UK from Madagascar. In 1883, when the French began their invasion of the island, the British Royal Navy had three ships in port, including HMS *Dragon*. However, despite the best efforts of the Navy captains, there was little political will in London to protect their outpost, which had diminished in strategic importance since the opening of the Suez Canal. The British largely exited, leaving the local army to fight the Franco–Hova wars over the following twelve years. The French were eventually victorious, but only after many thousands of lives had been lost.

The HMS *Colossus* was built in the Portsmouth Dockyard and commissioned in 1886. She was arguably the first truly modern warship, boasting steel construction, steam-only propulsion and a pair of gun turrets. She was notably fast through the water but had poor manoeuvrability and was decommissioned in 1901 and scrapped in 1908.

Quinton's New Hippodrome is based on Ginnett's Hippodrome, opened in 1880 by Frederick Ginnett. It was situated next to the Portsmouth Town railway station and had an eventful history through the 1880s, including being burned down and rebuilt, and changing name several times.

Miss La La was a stage name of a circus performer whose real name may have been Olga Brown. She was born in Szczecin in Prussia (now in Poland) in 1858. Her feats of strength and skill as an acrobat earned her a level of fame unusual for a Black woman, such that painter Edgar Degas became fascinated by her. You can see his painting of her in the National Gallery in London. She often performed with her partner Theophila Szterker, together becoming known as The Two Butterflies. Shortly after Szterker fell to her death in 1888, Brown ceased performing and married Emanuel Woodson, an African American contortionist. She became a mother to three daughters, living until at least 1919.

Nicolaev (or Mykolaiv) is a Black Sea port city in Ukraine. During the nineteenth century, it was part of the Russian empire. In 1834, its Jewish population was expelled by force and removed to the 'Pale of Settlement' to the west. Over the following years, many of them, like Jacob and Lilya Kleiner, fled across Europe, trying to escape from persecution. Jews were not permitted back until the 1860s. During the Second World War, the city was occupied by German forces, and in the autumn of 1941, nearly 36,000 citizens, almost all of them Jews, were murdered.

In the latter part of the nineteenth century, the punishment for male homosexual acts was brutal; a minimum of ten years in prison and, more commonly, life. Even minor indiscretions – embracing or kissing – could be punished by months of hard labour. Gay clubs, known as 'molly-houses' were often well-known to the police, who tolerated or raided them according to political whim. It was a very precarious life for a gay man. Homosexual acts remained a criminal act in the UK until 1967, but in the Royal Navy were illegal until 2000, and were still considered grounds for dismissal until 2016.

Acknowledgements

THIS IS THE LAST in the Leo Stanhope series.

I started writing about Leo because I care about the right of every person to decide who they are. My research told me that the topic of gender identity is absent from nineteenth-century British literature even though there were numerous examples of real trans people in Victorian times. Some of them became the subject of salacious press attention after their deaths, such as James Barry, who was a top surgeon in the British Army, and Harry Stokes, who fixed chimneys and fireplaces. And yet the novelists and playwrights of the time ignored them.

Perhaps, I thought, it was time to put trans people back.

But I am not trans. I'm an ally with the best of intentions, but still, a cis man writing about a trans man. Did I have the right to do this? I'm still not certain.

In my earliest attempts, I tried making Leo a lesser character, a friend of the main protagonist, but he refused to be sidelined. He kept hogging the limelight. So, I surrendered and made him the central character in the first of these novels, *The House on Half Moon Street*, giving myself three rules. First, as a historical series, Leo's experience would be somewhat removed from the present-day lives of trans people. Second, my stories wouldn't be about *being* or *becoming* trans, they would be about a man who *happened* to be trans. Leo's criminal cases are neither caused by, nor solved by, his gender identity. He has a unique perspective but being trans is just one part of who he is, not the sum of it. And finally, I sought the views of trans people, who gave me wonderful insights and were very supportive of my endeavours.

And now, you are holding the fourth and last of them. I hope you've enjoyed reading about Leo as much as I've enjoyed writing about him. But I feel I've achieved what I set out to do, and it's time to move on. I remain fascinated by gender identity in all its forms, and I can't wait to read the stories of other, better qualified writers. I have no doubt they will be as bright as fireworks, lighting up the sky.

Many skilled people have made this journey possible. My huge thanks to Carrie Plitt at Felicity Bryan Associates and the brilliant folks at Bloomsbury Raven, including Alison Hennessey, Sara Helen Binney, Ella Harold, Lilidh Kendrick and numerous others. Also, thanks to Dr Paul Vlitos and Prof Patricia Pullman at the University of Surrey for their expertise and advice, and everyone who helped with the research, including the British Library, Gladstone's Library, the Women's Library at the London School of Economics, the National Museum of the Royal Navy, the National Archives and many, many others. Also, thanks to my friend Magda Adamska for her help with the Polish tattoos, and Paula Akpan for her expert advice.

Also, my eternal respect and gratitude to the Beaumont Society, a charity doing important work supporting the trans community and advising on trans issues. You can find them at www.beaumontsociety.org.uk.

And finally, I'm forever grateful to my wonderful sons, Seth and Caleb, and my inestimable wife, Michelle, all of whom I love beyond measure.

A Note on the Type

The text of this book is set in Bembo, which was first used in 1495 by the Venetian printer Aldus Manutius for Cardinal Bembo's *De Aetna*. The original types were cut for Manutius by Francesco Griffo. Bembo was one of the types used by Claude Garamond (1480–1561) as a model for his Romain de l'Université, and so it was a forerunner of what became the standard European type for the following two centuries. Its modern form follows the original types and was designed for Monotype in 1929.